Beric the Briton

A Story of the Roman Invasion

G. A. Henty

Alpha Editions

This edition published in 2021

ISBN : 9789354842658

Design and Setting By
Alpha Editions
www.alphaedis.com
Email - info@alphaedis.com

As per information held with us this book is in Public Domain.
This book is a reproduction of an important historical work. Alpha Editions uses the best technology to reproduce historical work in the same manner it was first published to preserve its original nature. Any marks or number seen are left intentionally to preserve its true form.

Contents

PREFACE. - 1 -

CHAPTER I A HOSTAGE - 2 -

CHAPTER II CITY AND FOREST - 15 -

CHAPTER III A WOLF HUNT - 29 -

CHAPTER IV AN INFURIATED PEOPLE - 43 -

CHAPTER V THE SACK OF CAMALODUNUM - 56 -

CHAPTER VI FIRST SUCCESSES - 70 -

CHAPTER VII DEFEAT OF THE BRITONS - 84 -

CHAPTER VIII THE GREAT SWAMPS - 96 -

CHAPTER IX THE STRUGGLE IN THE SWAMP - 110 -

CHAPTER X BETRAYED - 123 -

CHAPTER XI A PRISONER - 137 -

CHAPTER XII A SCHOOL FOR GLADIATORS - 152 -

CHAPTER XIII A CHRISTIAN - 169 -

CHAPTER XIV ROME IN FLAMES - 183 -

CHAPTER XV THE CHRISTIANS TO THE LIONS - 196 -

CHAPTER XVI IN NERO'S PALACE - 211 -

CHAPTER XVII BETROTHAL - 224 -

CHAPTER XVIII THE OUTBREAK - 237 -

CHAPTER XIX OUTLAWS - 251 -

CHAPTER XX MOUNTAIN WARFARE - 264 -

CHAPTER XXI OLD FRIENDS - 277 -

PREFACE.

MY DEAR LADS,

My series of stories dealing with the wars of England would be altogether incomplete did it not include the period when the Romans were the masters of the country. The valour with which the natives of this island defended themselves was acknowledged by the Roman historians, and it was only the superior discipline of the invaders that enabled them finally to triumph over the bravery and the superior physical strength of the Britons. The Roman conquest for the time was undoubtedly of immense advantage to the people--who had previously wasted their energies in perpetual tribal wars--as it introduced among them the civilization of Rome. In the end, however, it proved disastrous to the islanders, who lost all their military virtues. Having been defended from the savages of the north by the soldiers of Rome, the Britons were, when the legions were recalled, unable to offer any effectual resistance to the Saxons, who, coming under the guise of friendship, speedily became their masters, imposing a yoke infinitely more burdensome than that of Rome, and erasing almost every sign of the civilization that had been engrafted upon them. How far the British population disappeared under the subsequent invasion and the still more oppressive yoke of the Danes is uncertain; but as the invaders would naturally desire to retain the people to cultivate the land for them, it is probable that the great mass of the Britons were not exterminated. It is at any rate pleasant to believe that with the Saxon, Danish, and Norman blood in our veins, there is still a large admixture of that of the valiant warriors who fought so bravely against Caesar, and who rose under Boadicea in a desperate effort to shake off the oppressive rule of Rome.

Yours truly,

G. A. Henty

CHAPTER I
A HOSTAGE

"It is a fair sight."

"It may be a fair sight in a Roman's eyes, Beric, but nought could be fouler to those of a Briton. To me every one of those blocks of brick and stone weighs down and helps to hold in bondage this land of ours; while that temple they have dared to rear to their gods, in celebration of their having conquered Britain, is an insult and a lie. We are not conquered yet, as they will some day know to their cost. We are silent, we wait, but we do not admit that we are conquered."

"I agree with you there. We have never fairly tried our strength against them. These wretched divisions have always prevented our making an effort to gather; Cassivelaunus and some of the Kentish tribes alone opposed them at their first landing, and he was betrayed and abandoned by the tribes on the north of the Thames. It has been the same thing ever since. We fight piecemeal; and while the Romans hurl their whole strength against one tribe the others look on with folded hands. Who aided the Trinobantes when the Romans defeated them and established themselves on that hill? No one. They will eat Britain up bit by bit."

"Then you like them no better for having lived among them, Beric?"

"I like them more, but I fear them more. One cannot be four years among them, as I was, without seeing that in many respects we might copy them with advantage. They are a great people. Compare their splendid mansions and their regular orderly life, their manners and their ways, with our rough huts, and our feasts, ending as often as not with quarrels and brawls. Look at their arts, their power of turning stone into lifelike figures, and above all, the way in which they can transfer their thoughts to white leaves, so that others, many many years hence, can read them and know all that was passing, and what men thought and did in the long bygone. Truly it is marvellous."

"You are half Romanized, Beric," his companion said roughly.

"I think not," the other said quietly; "I should be worse than a fool had I lived, as I have done, a hostage among them for four years without seeing that there is much to admire, much that we could imitate with advantage, in their life and ways; but there is no reason because they are wiser and far more polished, and in many respects a greater people than we, that they should come here to be our masters. These things are desirable, but they are as nothing to freedom. I have said that I like them more for being among them.

I like them more for many reasons. They are grave and courteous in their manner to each other; they obey their own laws; every man has his rights; and while all yield obedience to their superiors, the superiors respect the rights of those below them. The highest among them cannot touch the property or the life of the lowest in rank. All this seems to me excellent; but then, on the other hand, my blood boils in my veins at the contempt in which they hold us; at their greed, their rapacity, their brutality, their denial to us of all rights. In their eyes we are but savages, but wild men, who may be useful for tilling the ground for them, but who, if troublesome, should be hunted down and slain like wild beasts. I admire them for what they can do; I respect them for their power and learning; but I hate them as our oppressors."

"That is better, Beric, much better. I had begun to fear that the grand houses and the splendour of these Romans might have sapped your patriotism. I hate them all; I hate changes; I would live as we have always lived."

"But you forget, Boduoc, that we ourselves have not been standing still. Though our long past forefathers, when they crossed from Gaul wave after wave, were rude warriors, we have been learning ever since from Gaul as the Gauls have learned from the Romans, and the Romans themselves admit that we have advanced greatly since the days when, under their Caesar, they first landed here. Look at the town on the hill there. Though 'tis Roman now 'tis not changed so much from what it was under that great king Cunobeline, while his people had knowledge of many things of which we and the other tribes of the Iceni knew nothing."

"What good did it do them?" the other asked scornfully; "they lie prostrate under the Roman yoke. It was easy to destroy their towns while we, who have few towns to destroy, live comparatively free. Look across at Camalodunum, Cunobeline's capital. Where are the men who built the houses, who dressed in soft garments, who aped the Romans, and who regarded us as well nigh savage men? Gone every one of them; hewn down on their own hearthstones, or thrust out with their wives and families to wander homeless--is there one left of them in yonder town? Their houses they were so proud of, their cultivated fields, their wealth of all kinds has been seized by the Romans. Did they fight any better for their Roman fashions? Not they; the kingdom of Cunobeline, from the Thames to the western sea, fell to pieces at a touch and it was only among the wild Silures that Caractacus was able to make any great resistance."

"But we did no better, Boduoc; Ostorius crushed us as easily as Claudius crushed the Trinobantes. It is no use our setting ourselves against change. All that you urge against the Trinobantes and the tribes of Kent the Silures might urge with equal force against us. You must remember that we were like them not so many ages back. The intercourse of the Gauls with us on this eastern sea coast, and with the Kentish tribes, has changed us greatly. We are no longer, like the western tribes, mere hunters living in shelters of boughs and roaming the forests. Our dress, with our long mantles, our loose vests and trousers, differs as widely from that of these western tribes as it does from the Romans. We live in towns, and if our houses are rude they are solid. We no longer depend solely on the chase, but till the ground and have our herds of cattle. I daresay there were many of our ancestors who set themselves as much against the Gaulish customs as you do against those of the Romans; but we adopted them, and benefited by them, and though I would exult in seeing the last Roman driven from our land, I should like after their departure to see us adopt what is good and orderly and decent in their customs and laws."

Beric's companion growled a malediction upon everything Roman.

"There is one thing certain," he said after a pause, "either they must go altogether, not only here but everywhere--they must learn, as our ancestors taught them at their two first invasions, that it is hopeless to conquer Britain--or they will end by being absolute masters of the island, and we shall be their servants and slaves."

"That is true enough," Beric agreed; "but to conquer we must be united, and not only united but steadfast. Of course I have learned much of them while I have been with them. I have come to speak their language, and have listened to their talk. It is not only the Romans who are here whom we have to defeat, it is those who will come after them. The power of Rome is great; how great we cannot tell, but it is wonderful and almost inconceivable. They have spread over vast countries, reducing peoples everywhere under their dominion. I have seen what they call maps showing the world as far as they know it, and well nigh all has been conquered by them; but the farther away from Rome the more difficulty have they in holding what they have conquered.

"That is our hope here; we are very far from Rome. They may send army after army against us, but in time they will get weary of the loss and expense when there is so little to gain, and as after their first invasions a long time elapsed before they again troubled us, so in the end they may abandon a useless enterprise. Even now the Romans grumble at what they call their exile, but they are obstinate and tenacious, and to rid our land of them for good it would be necessary for us not only to be united among ourselves when we rise against them, but to remain so, and to oppose with our whole force the fresh armies they will bring against us.

"You know how great the difficulties will be, Boduoc; we want one great leader whom all the tribes will follow, just as all the Roman legions obey one general; and what chance is there of such a man arising--a man so great, so wise, so brave, that all the tribes of Britain will lay aside their enmities and jealousies, and submit themselves to his absolute guidance?"

"If we wait for that, Beric, we may wait for ever," Boduoc said in a sombre tone, "at any rate it is not while we are tranquil under the Roman heel that such a man could show himself. If he is to come to the front it must be in the day of battle. Then, possibly, one chief may rise so high above his fellows that all may recognize his merits and agree to follow him."

"That is so," Beric agreed; "but is it possible that even the greatest hero should find support from all? Cassivelaunus was betrayed by the Trinobantes. Who could have united the tribes more than the sons of Cunobeline, who reigned over well nigh all Britain, and who was a great king ruling wisely and well, and doing all in his power to raise and advance the people; and yet, when the hour came, the kingdom broke up into pieces. Veric, the chief of the Cantii, went to Rome and invited the invader to aid him against his rivals at home, and not a man of the Iceni or the Brigantes marched to the aid of Caractacus and Togodamnus. What wonder, then, that these were defeated. Worse than all, when Caractacus was driven a fugitive to hide among the Brigantes, did not their queen, Cartismandua, hand him over to the Romans? Where can we hope to find a leader more fitted to unite us than was Caractacus, the son of the king whom we all, at least, recognized and paid tribute to; a prince who had learned wisdom from a wise father, a warrior enterprising, bold, and indomitable--a true patriot?

"If Caractacus could not unite us, what hope is there of finding another who would do so? Moreover, our position is far worse now than it was ten years ago. The Belgae and Dumnonii in the southwest have been crushed after thirty battles; the Dobuni in the centre have been defeated and garrisoned; the Silures have set an example to us all, inflicting many defeats on the Romans; but their power has at last been broken. The Brigantes and ourselves have both been heavily struck, as we deserved, Boduoc, for standing aloof from Caractacus at first. Thus the task of shaking off the Roman bonds is far more difficult now than it was when Plautius landed here twenty years ago. Well, it is time for me to be going on. Won't you come with me, Boduoc?"

"Not I, Beric; I never want to enter their town again save with a sword in one hand and a torch in the other. It enrages me to see the airs of superiority they give themselves. They scarce seem even to see us as we walk in their streets; and as to the soldiers as they stride along with helmet and shield, my fingers itch to meet them in the forest. No; I promised to walk so far with you, but I go no farther. How long will you be there?"

"Two hours at most, I should say."

"The sun is halfway down, Beric; I will wait for you till it touches that hill over there. Till then you will find me sitting by the first tree at the spot where we left the forest."

Beric nodded and walked on towards the town. The lad, for he was not yet sixteen, was the son of Parta, the chieftainess of one of the divisions of the great tribe of the Iceni, who occupied the tract of country now known as Suffolk, Norfolk, Cambridge, and Huntingdon. This tribe had yielded but a nominal allegiance to Cunobeline, and had held aloof during the struggle between Caractacus and the Romans, but when the latter had attempted to establish forts in their country they had taken up arms. Ostorius Scapula, the Roman proprietor, had marched against them and defeated them with great slaughter, and they had submitted to the Roman authority. The Sarci, the division of the tribe to which Beric belonged, had taken a leading part in the rising, and his father had fallen in the defence of their intrenchments.

Among the British tribes the women ranked with the men, and even when married the wife was often the acknowledged chief of the tribe. Parta had held an equal authority with her husband, and at his death remained sole head of the subtribe, and in order to ensure its obedience in the future, Ostorius had insisted that her only son Beric, at that time a boy of eleven, should be handed over to them as a hostage.

Had Parta consulted her own wishes she would have retired with a few followers to the swamps and fens of the country to the north rather than surrender her son, but the Brigantes, who inhabited Lincolnshire, and who ranged over the whole of the north of Britain as far as Northumberland, had also received a defeat at the hands of the Romans, and might not improbably hand her over upon their demand. She therefore resigned herself to let Beric go.

"My son," she said, "I need not tell you not to let them Romanize you. You have been brought up to hate them. Your father has fallen before their weapons, half your tribe have been slain, your country lies under their feet. I will not wrong you then by fearing for a moment that they can make a Roman of you.

"You have been brought up to lie upon the bare ground, to suffer fatigue and hardship, hunger and thirst, and the rich food and splendid houses and soft raiment of the Romans should have no attraction for you. I know not how long your imprisonment among them may last. For the present I have little hope of another rising; but should I see a prospect of anything like unity among our people, I will send Boduoc with a message to you to hold yourself in readiness to escape when you receive the signal that the time has come. Till then employ your mind in gaining what good you may by your residence among them; there must be some advantage in their methods of warfare which has enabled the people of one city to conquer the world.

"It is not their strength, for they are but pigmies to us. We stand a full head above them, and even we women are stronger than Roman soldiers, and yet they defeat us. Learn then their language, throw your whole mind into that at first, then study their military discipline and their laws. It must be the last as much as their discipline that has made them rulers over so vast an empire. Find out if you can the secret of their rule, and study the training by which their soldiers move and fight as if bound together by a cord, forming massive walls against which we break ourselves in vain. Heed not their arts, pay no attention to their luxuries, these did Cunobeline no good, and did not for a day delay the destruction that fell upon his kingdom. What we need is first a knowledge of their military tactics, so that we may drive them from the land; secondly, a knowledge of their laws, that we may rule ourselves wisely after they have gone. What there is good in the rest may come in time.

"However kind they may be to you, bear always in mind that you are but a prisoner among the oppressors of your country, and that though, for reasons of policy, they may treat you well, yet that they mercilessly despoil and ill treat your countrymen. Remember too, Beric, that the Britons, now that Caractacus has been sent a prisoner to Rome, need a leader, one who is not only brave and valiant in the fight, but who can teach the people how to march to victory, and can order and rule them well afterwards. We are part of one of our greatest tribes, and from among us, if anywhere, such a leader should come.

"I have great hopes of you, Beric. I know that you are brave, for single handed you slew with an arrow a great wolf the other day; but bravery is common to all, I do not think that there is a coward in the tribe. I believe you are intelligent. I consulted the old Druid in the forest last week, and he prophesied a high destiny for you; and when the messenger brought the Roman summons for me to deliver you up as a hostage, it seemed to me that this was of all things the one that would fit you best for future rule. I am not ambitious for you, Beric. It would be nought to me if you were king of all the Britons. It is of our country that I think. We need a great leader, and my prayer to the gods is that one may be found. If you should be the man so much the better; but if not, let it be another. Comport yourself among them independently, as one who will some day be chief of a British tribe, but be not sullen or obstinate. Mix freely with them, learn their language, gather what are the laws under which they live, see how they build those wonderful houses of theirs, watch the soldiers at their exercises, so that when you return among us you can train the Sarci to fight in a similar manner. Keep the one purpose always in your mind. Exercise your muscles daily, for among us no man can lead who is not as strong and as brave as the best who follow him. Bear yourself so that you shall be in good favour with all men."

Beric had, to the best of his power, carried out the instructions of his mother. It was the object of the Romans always to win over their adversaries if possible, and the boy had no reason to complain of his treatment. He was placed in the charge of Caius Muro, commander of a legion, and a slave was at once appointed to teach him Latin. He took his meals with the scribe and steward of the household, for Caius was of noble family, of considerable wealth, and his house was one of the finest in Camalodunum. He was a kindly and just man, and much beloved by his troops. As soon as Beric had learned the language, Caius ordered the scribe to teach him the elements of Roman law, and a decurion was ordered to take him in hand and instruct him in arms.

As Beric was alike eager to study and to exercise in arms, he gained the approval of both his teachers. Julia, the wife of Caius, a kindly lady, took a great fancy to the boy. "He will make a fine man, Caius," she said one day when the boy was fourteen years old. "See how handsome and strong he is; why, Scipio, the son of the centurion Metellus, is older by two years, and yet he is less strong than this young Briton."

"They are a fine race, Julia, though in disposition as fierce as wild cats, and not to be trusted. But the lad is, as you say, strong and nimble. I marked him practising with the sword the other day against Lucinus, who is a stout soldier, and the man had as much as he could do to hold his own against him. I was surprised myself to see how well he wielded a sword of full weight, and how active he was. The contest reminded me of a dog and a wild cat, so nimble were the boy's springs, and so fierce his attacks. Lucinus fairly lost his temper at last, and I stopped the fight, for although they fought with blunted weapons, he might well have injured the lad badly with a downright cut, and that would have meant trouble with the Iceni again."

"He is intelligent, too," Julia replied. "Sometimes I have him in while I am working with the two slave girls, and he will stand for hours asking me questions about Rome, and about our manners and customs."

"One is never sure of these tamed wolves," Caius said; "sometimes they turn out valuable allies and assistants, at other times they grow into formidable foes, all the more dangerous for what they have learned of us. However, do with him as you like, Julia; a woman has a lighter hand than a man, and you are more likely to tame him than we are. Cneius says that he is very eager to learn, and has ever a book in his hand when not practising in arms."

"What I like most in him," Julia said, "is that he is very fond of our little Berenice. The child has taken to him wonderfully, and of an afternoon, when he has finished with Cneius, she often goes out with him. Of course old Lucia goes with them. It is funny to hear them on a wet day, when they cannot go out, talking together--she telling him stories of Rome and of our kings and consuls, and he telling her tales of hunting the wolf and wild boar, and legends of his people, who seem to have been always at war with someone."

After Beric had resided for three years and a half at Camalodunum a great grief fell on the family of Caius Muro, for the damp airs from the valley had long affected Julia and she gradually faded and died. Beric felt the loss very keenly, for she had been uniformly kind to him. A year later Suetonius and the governor of the colony decided that as the Sarci had now been quiet for nearly five years, and as Caius reported that their young chief seemed to have become thoroughly Romanized, he was permitted to return to his tribe.

The present was his first visit to the colony since he had left it four months before. His companion, Boduoc, was one of the tribesmen, a young man six years his senior. He was related to his mother, and had been his companion in his childish days, teaching him woodcraft, and to throw the javelin and use the sword. Together, before Beric went as hostage, they had wandered through the forest and hunted the wolf and wild boar, and at that time Boduoc had stood in the relation of an elder brother to Beric. That relation had now much changed. Although Boduoc was a powerful young man and Beric but a sturdy stripling, the former was little better than an untutored savage, and he looked with great respect upon Beric both as his chief and as possessing knowledge that seemed to him to be amazing.

Hating the Romans blindly he had trembled lest he should find Beric on his return completely Romanized. He had many times, during the lad's stay at Camalodunum, carried messages to him there from his mother, and had sorrowfully shaken his head on his way back through the forest as he thought of his young chief's surroundings. Beric had partially adopted the Roman costume, and to hear him talking and jesting in their own language to the occupants of the mansion, whose grandeur and appointments filled Boduoc with an almost superstitious fear, was terrible to him. However, his loyalty to Beric prevented him from breathing a word in the tribe as to his fears, and he was delighted to find the young chief return home in British garb, and to discover that although his views of the Romans differed widely from his own, he was still British at heart, and held firmly the opinion that the only hope for the freedom of Britain was the entire expulsion of the invaders.

He was gratified to find that Beric had become by no means what he considered effeminate. He was built strongly and massively, as might be expected from such parents, and was of the true British type, that had so surprised the Romans at their first coming among them, possessing great height and muscular power, together with an activity promoted by constant exercise.

Beric had fallen back upon the customs of his people as thoroughly as if he had never dwelt in the stately Roman town. He was as ready as before to undertake the longest hunting expeditions, to sleep in the forest, to go from sunrise to sunset without breaking his fast. When not engaged in hunting he practised incessantly hurling the javelin and other warlike exercises, while of an evening he frequently related stories of Roman history to any chiefs or other guests of his mother, on which occasions the humbler followers would gather thickly in the background, evincing an interest even greater than that which they felt in the songs and legends of the bards.

Beric generally chose stories relating to periods when Rome was hardly pressed by her foes, showing how the intense feeling of patriotism, and the obstinate determination to resist, in spite of all dangers, upon the part of the population, and the discipline and dogged valour of the soldiers, saved her from destruction. He was cautious to draw no parallel openly to the case of Britain. He knew that the Romans were made acquainted, by traitors in their pay, with much that passed among the native tribes, and that at first they were sure to interest themselves in his proceedings. At present there could be no thought of a rising, and the slightest sign of disaffection might bring disaster and ruin upon his tribe. Only when some unexpected event, some invasion of the rights of the Britons even more flagrant than those that had hitherto taken place, should stir the smouldering fire of discontent, and fan it into a fierce flame of revolt from end to end of Britain, could success be hoped for.

No Roman could have found fault with Beric's relation of their prowess or their valour; for he held them up to the admiration of his hearers. "No wonder Rome is great and powerful," he said, "when its people evince so deep a love of country, so resolute a determination in the face of their enemies, so unconquerable a spirit when misfortune weighs upon them."

To the men he addressed all this was new. It was true that a few princes and chiefs had visited Rome, occasionally as travellers desiring to see the centre of her greatness, more often as exiles driven from Britain by defeat in civil strife, but these had only brought back great tales of Rome's magnificence, and the Britons knew nothing of the history of the invaders, and eagerly listened to the stories that Beric had learned from their books in the course of his studies. The report of his stories spread so far that visits were paid to the village of Parta by chiefs and leading men from other sections of the Iceni to listen to them.

Oratory was among the Britons, as among most primitive tribes, highly prized and much cultivated. Oral tradition among such peoples takes the place of books among civilized nations. Story and legend are handed down from father to son, and the wandering bard is a most welcome guest. Next only to valour oratory sways and influences the minds of the people, and a Ulysses had greater influence than an Ajax. From his earliest childhood Beric had listened to the stories and legends told by bards in the rough palace of his father, and his sole schooling before he went to Camalodunum had been to learn these by heart, and to repeat them with due emphasis and appropriate gesture. His father had been one of the most eloquent and influential of the chiefs of the Iceni, and had early impressed upon him the importance of cultivating the power of speech.

His studies in Roman history, too, had taught him the power exercised by men with the gift of moving multitudes by their words; he had learned from books how clearly and distinctly events could be described by a careful choice of words, and attention to form and expression, so that almost unconsciously to himself he had practised the art in his relations of the tales and legends of British history to Berenice and her mother. Thus, then, the manner no less than the matter of his recitals of Roman story, gained him a high estimation among his hearers, and he was already looked upon as a young chief likely to rise to a very high position among the Iceni. Among the common herd his glowing laudations of Roman patriotism, devotion, and sacrifice, caused him to be regarded with disfavour, and the epithet "the Roman" was frequently applied to him. But the wiser spirits saw the hidden meaning of his stories, and that, while holding up the Romans as an example, he was endeavouring to teach how much can be done by patriotism, by a spirit of self sacrifice, and by unity against a common foe. Parta was also proud of the congratulations that distinguished chiefs, famed for their wisdom throughout the tribe, offered to her on the occasion of their visits.

"Beric will be a great chief," one of the wisest of these said to her; "truly his sojourn among the Romans has done great things for him. It would be well, indeed, if every noble youth throughout the island were to have such schooling, if he had your son's wit in taking advantage of it. He will be a great orator; never among our bards have I heard narrations so clear and so well delivered; although the deeds he praises are those of our oppressors, one cannot but feel a thrill of enthusiasm as he tells them. Yea, for the moment I myself felt half a Roman when he told us of the brave youth who thrust his hand into the flames, and suffered it to be consumed in order to impress the invader with a knowledge of the spirit that animated the Romans, and of the three men who held against a host the bridge that their friends were breaking down behind them.

"If he could stir me thus by his tales of the deeds of our enemies, what will it be when some day he makes the heroes of Britain his theme, and calls upon his countrymen to imitate their deeds! I have heard him called 'the Roman,' Parta. Now that I have listened to him I know that he will, when the time comes, be one of Rome's most formidable foes. I will tell you now that Prasutagus, our king, and his queen Boadicea, spoke to me about Beric, and begged me to come hither to see for myself this youth of whom they had heard reports from others, some saying that he had returned a Roman heart and soul, while others affirmed that, while he had learned much from them, he had forgotten nothing of the injuries he had received at their hands in the death of his father, and the disaster of the tribe. I shall know now what to tell them. To Prasutagus, whose fear of the Romans is even greater than his hatred for them, I shall say that the lad is full of the glories of Roman story, and that there is no fear of his doing or saying aught that will excite the anger or suspicion of the Romans. To Boadicea, who hates the Romans far more than she fears them, I shall tell the truth, and shall inform her that when the time comes, as assuredly it some day will, that the Iceni are called upon to defend their liberties against Rome, in Beric she will find a champion of whom I predict that he will be worthy to take his place in our history by the side of Caractacus and Cassivelaunus. May our gods avert that, like them, he fall a victim to British treachery!"

After leaving Boduoc, Beric crossed the bridge built by the Romans over the Stour, and entered the city. Camalodunum was the chief seat of the Roman power in England. Although but so short a time had elapsed since Claudius had occupied it, it was already a large city. A comparatively small proportion, however, was Roman work, but all bore the impress of Roman art and civilization, for Cunobeline, whose capital it had been, was a highly enlightened king, and had introduced Roman ways and methods among his people. Men instructed in their arts and architecture had been largely employed in the building of the town, and its edifices would have borne comparison with those in minor towns in the Roman provinces.

The conquerors, therefore, found much of their work done for them. The original possessors of the houses and of the highly cultivated lands lying round the town were ejected wholesale, and the Romans, establishing themselves in their abodes and farms, then proceeded to add to, embellish, and fortify the town. The 2nd, 9th, and 14th Legions were selected by Claudius to found what was called the colony, and to take possession of the surrounding country. Plautius was appointed propraetor, or governor, and establishing himself in the royal palace of Cunobeline, his first step was to protect the city from renewed attacks by the Britons. He accordingly erected vast works to the westward of the town, extending from the sea to the river, by which means he not only protected the city from attack, but gained, in case of an assault by overpowering numbers, the means of retiring safely to Mersea Island, lying a short distance from the shore.

A council house and a tribunal were erected for the Roman magistrates; temples, a theatre, and baths raised. The civilian population increased rapidly.

Architects, artists, and musicians, decorators, skilled artisans, and traders were attracted from the mainland to the rising city, which rapidly increased in wealth and importance. Conspicuous on the most elevated position stood a temple erected to the honour of Claudius, who was raised by the grateful legionaries to divine rank. So strong and populous was the city that the Trinobantes, during the years that had elapsed since the Romans took possession of it, remained passive under the yoke of their oppressors, and watched, without attempting to take part in them, the rising of the Iceni and Brigantes, the long and desperate war of the Silures and Ordovices under Caractacus, and the reduction of the Belgae and Dumnonii from Hampshire to Cornwall by Vespasian. Yet, had their spirit remained unbroken, there was an opportunity for revenge, for a large part of the veteran legionaries had been withdrawn to take part in the struggle against the western tribes. The tribe had, however, been disarmed, and with Camalodunum on the north, and the rising towns of London and Verulamium on the south, they were cut off from other tribes, and could not hope for final success, unless the powerful Iceni, who were still semi-independent, rose in the national cause. Whether their easy defeat of this tribe soon after the occupation of Camalodunum had rendered the Romans contemptuous of their fighting powers, or that they deemed it wiser to subdue the southwest and west of England, and to strike a heavy blow at the Brigantes to the north before interfering with a powerful tribe so close to their doors, is uncertain; but doubtless they felt that so long as Prasutagus reigned there was little fear of trouble in that quarter, as that king protested himself the friend and ally of Rome, and occupied himself wholly in acquiring wealth and adding to his personal possessions.

The scene in Camalodunum was a familiar one to Beric. The streets were thronged with people. Traders from Gaul and Italy, Roman artisans and workmen, haughty legionaries with shield and helmet, civil officials, Greek players, artists and decorators, native tribesmen, with the products of their fields or the spoils of the chase, walking with humble mien; and shopkeepers sitting at the open fronts of their houses, while their slaves called the attention of passersby to the merits of the goods. Here were the rich products of Eastern looms, there the cloths and linen of Rome, further on a smith's shop in full work, beyond that a silversmith's, next door to which was a thriving trader who sold unguents and perfumes, dyes for the ladies' cheeks and pigments for their eyebrows, dainty requisites for the toilette, and perfumed soap. Bakers and butchers, vendors of fish and game, of fruit, of Eastern spices and flavourings abounded.

Druggists and dealers in dyes for clothing and in the pigments used in wall decorations and paintings were also to be found; and, in fact, this Roman capital of a scarcely subjugated country contained all the appliances for luxury and comfort that could be found in the cities of the civilized provinces.

The only shops at which Beric paused were those of the armourers and of the scribes, at some of which were exhibited vellums with the writings of the Greek and Roman poets and historians; and Beric muttered to himself, "If I am ever present at the sack of Camalodunum these shall be my share of the spoil, and I fancy that no one is likely to dispute their possession with me."

But he did not linger long. Boduoc would be waiting for him, and he could not hurry over his visit, the first he had paid since his absence; therefore he pushed on, with scarce a glance at the stately temple of Claudius, the magnificent baths or other public buildings, until he arrived at the villa of Caius Muro, which stood somewhat beyond the more crowded part of the town.

CHAPTER II
CITY AND FOREST

The house of Caius Muro had been built six years before on the model of one owned by him in the Tuscan hills. Passing through the hall or vestibule, with its mosaic pavement, on which was the word of welcome, "Salve!" Beric entered the atrium, the principal apartment in the house. From each side, at a height of some twenty feet from the ground, extended a roof, the fall being slightly to the centre, where there was an aperture of about eight feet square. Through this light and air made their way down to the apartment, the rainfall from the roofs and opening falling into a marble tank, called the impluvium, below the level of the floor, which was paved with squares of coloured marble. On either side of the atrium were the small sleeping chambers, the bed places being raised and covered with thick mats and rugs.

The walls of the bed chambers as well as of the atrium were painted in black, with figures and landscapes in colour. On the centre of the side facing the vestibule was the tablinum, the apartment of Caius Muro himself. This formed his sitting room and study. The floor was raised about a foot above that of the atrium, and it was partly open both on that side and on the other, looking into the peristylium, so that, while at work, he commanded a view of all that was going on in the atrium and in the courtyard. In the centre of this was a fountain surrounded by plants. From the courtyard opened the triclinium, or dining room, and also rooms used as storerooms, kitchen, and the sleeping places of the slaves.

At the back of the peristylium was the oecus, or state apartment, where Caius received distinguished guests, and where, in the lifetime of Julia, entertainments were given to the ladies of the colony. Like the triclinium, this room was also partially open at both ends, affording the guests a view of the graceful fountain on the one side and of the garden on the other. In winter wooden frames, with heavy hangings, were erected across these openings and that of the tablinum, for the Romans soon found the necessity for modifying the arrangements which, although well suited for an Italian climate, were wholly unfit for that of Britain. The opening in the centre of the atrium was then closed with an awning of oiled canvas, which admitted a certain amount of light to pass, but prevented the passage of rain and snow, and kept out much of the cold. There was a narrow passage between the atrium and the peristylium; this was called the fauces. Above the chambers round the atrium was a second story, approached by a staircase from the peristylium; here were the apartments of the ladies and of the female slaves.

As Beric entered the atrium, a man, who was reading a roll of parchment, rose to his feet.

"Welcome, Beric!" he said warmly.

"All hail, preceptor!" the lad replied. "Are all well here?"

"All well, Beric. We had looked to see you before, and Berenice has been constantly asking me when you were coming."

"I had been absent over four years, you see," Beric replied, "and it was not easy to get away from home again. Now I must speak to Caius." He crossed the apartment, and stood at the entrance to the tablinum. Caius looked up from a military treatise he was perusing.

"Ah, Beric! it is you! I am glad to see you again, though I am sorry to observe that you have abandoned our fashions and taken to the native garb again."

"It was necessary, Caius," Beric said. "I should have lost all influence with the tribe had I not laid aside my Roman dress. As it is, they regard me with some doubt, as one too enamoured of Roman customs."

"We have heard of you, Beric, and, indeed, report says that you speak well of us, and are already famous for your relations of our history."

"I thought it well that my countrymen should know your great deeds," Beric said, "and should see by what means you have come to rule the world. I received nought but kindness at your hands, and no prisoner's lot was ever made more easy than mine. To you and yours I am deeply grateful. If your people all behaved as kindly towards the natives of this country as you did to me, Britain would be conquered without need of drawing sword from scabbard."

"I know not that, Beric; to rule, one should be strong as well as kind. Still, as you know, I think that things might have been arranged far less harshly than they have been. It was needful that we should show ourselves to be masters; but I regret the harshness that has been too often used, and I would that not one of us here, from the governor down to the poorest soldier, was influenced by a desire for gain, but that each was animated, as he assuredly should be, only by a desire to uphold the glory and power of Rome. But that would be expecting too much from human nature, and even among you there are plenty ready to side against their countrymen for the sake of Roman gold. In that they have less excuse than we. Custom and habit have made our wants many, and all aim at attaining the luxuries of the rich. On the other hand, your wants are few, and I see not that the piling up of wealth adds in any way to your happiness."

"That is true, Caius. I quite agree with you that it is far more excusable for a Roman to covet wealth than for a Briton; and while I blame many officials and soldiers for the harshness with which they strive to wring all their possessions from my countrymen, I deem their conduct as worthy and honourable when compared with that of Britons who sell their country for your gold."

"We must take the world as we find it, Beric. We may regret that greed and the love of luxury should influence men, as we may grieve that they are victims of other base passions; but it is of no use quarrelling with human nature. Certain it is that all vices bring their own punishment, and that the Romans were a far nobler race when they were poor and simple, in the days of the early consuls, than they are now, with all their power, their riches, and their luxuries. Such is the history of all peoples--of Egypt, of Persia, of Greece, and Carthage; and methinks that Rome, too, will run the course of other nations, and that some day, far distant maybe, she will sink beneath the weight of her power and her luxury, and that some younger and more vigorous people will, bit by bit, wrest her dominions from her and rule in her place.

"As yet, happily, I see no signs of failing in her powers. She is still vigorous, and even in the distant outskirts of the empire the wave of conquest flows onward. Happily for us, I think, it can flow no farther this way; there is but one island beyond this to conquer, and then, as in Western Gaul and Iberia, the ocean says to Rome, 'Thou shalt go no farther.' Would that to the south, the east, and north a similar barrier checked our progress, then we could rest and be content, and need no longer waste our strength in fresh conquests, or in opposing the incursions of hordes of barbarians from regions unknown to us even by report. I could wish myself, Beric, that nature had placed your island five days' sail from the coasts of Gaul, instead of placing it within sight. Then I might have been enjoying life in my villa among the Tuscan hills with my daughter, instead of being exposed at any moment to march with the Legion against the savage mountaineers of the west. Ah! here comes Berenice," he broke off, as his daughter, attended by her old nurse, entered the atrium from the vestibule. She hastened her steps as she saw Beric standing before her father in the tablinum.

"I knew you would come back, Beric, because you promised me; but you have been a long time in keeping your word."

"I am not my own master at home, any more than I was here, Berenice," he said, "and my mother would not hear before of my leaving her. I have only come now for an hour's visit, to see that all goes well in this house, and to tell you that I had not forgotten my promise; the next time I hope to pay a longer visit. At daybreak tomorrow we have a party to hunt the wolves, which have so multiplied as to become a danger in the forests of late."

"I should like to go out to see a wolf hunt, Beric."

"I fear that would not be possible," he said; "the woods are thick and tangled, and we have to force our way through to get to their lair."

"But last winter they came close to the town, and I heard that some came even into the streets."

"Yes, they will do so when driven by hunger; but they were hunting then and not being hunted. No, Berenice, I fear that your wish to see a wolf hunt cannot be gratified; they are savage beasts, and are great trouble and no loss to us. In winter they carry off many children, and sometimes devour grown up people, and in times of long snow have been known to attack large parties, and, in spite of a stout resistance by the men, to devour them. In summer they are only met singly, but in winter they go in packs and kill numbers of our cattle."

"I should like to go into the woods," the girl said earnestly, "I am tired of this town. My father says he will take me with him some day when he goes west, but so far I have seen nothing except this town and Verulamium, and the country was all just as it is here, fields and cultivation. We could see the forests in the distance, but that was all. My father says, that if we went west, we should travel for miles through the forest and should sleep in tents, but that we cannot do it till everything is quiet and peaceful. Oh, Beric! I do wish the Britons would not be always fighting."

Beric smiled. "The British girls, Berenice, say they wish the Romans would not be always fighting."

"It is very troublesome," she said pettishly. "I should like everyone to be friends, and then there would be no need to have so many soldiers in Britain, and perhaps the emperor would order our legions home. Father says that we ought to look upon this as home now, for that the legion may remain here for years and years; but he said the other day that he thought that if everything was quiet here he should, when I am sixteen years old, obtain leave from the governor, and go back to Rome for two or three years, and I think, though he has not said so outright, that he will perhaps retire and settle there."

"It would be much the best for you," Beric said earnestly. "I should be sorry, because you have been very kind to me, and I should grieve were you to leave me altogether; but there may be trouble here again some day, and I think it would be far better for you to be back in Rome, where you would have all the pleasures and delights of the great capital, and live in ease and comfort, without the risk of your father having to march away to the wars. I know that if I were your father I would take you back. He says that his villa there is exactly like this, and you have many relations there, and there must be all sorts of pleasures and grand spectacles far beyond anything there is here. I am sure it would be better for you, and happier."

"I thought that you would be quite sorry," she said gravely.

"So I shall be very sorry for myself," Beric said; "as, next to my own mother, there is no one I care for so much as you and your father. I shall miss you terribly; but yet I am so sure that it would be best for you to be at home with your own people, that I should be glad to hear that your father was going to take you back to Rome."

But Berenice did not altogether accept the explanation. She felt really hurt that Beric should view even the possibility of her going away with equanimity, and she very shortly went off to her own apartment; while a few minutes later, Beric, after bidding goodbye to Caius, started to rejoin Boduoc, whom he found waiting at the edge of the forest.

That evening Berenice said to her father, "I was angry with Beric today, father."

"Were you, child? what about?"

"I told him that perhaps in another three years, when I was sixteen, you would take me to Rome, and that I thought, perhaps, if we went there you would not come back again; and instead of being very much grieved, as I thought he would, he seemed quite pleased at the idea. Of course he said he was sorry, but he did not really seem to be, and he says he thought it would be very much better for me. I thought he was grateful, father, and liked us very much, and now I am quite disappointed in him."

Caius was silent for a minute or two.

"I do not think Beric is ungrateful," he said, "and I am sure that he likes us, Berenice."

"He said he did, father, that he cared for us more than anyone except his mother; but if he cared for us, surely he would be very, very sorry for us to go away."

"Beric is a Briton, my dear, and we are Romans. By this time he must have thoroughly learned his people's feelings towards us. I have never believed, as some do, that Britain is as yet completely conquered, and that when we have finished with the Silures in the west our work will be completely done.

"Beric, who knows his countrymen, may feel this even more strongly than I do, and may know that, sooner or later, there will be another great effort on the part of the Britons to drive us out. It may be a year, and it may be twenty, but I believe myself that some day we shall have a fierce struggle to maintain our hold here, and Beric, who may see this also, and who knows the feeling of his countrymen, may wish that we should be away before the storm comes.

"There is but little doubt, Berenice, that we despise these people too much, still less that we treat them harshly and cruelly. Were I propraetor of Britain, I would rule them differently. I am but the commander of a legion, and my duty is but to rule my men. I would punish, and punish sternly, all attempts at rising; but I would give them no causes for discontent. We treat them as if their spirit were altogether broken, as if they and their possessions were but our chattels, as if they possessed no rights, not even the right to live. Some day we shall find our mistake, and when the time comes the awakening will be a rude one. It is partly because I see dimly the storm gathering in the distance that I long to be home again. As long as your mother lived this seemed a home to me, now I desire rest and quiet. I have done my share of fighting, I have won honour enough, and I may look before long to be a general; but I have had enough of it, and long for my quiet villa in the Alban hills, with an occasional visit to Rome, where you can take part in its gaieties, and I can have the use of the libraries stored with the learning of the world. So do not think harshly of Beric, my child; he may see the distant storm more plainly than I do. I am sure that he cares for us, and if he is glad at the news that we are going, it is because he wishes us away and in safety before the trouble comes.

"Nero has come to the imperial throne, and the men he is sending hither are of a widely different stamp from the lieutenants of Claudius. The latter knew that the Britons can fight, and that, wild and untutored as they are, it needed all the skill and courage of Ostorius and Vespasian to reduce them to order. The newcomers regard them as slaves to be trampled upon, robbed, and ill used as they choose. I am sure they will find their mistake. As long as they deal only with the tribes thoroughly subdued, the Trinobantes, the Cantii, the Belgae, and the Dumnonii, all may be quiet; they dare not move. But the Iceni and Brigantes, although they both have felt the weight of our swords, are still partly independent, and if pressed too severely will assuredly revolt, and if they give the signal all Britain may be up in arms again. I am scoffed at if I venture to hint to these newcomers that there is life yet in Britain. Dwelling here in a Roman city, it seems to them absurd that there can be danger from the savages who roam in the forests that stretch away from beyond the river at our very feet to the far distant north, to regions of which we are absolutely ignorant. I regard what Beric has said as another warning."

"But I thought that Beric was our friend, father, and you told me you had heard that he was teaching his countrymen how great is our history."

"Beric is a Briton in the midst of Britons, child. He is a partially tamed wolf cub, and had he been sent to Rome and remained there he would have done credit to our teaching. He is fond of study, and at the same time fond of arms; he might have turned out a wise citizen or a valiant soldier. But this was not done. He has gone back again among the wolves, and whatever his feelings towards us personally may be, he must side with his own people. Did they suspect him of being Roman at heart they would tear him in pieces. I believe that as he knows our strength, and that in the end we must conquer, his influence will always be on the side of peace; but if arms are taken up he will have no choice but to side with his countrymen, and should it be another ten years before the cloud bursts, he may be one of our most formidable opponents. Don't blame him, child; he only shows his regard for you, by wishing you back safely in Rome before trouble arises."

"You are just in time, Beric," Boduoc said as the young chief joined him. "The sun is but a hand's breadth above that hill. Here are your spear and sword where you hid them, though why you should have done it I know not, seeing that they have not yet ventured to order us to disarm."

"And if they did we should not obey them, Boduoc; but as the Trinobantes have long been forbidden to carry arms, it might have caused trouble had I gone armed into the town, and we don't want trouble at present. I went on a peaceful visit, and there was no occasion for me to carry my weapons. But give me a piece of that deer flesh and an oaten cake; we have a long march before us."

"Why, did you not eat with them?"

"No. I was, of course, invited, but I had but a short time to stop and did not wish it to seem as if I had come for a taste of Roman dainties again."

As soon as the meal was eaten they set out. It was but a track through the forest, for although the trees had been cleared away for a width of twenty feet there was but little traffic, for the road was seldom traversed, save by an occasional messenger from Prasutagus. It had been used by the legions at the time that Ostorius had built a line of forts stretching from the Nen to the Severn, and by it they had advanced when the Iceni had risen; but from that time it had been unused by them, as the Iceni had paid their tribute regularly, and held aloof from all hostile movements against them. Prasutagus was always profuse in his assurance of friendship towards Rome, and save that the Roman officers visited his capital once a year to receive their tribute, they troubled but little about the Iceni, having their hands occupied by their wars in the south and west, while their main road to the north ran far to the west of Camalodunum.

"We shall arrive about midnight," Beric said as they strode along.

"We may or we may not," Boduoc said curtly.

"What is to prevent us, Boduoc?"

"Well, the wolves may prevent us, Beric; we heard them howling several times as we came along this morning. The rapacious brutes have not been so bold for years, and it is high time that we hunted them down, or at any rate made our part of the country too hot to hold them. I told Borgon before I started that if we did not return by an hour after midnight it would be because we had been obliged to take to a tree, and that he had better bring out a party at the first break of day to rescue us."

"But we have never had any trouble of that kind while we have been hunting, Boduoc."

"No; but I think there must have been some great hunts up in Norfolk, and that the brutes have come south. Certain it is that there have in the last week been great complaints of them, and, as you know, it was for that reason that your mother ordered all the men of the tribe to assemble by tomorrow morning to make war against them. The people in the farms and villages are afraid to stay out after nightfall. No man with arms in his hands fears a wolf, or even two or three of them, in the daytime; but when they are in packs they are formidable assailants, even to a strong party. Things are getting as bad now as they were twenty years ago. My father has told me that during one hard winter they destroyed full half our herds, and that hundreds of people were devoured by them. They had to erect stockades round the villages and drive in all the cattle, and half the men kept guard by turns, keeping great fires alight to frighten them away. When we have cleared the land of those two legged wolves the Romans, we shall have to make a general war upon them, for truly they are becoming a perfect scourge to the land. It is not like the wild boar, of which there might with advantage be more, for they do but little harm, getting their food for the most part in the woods, and furnishing us with good eating as well as good sport. But the wolves give us nothing in return, and save for the sport no one would trouble to hunt them; and it is only by a general order for their destruction, or by the offer of a reward for their heads, that we shall get rid of them."

"Well, let us press on, Boduoc. I would not that anything should occur to prevent us starting with the rest in the morning."

"We are walking a good pace now," Boduoc said, "and shall gain but little by going faster. One cannot run for six hours; and besides it is as much as we can do to walk fast in the dark. Did we try to run we should like enough fall over a stump or root, and maybe not arrive there even though the wolves stopped us not."

For two hours more they strode along. Boduoc's eyes had been trained by many a long night spent among the woods, and dark as it was beneath the overarching trees, he was able to discern objects around him, and kept along in his regular stride as surely and almost as noiselessly as a wild beast; but the four years spent in the Roman town had impaired Beric's nocturnal vision; and though he had done much hunting since his return home, he was far from being able to use his eyes as his companion did, and he more than once stumbled over the roots that crossed the path.

"You will be on your head presently," Boduoc growled.

"It is all very well for you, Boduoc, who have the eyes of a cat; but you must remember we are travelling in the dark, and although I can make out the trunks on either hand the ground is all black to me, and I am walking quite at hazard."

"It is not what I should call a light night," Boduoc admitted.

"Well, no, considering that there is no moon, and that the clouds that were rising when the sun went down have overspread all the sky. I don't see that it could well be darker."

"Well we will stop at that hut in the little clearing, somewhere about half a mile on, and get a couple of torches. If you were to fall and twist your foot you would not be able to hunt tomorrow."

"What is that?" Beric exclaimed as a distant cry came to their ears.

"I think it is the voice of a woman," Boduoc said. "Or maybe it is one of the spirits of evil."

Beric during his stay among the Romans had lost faith in most of his superstitions. "Nonsense, Boduoc! it was the cry of a woman; it came from ahead. Maybe some woman returning late has been attacked by wolves. Come along," he shouted, and he started to run, followed reluctantly by his companion.

"Stop, Beric, stop!" he said in a short time, "I hear other sounds."

"So do I," Beric agreed, but without checking his pace. "My eyes may be dull, Boduoc, but they are not so dull as your ears. Why, don't you know the snarling of wolves when you hear them?"

Again the loud cry of distress came on the night air. "They have not seized her yet," Beric said. "Her first cry would have been her last had they done so. She must be in that hut, Boduoc, and they are trying to get at her. Maybe her husband is away."

"It is wolves," Boduoc agreed in a tone of relief. "Since that is all I am ready for them; but sword and spear are of no avail against the spirits of the air. We must be careful though, or instead of us attacking we may be attacked."

Beric paid no attention. They had as they passed the hut that morning stopped for a drink of water there, and he saw now before his eyes the tall comely young woman with a baby in her arms and two children hanging to her skirts. In a short time they stood at the edge of the little clearing by the side of the path. It was lighter here, and he could make out the outline of the rude hut, and, as he thought, that of many dark figures moving round it. A fierce growling and snarling rose from around the hut, with once or twice a sharp yell of pain.

"There are half a dozen of them on the roof," Boduoc said, "and a score or more round the hut. At present they haven't winded us, for the air is in our faces."

"I think we had best make a rush at them, Boduoc, shouting at the top of our voices as we go, and bidding the woman stand in readiness to unbar the door. They will be scared for a moment, not knowing how many of us there may be, and once inside we shall be safe from them."

"Let us get as near as we can before we begin to shout, Beric. They may run back a few paces at our voice, but will speedily rally."

Holding their spears in readiness for action they ran forward. When within thirty yards of the hut Boduoc raised his voice in a wild yell, Beric adding his cry and then shouting, "Unbar your door and stand to close it as we enter."

There was, however, no occasion for haste. Boduoc's sudden yell completely scared the wolves, and with whimpers of dismay they scattered in all directions. The door opened as Beric and his companion came up, and they rushed in and closed it after them. A fire burned on the hearth. A dead wolf lay on the ground, the children crouched in terror on a pile of rushes, and a woman stood with a spear in her hand.

"Thanks to our country's gods you have come!" she said. "A few minutes later and all would have been over with me and my children. See, one has already made his way through the roof, and in half a dozen places they have scratched holes well nigh large enough to pass through."

"We heard your cry," Beric said, "and hastened forward at the top of our speed."

"It was for you that I called," the woman said. "By what you said this morning I judged you would be returning about this hour, and it was in hopes you might hear me that I cried out, for I knew well that no one else would be likely to be within earshot."

"Where is your husband?" Beric asked.

"He started this afternoon for Cardun. He and all the able bodied men were ordered to assemble there tonight in readiness to begin the war against the wolves at daybreak. There is no other house within a mile, and even had they heard me there they could have given me no assistance, seeing there are but women and children remaining behind."

"They are coming again," Boduoc broke in; "I can hear their feet pattering on the dead leaves. Which shall we do, Beric, pile more wood on the fire, or let it go out altogether? I think that we shall do better without it; it is from the roof that they will attack, and if we have a light here we cannot see them till they are ready to leap down; whereas, if we are in darkness we may be able to make them out when they approach the holes, or as they pass over any of the crevices."

"I don't know, Boduoc; I think we shall do better if we have light. We may not make them out so well, but at least we can use our spears better than we could in the dark, when we might strike them against the rafters or thick branches."

The woman at once gathered some of the pieces of wood that had fallen through as the wolves made the holes and put them on the hearth, where they soon blazed up brightly.

"I will take this big hole," Boduoc said, "it is the only one by which they can come down at present. Do you try and prevent them from enlarging any of the others."

There was a sudden thump overhead, followed almost immediately by several others.

"They get up by the wood pile," the woman said. "It is against that side of the hut, and reaches nearly up to the eaves.

There was a sharp yell as Boduoc thrust his spear up through the hole when he saw a pair of eyes, shining in the firelight, appear at the edge. At the same moment there was a sound of scraping and scratching at some of the other holes. The roof was constructed of rough poles laid at short distances apart, and above these were small branches, on which was a sort of thatch of reeds and rushes. Standing close under one of the holes Beric could see nothing, but from the sound of the scratching he could tell from which side the wolf was at work enlarging it. He carefully thrust the point of his spear through the branches and gave a sudden lunge upwards. A fierce yell was heard, followed by the sound of a body rolling down the roof, and then a struggle accompanied by angry snarling and growling outside.

"That is one less, Beric," Boduoc said. "I fancy I only scratched mine. Ah!" he exclaimed suddenly, as without the least warning a wolf sprang down through the hole. Before it could gather its legs under it for a fresh spring Beric and the woman both thrust their spears deeply into it, Boduoc keeping his eyes fixed on the hole, and making a lunge as another wolf peered down in readiness to spring after the one that had entered.

For hours the fight went on. Gradually the holes, in spite of the efforts of the defenders, were enlarged, and the position became more and more critical. At least twenty of the wolves were slain; but as the attack was kept up as vigorously as at first, it was evident that fresh reinforcements had arrived to the assailants.

"We cannot keep them out much longer, Beric," Boduoc said at last. "It seems to me that our only plan is to fire the hut, and then, each taking a child, to make a rush across to the trees and climb them. The sudden burst of fire will drive them back for a little, and we may make good our retreat to the trees."

"What time is it, think you, Boduoc?"

"It must be two or three hours past midnight, and if Borgon carried out my instructions help ought to be near at hand. I would that we could let them know of our peril."

"There is a cow horn," the woman said, pointing to the corner of the hut. "My husband uses it for calling in the cattle."

Boduoc seized the horn and blew a deep hollow blast upon it. There was a sudden pattering of feet overhead and then silence.

"That has scared them," Beric said. "Blow again, Boduoc; if we can but gain half an hour our friends may be up."

Again and again the hoarse roar of the cow horn rose, but the wolves speedily recovered from their scare and crowded on the roof.

"We can't hold out much longer," Beric said, as two wolves that leapt down together had just been despatched. "Get a brand from the fire." At this moment there was a sudden scuffle overhead, and the three defenders stood, spear in hand, ready to repel a fresh attack; but all was quiet; then a loud shout rose on the air.

"Thank the gods, here they are!" Boduoc said. He listened a moment, but all was still round the hut; then he threw the door open as a score of men with lighted torches came running towards it, and raised a shout of satisfaction as the light fell upon Beric.

"Thanks for your aid, my friends!" he said as they crowded round him; "never was a shout more welcome than yours. You were just in time, as you may see by looking at the roof. We were about to fire it and make for the trees, though I doubt if one of us would have reached them."

As the men entered the hut and looked at the ragged holes in the roof and the bodies of nine wolves stretched on the ground, they saw that they had, indeed, arrived only just in time. Among the rescuing party was the man to whom the hut belonged, whose joy at finding his wife and children unhurt was great indeed; and he poured forth his thanks to Beric and Boduoc when he learned from his wife that they had voluntarily abandoned the wood, where they could have been secure in the shelter of a tree, in order to assist her in defending the hut against the wolves.

"You must all come with us," Beric said; "the wolves may return after we have gone. When our hunt is over I will send some men to help you to repair your roof. Where are the cattle?"

"They are safe in a stockade at the next village," the man said. "We finished it only yesterday, and drove in all the cattle from the forests, and collected great quantities of wood so that the women might keep up great bonfires if the wolves tried to break in."

A few minutes later the party started on their return. As they walked they could sometimes hear the pattering of footsteps on the falling leaves, but the torches deterred the animals from making an attack, and after three hours' walking they arrived at Cardun. The village stood on a knoll rising from swamps, through which a branch of the Stour wound its way sluggishly. Round the crest of the knoll ran two steep earthen banks, one rising behind the other, and in the inclosed space, some eight acres in extent, stood the village. The contrast between it and the Roman city but two-and-twenty miles away was striking. No great advance had been made upon the homes that the people had occupied in Gaul before their emigration. In the centre stood Parta's abode, distinguished from the rest only by its superior size. The walls were of mud and stone, the roof high, so as to let the water run more easily off the rough thatching. It contained but one central hall surrounded by half a dozen small apartments.

The huts of the people consisted but of a single room, with a hole in the roof by which the smoke of the fire in the centre made its way out. The doorway was generally closed by a wattle secured by a bar. When this was closed light only found its way into the room through the chinks of the wattle and the hole in the roof. In winter, for extra warmth, a skin was hung before the door. Beyond piles of hides, which served as seats by day and beds at night, there was no furniture whatever in the rooms, save a few earthen cooking pots.

Parta's abode, however, was more sumptuously furnished. Across one end ran a sort of dais of beaten earth, raised a foot above the rest of the floor. This was thickly strewn with fresh rushes, and there was a rough table and benches. The walls of the apartment were hidden by skins, principally those of wolves.

The fireplace was in the centre of the lower part of the hall, and arranged on a shelf against the wall were cooking pots of iron and brass; while on a similar shelf on the wall above the dais were jugs and drinking vessels of gold. Hams of wild boar and swine hung from the rafters, where too were suspended wild duck and fish, and other articles of food. Parta's own apartment led from the back of the dais. That of Beric was next to it, its separate use having been granted to him on his return from Camalodunum, not without some scoffing remarks upon his effeminacy in requiring a separate apartment, instead of sleeping as usual on the dais; while the followers and attendants stretched themselves on the floor of the hall.

CHAPTER III
A WOLF HUNT

Shouts of welcome saluted Beric as with his party he crossed the rough bridge over the stream and descended the slope to the village. Some fifteen hundred men were gathered here, all armed for the chase with spears, javelins, and long knives. Their hair fell over their necks, their faces were, according to the universal custom, shaved with the exception of the moustache. Many of them were tattooed--a custom that at one time had been universal, but was now dying out among the more civilized. Most of them were, save for the mantle, naked from the waist up, the body being stained a deep blue with woad--a plant largely cultivated for its dye. This plant, known as Isatis tinctoria, is still grown in France and Flanders. It requires rich ground and grows to a height of three or four feet, bearing yellow flowers. The dye is obtained from the leaves, which are stripped two or three times in the season. They are partially dried, and are then pounded or ground, pressed into a mass with the hands or feet, and piled in a heap, when fermentation takes place. When this process is completed the paste is cut up, and when placed in water yields a blue dye. It can also be prepared by laying it in the water in the first place and allowing it to ferment there. The water, which becomes a deep blue, is drawn off and allowed to settle, the dye remaining at the bottom. Fresh water is then added to the leaves, which are again stirred up and the operation is repeated.

Passing through the crowd of tribesmen, Beric entered his mother's abode, walked up to the dais, and saluted her by a deep bow. Parta was a woman of tall stature and of robust form. Her garment was fastened at each shoulder by a gold brooch. A belt studded and clasped by the same metal girded it in at the waist, and it then fell in loose folds almost to her feet. She had heavy gold bracelets on her arms.

"You are late, Beric," she said sternly. "Our tribesmen have been waiting nigh an hour for you. I only heard at daybreak that Borgon had gone out to search for you with a party."

"It was well that he did, mother, for Boduoc and I were besieged in a hut by a pack of wolves, who would shortly have made an end of us had not rescue arrived."

"What were you doing in the hut?" she asked. "You told me you should leave the Romans' town before sunset and make your way straight back here."

Beric shortly related the circumstances of the fight.

"It is well that it is no worse," she said; "but Boduoc ought to have known better than to have allowed you to leave the trees, where you would at least have been safe from the wolves. What mattered the life of a woman in comparison to yours, when you know my hopes and plans for you? But stay not talking. Magartha has some roasted kid in readiness for you. Eat it quickly, and take a horn of mead, and be gone. An hour has been wasted already."

A few minutes sufficed for Beric to satisfy his hunger. Then he went out and joined two or three minor chiefs of experience who had charge of the hunt. The greater portion of the tribesmen had already started. Almost every man had brought with him one or more large dogs trained in hunting the wolf and boar, and the woods beyond the swamp rang with their deep barking. Instructions had already been given to the men. These proceeded in parties of four, each group taking its post some fifty yards from the next. Those who had the farthest to go had started before daybreak, and it was another two hours before the whole were in position, forming a long line through the forest upwards of ten miles in length. A horn was sounded in the centre where the leaders had posted themselves, and the signal was repeated at points along the line, and then, with shouts on the part of the men and fierce barkings on that of the dogs, the whole moved forward. The right of the line rested on the Stour, the left upon the Orwell; and as they passed along through the forest the line contracted. At times wild boars made a dash to break through it. Many of these were slain, till the chiefs considered that there was a sufficient supply of food, and the rest were then allowed to pass through.

No wolves were seen until they neared the point where the two rivers unite, by which time the groups were within a few paces of each other. Then among the trees in front of them a fierce snarling and yelping was heard. The dogs, which had hitherto been kept in hand, were now loosed, and with a shout the men rushed forward both on the bluffs in the centre and along the low land skirting the rivers on either side. Soon the wolves came pouring down from the wooded bluff, and engaged in a furious conflict with the dogs. As the men ran up, a few of the wolves in their desperation charged them and endeavoured to break through, but the great majority, cowed by the clamour and fierce assault, crouched to the earth and received their death blow unresistingly. Some took to the water, but coracles had been sent down to the point the evening before, and they were speedily slain. Altogether some four or five hundred wolves were killed.

It was now late in the afternoon. Wood was collected and great fires made, and the boars' flesh was soon roasting over them. At daybreak they started again, and retracing their steps formed a fresh line at the point where the last beat had begun, this time beating in a great semicircle and driving the wolves down on to the Stour. So for a fortnight the war went on. Only such deer and boar as were required for food were killed; but the wolves were slain without mercy, and at the end of the operations that portion of the country was completely cleared of these savage beasts, for those who had escaped the beating parties had fled far away through the forest to more quiet quarters.

The work had been laborious; for each day some forty miles had been traversed in the march from the last place of slaughter to the next beat, and in the subsequent proceedings. It had, however, been full of interest and excitement, especially during the second week, when, having cleared all the country in the neighbourhood of the rivers, the men were ranged in wide circles some ten miles in diameter, advancing gradually towards a centre. Occasionally many of the wolves escaped before the lines had narrowed sufficiently for the men to be near enough to each other to oppose a successful resistance, but in each case the majority continued to slink from the approaching noises until the cordon was too close for them to break through.

Altogether over four thousand wolves were slain. All those whose coats were in good condition were skinned, the skins being valuable for linings to the huts, for beds, and winter mantles. Many men had been bitten more or less severely by them, but none had been killed; and there was much rejoicing at the complete clearance from the district of a foe that had, since the arrival of the large packs from the north, made terrible inroads among the herds of cattle and swine, and had killed a considerable number of men, women, and children. The previous winter had been a very severe one, and had driven great numbers of wolves down from North Britain. The fighting that had been going on for years in the south and west, and at times in the midlands, had put a stop to the usual chases of wolves in those districts, and they had consequently multiplied exceedingly and had become a serious scourge even before the arrival of the fresh bands from the north. However, after so great a slaughter it was hoped that for a time at least they would not again make their appearance in that neighbourhood.

Returning home at the end of their expedition Beric was surprised as he entered the hall to see a Druid standing upon the dais conversing with his mother, who was pacing up and down with angry gestures. That their conference was an important one he did not doubt; for the Druids dwelt in the recesses of the forests or near their temples, and those who wished to consult them must journey to them to ask their counsel beneath a sacred oak or in the circle of the magic stones. When great events were impending, or when tribes took up arms against each other, the Druids would leave their forest abodes, and, interposing between the combatants, authoritatively bid them desist. They acted as mediators between great chiefs, and were judges upon all matters in dispute. He was sure, therefore, that the Druid was the bearer of news of importance. He stood waiting in the centre of the hall until his mother's eye fell upon him.

"Come hither, Beric," she said, "and hear the news that the holy Druid has brought. Think you not that the Romans have carried their oppression far enough when they have seized half the land of our island, enslaved the people, and exacted tribute from the free Britons? What think you, now? The Roman governor Severus, knowing that it is our religion as well as love of our country that arms us against them, and that the Druids ever raise their voices to bid us defend our altars and our homes, have resolved upon an expedition against the Sacred Island, and have determined to exterminate our priests, to break down our altars, and to destroy our religion. Ten days since the legion marched from Camalodunum to join the army he is assembling in the west. From all other parts he has drawn soldiers, and he has declared his intention of rooting out and destroying our religion at its centre."

"The news is terrible," the Druid said, "but our gods will fight for us, and doubtless a terrible destruction will fall upon the impious men who thus dream of profaning the Sacred Island; but it may be otherwise, or perchance the gods may see that thus, and thus only, can the people of Britain be stirred to take up arms and to annihilate the worshippers of the false gods of Rome. Assuredly we are on the eve of great events, and every Briton must prepare to take up arms, either to fall upon the legions whom our gods have stricken or to avenge the insult offered to our faith."

"It is terrible news, indeed," Beric said; "and though I am but a lad, father, I am ready when the call comes to fight in the front ranks of the Iceni with our people. My father fell fighting for his country by the sword of the Romans, and I am ready to follow his example when my mother shall say, 'Go out to war.'"

"For the present, Beric, we must remain quiet; we must await news of the result of this expedition; but the word has gone round, and I and my brethren are to visit every chief of the Iceni, while the Druids of the north stir up the Brigantes; the news, too, that the time of their deliverance is at hand, and that they must hold themselves in readiness to rise against the oppressors, is passing through the Trinobantes and the tribes of the south and southwest. This time it must be no partial rising, and we must avoid the ruinous error of matching a single tribe against the whole strength of the Romans. It must be Britain against Rome--a whole people struggling for their homes and altars against those who would destroy their religion and reduce them to slavery."

"I would that it could have been postponed for a time, father," Beric said. "During the four years I passed as a hostage at Camalodunum I have been learning the tactics that have enabled the Romans to conquer us. I have learned their words of command, and how the movements were executed, and I hope when I become a man to train the Sarci to fight in solid order, to wheel and turn as do the Romans, so that we might form a band which might in the day of battle oppose itself to the Roman onset, check pursuit, and perhaps convert a reverse into a victory."

"Heed not that," the Druid said enthusiastically. "It would be useful indeed, but there is but scant time for it now. Our gods will fight for us. We have numbers and valour. Our warriors will sweep their soldiers aside as a wave dashes over a rock."

The conversation between the Druid and Parta had been heard by others in the hall, and the news spread rapidly among the tribesmen as they returned from the chase. Shouts of fury and indignation rose outside, and several of the minor chiefs, followed by a crowd of excited men, poured into the hall, demanding with loud shouts that war should be declared against the Romans. The Druid advanced to the edge of the dais.

"Children," he said, "the time has not yet come, nor can the Sarci do aught until the word is given by Prasutagus, and the whole of the Iceni rise in arms, and not the Iceni alone, but Britons from sea to sea. Till then hold yourselves in readiness. Sharpen your arms and prepare for the contest. But you need a chief. In the ordinary course of things years would have elapsed before Beric, the son of your last brave prince, would have been associated with his mother in the rule of the tribe; but on the eve of such a struggle ordinary customs and usages must be set at nought. I therefore, in virtue of my sacred authority, now appoint Beric as chief next to his mother in the tribe, and I bid you obey him in all things relating to war. He has learned much of Roman ways and methods, and is thus better fitted than many far older than he to instruct you how best to stand their onset, and I prophesy that under him no small honour and glory will fall to the tribe, and that they will bear a signal share in avenging our gods and winning our freedom. Come hither, Beric;" and the Druid, laying a hand upon the lad's head, raised the other to heaven and implored the gods to bestow wisdom and strength upon him, and to raise in him a mighty champion of his country and faith. Then he uttered a terrible malediction upon any who should disobey Beric's orders, or question his authority, who should show faint heart in the day of battle, or hold his life of any account in the cause of his country.

"Now," he concluded, "retire to your homes. We must give no cause or pretext for Roman aggression until the signal is given. You will not be idle. Your young chief will teach you somewhat of the discipline that has rendered the Roman soldiers so formidable, so that you may know how to set yourselves in the day of battle, how to oppose rank to rank, to draw off in good order, or to press forward to victory. The issue is ever in the hands of the gods, but we should do all we can to deserve it. It is good to learn even from our enemies. They have studied war for ages, and if they have conquered brave peoples, it has not been by superior valour, but because they have studied war, while others have trusted solely to their native valour. Therefore deem not instruction useless, or despise methods simply because you do not understand them. None could be braver than those who fought under Caractacus, yet they were conquered, not by the valour, but by the discipline of the Romans. It was the will of the gods that your young chief should dwell for four years a hostage among the Romans, and doubtless they willed it should be so in order that he might be fitted to be a worthy champion of his country, and so to effect what even the valour of Caractacus failed to do. The gods have spoken by me. See that you obey them, and woe to the wretch who murmurs even in his own heart against their decrees!"

As he concluded a loud shout was raised throughout the crowded hall, and swelled into a mighty roar outside, for those at the open door had passed his words to the throng of tribesmen outside. When the shout subsided, Beric added a few words, saying, that although he regretted he had not yet come to his full strength, and that thus early he should be called upon to lead men, he accepted the decree of the gods, and would strive not to be wanting in the day of trial. In matters connected with war he had learned much from the Romans, who, oppressors as they were and despisers of the gods of Britain, were skilled beyond all others in such matters. In all other respects he had happily his mother's counsel and guidance to depend upon, and before assuming any civil authority he should wait until years had taught him wisdom, and should then go through all the usual ceremonies appointed by their religion, and receive his instalment solemnly in the temple at the hands of the Druids.

That night there was high feasting at Cardun. A bullock and three swine were slain by order of Parta, and a number of great earthen jars of mead broached, and while the principal men of the tribe feasted in the hall, the rest made merry outside. The bard attached to Parta's household sang tales of the glories of the tribe, even the women from the villages and detached huts for a large circle round came in, happy that, now the wolves had been cleared away, they could stir out after nightfall without fear. After entertaining their guests in the hall, Parta and her son went round among the tribesmen outside and saw that they had all they needed, and spoke pleasantly even to the poorest among them.

It was long before Beric closed his eyes that night. The events of the day had been a complete surprise to him. He had thought that in the distant future he should share with his mother in the ruling of the tribe, but had never once dreamed of its coming for years. Had it not been for the news that they had heard of the intended invasion of the Holy Isle he should not have regretted his elevation, for it would have given him the means and opportunity to train the tribesmen to fight in close order as did the Romans. But now he could not hope that there would be time to carry this out effectually. He knew that throughout Britain the feeling of rage and indignation at this outrage upon the gods of their country would raise the passions of men to boiling point, and that the slightest incident would suffice to bring on a general explosion, and he greatly feared that the result of such a rising would in the end be disastrous.

His reading had shown him how great was the power of Rome, and how obstinately she clung to her conquests. His countrymen seemed to think that were they, with a mighty effort, to free Britain of its invaders, their freedom would be achieved; but he knew that such a disaster would arouse the Roman pride, and that however great the effort required, fresh armies would be despatched to avenge the disaster and to regain the territory lost.

"The Britons know nothing of Roman power," he said to himself. "They see but twenty or thirty thousand men here, and they forget that that number have alone been sent because they were sufficient for the work, and that Rome could, if need be, despatch five times as many men. With time to teach the people, not of the Sarci tribe only, but all the Iceni, to fight in solid masses, and to bear the brunt of the battle, while the rest of the tribes attacked furiously on all sides, we might hope for victory; but fighting without order or regularity, each man for himself, cannot hope to prevail against their solid mass.

"If I could have gained a name before the time came, so that my voice might have had weight and power in the councils of the chiefs, I might have done something. As it is, I fear that a rising now will bring ruin and slavery upon all Britain."

Beric thought but little of himself, or of the personal danger he should encounter. The Britons were careless of their lives. They believed implicitly in a future life, and that those who fell fighting bravely for their country would meet with reward hereafter; hence, as among the Gauls, cowardice was an almost unknown vice.

Beric had faith in the gods of his country, while he had none whatever in those of Rome, and wondered how a mighty people could believe in such deities; but, unlike the Britons in general, he did not believe that the gods interfered to decide the fate of battles.

He saw that the Romans, with their false gods, had conquered all other nations, and that so far they had uniformly triumphed over his own. Therefore, mighty as he believed the gods to be, he thought that they concerned themselves but little in the affairs of the world, and that battles were to be won solely by valour, discipline, and numbers. Numbers and valour the British had, but of discipline they were absolutely ignorant, and it was this that gave so tremendous an advantage to the Romans. Hence Beric felt none of the exultation and excitement that most British lads of his age would have done on attaining to rank and command in the tribe to which they belonged.

The Britons despised the Romans as much for their belief in many gods as for their luxury, and what they considered their effeminacy. The religion of the Britons was a pure one, though disfigured by the offering of human sacrifices. They believed in one great Supreme Spirit, whose power pervaded everything. They thought of him less as an absolute being than as a pervading influence. They worshipped him everywhere, in the forests and in the streams, in the sky and heavenly bodies. Through the Druids they consulted him in all their undertakings. If the answer was favourable, they followed it; if unfavourable, they endeavoured to change it by sacrifices and offerings to the priests. They believed firmly in a life after death, when they held that the souls of all brave and good men and women would be transported at once to an island far out in the Atlantic, which they called the Happy Island. The highest places would be theirs who had fought valiantly and died in battle; but there was room for all, and all would be happy. Holding this idea firmly, the Britons sought rather than avoided death. Their lives in their separate tribes were quiet and simple, except when engaged in the chase or war. They were averse to labour. They were domestic, virtuous, frank, and straightforward. The personal property of a stranger was sacred among them, and the most lavish hospitality was exercised. It was not strange that a simple hardy people, believing firmly in the one supreme god, should have regarded with contempt alike the luxury of the Romans and their worship of many gods in the likenesses of men and women, and that the more Beric had seen of the learning and wisdom of the Romans in other directions, the more he should wonder that such a people should be slaves to what seemed to him childish superstitions.

The next morning, after a consultation with some of the minor chiefs, a hundred men were summoned to attend on the following day. They were picked out from families where there were two or more males of working age, so that there would be as little disturbance of labour as possible. It was principally in companies of a hundred that Beric had seen the Romans exercised, and he had learned every order by heart from first to last. The manoeuvres to be taught were not of a complicated nature. To form in fighting order six deep, and to move in column, were the principal points; but when the next day the band assembled, Beric was surprised and vexed to find that the operations were vastly more difficult than he expected. To begin with, every man was to have his place in the line, and the tribesmen, though eager to learn, and anxious to please their young chief, could not see that it mattered in what order they stood. When, however, having arranged them at first in a line two deep, Beric proceeded to explain how the spears were to be held, and in what order the movements were to be performed,--the exercise answering to the manual and platoon of modern days,--the tribesmen were unable to restrain their laughter. What difference could it make whether the hands were two feet apart or three, whether the spears were held upright or sloped, whether they came down to the charge one after another or all together? To men absolutely unaccustomed to order of any kind, but used only to fight each in the way that suited him best, these details appeared absolutely ludicrous.

Beric was obliged to stop and harangue them, pointing out to them that it was just these little things that gave the Romans their fighting power; that it was because the whole company moved as one man, and fought as one man, each knowing his place and falling into it, however great the confusion, however sudden the alarm, that made them what they were.

"Why do they conquer you?" he said. "Chiefly because you can never throw them into confusion. Charge down upon them and break them, and they at once reunite and a solid wall opposes your scattered efforts. You know how cattle, when wolves attack them, gather in a circle with their horns outwards, and so keep at bay those who could pull them down and rend them separately. At present it seems ridiculous to you that every position of the hand, every movement of the arm, should be done by rule; but when you have practised them these will become a second nature; so with your other movements. It seems folly to you to do with measured steps what it seems you could do far more quickly by running together hastily; but it is not so. The slowest movement is really the quickest, and it has the advantage that no one is hurried, that everything is done steadily and regularly, and that even in the greatest heat and confusion of a battle every man takes his place, as calm and ready to fight as if no foe were in sight. Now let us try this again. At the end of the day I shall pick out some of those who are quickest and most attentive, and make of them officers under me. They will have more work to do, for they will have to understand and teach my orders, but also they will gain more honour and credit."

For hours the drill went on; then they broke off for dinner and again worked until evening, and by that time had made sufficient progress in their simple movements to begin to feel that there was after all something more in it than they had fancied. For the first hour it had seemed to them a sort of joke--a mere freak on the part of their young chief; but they were themselves surprised to find by the end of the day how rapidly they were able to change from their rank two deep into the solid formation, and how their spears rose and fell together at the order. Beric bade them by the next morning provide themselves with spears six feet longer. Britons were more accustomed to fight with javelin than with spear, and the latter weapons were shorter and lighter than those of the Romans. Beric felt that the advantage should be the other way, for the small shields carried by the Britons were inferior as defensive weapons to those of the Romans, and to preserve the balance it was necessary therefore to have longer spears; the more so since the Britons were taller, and far more powerful men than their foes, and should therefore be able, with practice, to use longer weapons.

The next day Beric chose Boduoc as his second in command, and appointed ten men sub-officers or sergeants. After a week of almost incessant work that would have exhausted men less hardy and vigorous, Beric was satisfied. The company had now come to take great interest in their work, and were able to go through their exercises with a fair show of regularity. Even the older chiefs, who had at first shaken their heads as they looked on, acknowledged that there was a great deal to be gained from the exercises. Parta was delighted. It was she who had foreseen the advantages that might be derived from Beric's stay among the Romans, and she entered heartily into his plans, ordering the men engaged to be fed from the produce of her flocks and herds.

When the week was over two hundred more men were summoned, a sufficient number of the brightest and most intelligent of the first company being chosen as their sub- officers. Before the drill commenced, however, the first company were put through their exercises in order that the newcomers might see what was expected of them, and how much could be done. This time several of the chiefs joined the companies in order that they might learn the words of command and be fitted to lead. This greatly encouraged Beric, who had foreseen that while he himself could command a company, he could do nothing towards controlling ten or fifteen companies unless these had each officers of rank and influence enough to control them.

The exercises after the first company had been drilled were carried on in the forest some miles away from the village, the men assembling there and camping beneath the trees, so that no rumour of gatherings or preparations for war should reach the Romans, although at present these were not in a position to make any eruption from Camalodunum, as the greater portion of the legionaries had marched with Suetonius.

Returning one day to Cardun with Boduoc, Beric was surprised to hear loud cries of lamentation. The women were running about with dishevelled hair and disordered garments. Fearful that something might have happened to his mother, he hurried on to the hall. Parta was sitting on the ground rocking herself to and fro in her grief, while the women were assembled round her uttering cries of anguish.

"What is the matter?" Beric asked as he hurried forward. The bard stepped forward to answer the question.

"My son," he said, "misfortune has fallen on the land. The gods have hidden their faces and refused to fight for their children. Woe and desolation have come upon us. The altars are thrown down and the priests slaughtered."

"Mona is taken!" Beric exclaimed.

"Yes, my son, Mona is taken. The Druid Boroc but an hour ago brought the news. The Romans having reached the strait, constructed flat bottomed boats, and in these approached the island, the horsemen towing their horses behind them. There were assembled the women of the Silures and the Druids from all parts of Britain, with many fugitives who had fled for shelter to the island. The Druids remained by their altars offering up human sacrifices, the men and women assembled on the beach waving torches, hurling imprecations upon the invaders, and imploring the gods to aid them and to crush the impious foe. For a time the Romans paused in mid channel, terrified at the spectacle, and the hopes of all that the gods had paralysed their arms rose high; but, alas! the halt was but temporary. Encouraging each other with shouts, they again advanced, and, leaping from their boats, waded through the water and set foot on the sacred soil.

"What was there to do? The men were few, and though the women in their despair rushed wildly at the enemy, it was all in vain; men and women were alike slaughtered; and then, moving forward, they advanced against the holy circle and slew the Druids upon the altars of the gods they served, and yet the gods were silent. They saw, they heard, but answered not; neither the clouds rained fire upon the invaders nor the earth shook. Ah! my son, evil days have fallen upon the land. What will be the end of them?"

Throughout the length and breadth of Britain a thrill of horror was felt at the news of the massacre of Druids at Mona, and everywhere it was followed by a stern determination to prepare for battle to clear the land of the Romans. The Druids went from tribe to tribe and from village to village stirring up men's hearts; the women, even more deeply excited than the men at the news of the calamity, behaved as if possessed, many going about the country calling upon the men to take up arms, and foretelling victory to the Britons and destruction to the Romans; even in the streets of Camalodunum at night their voices were heard crying out curses upon the Romans and predicting the destruction of the city.

A week after the news came, Beric, in fulfilment of the promise he had given to Berenice, paid another visit to Camalodunum. There were no signs in its busy streets of uneasiness or fear. The new propraetor Catus Decianus, who commanded in the absence of Suetonius, was holding a sort of court there, and the bearing of the Romans seemed even more arrogant and insolent than usual. The news of the destruction of the Druids at Mona had by them been hailed as a final and most crushing blow to the resistance of the Britons. Since their gods could not protect their own altars what hope could there be for them in the future? Decianus, a haughty tyrant who had been sent to Britain by Nero as a mark of signal favour, in order that he might enrich himself by the spoils of the Britons, was levying exactions at a rate hitherto unknown, treating the people as if they were but dirt under his feet. His lieutenants, all creatures of Nero, followed his example, and the exasperation of the unfortunate Trinobantes, who were the chief victims, had reached such a point that they were ready for revolt whensoever the signal might come.

On arrival at the house of Caius Muro, Beric found Berenice at home; she received him with joy. "I am glad that you have come, Beric; it is so dull now that father has gone away to the war. I have been expecting you here for the last fortnight. I suppose you have been amusing yourself too much to give a thought to me."

"I have been very busy, Berenice. I am a chief now, and have had much to do in the tribe. Among other things we have been having great war with the wolves."

"Yes, you told me when you were last here that you were going to set out next day on an expedition against them."

"They began first, as it turned out," he said smiling, "and very nearly made a meal of me that night on my way homeward."

"Sit down and tell me all about it," she said. "You know I love stories."

Beric recited to her the story of the fight at the hut.

"And there was a woman there! How terrible it must have been for her to be alone with her children before you arrived, and to think of her killing wolves with the spear. How different your women must be from us, Beric, for we are only taught to embroider, to dress ourselves, and to care for pretty things. Why, I should be frightened out of my life at the sight of a wolf if I were all alone and had no one to protect me."

"Our women are brought up differently, Berenice. We regard them as altogether our equals, and many of our tribes are ruled by women. My own, you know, for example. They do not go into battle with the men; but when a camp is attacked they are ready to fight in its defence, and being brought up to lead a vigorous life, they are well nigh as strong as we are. Among all the Gaulish nations the women are held in high respect. Of course with you this is so sometimes. Your father was wont to listen to the opinions of your mother; but you know that is not often so, and that with many Romans women are looked upon as inferior creatures, good only for dress and pleasure, useful in ordering a house and in managing the slaves, but unfit to take part in public life, and knowing nothing of aught save domestic affairs. And what has been going on here, Berenice?"

"Nothing," the girl said; "at least I have been doing nothing. I went to the footraces the other day, and saw the propraetor, but I don't like him. I think that he is a bad man, and I hear stories among the ladies of his being cruel and greedy; and there have been mad women going about at night shrieking and crying; I have heard them several times myself. Some of the ladies said they wish that my father was back here with his legion, for that there are but few soldiers, and if Decianus continues to treat the people so badly there may be trouble. What do you think, Beric?"

"I cannot say," he replied. "It seems to me that the Romans are bent upon crushing us down altogether. They have just captured our Holy Island, slaying the priests and priestesses, and overthrowing the altars, while Nero's officers wring from the people the last coin and the last animal they possess. I fear that there will be trouble, Berenice. No men worthy of the name could see their gods insulted and themselves despoiled of all they possess without striking a blow in defence."

"But they will only bring more trouble upon themselves," the girl said gravely. "I have heard my father lament that they forced us to fight against them, though you know he held that it was our fault more than theirs, and that if they were ruled kindly and wisely, as were the people in Southern Gaul, where the legion was stationed before it came over here, they would settle down and live peaceably, and be greatly benefited by our rule."

"If you treat a man as you would a dog you must not be surprised if he bites you," Beric said. "Some of your people not only think that we are dogs, but that we are toothless ones. Mayhap they will find their mistake some day."

"But you will never fight against us, Beric," the girl said anxiously, "after living so long among us?"

"I would not fight against your father or against those who have treated me well," he replied; "but against those who ill treat and abuse us I would fight when my countrymen fought. Yet if I could ever do you a service, Berenice, I would lay down my life to do it."

The event seemed so improbable to the girl that she passed over the promise without comment.

"So you are a chief, Beric! But I thought chiefs wore golden bracelets and ornaments, and you are just as you were when you came here last."

"Because I come here only as a visitor. If I came on a mission from the queen, or as one of a deputation of chiefs, I should wear my ornaments. I wear them at home now, those that my father had."

Beric stayed for some hours chatting with Berenice, and his old instructor, who had been left by Caius in charge of the household. As he walked home he wondered over the careless security of the Romans, and vowed that should opportunity occur he would save Berenice from the fate that was likely to fall upon all in Camalodunum should the Britons rise.

CHAPTER IV
AN INFURIATED PEOPLE

"A fresh misfortune has occurred," was the greeting with which Beric's mother met him on his return home. "Prasutagus is dead; and this is not the worst, he has left half his estates to the Roman Emperor."

"To the Roman Emperor!" Beric repeated; "is it possible, mother?"

"It is true, Beric. You know he has always tried to curry favour with the Romans, and has kept the Iceni from joining when other tribes rose against Rome. He has thought of nothing but amassing wealth, and in all Britain there is no man who could compare with him in riches. Doubtless he felt that the Romans only bided their time to seize what he had gathered, and so, in order that Boadicea and his daughters should enjoy in peace a portion of his stores, he has left half to Nero. The man was a fool as well as a traitor. The peasant who throws a child out of the door to the wolves knows that it does but whet their appetite for blood, and so it will be in this case. I hear Prasutagus died a week since, though the news has come but slowly, and already a horde of Roman officials have arrived in Norfolk, and are proceeding to make inventories of the king's possessions, and to bear themselves as insolently as if they were masters of all. Trouble must come, and that soon. Boadicea is of different stuff to her husband; she will not bear the insolence of the Romans. It would have been well for the Iceni had Prasutagus died twenty years ago and she had ruled our country."

"The gods have clearly willed, mother, that we should rise as one people against the Romans. It may be that it was for this that they did not defend their shrines from the impious hands of the invaders. Nought else stirred the Britons to lay aside their jealousies and act as one people. Now from end to end of the island all are burning for vengeance. Just at this moment, comes the death of the Romans' friend Prasutagus, and the passing of the rule of the Iceni into the hands of Boadicea. With the Romans in her capital the occasion will assuredly not long be wanting, and then there will be such a rising as the Romans have never yet seen; and then, their purpose effected, the gods may well fight on our side. I would that there had been five more years in which to prepare for the struggle, but if it must come it must. This Catus Decianus is just the man to bring it on. Haughty, arrogant, and greedy, he knows nothing of us, and has never faced the Britons in arms. Had Suetonius been here he would not have acted thus with regard to the affairs of Prasutagus. Had Caius Muro not been absent his voice might have been raised in warning to the tyrant; but everything seems to conspire together, mother, to bring on the crisis."

"The sooner the better," Parta exclaimed vehemently. "It is true that in time you might teach the whole Iceni to fight in Roman methods, but what is good for the Romans may not be good for us. Moreover, every year that passes strengthens their hold on the land. Their forts spring up everywhere, their cities grow apace; every month numbers flock over here. Another five years, my son, and their hold might be too strong to shake off."

"That is so, mother. Thinking of ourselves I thought not of them; it may be that it were better to fight now than to wait. Well, whenever the signal is given, and from wheresoever it comes, we are ready."

Since the news of the capture of Mona had arrived, the tribesmen had drilled with increased alacrity and eagerness. Every man saw that the struggle with Rome must ere long take place, and was eager to take a leading share in the conflict. It was upon them that the blow had fallen most heavily in the former partial rising, and they knew that the other tribes of the Iceni held that their defence of their camp should not have been overborne by the Romans as it was; hence they had something of a private wrong as well as a national one to avenge. Another fortnight was spent in constant work, until one day the news came that Boadicea's daughters had been most grossly insulted by the Roman officers, and that the queen herself had started for Camalodunum to demand from Decianus a redress of their wrongs and the punishment of the offenders. The excitement was intense. Every man felt the outrage upon the daughters of their queen as a personal injury, and when Beric took his place before the men of the tribe, who were drawn up in military order, a shout arose: "Lead us to Camalodunum! Let us take vengeance!"

"Not yet," Beric cried. "The queen has gone there; we must wait the issue. Not until she gives the orders must we move. A rising now would endanger her safety. We must wait, my friends, until all are as ready as we are; when the time comes you will not find me backward in leading you."

Three days later came news that seemed at first incredible, but which was speedily confirmed. Decianus had received the queen, had scoffed at her complaints, and when, fired with indignation, she had used threats, he had ordered his soldiers to strip and scourge her, and the sentence had actually been carried into effect. Then the rage of the tribesmen knew no bounds, and it needed the utmost persuasions of Parta herself to induce them to wait until news came from the north.

"Fear not," she said, "that your vengeance will be baulked. Boadicea will not submit to this double indignity, of that you maybe sure. Wait until you hear from her. When measures are determined upon in this matter the Iceni must act as one man. We are all equally outraged in the persons of our queen and her daughters; all have a right to a share in avenging her insults. We might spoil all by moving before the others are ready. When we move it must be as a mighty torrent to overwhelm the invaders. Not Camalodunum only, but every Roman town must be laid in ruins. It must be a life and death struggle between us and Rome; we must conquer now or be enslaved for ever."

It was not long before messengers arrived from Boadicea, bidding the Sarci prepare for war, and summoning Parta and her son to a council of the chiefs of the tribe, to be held under a well known sacred oak in the heart of the forest, near Norwich. Parta's chariot was at once prepared, together with a second, which was to carry Boduoc and a female attendant of Parta, and as soon as the horses were harnessed they started. Two long days' journey brought them to the place of meeting. The scene was a busy one. Already fully two score of the chiefs had arrived. Parta was received with great marks of respect. The Sarci were the tribe lying nearest to the Romans, and upon them the brunt of the Roman anger would fall, as it had done before; but her appearance in answer to the summons showed, it was thought, their willingness to join in the general action of the tribe.

Beric was looked at curiously. His four years' residence among the Romans caused him to be regarded with a certain amount of suspicion, which had been added to by rumours that he had been impressing upon the tribe the greatness and power of Rome. Of late there had been reports brought by wandering bards that the Sarci were being practised in the same exercises as those of the Roman soldiers, and there were many who thought that Beric, like Cogidinus, a chief of the Regi of Sussex, had joined himself heart and soul to Rome, and was preparing his tribe to fight side by side with the legions. On the other hand many, knowing that Parta had lost her husband at the hands of the Romans, and hated them with all her heart, held that she would never have divided her power with Beric, or suffered him to take military command of the tribe, had she not been assured of his fidelity to the cause of Britain.

Beric was dressed in the full panoply of a chief. He wore a short skirt or kilt reaching to his knees. Above it a loose vest or shirt, girt in by a gold belt, while over his shoulders he wore the British mantle, white in colour and worked with gold. Around his neck was the torque, the emblem of chieftainship. On his left arm he carried a small shield of beaten brass, and from a baldric covered with gold plates hung the straight pointless British sword that had been carried by his father in battle. Even those most suspicious of him could not deny that he was a stalwart and well built youth, with a full share of pith and muscle, and that his residence among the Romans had not given him any airs of effeminacy. The only subject of criticism was that his hair was shorter than that of his countrymen, for although he had permitted it to grow since he left Camalodunum, where he had worn it short, in Roman fashion, it had not yet attained its full length.

Beric felt a stranger among the others. Since his return home there had been no great tribal gathering, for Prasutagus had for some time been ill, and had always discouraged such assemblages both because they were viewed with jealousy by the Romans and because he begrudged the expenses of entertaining. Parta, who was personally known to almost all present, introduced Beric to them.

"My son is none the less one of the Iceni for his Roman training," she said; "he has learned much, but has forgotten nothing. He is young, but you will find him a worthy companion in arms when the day of battle comes."

"I am glad to hear what you say, Parta," Aska, one of the older chiefs, said. "It would be unfair to impute blame to him for what assuredly was not his fault, but I feared that they might have taught him to despise his countrymen."

"It is not so, sir," Beric said firmly. "Happily I fell into good hands. Caius Muro, the commander of the 12th Legion, in whose charge I was, is a just as well as a valiant man, and had me instructed as if I had been his own son, and I trust that I am none the less a true Briton because I except him and his from the hatred I bear the Romans. He never said a word to me against my countrymen, and indeed often bewailed that we were not treated more wisely and gently, and were not taught to regard the Romans as friends and teachers rather than oppressors."

"Well spoken, young chief!" the other said; "ingratitude is, of all sins, the most odious, and you do well to speak up boldly for those who were kind to you. Among all men there are good and evil, and we may well believe, even among the Romans, there are some who are just and honourable. But I hear that you admire them greatly, and that you have been telling to your tribe tales of their greatness in war and of their virtues."

"I have done so," Beric replied. "A race could not conquer the world as the Romans have done unless they had many virtues; but those that I chiefly told of are the virtues that every Briton should lay to heart. I spoke of their patriotism, of the love of country that never failed, of the stern determination that enabled them to pass through the gravest dangers without flinching, and to show a dauntless face to the foe even when dangers were thickest and the country was menaced with destruction. Above all, how in Rome, though there might be parties and divisions, there were none in the face of a common enemy. Then all acted as one man; there was no rivalry save in great deeds. Each was ready to give life and all he possessed in defence of his country. These were lessons which I thought it well that every Briton should learn and take to heart. Rome has conquered us so far because she has been one while we are rent into tribes having no common union; content to sit with our arms folded while our neighbours are crushed, not seeing that our turn will come next. It was so when they first came in the time of our forefathers, it has been so in these latter times; tribe after tribe has been subdued; while, had we been all united, the Romans would never have obtained a footing on our shore. No wonder the gods have turned away their faces from a people so blind and so divided when all was at stake. Yes, I have learned much from the Romans. I have not learned to love them, but I have learned to admire them and to regret that in many respects my own countrymen did not resemble them."

There was a murmur of surprise among the chiefs who had by this time gathered round, while angry exclamations broke from some of the younger men; but Aska waved his hand.

"Beric speaks wisely and truly," he said; "our dissensions have been our ruin. Still more, perhaps, the conduct of those who should have led us, but who have made terms with Rome in order to secure their own possessions. Among these Prasutagus was conspicuous, and we ourselves were as much to blame as he was that we suffered it. If he knows what is passing here he himself will see how great are the misfortunes that he has brought upon his queen, his daughters, and the tribe. Had we joined our whole forces with those of Caractacus the Brigantes too might have risen. It took all the strength of the Romans to conquer Caractacus alone. What could they have done had the Brigantes and we from the north, and the whole of the southern tribes, then unbroken, closed down upon them? It is but yesterday since Prasutagus was buried. The grass has not yet begun to shoot upon his funeral mound and yet his estates have been seized by the Romans, while his wife and daughters have been insulted beyond measure.

"The young chief of the Sarci has profited by his sojourn among the Romans. The Druids have told me that the priest who has visited the Sarci prophesies great things of him, and for that reason decided that, young as he was, he should share his mother's power and take his place as leader of the tribe in battle, and that he foresaw that, should time be given him to ripen his wisdom and establish his authority, he might some day become a British champion as powerful as Cunobeline, as valiant as Caractacus. These were the words of one of the wisest of the Druids. They have been passed round among the Druids, and even now throughout Britain there are many who never so much as heard of the name of the Sarci, who yet believe that, in this young chief of that tribe, will some day be found a mighty champion of his country. Prasutagus knew this also, for as soon as Beric returned from Camalodunum he begged the Druids to find out whether good or evil was to be looked for from this youth, who had been brought up among the Romans, and their report to him tallied with that which I myself heard from them. It was for that reason that Boadicea sent for him with his mother, although so much younger than any here, and belonging to a tribe that is but a small one among the Iceni. I asked these questions of him, knowing that among some of you there were doubts whether his stay with the Romans had not rendered him less a Briton. He answered as I expected from him, boldly and fearlessly, and, as you have heard wisely, and I for one believe in the predictions of the Druids. But here comes the queen."

As he spoke a number of chariots issued from the path through the forest into the circular clearing, in the centre of which stood the majestic oak, and at the same moment, from the opposite side, appeared a procession of white robed Druids singing a loud chant. As the chariots drew up, the queen and her two daughters alighted from them, with a number of chiefs of importance from the branches of the tribe near her capital. Beric had never seen her before, and was struck with her aspect. She was a tall and stately woman, large in her proportions, with her yellow hair falling below her waist. She wore no ornaments or insignia of her high rank; her dress and those of her daughters were careless and disordered, indicative of mourning and grief, but the expression of her face was that of indignation and passion rather than of humiliation.

Upon alighting she acknowledged the greeting of the assembled chiefs with a slight gesture, and then remained standing with her eyes fixed upon the advancing Druids. When these reached the sacred tree they encircled it seven times, still continuing their chanting, and then ranged themselves up under its branches with the chief Druid standing in front. They had already been consulted privately by the queen and had declared for war; but it was necessary that the decision should be pronounced solemnly beneath the shade of the sacred oak.

"Why come you here, woman?" the chief priest asked, addressing the queen.

"I come as a supplicant to the gods," she said; "as an outraged queen, a dishonoured woman, and a broken hearted mother, and in each of these capacities I call upon my country's gods for vengeance." Then in passionate words she poured out the story of the indignities that she and her daughters had suffered, and suddenly loosening her garment, and suffering it to drop to her waist, she turned and showed the marks of the Roman rods across her back, the sight eliciting a shout of fury from the chiefs around her.

"Let all retire to the woods," the Druids said, "and see that no eye profanes our mysteries. When the gods have answered we will summon you."

The queen, followed by all the chiefs, retired at once to the forest, while the Druids proceeded to carry out the sacred mysteries. Although all knew well what the decision would be, they waited with suppressed excitement the summons to return and hear the decision that was to embark them in a desperate struggle with Rome. Some threw themselves down under the trees, some walked up and down together discussing in low tones the prospects of a struggle, and the question what tribes would join it. The queen and her daughters sat apart, none venturing to approach them. Parta and three other female chiefs sat a short distance away talking together, while two or three of the younger chiefs, their attitude towards Beric entirely altered by the report of the Druids' predictions concerning him, gathered round him and asked questions concerning the Romans' methods of fighting, their arms and power. An hour after they had retired a deep sound of a conch rose in the air. The queen and her daughters at once moved forward, followed by the four female chiefs, behind whom came the rest in a body. Issuing from the forest they advanced to the sacred oak and stood in an attitude of deep respect, while the chief Druid announced the decision of the gods.

"The gods have spoken," he said. "Too long have the Iceni stood aloof from their countrymen, therefore have the gods withdrawn their faces from them; therefore has punishment and woe fallen upon them. Prasutagus is dead; his queen and his daughters have suffered the direst indignities; a Roman has seized the wealth heaped up by inglorious cowardice. But the moment has come; the gods have suffered their own altars to be desecrated in order that over the whole length and breadth of the land the cry for vengeance shall arise simultaneously. The cup is full; vengeance is at hand upon the oppressors and tyrants, the land reeks with British blood. Not content with grasping our possessions, our lives and the honour of our women are held as nought by them, our altars are cold, our priests slaughtered. The hour of vengeance is at hand. I see the smoke of burning cities ascending in the air. I hear the groans of countless victims to British vengeance. I see broken legions and flying men.

"To arms! the gods have spoken. Strike for vengeance. Strike for the gods. Strike for your country and outraged queen. Chiefs of the Iceni, to arms! May the curse of the gods fall upon an enemy who draws back in the day of battle! May the gods give strength to your arms and render you invincible in battle! The gods have spoken."

A mighty shout was raised by his hearers; swords were brandished, and spears shaken, and the cry "To arms! the gods have spoken," was repeated unanimously. As the Druids closed round their chief, who had been seized with strong convulsions as soon as he had uttered the message of the gods, Boadicea turned to the chiefs and raised her arm for silence.

"I am a queen again; I reign once more over a race of men. No longer do I feel the smart of my stripes, for each shall ere long be washed out in Roman blood; but before action, counsel, and before counsel, food, for you have, many of you, come from afar. I have ordered a feast to be prepared in the forest."

She led the way across the opposite side of the glade, where, a few hundred yards in the forest, a number of the queen's slaves had prepared a feast of roasted sheep, pig, and ox, with bread and jars of drink formed of fermented honey, and a sort of beer. As soon as the meal was concluded the queen called the chiefs round her, and the assembly was joined by the Druids.

"War is declared," she said; "the question is shall we commence at once, or shall we wait?"

There was a general response "At once!" but the chief Druid stepped forward and said: "My sons, we must not risk the ruin of all by undue haste; this must be a national movement if it is to succeed. For a fortnight we must keep quiet, preparing everything for war, so that we may take the field with every man capable of bearing arms in the tribe. In the meantime we, with the aid of the bards, will spread the news of the outrages that the Romans have committed upon the queen and her daughters far and wide over the land. Already the tribes are burning with indignation at the insults to our gods and the slaughter of our priests at Mona, and this news will arouse them to madness, for what is done here today may be done elsewhere tomorrow, and all men will see that only in the total destruction of the Romans is there a hope of freedom. All will be bidden to prepare for war, and, when the news comes that the Iceni have taken up arms, to assemble and march to join us. On this day fortnight, then, let every chief with his following meet at Cardun, which is but a short march from Camalodunum. Then we will rush upon the Roman city, the scene of the outrage to your queen, and its smoke shall tell Britain that she is avenged, and Rome that her day of oppression is over."

The decision was received with satisfaction. A fortnight was none too long for making preparations, assembling the tribesmen, and marching to the appointed spot.

"One thing I claim," Boadicea said, "and that is the right to fall upon and destroy instantly the Romans who installed themselves in my capital, and who are the authors of the outrages upon my daughters. So long as they live and lord it there I cannot return."

"That is right and just," the Druid said. "Slay all but ten, and hand them over bound to us to be sacrificed on the altars of the gods they have insulted."

"I will undertake that task, as my tribe lies nearest the capital," one of the chiefs said. "I will assemble them tonight and fall upon the Romans at daybreak."

"See that none escape," the Druid said. "Kill them and all their slaves and followers. Let not one live to carry the news to Camalodunum."

"I shall be at the meeting place and march at your head," the queen said to the chiefs; "that victory will be ours I do not doubt; but if the gods will it otherwise I swear that I shall not survive defeat. Ye gods, hear my vow."

The council was now over, and the queen mingled with the chiefs, saying a few words to each. Beric was presented to her by his mother, and Boadicea was particularly gracious to him. "I have heard great things predicted of you, Beric. The gods have marked you out for favour, and their priests tell me that you will be one day a great champion of the Britons. So may it be. I shall watch you on the day of battle, and am assured that none among the Iceni will bear themselves more worthily."

An hour later the meeting broke up, and Parta and Beric returned to Cardun, where they at once began to make preparations for the approaching conflict. Every man in the tribe was summoned to attend, and the exercises went on from daybreak till dusk, while the women cooked and waited upon the men. Councils were held nightly in the hall, and to each of the chiefs was assigned a special duty, the whole tribe being treated as a legion, and every chief and fighting man having his place and duty assigned to him.

In Camalodunum, although nothing was known of the preparations that were being made, a feeling of great uneasiness prevailed. The treatment of Boadicea had excited grave disapproval upon the part of the great majority of the inhabitants, although new arrivals from Gaul or Rome and the officials in the suite of Decianus lauded his action as an act of excellent policy.

"These British slaves must be taught to feel the weight of our arm," they said, "and a lesson such as this will be most useful. Is it for dogs like these to complain because they are whipped? They must be taught to know that they live but at our pleasure; that this island and all it contains is ours. They have no rights save those we choose to give them."

But the older settlers viewed the matter very differently. They knew well enough that it was only after hard fighting that Vespasian had subdued the south, and Ostorius crushed Caractacus. They knew, too, that the Iceni gave but a nominal submission to Rome, and that the Trinobantes, crushed as they were, had been driven to the verge of madness by extortion. Moreover the legions were far away; Camalodunum was well nigh undefended, and lay almost at the mercy of the Britons should they attack. They, therefore, denounced the treatment of Boadicea as not only brutal but as impolitic in the extreme.

The sudden cessation of news from the officials who had gone to take possession of the estate of Prasutagus caused considerable uneasiness among this section of the inhabitants of Camalodunum. Messengers were sent off every day to inquire as to what had taken place after the return of Boadicea, but none came back. The feeling of uneasiness was heightened by the attitude of the natives. Reports came in from all parts of the district that they had changed their attitude, that they no longer crouched at the sight of a Roman but bore themselves defiantly, that there were meetings at night in the forest, and that the women sang chants and performed dances which had evidently some hidden meaning.

Decianus, conscious perhaps that his action was strongly disapproved by all the principal inhabitants of the town, and that, perhaps, Suetonius would also view it in the same light when it was reported to him, had left the city a few days after the occurrence and had gone to Verulamium. His absence permitted the general feeling of apprehension and discontentment more open expression than it would otherwise have had. Brave as the Romans were, they were deeply superstitious, and a thrill of horror and apprehension ran through the city when it was reported one morning that the statute of Victory in the temple had fallen to the ground, and had turned round as if it fled towards the sea. This presage of evil created a profound impression.

"What do you think of it, Cneius?" Berenice asked; "it is terrible, is it not? Nothing else is spoken of among all the ladies I have seen today, and all agree it forbodes some terrible evil."

"It may, or it may not," the old scribe said cautiously; "if the statue has fallen by the action of the gods the omen is surely a most evil one."

"But how else could it have fallen, Cneius?"

"Well, my dear, there are many Britons in the town, and you know they are in a very excited state; their women, indeed, seem to have gone well nigh mad with their midnight singing and wailing. It is possible--mind, I do not for a moment say that it is so, for were the suggestion to occur to the citizens it would lead to fresh oppressions and cruelties against the Britons--but it is just possible that some of them may have entered the temple at night and overthrown Victory's image as an act of defiance. You know how the women nightly shriek out their prophecies of the destruction of this town."

"But could they destroy it, Cneius? Surely they would never dare to attack a great Roman city like this!"

"I don't know whether they dare or not, Berenice, but assuredly Decianus is doing all in his power to excite them to such a pitch of despair that they might dare do anything; and if they dare, I see nothing whatever to prevent them from taking the city. The works erected after Claudius first founded the colony are so vast that they would require an army to defend them, while there are but a few hundred soldiers here. What could they do against a horde of barbarians? I would that your father were back, and also the two legions who marched away to join Suetonius. Before they went they ought to have erected a central fort here, to which all could retire in case of danger, and hold out until Suetonius came back to our assistance; but you see, when they went away none could have foreseen what has since taken place. No one could have dreamt that Decianus would have wantonly stirred up the Iceni to revolt."

"But you don't think they have revolted?"

"I know nothing of it, Berenice, but I can put two and two together. We have heard nothing for a week from the officials who went to seize the possessions of Prasutagus. How is it that none of our messengers have returned? It seems to me almost certain that these men have paid for their conduct to the daughters of Boadicea with their lives."

"But Beric is with the Iceni. Surely we should hear from him if danger threatened."

"He is with them," Cneius said, "but he is a chief, and if the tribe are in arms he is in arms also, and cannot, without risking the forfeit of his life for treachery, send hither a message that would put us on our guard. I believe in the lad. Four years I taught him, and I think I know his nature. He is honest and true. He is one of the Iceni and must go with his countrymen; but I am sure he is grateful for the kindness he received here, and has a real affection for you, therefore I believe, that should my worst fears be verified, and the Iceni attack Camalodunum, he will do his utmost to save you."

"But they will not kill women and girls surely, even if they did take the city?"

"I fear that they will show slight mercy to any, Berenice; why should they? We have shown no mercy to them; we have slaughtered their priests and priestesses, and at the storm of their towns have put all to death without distinction of age or sex. If we, a civilized people, thus make war, what can you expect from the men upon whom we have inflicted such countless injuries?"

The fall of the statue of Victory was succeeded by other occurrences in which the awestruck inhabitants read augury of evil. It was reported that strange noises had been heard in the council house and theatre, while men out in boats brought back the tale that there was the appearance of a sunken town below the water. It was currently believed that the sea had assumed the colour of blood, and that there were, when the tide went out, marks upon the sand as if dead bodies had been lying there. Even the boldest veterans were dismayed at this accumulation of hostile auguries. A council of the principal citizens was held, and an urgent message despatched to Decianus, praying that he would take instance measures for the protection of the city. In reply to this he despatched two hundred soldiers from Verulamium, and these with the small body of troops already in the city took possession of the Temple of Claudius, and began to make preparations for putting it into a state of defence.

Still no message had come from Norwich, but night after night the British women declared that the people of Camalodunum would suffer the same fate that had already overwhelmed those who had ventured to insult the daughters of the queen of the Iceni. A strange terror had now seized the inhabitants of the town. The apprehension of danger weighted upon all, and the peril seemed all the more terrible inasmuch as it was so vague. Nothing was known for certain. No message had come from the Iceni since the queen quitted the town, and yet it was felt that among the dark woods stretching north a host of foes was gathering, and might at any moment pour down upon the city. Orders were issued that at the approach of danger all who could do so were to betake themselves at once to the temple, which was to act as a citadel, yet no really effective measures were taken. There was, indeed, a vague talk of sending the women and children and valuables away to the legion, commanded by Cerealis, stationed in a fortified camp to the south, but nothing came of it; all waited for something definite, some notification that the Britons had really revolted, and while waiting for this nothing was done.

One evening a slave brought in a small roll of vellum to Cneius. It had been given him at the door, he said, by a Briton, who had at once left after placing it in his hands. The scribe opened it and read as follows:--

"To Cneius Nepo, greeting--Obtain British garb for yourself and Berenice. Let her apparel be that of a boy. Should anything unusual occur by night or day, do you and she disguise yourselves quickly, and stir not beyond the house. It will be best for you to wait in the tablinum; lose no time in carrying out this instruction."

There was no signature, nor was any needed.

"So the storm is about to burst," Cneius said thoughtfully when he had read it. "I thought so. I was sure that if the Britons had a spark of manhood left in them they would avenge the cruel wrongs of their queen. I am rejoiced to read Beric's words, and to see that he has, as I felt sure he had, a grateful heart. He would save us from the fate that he clearly thinks is about to overwhelm this place. The omens have not lied then--not that I believe in them; they are for the most part the offspring of men's fancy, but at any rate they will come true this time. I care little for myself, but I must do as he bids me for the sake of the girl. I doubt, though whether Beric can save her. These people have terrible wrongs to avenge, and at their first outburst will spare none. Well, I must do my best, and late as it is I will go out and purchase these garments. It is not likely that the danger will come tonight, for he would have given us longer notice. Still he may have had no opportunity, and may not have known until the last moment when the attack was to take place. He says 'lose no time.'"

Cneius at once went to one of the traders who dealt with the natives who came into the town, and procured the garments for himself and Berenice. The trader, who knew him by sight, remarked, "Have you been purchasing more slaves?"

"No, but I have need for dresses for two persons who have done me some service."

"I should have thought," the trader said, "they would have preferred lighter colours. These cloths are sombre, and the natives, although their own cloths are for the most part dark, prefer, when they buy of me, brighter colours."

"These will do very well," Cneius said. "just at present Roman colours and cloths are not likely to be in demand among them."

"No, the times are bad," the trader said; "there has been scarce a native in my shop for the last ten days, and even among the townspeople there has been little buying or selling."

Cneius returned to the house, a slave carrying his purchases behind him. On reaching home he took the parcel from him, and carried it to his own cubicule, and then ordered a slave to beg Berenice to come down from her apartment as he desired to speak with her.

CHAPTER V
THE SACK OF CAMALODUNUM

Upon the morning of the day fixed for the gathering of the Iceni preparations were begun early at Cardun. Oxen and swine were slaughtered, great fires made, and the women in the village were all employed in making and baking oaten cakes upon the hearth. For some days many of them had been employed in making a great store of fermented honey and water. Men began to flock in from an early hour, and by midday every male of the Sarci capable of bearing arms had come in. Each brought with him a supply of cooked meat and cakes sufficient to last for three or four days. In the afternoon the tribes began to pour in, each tribe under its chiefs. There was no attempt at order or regularity; they came trooping in in masses, the chiefs sometimes in chariots sometimes on horseback, riding at their head. Parta welcomed them, and food was served out to the men while the chiefs were entertained in the hall. Beric, looking at the wild figures, rough and uncouth but powerful and massive in frame, was filled with regret that these men knew nothing of discipline, and that circumstances had forced on the war so suddenly.

The contrast between these wild figures and the disciplined veterans of Rome, whom he had so often watched as they performed their exercises, was striking indeed. Far inferior in height and muscular power to the tribesmen, the legionaries bore themselves with a proud consciousness in their fighting power that alone went a long way towards giving them victory. Each man trusted not only in himself, but on his fellows, and believed that the legion to which he belonged was invincible. Their regular arms, their broad shields and helmets, all added to their appearance, while their massive formation, as they stood shoulder to shoulder, shield touching shield, seemed as if it could defy the utmost efforts of undisciplined valour. However, Beric thought with pride that his own tribe, the sixteen hundred men he had for six weeks been training incessantly, would be a match even for the Roman veterans. Their inferiority in the discipline that was carried to such perfection among the Romans would be atoned for by their superior strength and activity. His only fear was, that in the excitement of battle they would forget their teaching, and, breaking their ranks, fight every man for himself. He had, however, spared no pains in impressing upon them that to do this would be to throw away all that they had learned.

"I have not taught you to fight in Roman fashion," he said, "merely that you might march in regular order and astonish the other tribesmen, but that you should be cool and collected, should be able patiently to stand the shock of the Roman legion, and to fight, not as scattered units, but as a solid whole.

You will do well to bear this in mind, for to those who disobey orders and break the line when engaged with the foe I will show no mercy. My orders will be given to each sergeant of ten men to run a spear through any man who stirs from his post, whether in advance or in retreat, whether to slay or to plunder. The time may come when the safety of the whole army depends upon your standing like a wall between them and the Romans, and the man who advances from his place in the ranks will, as much as the man who retreats, endanger the safety of all."

Over and over again had he impressed this lesson upon them. Sometimes he had divided them in two parts, and engaged in mimic fight. The larger half, representing the tribesmen, advanced in their ordinary fashion with loud shouts and cries, while the smaller section maintained their solid formation, and with levelled spears, five deep, waited the attack. Even those who were least impressed with the advantages of the exercises through which they had been going, could not but feel how immensely superior was the solid order, and how impossible would it have been for assailants to burst through the hedge of pointed weapons.

By sunset well nigh thirty thousand men had arrived, each subtribe passing through the village and taking up its post on the slopes around it, where they were at once supplied with food by the women.

With the fighting men were large numbers of women, for these generally accompanied the Britons on their warlike expeditions. Just at sunset a shout arose from the tribesmen on the north side of the village, and Boadicea, with her daughters and chief councillors, drove into the village. Her mien was proud and lofty. She carried a spear in her hand and a sword in her girdle. She had resumed her royal ornaments, and a fillet of gold surrounded her head. Her garments were belted in with a broad girdle of the same metal, and she wore heavy gold armlets and bracelets. She looked with pride upon the tribesmen who thronged shouting to greet her, and exclaimed as she leapt from her chariot, "The day of vengeance is at hand."

The fires blazed high all that night round Cardun. Numbers of bards had accompanied the tribes, as not only had those who lived in the households of the principal chiefs come in, but many had been attracted from the country lying near their borders. At every fire, therefore, songs were sung and tales told of the valour and glory of the heroes of old. Mingled with these were laments over the evil days that had befallen Britain, and exhortations to their hearers to avenge the past and prove themselves worthy of their ancestors.

In similar manner the night was passed in Parta's hall. Here the chief bards were assembled, with all the tribal leaders, and vied with each other in their stirring chants. Beric moved about among the guests, seeing that their wants were supplied, while Parta herself looked after those who were gathered on the dais. Beric learned from the old chief Aska, who had first spoken to him on the day of their arrival at the sacred oak, that all Britain was ripe for the rising, and that messengers had been received not only from the Brigantes, but from many of the southern and western tribes, with assurances that they would rise as soon as they heard that the Iceni had struck the first blow.

"The Trinobantes will join us at Camalodunum. All goes well. Suetonius, with the legions, is still in the far west. We shall make an end of them here before he can return. By that time we shall have been joined by most of the tribes, and shall have a force that will be sufficient to destroy utterly the army he is leading. That done, there will be but the isolated forts to capture and destroy, and then Britain will be free from the invader. You think this will be so, Beric?"

"I hope and trust so," Beric replied. "I think that success in our first undertakings is a certainty, and I trust we may defeat Suetonius. With such numbers as we shall put in the field we ought surely to be able to do so. It is not of the present I think so much as of the future. Rome never submits to defeat, and will send an army here to which that of Suetonius would be but a handful. But if we remain united, and utilize the months that must elapse before the Romans can arrive in preparing for the conflict, we ought to be victorious."

"You feel sure that the Romans will try to reconquer Britain?"

"Quite sure. In all their history there is not an instance where they have submitted to defeat. This is one of the main reasons of their success. I am certain that, at whatever sacrifices, they will equip and send out an army that they will believe powerful enough for the purpose."

"But they were many years after their first invasion before they came again."

"That is true; but in those first two invasions they did not conquer. In the first they were forced to retire, and therefore came again; in the second they had success enough to be able to claim a victory and so to retire with honour. Besides, Rome is vastly stronger and more powerful now than she was then. Believe me, Aska, the struggle will be but begun when we have driven the last Roman from the island."

"We must talk of this again," Aska said, "as it is upon us that the brunt of this struggle will fall. We shall have the chief voice and influence after it is over, and Boadicea will stand in the place that Cunobeline held, of chief king of the island. Then, as you say, much will depend on the steps we take to prepare to resist the next invasion; and young as you are, your knowledge of

Roman ways will render your counsels valuable, and give great weight to your advice."

"I do not wish to put myself in any way in the foreground," Beric said. "I am still but a boy, and have no wish to raise my voice in the council of chiefs; but what I have learned of Roman history and Roman laws I would gladly explain to those who, like yourself, speak with the voice of authority, and whose wisdom all recognize."

In the morning Boadicea said that reports had been brought to her of the manner in which Beric had been teaching the Sarci to fight in Roman fashion, and that she should be glad to see the result.

Accordingly the tribesmen proceeded to the open fields a mile away, where they had been accustomed to drill, and they were followed by the whole of those gathered round the village. The queen and Parta drove out in their chariots. When they reached the spot the chiefs of the other tribes, at Beric's request, called upon their men to draw off and leave a space sufficient for the exercises. This left the Sarci standing in scattered groups over the open space, at one end of which Boadicea and all the chiefs were gathered.

"They are now in the position, queen," Beric said, "of men unsuspecting danger. I shall now warn them that they are about to be attacked, and that they are to gather instantly to repel the enemy."

Taking the conch slung over his shoulder Beric applied it to his lips and blew three short notes. The tribesmen ran together; there was, as it seemed to the lookers on, a scene of wild confusion for a minute, and then they were drawn up in companies, each a hundred strong, in regular order. A short blast and a long one, and they moved up together into a mass five deep; a single note, and the spears fell, and an array of glistening points shone in front of them.

A shout of surprise and approval rose from the tribesmen looking on. To them this perfect order and regularity seemed well nigh miraculous.

Beric now advanced to the line. At his order the two rear ranks stepped backwards a few feet, struck their spears in the ground, and then discharged their javelins--of which each man carried six--over the heads of the ranks in front, against the enemy supposed to be advancing to attack them. Then seizing their spears they fell into line again, and at another order the whole advanced at a quick pace with levelled spears to the charge, and keeping on till within a few paces of where the queen was standing, halted suddenly and raised their spears. Again a roar of applause came from the tribesmen.

"It is wonderful," the queen said. "I had not thought that men could be taught so to move together; and that is how the Romans fight, Beric?"

"It is, queen," Beric said. "The exercises are exactly similar to those of the Romans. I learnt them by heart when I was among them, and the orders are exactly the same as those given in the legions--only, of course, they are performed by trained soldiers more perfectly than we can as yet do them. It is but two months since we began, and the Romans have practised them for years. Had I time you would have seen them much more perfect than at present."

"You have performed marvels," she said. "I wish that you had had more time, and that all the Iceni, and not the Sarci only could have thus learned to meet the enemy. Do you not think so, chiefs?"

"It is wonderful," one of the chiefs said; "but I think that it is not so terrifying to a foe as the rush of our own men. It is better for resistance, but not so good for attack. Still it has great merits; but I think it more suited for men who fight deliberately, like the Romans, than for our own tribesmen, who are wont to rely for victory each upon his own strength and valour."

"What say you, Beric?" the queen asked.

"It would be presumptuous for me to give my opinion against that of a great chief," Beric said quietly; "But, so far, strength and valour have not in themselves succeeded. The men of Caractacus had both, but they were unavailing against the solid Roman line. We have never yet won a great victory over the Romans, and yet we have fought against them valiantly. None can say that a Briton is not as brave and as strong as a Roman. In our battles we have always outnumbered them. If we have been beaten, therefore, it has been surely because the Roman method of fighting is superior to our own."

There was a murmur of assent from several of the chiefs.

"Beric's argument is a strong one," the queen said to the one who had spoken; "and I would that all the Iceni had learnt to fight in this fashion. However, we shall have opportunities of seeing which is right before we have finished with the Romans. March your men back again, Beric."

Beric sounded his horn, and the line, facing half round, became a column, and marched in regular order back to the village. The morning meal was now taken, and at midday the march began. Boadicea with her daughters, Parta and other women of rank, went first in their chariots; and the Sarci, who, as lying next to the enemy's country, were allowed the post of honour, followed in column behind her, while the rest of the tribesmen made their way in a miscellaneous crowd through the forest. They halted among the trees at a distance of four miles from Camalodunum, and then rested, for the attack was not to take place until daybreak on the next morning.

Late that evening two or three women of the Trinobantes came out, in accordance with a preconcerted arrangement, to tell them that there was no suspicion at Camalodunum of the impending danger; and that, although there was great uneasiness among the inhabitants, no measures for defence had been taken, and that even the precaution of sending away the women and children had not been adopted.

No fires had been lighted; the men slept in the open air, simply wrapping themselves in their mantles and lying down under the trees. Beric had a long talk with Boduoc and ten of the tribesmen of the latter's company.

"You understand," Beric said at last, "that if, as I expect, the surprise will be complete and no regular resistance be offered, I shall sound my horn and give the signal for the tribe to break ranks and scatter. You ten men will, however, keep together, and at once follow Boduoc and myself. As soon as we enter the house to which I shall lead you, you will surround the two persons I shall place in your charge, and will conduct them to the spot where the chariot will be waiting. You will defend them, if necessary, with your lives, should any disobey my order to let you pass through with them. As soon as they are placed in the chariot you will be free to join in the sack, and if you should be losers by the delay, I will myself make up your share to that of your comrades. You are sure, Boduoc, that all the other arrangements are perfect?"

"Everything is arranged," Boduoc said. "My brother, who drives the chariot that brought your mother's attendants, quite understands that he is to follow as soon as we move off, and keeping a short way behind us is to stop in front of the last house outside the gate until we come. As soon as he has taken them up he will drive off and give them into the charge of our mother, who has promised you to have everything in readiness for them; the skins for beds, drinking vessels, food, and everything else necessary was taken there two days ago. My sisters will see to the comfort of the young lady, and you can rely upon my mother to carry out all the orders you have given her. Our hut lies so deeply in the forest that there is little chance of anyone going near it, especially as the whole of the men of the tribe are away."

Two hours before daylight the Iceni moved forward. They were to attack at a number of different points, and each chief had had his position allotted to him. The Sarci were to move directly against the northern gate and would form the centre of the attack. Each man, by Beric's order, carried a faggot so that these could be piled against the wall by the gate and enable them to effect an entrance without the delay that would be incurred in breaking down the massive gates. They passed quietly through the cultivated fields, and past the houses scattered about outside the walls, whose inhabitants had withdrawn into the city since the alarm spread. They halted at a short distance from the gate, for sentries would be on guard there, and remained for nearly an hour, as many of the other tribesmen had a considerably longer distance to go to reach their appointed stations. A faint light was beginning to steal over the sky when, far away on their right, a horn sounded. It was repeated again and again, each time nearer, and ran along far to the left; then, raising their war cry, the Sarci dashed forward to the gate.

The shouts of the sentinels on the walls had arisen as soon as the first horn sounded, and had scarcely died away when the Sarci reached the gate. Each man as he arrived threw down his faggot, and the pile soon reached the top of the wall. Then Beric led the way up and stood on the Roman work. The sentries, seeing the hopelessness of resistance, had already fled, and the Sarci poured in. A confused clamour of shouts and cries rose from the town, above which sounded the yells of the exulting Iceni. Beric gave the signal for the Sarci to scatter, and the tribesmen at once began to attack the houses. Placing himself at the head of Boduoc's chosen party, Beric ran forward. Already from some of the houses armed men were pouring out, but disregarding these Beric pressed on until he reached the house of Caius Muro. His reason for haste was that, standing rather on the other side of the town, it was nearer the point assailed by one of the other divisions of the tribe than to the north gate, and he feared that others might arrive there before him. Reaching the door he beat upon it with the handle of his sword.

"Open, Cneius," he shouted, "it is I, Beric."

The door was opened at once, and he ran forward into the atrium, which was filled with frightened slaves, who burst into cries of terror as, followed by his men, he entered. "Where are you, Cneius?" Beric shouted.

"I am here," the scribe replied from his cubicule, "I will be with you in a moment; it is but a minute since we were awoke by the uproar."

"Be quick!" Beric said, "there is not a moment to be lost.

"Run up to the women's apartments," he said to a slave, "and tell your mistress to hurry down, for that every minute is precious."

Almost immediately Berenice came down the stairs in her disguise as a British boy, and at the same moment Cneius issued from his room.

"Come, Berenice," Beric said, "there is not a moment to be lost; the town is in our hands, and if others of the tribe arrive I might not be able to save you."

Hurrying them from the house he ordered the men to close round them, and then started on his way back. A terrible din was going on all round; yells, shouts, and screams arising from every house. flames were bursting up at a dozen points. To his great satisfaction Beric reached the point where the Sarci were at work, breaking into the houses, before he encountered any of the other Iceni. The men were too busy to pay any attention to the little group of their own tribesmen; passing through these they were soon at the gate. It already stood open, the bolts having been drawn by those who first entered. Fifty yards from the wall stood the chariot.

"Now you can leave us," Beric said to his followers, "I will rejoin you soon."

Berenice was crying bitterly, horror stricken at the sounds she had heard, though happily she had seen nothing, being closely shut in by the tall forms of her guard.

"Thanks be to the gods that I have saved you, Berenice," Beric said, "and you also, Cneius! Now I must commit you to the care of the driver of the chariot, who is one of my tribesmen. He will take you to a retreat where you will, I trust, be in perfect safety until the troubles are over. His mother has promised to do all in her power for your comfort. You will find one of our huts but a rough abode, but it will at least be a shelter."

"Cannot you come with us, Beric?" the girl sobbed.

"That I cannot do, Berenice. I am a Briton and a chief, and I must be with my tribe. And now I must away. Farewell, Berenice! may your gods and mine watch over you! Farewell, my kind teacher!"

He took off the torque, the collar formed of a number of small metal cords interlaced with each other, the emblem of rank and command, and handed it to the driver. "You will show this, Runoc, to any you meet, for it may be that you will find parties of late comers on the road. This will be a proof that you are journeying on my business and under my orders. Do not stop and let them question you, but drive quickly along, and if they should shout and bid you stop, hold up the torque and shout, 'I travel at speed by my chief's orders.'

"Do you both sit down in the chariot," he said to the others. "Then as you journey rapidly along it will be supposed that you are either wounded or messengers of importance. Farewell!"

Cneius and the girl had already mounted the chariot, and the driver now gave the horses rein and started at full speed. Beric turned and re-entered the town slowly. In those days pity for the vanquished was a sentiment but little comprehended, and he had certainly not learned it among the Romans, who frequently massacred their prisoners wholesale. Woe to the vanquished! was almost a maxim with them. But Beric shrank from witnessing the scene, now that the tables were turned upon the oppressors. Nationally he hated the Romans, but individually he had no feeling against them, and had he had the power he would at once have arrested the effusion of blood. He wished to drive them from the kingdom, not to massacre them; but he knew well that he had no power whatever in such a matter. Even his own tribesmen would not have stayed their hand at his command. To slay a Roman was to them a far more meritorious action than to slay a wolf, and any one who urged mercy would have been regarded not only as a weakling but as a traitor.

Already the work was well nigh done. Pouring in on all sides into the city the Iceni had burst into the houses and slain their occupants whether they resisted or not. A few men here and there sold their lives dearly, but the great majority had been too panic stricken with the sudden danger to attempt the slightest resistance. Some of the inhabitants whose houses were near the temple had fled thither for refuge before the assailants reached them, but in half an hour from the striking of the first blow these and the troops there were the sole survivors of the population of Camalodunum. For the present the temple was disregarded. It was known that the garrison did not exceed four hundred men, and there was no fear of so small a body assuming the offensive.

The work of destruction had commenced. There was but little plundering, for the Britons despised the Roman luxuries, of the greater part of which they did not even comprehend the use. They were Roman, and therefore to be hated as well as despised. Save, therefore, weapons, which were highly prized, and gold ornaments, which were taken as trinkets for the women at home, nothing was saved. As the defenders of each house were slain, fire was applied to hangings and curtains, and then the assailants hurried away in search of fresh victims. Thus the work of destruction proceeded concurrently with that of massacre, and as the sun rose vast columns of smoke mounting upwards conveyed the news to the women of the Iceni and Trinobantes for a circle of many miles round, that the attack had been successful, and that Camalodunum, the seat of their oppressors, was in flames. Beric, as he made his way towards the centre of the town, sighed as he passed the shop where two months before he had stopped a moment to look at the rolls of vellum.

The destruction of the monuments of Roman luxury; the houses with their costly contents; and even the Palace of Cunobeline, which had been converted into the residence of the Roman governor, had not affected him; but he mourned over the loss of the precious manuscripts which had contained such a wealth of stored up learning. Already the house was wrapped in flames, which were rushing from the windows, and the prize which he had looked upon as his own special share of the plunder had escaped him.

At the edge of the broad open space that surrounded the Temple of Claudius the Britons were gathering thickly. Beric applied his horn to his lips, and in a few minutes the Sarci gathered round him. Bidding them stand in order he moved away to see what disposition was being made for the attack on the temple, but at present all were too excited with their success for any to assume the lead or give orders. At the first rush parties of the Britons had made for the temple, but had been received with showers of darts and stones, and had been met on the steps by the Roman soldiers and roughly repulsed. Walking round he came upon the chariot of Boadicea. The queen was flushed with excitement and gratified vengeance, and was shaking her spear menacingly towards the temple; her eye presently fell upon Beric.

"The work has begun well, my young chief, but we have still to crush the wolves in their den. It is a strong place, with its massive walls unpierced save by the doorway at each end; but we will have them out if to do so we are forced to tear it down stone by stone."

"I trust that we shall not be as long as that would take, queen," Beric said, "for we have other work to do."

Just at this moment one of the chiefs of the Trinobantes came up. "Queen Boadicea," he said, "we crave that we may be allowed to storm the temple. It is built on our ground as a sign of our subjection, and we would fain ourselves capture it."

"Be it so," the queen replied. "Do you undertake the task at once."

The Trinobantes, who had joined the Iceni in the attack on the town, presently gathered with loud shouts, and under their chiefs rushed at the temple. From the roof darts and stones were showered down upon them; but though many were killed they swarmed up the broad steps that surrounded it on all sides and attacked the doors. Beric shook his head, and returning to his men led them off down one of the broad streets to an open space a short distance away.

"This will be our gathering place," he said. "Do not wander far away, and return quickly at the sound of my horn. We may be wanted presently. I do not think that the Trinobantes will take the temple in that fashion."

They had indeed advanced entirely unprovided with proper means of assault. The massive gates against which the Romans had piled stones, casks of provisions, and other heavy articles were not to be broken down by such force as the Britons could bring against them. In vain these chopped with their swords upon the woodwork. The gates were constructed of oak, and the weapons scarce marked them. In vain they threw themselves twenty abreast against them. The doors hardly quivered at the shock, and in the meantime the assailants were suffering heavily, for from openings in the roof, extending from the building itself to the pillars that surrounded it, the Romans dropped missiles upon them.

For some time the Trinobantes persevered, and then their chiefs, seeing that the attempt was hopeless, called off their followers. No fresh attempt was made for a time, and Boadicea established herself in one of the few houses that had escaped the flames, and there presently the chiefs assembled. Various suggestions were made, but at last it was decided to batter in the doors with a heavy tree, and a strong party of men were at once despatched to fell and prepare two of suitable size. The operation was a long one, as the trees when found had to be brought down by lighting fires against the trunks, and it was nightfall before they fell and the branches were cut off. It was decided, therefore, to postpone the attack until the next day.

Beric had not been present at the council, to which only a few of the leading chiefs had been summoned; but he doubted, when he heard what had been decided upon, whether the attack would be successful. It was settled that the Trinobantes were to attack the door at one end of the temple, and the Iceni that at the other. Late in the evening the chariot returned, and Beric was greatly relieved to hear that the fugitives had been placed in safety and that the journey had been made without interference. He was glad to recover his torque, for its absence would have excited surprise when men's minds were less occupied and excited. Not until he recovered it could he go to see Parta, who was lodged with the queen, but as soon as he recovered it he went in. Every sign of Roman habitation and luxury had been, as far as possible, obliterated by order of Boadicea before she entered the house. Hangings had been pulled down, statues overthrown, and the paintings on the plaster chipped from the walls.

"What have you been doing all day, Beric?" his mother asked. "I looked to see you long before this, and should have thought that some accident had befallen you had I not known that the news would have been speedily brought me had it been so."

"I have been looking after the tribesmen, mother. I should have come in to see you, but did not wish to intrude among the chiefs in council with the queen. You represented the Sarci here, and had we been wanted you would have sent for me. Who are to attack the temple tomorrow?"

"Not the Sarci, my son. Unser begged that he and his tribe might have the honour, and the queen and council granted it to him."

"I am glad of it, mother. The duty is an honourable one, but the loss will be heavy, and others can do the work as well as we could, and I want to keep our men for the shock of battle with the legions. Moreover, I doubt whether the doors will be battered down in the way they propose."

"You do, Beric! and why is that?" The speaker was Aska, who had just left the group of chiefs gathered round the queen at the other end of the apartment, and had come close without Beric hearing him.

The lad coloured. "I spoke only for my mother's hearing, sir," he said. "To no one else should I have ventured to express an opinion on a course agreed upon by those who are older and wiser than myself."

"That is right, Beric; the young should be silent in the presence of their elders; nevertheless I should like to know why you think the assault is likely to fail."

"It was really not my own opinion I was giving, sir. I was thinking of the manner in which the Romans, who are accustomed to besiege places with high walls and strong gates, proceed. They have made these matters a study, while to us an attack upon such a place is altogether new, seeing that none such exist in Britain save those the Romans have erected."

"How would they proceed, Beric?"

"They would treat an attack upon such a place as a serious matter, not to be undertaken rashly and hastily, but only after great preparation. In order to batter down a gate or a wall they use heavy beams, such as those that have been prepared for tomorrow, but they affix to the head a shoe of iron or brass. They do not swing it upon men's arms, seeing that it would be most difficult to get so many men to exercise their strength together, and indeed could not give it the momentum required."

"But we propose to have the beam carried by fifty men, and for all to rush forward together and drive it against the door."

"If the door were weak and would yield to the first blow that might avail," Beric said; "but unless it does so the shock will throw down the tree and the men bearing it. Many will be grievously hurt. Moreover, if, as will surely be the case, many of the bearers fall under the darts of the Romans as they approach, others will stumble over their bodies, and the speed of the whole be greatly checked."

"Then can you tell me how the Romans act in such a case, Beric?"

"Yes, sir. I have frequently heard relations of sieges from soldiers who have taken part in them. They build, in the first place, movable towers or sheds running on wheels. These towers are made strong enough to resist the stones and missiles the besieged may hurl against them. Under cover of the shelter men push up the towers to the door or wall to be battered; the beam is then slung on ropes hanging from the inside of the tower. Other ropes are attached; numbers of men take hold of these, and working together swing the beam backwards and forwards, so that each time it strikes the wall or door a heavy blow. As the beam is of great weight, and many men work it, the blows are well nigh irresistible, and the strongest walls crumble and the most massive gates splinter under the shock of its iron head."

"The Romans truly are skilled warriors," Aska said. "We are but children in the art of war beside them, and methinks it would be difficult indeed for us to construct such a machine, though mayhap it could be done had we with us many men skilled in the making of chariots. But sometimes, Beric, they must have occasion to attack places where such machines could not well be used."

"In that case, sir, they sometimes make what they call a tortoise. The soldiers link their broad shields together, so as to form a complete covering, resembling the back of a tortoise, and under shelter of this they advance to the attack. When they reach the foot of the wall all remain immovable save those in the front line, who labour with iron bars to loosen the stones at the foot of the wall, protected from missiles from above by the shields of their comrades. From time to time they are relieved by fresh workers until the foundations of the wall are deeply undermined. As they proceed they erect massive props to keep up the wall, and finally fill up the hole with combustibles. After lighting these they retire. When the props are consumed the wall of course falls, and they then rush forward and climb the breach."

"Truly, Beric, you have profited by your lessons," Aska said, laying his hand kindly on the lad's shoulder. "The Druids spoke wisely when they prophesied a great future for you. Before we have done we may have many Roman strongholds to capture, and when we do I will see that the council order that your advice be taken as to how they shall be attacked; but in this matter tomorrow things must remain as they are. Unser is a proud chief, and headstrong, and would not brook any interference. Should he be repulsed in the assault, I will advise the queen to call up the Sarci, and allow you to proceed in your own manner."

"I will do my best, sir; but time is needed for proceeding according to the first Roman method, and our shields are too small for the second. The place should be taken by tomorrow night, for Cerealis will assuredly move with his legion to relieve it as soon as he hears the news of our attack."

"That is what has been in our minds," Aska said. "Well, what do you say, Beric? After what I saw the other day of the movements you have taught your tribe I should be sorry to have their ranks thinned in a hopeless attack upon the temple. I would rather that we should leave it for the present and march out to meet Cerealis, leaving a guard here to keep the Romans hemmed in until we have time to deal with them."

Beric stood for a minute or two without answering, and then said, "I will undertake it, sir, with the Sarci should Unser's attack fail."

CHAPTER VI
FIRST SUCCESSES

Upon leaving his mother, Beric returned to the spot where the Sarci were lying. Some of the chiefs were sitting round a fire made of beams and woodwork dragged from the ruins of the Roman houses.

"We must be up an hour before daybreak; I think that there will be work for us tomorrow. If Unser and his tribe fail in capturing the temple we are to try; and there will be preparations to make." And he explained the plan upon which he had determined.

Daylight was just breaking when the Sarci entered the forest four miles from Camalodunum. Here they scattered in search of dry wood. In two hours sufficient had been gathered for their purpose, and it was made up into two hundred great faggots nearly four feet across and ten in length, in weight as much as a strong man could carry on his head. With these they returned to the city. It needed no questions as to the result of the attack, which had just terminated with the same fortune that had befallen that on the day previous. Unser had been killed, and large numbers of his men had fallen in their vain attempts to hew down the gates. The battering rams had proved a complete failure. Many of the fifty men who carried the beam had fallen as they advanced. The others had rushed at the gate door, but the recoil had thrown them down, and many had had their limbs broken from the tree falling on them. Attempts had been made to repeat the assault; but the Romans having pierced the under part of the roof in many places, let fall javelins and poured down boiling oil; and at last, having done all that was possible, but in vain, the tribesmen had fallen back.

Beric proceeded at once to the queen's. A council was being held, and it had just been determined to march away to meet Cerealis when Beric entered. Aska left his place in the circle of chiefs as soon as he saw him enter the door.

"Are you ready to undertake it, Beric? Do not do so unless you have strong hopes of success. The repulses of yesterday and today have lowered the spirits of our men, and another failure would still further harm us."

"I will undertake it, Aska, and I think I can answer for success; but I shall need three hours before I begin."

"That could be spared," the chief said. "Cerealis will not have learned the news until last night at the earliest--he may not know it yet. There is no fear of his arriving here until tomorrow." Then he returned to his place.

"Before we finally decide, queen," he said, "I would tell you that the young chief Beric is ready to attack the place with the Sarci. He has learned much of the Roman methods, and may be more fortunate than the others have been. I would suggest that he be allowed to try, for it will have a very ill effect upon the tribes if we fail in taking the temple, which is regarded as the symbol of Roman dominion. I will even go so far as to say that a retreat now would go very far to mar our hopes of success in the war, for the news would spread through the country and dispirit others now preparing to join us."

"Why should Beric succeed when Unser has failed?" one of the chiefs said. "Can a lad achieve a success where one of our best and bravest chiefs has been repulsed?"

"I think that he might," Aska replied. "At any rate, as he is ready to risk his life and his tribe in doing so, I pray the queen to give her consent. He demands three hours to make his preparations for the attack."

"He shall try," Boadicea said decidedly. "You saw the other day, chiefs, how well he has learned the Roman methods of war. He shall have an opportunity now of turning his knowledge to account. Parta, you are willing that your son should try?"

"Certainly I am willing," Parta said. "He can but die once; he cannot die in a nobler effort for his country."

"Then it is settled," the queen said. "The Sarci will attack in three hours."

As soon as Beric heard the decision he hurried away and at once ordered the tribesmen to scatter through the country and to kill two hundred of the cattle roaming at present masterless, to strip off their hides, and bring them in. They returned before the three hours expired, bringing in the hides. In the meantime Beric had procured from a half consumed warehouse a quantity of oil, pitch, and other combustibles, and had smeared the faggots with them. On the arrival of the men with the hides, these were bound with the raw side upwards over the faggots.

Two hundred of the strongest men of the tribe were then chosen and divided into two parties, and the rest being similarly divided, took their station at the ends of the square facing the gates. When Beric sounded his horn the faggot bearers raised their burdens on to their heads and formed in a close square, ten abreast, with the faggots touching each other. Beric himself commanded the party facing the principal entrance, and holding a blazing torch in each hand, took his place in the centre of the square, there being ample room for him between the lines of men. The rest of the tribe were ordered to stand firmly in order until he gave the signal for the advance. Then he again sounded his horn, and the two parties advanced from the opposite ends of the square.

As soon as they came within reach the Romans showered down darts and javelins; but these either slipped altogether from the surface of the wet hides, or, penetrating them, went but a short distance into the faggots; and the British tribesmen raised shouts of exultation as the two solid bodies advanced unshaken to the steps of the temple. Mounting these they advanced to the gates. In vain the Romans dropped their javelins perpendicularly through the holes in the ceiling of the colonnade, in vain poured down streams of boiling oil, which had proved so fatal to the last attack. The javelins failed to penetrate, the oil streamed harmless off the hides. The men had, before advancing, received minute instructions. The ten men in the front line piled their faggots against the door, and then keeping close to the wall of the temple itself, slipped round to the side colonnade.

The operation was repeated by the next line, and so on until but two lines remained. Then the two men at each end of these lines mounted the pile of faggots and placed their burdens there, leaving but six standing. In their centre Beric had his place, and now, kneeling down under their shelter, applied his torches to the pile. He waited till he saw the flames beginning to mount up. Then he gave the word; the six men dropped their faggots to the ground, and with him ran swiftly to the side colonnade, where they were in shelter, as the Romans, knowing they could not be attacked here, had made no openings in the ceiling above. The Britons were frantic with delight when they saw columns of smoke followed by tongues of flames mounting from either end of the temple. Higher and higher the flames mounted till they licked the ceiling above them.

For half an hour the fire continued, and by the end of that time there was but a glowing mass of embers through which those without could soon see right into the temple. The doors and the obstacles behind them had been destroyed. As soon as he was aware by the shouts of his countrymen that the faggots were well in a blaze, Beric had sounded his horn, and he and the tribesmen from both colonnades had run across the open unmolested by the darts of the Romans, who were too panic stricken at the danger that threatened them to pay any heed to their movements. Beric was received with loud acclamations by the Iceni, and was escorted by a shouting multitude to the queen, who had taken her place at a point where she could watch the operations. She held out her hand to him. "You have succeeded, Beric," she said; "and my thanks and those of all here--nay, of all Britain--are due to you. In half an hour the temple will be open to attack."

"Hardly in that time, queen," he replied. "The faggots will doubtless have done their work by then, but it will be hours before the embers and stonework will be sufficiently cool to enable men to pass over them to the assault."

"We can wait," the queen said. "A messenger, who left the camp of Cerealis at daybreak, has just arrived, and at that hour nothing was known to the Romans of our attack here. They will not now arrive until tomorrow."

Not until the afternoon was it considered that the entrances would be cool enough to pass through. Then the Sarci prepared for the attack, binding pieces of raw hide under their feet to protect them from the heated stonework. They were formed ten abreast. Beric took his place before the front line of one of the columns, and with levelled spears they advanced at a run towards the doors. A shower of missiles saluted them from the roof. Some fell, but the rest, pressing on in close order, dashed through the gateway and flung themselves upon the Roman soldiers drawn up to oppose their passage. The resistance was feeble. The Romans had entirely lost heart and could not for a moment sustain the weight of the charge. They were swept away from the entrance, and the Britons poured in.

Standing in groups the Romans defended themselves in desperation; but their efforts were vain, and in five minutes the last defender of the place was slain. As soon as the fight was over the whole of the Iceni rushed tumultuously forward with exultant shouts and filled the temple; then a horn sounded and a lane was made, as Boadicea, followed by her chiefs and chieftainesses, entered the temple. The queen's face was radiant with triumph, and she would have spoken but the shouting was so loud that those near her could not obtain silence. They understood, however, when advancing to the statues of the gods that stood behind the altars, she waved her spear. In an instant the tribesmen swarmed round the statues, ropes were attached to the massive figures, and Jupiter, Mars, and Minerva fell to the ground with a crash, as did the statue of the Emperor Claudius.

A mighty shout hailed its downfall. The gods of the Britons, insulted and outraged, were avenged upon those of Rome; the altars of Mona had streamed with the blood of the Druids, those of Camalodunum were wet with the gore of Roman legionaries. The statues were broken to pieces, the altars torn down, and then the chiefs ordered the tribesmen to fetch in faggots. Thousands went to the forest, while others pulled down detached houses and sheds that had escaped the flames, and dragged the beams and woodwork to the temple. By nightfall an enormous pile of faggots was raised round each of the eight interior columns that in two lines supported the roof. Torches were applied by Boadicea, her two daughters and some of the principal Druids, and in a short time the interior of the temple was a glowing furnace. The beams of the ceiling and roof soon ignited and the flames shot up high into the air.

All day the Trinobantes had been pouring in, and a perfect frenzy of delight reigned among the great crowd looking on at the destruction of the temple that had been raised to signify and celebrate the subjugation of Britain. Women with flowing hair performed wild dances of triumph; some rushed about as if possessed with madness, uttering prophecies of the total destruction of the Romans; others foamed at the mouth and fell in convulsions, while the men were scarcely less excited over their success. Messengers had already brought in news that at midday Cerealis had learned that Camalodunum had been attacked, and that the legion was to start on the following morning to relieve the town.

The news had been taken to him by one of the Trinobantes, who had received his instructions from Aska. He was to say that the town had suddenly been attacked and that many had fallen; but the greater portion of the population had escaped to the temple, which had been vainly attacked by the Iceni. The object of this news was to induce Cerealis to move out from his fortified camp. The chiefs felt the difficulty of assaulting such a position, and though they had dreaded the arrival of Cerealis before the temple was taken, they were anxious that he should set out as soon as they saw that Beric's plan of attack had succeeded, and that the temple was now open to their assault.

At midnight the roof of the temple fell in, and nothing remained but the bare walls and the columns surrounding them. The chiefs ordered their followers to make their way through the still burning town and to gather by tribes outside the defensive works, and there lie down until morning, when they would march to meet the legion of Cerealis. At daybreak they were again afoot and on the march southward, swollen by the accession of the Trinobantes and by the arrival during the last two days of tribes who had been too late to join the rest at Cardun. The British force now numbered at least fifty thousand.

"It is a great army, Beric," Boduoc said exultingly as they moved forward.

"It is a great host," Beric replied. "I would that it were an army. Had they all even as much training as our men I should feel confident in the future."

"But surely you are confident now, Beric; we have begun well."

"We have scarcely begun at all," Beric said. "What have we done? Destroyed a sleeping town and captured by means of fire a temple defended by four hundred men. We shall win today, that I do not doubt. The men are wrought up by their success, and the Romans are little prepared to meet such a force--I doubt not that we shall beat them, but to crush a legion is not to defeat Rome. I hope, Boduoc, but I do not feel confident. Look back at the Sarci and then look round at this disordered host. Well, the Romans in discipline and order exceed the Sarci as much as we exceed the rest of the Iceni. They will be led by generals trained in war; we are led by chiefs whose only idea of war is to place themselves at the head of their tribe and rush against the enemy. Whether courage and great numbers can compensate for want of discipline remains to be seen. The history of Rome tells me that it has never done so yet."

After five hours' marching some fleet footed scouts sent on ahead brought in the news that the Romans were approaching. A halt was called, and the chiefs assembled round the queen's chariot in council. Beric was summoned by a messenger from the queen.

"You must always attend our councils," she said when he came up. "You have proved that, young as you are, you possess a knowledge of war that more than compensates for your lack of years. You have the right, after capturing the temple for us, to take for the Sarci the post of honour in today's battle. Choose it for yourself. You know the Romans; where do you think we had better fight them?"

"I think we could not do better than await them here," he said. "We stand on rising ground, and one of the Trinobantes to whom I have just spoken says that there is a swamp away on the left of our front, so that the Roman horsemen cannot advance in that direction. I should attack them in face and on their left flank, closing in thickly so as to prevent their horsemen from breaking out on to the plain at our right and then falling upon us in our rear. Since you are good enough to say that I may choose my post for the Sarci, I will hold them where they stand; then, should the others fail to break the Roman front, we will move down upon them and check their advance while the rest attack their flanks."

This answer pleased some of the chiefs, who felt jealous of the honour the small tribe had gained on the previous day. They were afraid that Beric would have chosen to head the attack.

"Does that plan please you?" Boadicea asked.

"It is as well as another," one of the chiefs said. "Let the Sarci look on this time while we destroy the enemy. I should have thought Beric would have chosen for his tribe the post of honour in the attack."

"The Romans always keep their best troops in reserve," Beric said quietly; "in a hard fight it is the reserve that decides the fate of the battle."

"Then let it be so," Boadicea said. "Is the swamp that you speak of deep?"

"It is not too deep for our men to cross," one of the chiefs of the Trinobantes said; "but assuredly a horseman could not pass through it."

"Very well, then, let the Trinobantes attack by falling upon the Romans on our right; the Iceni will attack them in front; and the Sarci will remain where they stand until Beric sees need for them to advance."

In a few minutes the Roman legion was seen advancing, with a portion of the cavalry in front and the rest in the rear. The queen, whose chariot was placed in front of the line, raised her spear. A tremendous shout was raised by the Britons, and with wild cries the tribes poured down to the attack, while the women, clustered on the slopes they had left, added their shrill cries of encouragement to the din. The Romans, who, believing that the Britons were still engaged in the attack on Camalodunum, had no expectation of meeting them on the march, halted and stood uncertain as the masses of Britons poured down to the attack. Then their trumpets sounded and they again advanced, the cavalry in the rear moving forward to join those in the advance, but before they accomplished this the Britons were upon them. Showers of darts were poured in, and the horsemen, unable to stand the onslaught, rode into the spaces between the companies of the infantry, who, moving outwards and forming a solid column on either flank, protected them from the assaults of their foes.

The Britons, after pouring in showers of javelins, flung themselves, sword in hand, upon the Roman infantry; but these with levelled spears showed so solid a front that they were unable to break through, while from behind the spearmen, the light armed Roman troops poured volleys of missiles among them. Boadicea called Beric to her side.

"It is as you said, Beric; the order in which the Romans fight is wonderful. See how steadily they hold together, it is like a wild boar attacked by dogs; but they will be overwhelmed, see how the darts fly and how bravely the Iceni are fighting."

The tribesmen, indeed, were attacking with desperate bravery. Seizing the heads of the spears they attempted to wrest them from their holders, or to thrust them aside and push forward within striking distance. Sometimes they partially succeeded, and though the first might fall others rushing in behind reached the Romans and pressed them backwards, but reserves were brought up and the line restored. Then slowly but steadily the Romans moved forward, and although partial success had at some points attended those who attacked them in flank, the front of the column with serried spears held its way on in spite of the efforts of the Britons to arrest the movement. Presently the supply of javelins of their assailants began to fail, and the assaults upon the head of the column to grow more feeble, while the shouts of the Roman soldiers rose above the cries of their assailants.

"Now it is time for us to move down," Beric said; "if we can arrest the advance their flanks will be broken in before long. Now, men," he shouted as he returned to his place at the head of the Sarci, "now is the time to show that you can meet the Romans in their own fashion. Move slowly down to the attack, let no man hasten his pace, but let each keep his place in the ranks. Four companies will attack the Romans in front, the others in column five deep will march down till they face the Roman flank, then they will march at it, spears down, and break it in."

Beric sounded his bugle, and ten deep the four hundred men moved steadily down to the attack of the Romans. The five front ranks marched with levelled spears, those behind prepared to hurl their darts over their heads. When within fifty yards of the enemy the Sarci raised their battle cry, and the Iceni engaged with the Romans in front, seeing the hedge of spears advancing behind them, hurriedly ran off at both flanks and the Sarci advanced to the attack.

The Romans halted involuntarily, astonished at the spectacle. Never before had they encountered barbarians advancing in formation similar to their own, and the sight of the tall figures advancing almost naked to the assault--for the Britons always threw off their garments before fighting--filled them with something like consternation. At the shouts of their officers, however, they again got into motion and met the Britons firmly. The additional length Beric had given to the spears of the Sarci now proved of vital advantage, and bearing steadily onward they brought the Romans to a standstill, while the javelins from the British rear ranks fell thick and fast among them. Gradually the Romans were pressed backwards, quickly as the gaps were filled up by those behind, until the charging shout of the Sarci on their flank was heard. Beric blew his horn, and his men with an answering shout pressed forward faster, their cries of victory rising as the Romans gave way.

Still the latter fought stubbornly, until triumphant yells and confused shouts told them that the flank had given way under the attack of the Britons. Then Beric's horn sounded again, the slow advance was converted into a charge, the ranks behind closed up, and before the weight and impetus of the rush the Roman line was broken. Then the impetuosity of the Sarci could no longer be restrained, in vain Beric blew his horn. Flinging down their spears and drawing their swords the Britons flung themselves on the broken mass, the other tribesmen pouring in tumultuously behind them.

For a few minutes a desperate conflict raged, each man fighting for himself, but numbers prevailed, the Roman shouts became feebler, the war cries of the Britons louder and more triumphant. In ten minutes the fight was over, more than two thousand Roman soldiers lay dead, while Cerealis and the cavalry, bursting their way through their assailants, alone escaped, galloping off at full speed towards the refuge of their fortified camp. The exultation of the Britons knew no bounds. They had for the first time since the Romans set foot on their shore beaten them in a fair fight in the open. There was a rush to collect the arms, shields, and helmets of the fallen Romans, and two of the Sarci presently brought the standards of the legion to Beric.

"Follow me with them," he said, and, extricating himself from the throng, ascended the slope to where Boadicea, surrounded with women who were dancing and joining in a triumphant chant of victory, was still standing in her chariot.

"Here are the Roman standards, the emblems of victory," Beric said as he approached the chariot.

Boadicea sprang down, and advancing to him, embraced him warmly. "The victory is yours, Beric," she said. "Keep these two eagles, and fix them in your hall, so that your children's children may point to them with pride and say, 'It was Beric, chief of the Sarci, who first overthrew the Romans in the field.' But there is no time to be lost;" and she turned to her charioteer, who carried a horn. "Sound the summons for the chiefs to assemble."

There were several missing, for the Britons had suffered heavily in their first attack.

"Chiefs," she said, "let us not lose an instant, but press on after the Romans. Let us strike before they recover from their confusion and surprise. Catus Decianus may be in their camp, and while I seek no other spoil, him I must have to wreak my vengeance on. See that a party remain to look to the wounded, and that such as need it are taken to their homes in wagons." The horns were at once sounded, the tribesmen flocked back to the positions from which they had charged, and resumed their garments. Then the march was continued.

They presented a strange appearance now. Almost every man had taken possession of some portion or other of the Romans' arms. Some had helmets, others shields, others breastplates, swords, or spears. The helmets, however, were speedily taken off and slung behind them, the heads of the Iceni being vastly larger than those of the Romans, the tallest of whom they overtopped by fully six inches. The arms of the officer who commanded under Cerealis were offered to Beric, but he refused them.

"I fight to drive the Romans from our land," he said, "and not for spoil. Nothing of theirs will I touch, but will return to the forest when all is over just as I left it."

By evening they approached the Roman camp. A portion of the legion had been left there when Cerealis set out, and in the light of the setting sun the helmets and spearheads could be seen above the massive palisades that rose on the top of the outworks. The Britons halted half a mile away, fires were lighted, and the men sat down to feast upon the meat that had been brought in wagons from Camalodunum. Then a council was held. As a rule, the British councils were attended by all able bodied men. The power of the chiefs, except in actual war, was very small, for the Britons, like their Gaulish ancestors, considered every man to be equal, and each had a voice in the management of affairs. Thus every chief had, before taking up arms, held a council of his tribesmen, and it was only after they had given their vote for war that he possessed any distinct power and control.

When the council began, one of the chiefs of the Trinobantes was asked first to give a minute description of the Roman camp. The works were formidable. Surrounding it was a broad and deep fosse, into which a stream was turned. Beyond this there was a double vallum or wall of earth so steep as to be climbed with great difficulty. In the hollow between the two walls sharp stakes were set thickly together. The second wall was higher than the first, and completely commanded it. Along its top ran a solid palisade of massive beams, behind which the earth was banked up to within some three and a half feet from the top, affording a stand for the archers, slingers, and spearmen.

The council was animated, but the great majority of chiefs were in favour of leaving this formidable position untouched, and falling upon places that offered a chance of an easier capture. The British in their tribal wars fought largely for the sake of plunder. In their first burst of fury at Camalodunum they had, contrary to their custom, sought only to destroy; but their thirst for blood was now appeased, they longed for the rich spoils of the Roman cities, both as trophies of victory and to adorn their women. The chiefs represented that already many of their bravest tribesmen had fallen, and it would be folly to risk a heavy loss in the attack upon such a position.

What matter, they argued, if two or three hundred Romans were left there for the present? They could do no harm, and could be either captured by force or obliged to surrender by hunger after Suetonius and the Roman army had been destroyed. Not a day should be lost, they contended, in marching upon Verulamium, after which London could be sacked, for, although far inferior in size and importance to Camalodunum and Verulamium, it was a rising town, inhabited by large numbers of merchants and traders, who imported goods from Gaul and distributed them over the country.

Beric's opinion was in favour of an instant assault, and in this he was supported by Aska and two or three of the older chiefs; but the majority were the other way, and the policy of leaving altogether the fortified posts garrisoned by the Romans to be dealt with after the Roman army had been met and destroyed was decided upon. One of the arguments employed was that while the capture of these places would be attended with considerable loss, it would add little to the effect that the news of the destruction of the chief Roman towns would have upon the tribes throughout the whole country, and would take so long that Suetonius might return in time to succour the most important places before the work was done. Aska walked away from the council with Beric.

"They have decided wrongly," he said.

"I do not think it much matters," Beric replied. "Everything hangs at present upon the result of our battle with Suetonius. If we win, all the detached forts must surrender; if we lose, what matters it?"

"You think we shall lose, Beric?"

"I do not say that," Beric said; "but see how it was today. The Iceni made no more impression upon the Roman column than if they had been attacking a wall. They hindered themselves by their very numbers, and by the time we meet the Romans our numbers will be multiplied by five, perhaps by ten. But shall we be any stronger thereby? Will not rather the confusion be greater? Today the Roman horse fled; but had they charged among us, small as was their number, what confusion would they have made in our ranks! A single Briton is a match for a single Roman, and more. Ten Romans fighting in order might repel the assault of a hundred, and as the numbers multiply so does the advantage of discipline increase. I hope for victory, Aska, but I cannot say that I feel confident of it."

Marching next morning against Verulamium, they arrived there in the afternoon and at once attacked it. The resistance was feeble, and bursting through in several places the Iceni and Trinobantes spread over the town, slaughtering all they found. Not only the Romans, but the Gauls settled in the city, and such Britons as had adopted Roman customs were put to the sword. The city was then sacked and set on fire. It was now decided that instead of turning towards London they should march west in order that they might be joined by other tribes on their way and meet Suetonius returning from Wales.

There was no haste in their movements. They advanced by easy stages, their numbers swelling every day, tribe after tribe joining them, as the news spread of the capture and destruction of the two chief Roman towns, and the defeat and annihilation of one of the legions. So they marched until, a fortnight after the capture of Verulamium, the news arrived that Suetonius, marching with all speed towards the east, had already passed them, gathering up on his way the garrisons of all the fortified posts. Then the great host turned and marched east again. Beric regretted deeply the course that had been taken. Had the garrisons all been attacked and destroyed separately, the army they would have to encounter would have been a little more than half the strength of that which Suetonius would be able to put into the field when he collected all the garrisons.

But the Britons troubled themselves in no way. They regarded victory as certain, and expressed exultation that they should crush all the Romans at one blow in the open field, instead of being forced to undertake a number of separate sieges. Still marching easily, they came down upon the valley of the Thames and followed it until they arrived at London. They had expected that Suetonius would give battle before they arrived there. He had indeed passed through the town a few days previously, but had disregarded the prayers of the inhabitants to remain for their protection. He allowed all males who chose to do so to enlist in the ranks and permitted others to accompany the army, but he wished before fighting to be joined by Cerealis and the survivors of his legion, and by the garrisons of other fortified posts. The Britons therefore fell upon London, slaughtered all the inhabitants, and sacked and burned the town. It was calculated that here and in the two Roman cities no less than 80,000 persons had been slain. This accomplished, the great host again set out in search of Suetonius. They were accompanied now by a vast train of wagons and chariots carrying the women and spoil.

Beric was not present at the sack of London. As they approached the town and it became known that Suetonius had marched away, and that there would be no resistance, he struck off north. Since they had left Verulamium the tribesmen had given up marching in military order. They were very proud of the credit they had gained in the battle with the Romans, but said that they did not see any use in marching tediously abreast when there was no enemy near. Beric having no power whatever to compel them, told them that of course they could do as they liked, but that they would speedily forget all they had learned. But the impatience of restraint of any kind, or of doing anything unless perfectly disposed to do it, which was a British characteristic, was too strong, and many were influenced by the scoffs of the newcomers, who, not having seen them in the day of battle, asked them scornfully if the Sarci were slaves that they should obey orders like Roman soldiers.

Boduoc, although he had objected to the drill at first, and had scoffed at the idea of men fighting any better because they all kept an even distance from each other, and marched with the same foot forward, had now become an enthusiast in its favour and raged at this falling away. But Beric said, "It is no use being angry, Boduoc. I was surprised that they consented at first, and I am not surprised that they have grown tired of it. It is the fault of our people to be fickle and inconstant, soon wearying of anything they undertake; but I do not think that it matters much now. We alone were able to decide the fight when there were but two thousand Roman spearmen; but when we meet Suetonius, he will have ten thousand soldiers under him, and our multitude is so great that the Sarci would be lost in the crowd. If the Britons cannot beat them without us, we should not suffice to change the fortunes of the day."

It was partly to escape the sight of the sack of London, partly because he was anxious to know how Berenice and Cneius Nepo were faring that Beric left the army, and drove north in a chariot. After two days' journey he arrived at the cottage of Boduoc's mother. The door stood open as was the universal custom in Britain, for nowhere was hospitality so lavishly practised, and it was thought that a closed door might deter a passerby from entering. His footsteps had been heard, for two dogs had growled angrily at his approach. The old woman was sitting at the fire, and at first he saw no one else in the hut.

"Good will to all here!" he said.

"It is the young chief!" the old woman exclaimed, and at once two figures rose from a pile of straw in a dark corner of the room.

"Beric?"

"Yes, it is I," he said. "How fares it with you, Berenice? You are well, Cneius, I hope? You have run no risks, I trust, since you have been here?"

"We are well, Beric," the girl said; "but oh the time has seemed so long! It is not yet a month since you sent us here, but it seems a year. She has been very kind to us, and done all that she could, and the girls, her daughters, have gone with me sometimes for rambles in the wood; but they cannot speak our language. Not another person has been here since we came."

"What is the news, Beric?" Cneius asked. "No word has reached us. The old woman and her daughters have learned something, for the eldest girl goes away sometimes for hours, and I can see that she tells her mother news when she returns."

Beric briefly told them what had happened, at which Berenice exclaimed passionately that the Britons were a wicked people.

"Then there will be a great battle when you meet Suetonius, Beric," Cneius said. "How think you will it go?"

"It is hard to say," Beric replied; "we are more than one hundred and fifty thousand men against ten thousand, but the ten thousand are soldiers, while the hundred and fifty thousand are a mob. Brave and devoted, and fearless of death I admit, but still a mob. I cannot say how it will go."

"How long shall we stay here, Beric?" Berenice asked. "When will you take me to my father?"

"If we are beaten, Berenice, you will rejoin him speedily; if we win--"

"He will not be alive," she broke in.

Beric did not contradict her, but went on, "I will see that you are placed on board a ship and sent to Gaul; it is for this I come here today. Cneius, in two or three days we shall meet Suetonius; if we win, I will return to you myself, or if I am killed, Boduoc or his brother, both of whom I shall charge with the mission, will come in my place and will escort you to the coast and see that you are placed on board ship. If we lose, it is likely that none of us will return. I shall give the old woman instructions that in that case her daughter is to guide you through the forest and take you on until you meet some Roman soldiers, or are within sight of their camp, then you will only have to advance and declare yourself."

Then he turned and spoke for some time to Boduoc's mother in her own language, thanking her for the shelter that she had given the fugitives, and giving instructions as to the future. He took a hasty meal, and started at once on his return journey in order to rejoin the Sarci as the army advanced from London. Berenice wept bitterly when he said goodbye, and Cneius himself was much affected.

"I view you almost as a son," he said; "and it is terrible to know that if you win in the battle, my patron Caius and my countrymen will be destroyed, while if they win, you may fall."

"It is the fortune of war, Cneius. You know that we Britons look forward to death with joy; that, unlike you, we mourn at a birth and feast at a burial, knowing that after death we go to the Happy Island where there is no more trouble or sorrow, but where all is peace and happiness and content; so do not grieve for me. You will know that if I fall I shall be happy, and shall be free from all the troubles that await this unfortunate land."

CHAPTER VII
DEFEAT OF THE BRITONS

London was but a heap of ashes when Beric arrived there. It had been a trading place rather than a town. Here were no Roman houses or temples with their massive stone work; it consisted only of a large collection of wooden structures, inhabited by merchants and traders. It lay upon a knoll rising above the low swampy ground covered by the sea at high water, for not till long afterwards did the Romans erect the banks that dammed back the waters and confined them within their regular channel. The opposite shore was similarly covered with water at high tide, and forests extended as far as the eye could reach. London, in fact, occupied what was at high water a peninsula, connected with the mainland only by a shoulder extending back to the hills beyond it, and separated by a deep channel on the west from a similar promontory.

It was a position that, properly fortified by strong walls across the isthmus, could have been held against a host, but the Romans had not as yet taken it in hand; later, however, they recognized the importance of the position, and made it one of the chief seats of their power. Even in the three days that he had been absent Beric found that the host had considerably increased. The tribes of Sussex and Kent, as they heard of the approach of the army, had flocked in to join it, and to share in the plunder of London.

Another day was spent in feasting and rejoicing, and then the army moved northward. It consisted now of well nigh two hundred thousand fighting men, and a vast crowd of women, with a huge train of wagons. Two days later, news reached them of the spot where Suetonius had taken up his position and was awaiting their attack, and the army at once pressed forward in that direction. At nightfall they bivouacked two miles away from it, and Beric, taking Boduoc with him, went forward to examine it. It was at a point where a valley opened into the plain; the sides of the valley were steep and thickly wooded, and it was only in front that an attack could well be delivered.

"What think you of it, Beric?" Boduoc asked.

"Suetonius relies upon our folly," Beric said; "he is sure that we shall advance upon him as a tumultous mob, and as but a small portion can act at once our numbers will count but little. The position would be a bad one had we any skill or forethought. Were I commander tomorrow I should, before advancing to the attack, send a great number round on either side to make their way through the woods, and so to attack on both flanks, and to pour down the valley in their rear, at the same time that the main body attacked in the front. Then the position would be a fatal one; attacked in front and rear and overwhelmed by darts from the woods on the flanks, their position would be well nigh desperate, and not a man should escape."

"But we must overwhelm them," Boduoc said. "What can ten thousand men do against a host like ours?"

"It may be so, Boduoc. Yet I feel by no means sure of it. At any rate we must prepare for defeat as well as victory. If we are beaten the cause of Britain will be lost. As we advance without order we shall fly without order, and the tribes will disperse to their homes even more quickly than they have gathered. Of one thing you may be sure, the Roman vengeance will be terrible. We have brought disgrace and defeat upon them. We have destroyed their chief cities. We have massacred tens of thousands. No mercy will be shown us, and chiefly will their vengeance fall upon the Iceni. When we return to the camp, go among the men and ask them whether they mean to fight tomorrow as they fought Cerealis, or whether they will fight in the fashion of the rest. I fear that, wild as all are with enthusiasm and the assurance of victory, they will not consent to be kept in reserve, but will be eager to be in the front of the attack. I will go with you, and will do my best to persuade them; but if they insist on fighting in their own way, then we will go to them one by one, and will form if we can a body, if only a hundred strong, to keep, and if needs be, retreat together. In speed we can outrun the heavy armed Roman soldiers with ease, but their cavalry will scour the plain. Keeping together, however, we can repel these with our lances, and make good our escape. We will first make for home, load ourselves with grain, and driving cattle before us, and taking our women and children, make for the swamps that lie to the northwest of our limits. There we can defend ourselves against the Romans for any length of time."

"You speak as if defeat were certain," Boduoc said reproachfully.

"Not at all, Boduoc; a prudent man prepares for either fortune, it is only the fool that looks upon one side only. I hope for victory, but I prepare for defeat; those who like to return to their homes and remain there to be slaughtered by the Romans, can do so. I intend to fight to the last."

Upon rejoining the Sarci, Beric called them together, and asked them whether they wished on the following day to rush into the battle, or to remain in solid order in reserve. The reply was, that they wished for their share of glory, and that did they hold aloof until the battle was done and the enemy annihilated they would be pointed out as men who had feared to take their share in the combat. When the meeting had dispersed Beric and Boduoc went among them; they said nothing about the advantage that holding together would be in case of defeat, but pointed out the honour they had gained by deciding the issue of the last battle, and begged them to remain in a solid body, so that possibly they might again decide the battle. As to disgrace, they had already shown how well they could fight, and that none could say that fear had influenced their decision. Altogether two hundred agreed to retain their ranks, and with this Beric was satisfied. He then went off to find his mother, who was as usual with the queen. She would not hear of any possibility of defeat.

"What!" she said. "Are Britons so poor and unmanly a race, that even when twenty to one they cannot conquer a foe? I would not believe it of them."

"I don't expect it, mother, but it is best to be prepared for whatever may happen." He then told her of the arrangements he had made.

"You may be right, Beric, in preparing for the worst, but I will take no part in it. The queen has sworn she will not survive defeat, nor shall I. I will not live to see my country bound in Roman chains. A free woman I have lived, and a free woman I will die, and shall gladly quit this troubled life for the shores of the Happy Island."

Beric was silent for a minute. "I do not seek to alter your determination, mother, but as for myself, so long as I can lift a sword I shall continue to struggle against the Romans. We shall not meet tomorrow; when the battle once begins all will be confusion, and there would be no finding each other in this vast crowd. If victory is ours, we shall meet afterwards; if defeat, I shall make for Cardun, where, if you change your mind, I shall hope to meet you, and then shall march with those who will for the swamps of Ely, where doubtless large numbers of fugitives will gather, for unless the Romans drive their causeways into its very heart they can scarce penetrate in any other way."

So sure were the Britons of victory that no council was held that night. There were the enemy, they had only to rush upon and destroy them. Returning to his men, Beric met Aska.

"I have just been over to your camp to see you, Beric. I have talked with Boduoc, who told me frankly that you did not share the general assurance of an easy victory. Nor do I, after what I saw the other day--how we dashed vainly against the Roman line. He tells me that your men, save a small party, have determined to fight tomorrow in the front line with the rest, and I lament over it."

"It would make no difference in the result," Beric said; "in so great a mass as this we should be lost, and even if we could make our way to the front, and fall upon the Romans in a solid body, our numbers are too small to decide the issue; but at least we might, had the day gone against us, have drawn off in good order."

"I will take my station with you," Aska said; "I have, as all the Iceni know, been a great fighter in my time; but I will leave it to the younger men tomorrow to win this battle. My authority may aid yours, and methinks that if we win tomorrow, none can say that you were wrong to stand aloof from the first charge, if Aska stood beside you."

Thanking the chief warmly for the promise, Beric returned to the Sarci. Feasting was kept up all night, and at daybreak the Britons were on foot, and forming in their tribes advanced within half a mile of the Roman position. Then they halted, and Boadicea with her daughters and the chiefs moved along their front exhorting them to great deeds, recalling to them the oppression and tyranny of the Romans, and the indignity that they had inflicted upon her and her daughters; and her addresses were answered by loud shouts from the tribesmen. In the meantime the wagons had moved out and drew up in a vast semicircle behind the troops, so as to enable the women who crowded them to get a view of the victory. So great was the following that the wagons were ranged four or five deep. Beric had drawn up the men who had agreed to fight in order, in a solid mass in front of the tribe. He was nearly on the extreme left of the British position. Aska had taken his place by his side. His mother, as in her chariot she passed along behind Boadicea, waved her hand to him, and then pointed towards the Romans.

"Look, Aska," he said presently; "do you see that deep line of wagons forming all round us? In case of disaster they will block up the retreat. A madness has seized our people. One would think that this was a strife of gladiators at Rome rather than a battle between two nations. There will be no retreat that way for us if disaster comes. We must make off between the horn of the crescent and the Romans. It is there only we can draw off in a body."

"That is so, Beric," the chief said; "but see! the queen has reached the end of the lines, and waves her spear as a signal."

A thundering shout arose, mingled with the shrill cries of encouragement from the women, and then like a torrent the Britons rushed to the attack in confused masses, each tribe striving to be first to attack the Romans. The Sarci from behind the company joined in the rush, and there was confusion in the ranks, many of the men being carried away by the enthusiasm; but the shouts and exhortations of Beric, Aska, and Boduoc steadied them again, and in regular order they marched after the host. In five minutes the uproar of battle swelled high in front. Beric marched up the valley until he arrived at the rear of the great mass of men who were swarming in front of the Roman line, each man striving to get to the front to hurl his dart and join in the struggle. The Romans had drawn up twelve deep across the valley, the heavy armed spearmen in front, the lighter troops behind, the latter replying with their missiles to the storm of darts that the Britons poured upon them. With desperate efforts the assailants strove to break through the hedge of spears; their bravest flung themselves upon the Roman weapons and died there, striving in vain to break the line.

For hours the fight continued, but the Roman wall remained unbroken and immovable. Fresh combatants had taken the place of those in front until all had exhausted their store of javelins. In vain the chiefs attempted to induce their followers to gather thickly together and to make a rush; the din was too great for their voices to be heard, and the tribesmen were half mad with fury at the failure of their own efforts to break the Roman line. Beric strove many times to bring up his company in a mass through the crowd to the front. The pressure was too great, none would give way where all sought to get near their foes, and rather than break them up he remained in the rear in spite of the eager cries of the men to be allowed to break up and push their way singly forward.

"What can you do alone," he shouted to them, "more than the others are doing? Together and in order we might succeed, broken we should be useless. If this huge army cannot break their line, what could two hundred men do?" At last, as the storm of javelins began to dwindle, a mighty shout rose from the Romans, and shoulder to shoulder with levelled spears they advanced, while the flanks giving way, the cavalry burst out on both sides and fell upon the Britons. For those in front, pressed by the mass behind them, there was no falling back, they fell as they stood under the Roman spears. Stubbornly for a time the tribesmen fought with sword and target; but as the line pressed forward, and the horsemen cut their way through the struggling mass, a panic began to seize them.

The tribes longest conquered by the Romans first gave way, and the movement rapidly spread. Many for some time desperately opposed the advance of the Romans, whose triumphant shouts rose loudly; but gradually these melted away, and the vast crowd of warriors became a mob of fugitives, the Romans pressing hotly with cries of victory and vengeance upon their rear. Beric's little band was swept away like foam before the wave of fugitives. For a time it attempted to stem the current; but when Beric saw that this was in vain he shouted to his tribesmen to keep in a close body and to press towards the left, which was comparatively free. Fortunately the Roman horse had plunged in more towards the centre, and the ground was open for their retreat.

Thousands of flying men were making towards the rear, but with a great effort they succeeded in crossing the tide of fugitives, and in passing through outside the semicircle of wagons. Here they halted for a moment while Beric, climbing on the end wagon, surveyed the scene. There was no longer any resistance among the Britons. The great semicircle within the line of wagons was crowded by a throng of fugitives behind whom, at a run now, the Roman legions were advancing, maintaining their order even at that rapid pace. Outside the sweep of wagons women with cries of terror were flying in all directions, and the horses, alarmed by the din, were plunging and struggling, while their drivers vainly endeavoured to extricate them from the close line of vehicles.

"All is lost for the present," he said to Aska, "let us make for the north; it is useless to delay, men; to try to fight would be to throw away our lives uselessly, we shall do more good by preserving them to fight upon another day. Keep closely together, we shall have the Roman cavalry upon us before long, and only by holding to our ranks can we hope to repel them."

Many of the women from the nearest wagons rushed in among the men, and, placing them in their centre, the band went off at a steady trot, which they could maintain for hours. The din behind was terrible, the shouts of the Romans mingled with the cries of the Britons and the loud shrieks of women. The plain was already thick with fugitives, consisting either of women from the outside wagons or men who had made their way through the mass of struggling animals. Here and there chariots were dashing across the plain at full gallop. Looking back from a rise of the ground a mile from the battlefield, they saw a few parties of the Roman horse scouring the plain; but the main body were scattered round the confused mass by the wagons.

"There will be but few escape," Aska said, throwing up his arms in despair; "the wagons have proved a death trap; had it not been for them the army would have scattered all over the country, and though the Roman horse might have cut down many, the greater number would have gained the woods and escaped; but the wagons held them just as a thin line of men will hold the wolves till the hunters arrive and hem them in."

The carts crowded with women, the plunging horses in lines three or four deep had indeed checked the first fugitives; then came the others crowding in upon them, and then before a gap wide enough to let them through could be forced, the Roman horse were round and upon them.

The pause that Beric made had been momentary, and the band kept on at their rapid pace until the woods were reached, and they were safe from pursuit; then, as they halted, they gave way to their sorrow and anguish. Some threw themselves down and lay motionless; others walked up and down with wild gestures; some broke into imprecations against the gods who had deserted them. Some called despairingly the names of wives and daughters who had been among the spectators in that fatal line of wagons. The women sat in a group weeping; none of them belonged to the Iceni, and their kinsfolk and friends had, as they believed, all perished in the fight.

"Think you that the queen has fallen?" Aska asked Beric.

"She may have made her way out," Beric said; "we saw chariots driving across the plain. She would be carried back by the first fugitives, and it may be that they managed to clear a way through the wagons for her and those with her. If she is alive, doubtless my mother is by her side."

"If the queen has escaped," Aska said, "it will be but to die by her own hand instead of by that of the Romans. I am sure that she will not survive this day. There is nothing else left for her, her tribe is destroyed, her country lost, herself insulted and humiliated. Boadicea would never demand her life from the Romans."

"My mother will certainly die with her," Beric said, "and I should say that all her party will willingly share her fate. For the chiefs and leaders there will be no mercy, and for a time doubtless all will be slaughtered who fall into the Roman hands; but after a time the sword will be stayed, for the land will be useless to them without men to cultivate it, and when the Roman hands are tired of slaying, policy will prevail. It were best to speak to the men, Aska, for us to be moving on; will you address them?"

The old chief moved towards the men, and raising his hand, called them to him. At first but few obeyed the summons, but as he proceeded they roused themselves and gathered round him, for his reputation in the tribe was great, and the assured tone in which he spoke revived their spirits.

"Men of the Sarci," he said, "this is no time for wailing or lamentation; the gods of Britain have deserted us, but of this terrible day's defeat none of the disgrace rests upon you. The honour of the victories we won was yours, and though but a small subtribe, the name of the Sarci rang through Britain as that of the bravest in the land. Had all of your tribe obeyed their young chief and fought together today as they have fought before, it may be that the defeat would have been averted; but you stood firmly by him when the others fell away, and you stand here without the loss of a man, safe in the forest and ready to meet the Roman again. You are fortunate in having such a leader. I may tell you that had his counsel prevailed you would not now be mourning a defeat. I, an old chief with long years of experience, believed what he said, young though he is, and saw that to fight in a confused multitude on such a field was to court almost certain defeat.

"Thus then I placed myself by his side, relying upon his skill in arms and your bravery, and throwing my fortune in with yours. I was not mistaken. Had you not firmly kept together and followed his instructions you too would have been inclosed in that vast throng of fugitives hemmed in among the wagons, slaughtered by the Roman footmen in their rear and cut down by their horse if they broke through the line of wagons. You may ask what is there to live for; you may say that the cause of Britain is lost, that your tribe is well nigh destroyed, that many of you have lost your wives and families as well. All this is true, but yet, men, all is not lost. Great as may have been the slaughter, large numbers must have escaped, and many of you have still wives and families at home. Before aught else is thought of these must be taken to a place of safety until the first outburst of Roman vengeance has passed.

"Had Beric been the sole leader of the Britons from the first there would be no need of fearing their vengeance, for in that case none of their women and children would have been slain, and they would be now in our hands as hostages; but that is past. I say it only to show you how wise and far seeing as well as how brave a leader in battle is this young chief of yours. While all others were dreaming only of an easy victory over the Romans he and I have been preparing for what had best be done in case of defeat. To return to your homes would be but to court death, and if we are to die at the hands of the Romans it is best that we should die fighting them to the end. We have therefore arranged that we will seek a refuge in the Fen country that forms the western boundary of the land of the Iceni; there we can find strongholds into which the Romans can never force their way; thence we can sally out, and in turn take vengeance. There will rally round you hundreds of other brave men till we grow to a force that may again make head against the Romans. There at least we shall live as free men and die as free men."

A shout of approval broke from the men.

"You need not starve," Aska went on. "The rivers abound with fish and the swamps with waterfowl. There are islands among the swamps where the land is dry, and we can construct huts. Three days since, when he foresaw that it might be that a refuge would be needed, Beric despatched a messenger home with orders that a herd of three hundred cattle and another of as many swine should be driven to the spot near the swamps for which we propose to make, and they will there be found awaiting you."

There was again a chorus of approval, and one of the men stepping forward said, "Beric is young, but he is a great chief. We will follow him wherever he will take us, and will swear to be faithful and obedient to him." Every man raised his right arm towards the sky, and with a loud shout swore to be faithful to Beric.

"You are right," Aska said. "It is of no use to obey a chief only when ranged in battle; it is that which has ruined our country. There is nothing slavish in recognizing that one man must rule, and in obeying when obedience is necessary for the sake of all. As one body led by one mind you may do much; as two hundred men swayed by two hundred minds you will do nothing. I shall be with Beric, and my experience may be of aid to him. And if I, a chief of high standing among the Iceni, am well content to recognize in him the leader of our party, you may well do the same. Now, Beric, step forward and say what is next to be done."

"I thank you," Beric said when the shout of acclamation that greeted him when he stepped forward had subsided, "for the oath you have sworn to be faithful to me. I pretend not to more wisdom than others, and feel that in the presence of one so full of years and experience as Aska it is a presumption for one of my age to give an opinion; but in one respect I know that I am more fitted than others to lead you. I have studied the records of the Romans, of their wars with the Gauls and other peoples, and I know that their greatest trouble was not in defeating armies in the field but of overcoming the resistance of those who took refuge in fastnesses and harassed them continually by sorties and attacks. I know where the Romans are strong and where they are weak; and it is by the aid of such knowledge that I hope that we may long retain our freedom, and may even in time become so formidable that we may be able to win terms not only for ourselves but for our countrymen.

"The first step is to gather at our place of refuge those belonging to us. Therefore do you choose among yourselves twenty swift runners and send them to our villages, bidding the wives and families of all here to leave their homes at once, taking only such gear as they can carry lightly, and to make with all speed for Soto, a village in the district of the Baci, and but a mile or two from the edge of the great swamp country. It is there that the herds have been driven, and there they will find a party ready to escort them. Let all the other women and children be advised to quit their homes also, and to travel north together with the old men and boys. Bid the latter drive the herds before them. It may be months before they can return to their homes. It were best that they should pass altogether beyond the district of our people, for it is upon the Iceni that the vengeance of the Romans will chiefly fall. By presents of cattle they can purchase an asylum among the Brigantes, and had best remain there till they hear that Roman vengeance is satisfied.

"Let them as they journey north advise all the people in our villages to follow their example. Let those who will not do this take shelter in the hearts of the forests. To our own people my orders are distinct: no herd, either of cattle or swine, is to be left behind. Let the Romans find a desert where they can gather no food; let the houses be burnt, together with all crops that have been gathered. Warn all that there must be no delay. Let the boys and old men start within five minutes from the time that you deliver my message, to gather the herds and drive them north. Let the women call their children round them, take up their babes, make a bundle of their garments, and pile upon a wagon cooking pots and such things as are most needed, and then set fire to their houses and stacks and granaries and go. Warn them that even the delay of an hour may be fatal, for that the Roman cavalry will be spreading like a river in flood over the country. Beg them to leave the beaten tracks and journey through the woods, both those who go north and those who will meet us at Soto. Quick! choose the messengers; and such of you as choose had best hand to the one who is bound for his village a ring or a bracelet, or some token that your wives will recognize, so that they may know that the order comes from you."

Twenty young men were at once chosen, and Boduoc and two of the older men divided the district of the Sarci among them, allotting to each the hamlets they should visit. As soon as this was decided the rest of the band gave the messengers their tokens to their families, and then the runners started at a trot which they could maintain for many hours. The rest of the band then struck off in the direction in which they were bound. With only an occasional half hour for food and a few hours at night for sleep they pressed northward. Fast as they went the news of the disaster had preceded them, carried by fugitives from the battle.

At each hamlet through which they passed, Aska repeated the advice that had been sent to the Iceni. "Abandon your homes, drive the swine and the cattle before you, take to the forests, journey far north, and seek refuge among the Brigantes. A rallying place for fighting men will be found at Soto, on the edge of the great swamps; let all who can bear arms and love freedom better than servitude or death gather there."

Upon the march swine were taken and killed for food without hesitation. Many were found straying in the woods untended, the herdsmen having fled in dismay when the news of the defeat reached them. As yet the full extent of the disaster was unknown. Some of the fugitives had reported that scarce a man had escaped; but the very number of fugitives who had preceded the band showed that this was an exaggeration. But it was not until long afterwards that the truth was known. Of the great multitude, estimated at two hundred and thirty thousand, fully a third had fallen, among whom were almost all the women and children whose presence on the battlefield had proved so fatal, and of whom scarce one had been able to escape; for the Romans, infuriated by the massacres at Camalodunum, Verulamium, and London had spared neither age nor sex.

On their arrival at Soto they obtained for the first time news of the queen. A chief of one of the northern subtribes of the Iceni had driven through on his chariot and had told the headman of the hamlet that he had been one of the few who had accompanied Boadicea in her flight.

At the call of the queen, he said, the men threw themselves on the line of wagons in such number and force that a breach was made through them, horses and wagons being overthrown and dragged bodily aside. The chariot with the queen and her two daughters passed through, with four others containing the ladies who accompanied her. Three or four chiefs also passed through in their chariots, and then the breach was filled by the struggling multitude, that poured out like a torrent. The chariots were well away before the Roman horse swept round the wagons, and travelled without pursuit to a forest twenty miles away. As soon as they reached this the queen ordered the charioteers to dig graves, and then calling upon the god of her country to avenge her, she and her daughters and the ladies with them had all drunk poison, brewed from berries that they gathered in the wood. The chiefs would have done so also, but the queen forbade them.

"It is for you," she said, "to look after your people, and to wage war with Rome to the last. We need but two men to lay us in our graves and spread the sods over us; so that after death at least we shall be safe from further dishonour at the hands of the Romans."

When they had drunk the poison the men were ordered to leave them for an hour and then to return. When they did so the ladies were all dead, lying in a circle round Boadicea. They were buried in the shallow holes that had been dug, the turf replaced, and dead leaves scattered over the spot, so that no Roman should ever know where the queen of the Iceni and her daughters slept.

Although Beric had given up all hope of again seeing his mother alive, the news of her death was a terrible blow to him, and he wept unrestrainedly until Aska placed a hand on his shoulder. "You must not give way to sorrow, Beric. You have her people to look to. She has gone to the Green Island, where she will dwell in happiness, and where your father has been long expecting her. It is not at a death that we Britons weep, knowing as we do that those that have gone are to be envied. Arouse yourself! there is much to be done. The cattle will probably be here in the morning. We have to question the people here as to the great swamps, and get them to send to the Fen people for guides who will lead us across the marshes to some spot where we can dwell above the level of the highest waters."

Beric put aside his private grief for the time, and several of the natives of the village who were accustomed to penetrate the swamps in search of game were collected and questioned as to the country. None, however, could give much useful information. There was a large river that ran through it, with innumerable smaller streams that wandered here and there. None had penetrated far beyond the margin, partly because they were afraid of losing their way, partly because of the enmity of the Fen people.

These were of a different race to themselves, and were a remnant of those whom the Iceni had driven out of their country, and who, instead of going west, had taken refuge in the swamps, whither the invaders had neither the power nor inclination to follow them.

"It is strange," Aska said, "that just as they fled before us centuries ago, so we have now to fly before the Romans. Still, as they have maintained themselves there, so may we. But it will be necessary that we should try and secure the goodwill of these people and assure them that we do not come among them as foes."

"There is no quarrel between us now," the headman of the hamlet said. "There has not been for many generations. They know that we do not seek to molest them, while they are not strong enough to molest us. There is trade between all the hamlets near the swamps and their people; they bring fish and wildfowl, and baskets which they weave out of rushes, and sell to us in exchange for woven cloth, for garments, and sometimes for swine which they keep upon some of their islands.

"It is always they who come to us, we go not to them. They are jealous of our entering their country, and men who go too far in search of game have often been shot at by invisible foes. They take care that their arrows don't strike, but shoot only as a warning that we must go no farther. Sometimes some foolhardy men have declared that they will go where they like in spite of the Fenmen, and they have gone, but they have never returned. When we have asked the men who come in to trade what has become of them they say 'they do not know, most likely they had lost their way and died miserably, or fallen into a swamp and perished there;' and as the men have certainly lost their lives through their own obstinacy nothing can be done."

"Then some of these men speak our tongue, I suppose?" Aska said.

"Yes, the men who come are generally the same, and these mostly speak a little of our language. From time to time some of our maidens have taken a fancy to these Fenmen, and in spite of all their friends could do have gone off. None of these have ever returned, though messages have been brought saying they were well. We think that the men who do the trading are the children of women who went to live among them years ago."

"Then it is through one of these men that we must open communications with them," Aska said.

"Some of them are here almost daily. No one has been today, and therefore we may expect one tomorrow morning. This is one of the chief places of trade with them. The women of the hamlets round bring here the cloth they have woven to exchange it for their goods, others from beyond them do the same, so that from all this part of the district goods are brought in here, while the fish and baskets of the Fenmen go far and wide."

CHAPTER VIII
THE GREAT SWAMPS

Soon after daybreak next morning the headman came into the hut he had placed at the disposal of Aska and Beric with news that two of the Fenmen had arrived. They at once went out and found that the two men had just laid down their loads, which were so heavy that Beric wondered they could possibly have been carried by them. One had brought fish, the other wildfowl, slung on poles over their shoulders. These men were much shorter than the Iceni, they were swarthier in complexion, and their hair was long and matted. Their only clothing was short kilts made of the materials for which they bartered their game.

"They both speak the language well," the headman said, "I will tell them what you want."

The men listened to the statement that the chiefs before them desired to find with their followers a refuge in the Fens, and that they were willing to make presents to the Fenmen of cattle and other things, so that there should be friendship between them, and that they should be allowed to occupy some island in the swamps where they might live secure from pursuit. The men looked at each other as the headman began to speak, shaking their heads as if they thought the proposal impossible.

"We will tell our people," they said, "but we do not think that they will agree; we have dwelt alone for long years without trouble with others. The coming of strangers will bring trouble. Why do they seek to leave their land?"

"Our people have been beaten in battle by the Romans," Aska said, taking up the conversation, "and we need a refuge till the troubles are over."

"The Romans have won!" one of the men exclaimed in a tone that showed he was no stranger to what was going on beyond the circle of the Fens.

"They have won," Aska repeated, "and there will be many fugitives who will seek for shelter in the Fens. We would fain be friends with your people, but shelter we must have. Our cause after all is the same, for when the Romans have destroyed the Iceni, and conquered all the countries round, they will hunt you down also, for they let none remain free in the lands where they are masters. The Fen country is wide, there must be room for great numbers to shelter, and surely there must be places where we could live without disturbance to your people."

"There is room," the man said briefly. "We will take your message to our people, our chiefs will decide."

Aska and Beric wore few other ornaments than those denoting their position and authority. Many of their followers, however, had jewels and bracelets, the spoil of the Roman towns. Beric left the group and spoke to Boduoc, who in two or three minutes returned with several rings and bracelets.

"You could have a score for every one of these," he said; "they are of no value to the men now, and indeed their possession would bring certain death upon any one wearing them did he fall into the hands of the Romans."

Beric returned to the Fenmen. "Here," he said, "are some presents for your chiefs, tell them that we have many more like them."

The men took them with an air of indifference.

"They are of no use," they said, "though they may please women. If you want to please men you should give them hatchets and arms."

"We will do that," Aska said, "we have more than we require;" for indeed after the battle with Cerealis and the sack of the towns all the men had taken Roman swords and carried them in addition to their own weapons, regarding them not only as trophies but as infinitely superior to their own more clumsy implements for cutting wood and other purposes. At a word from Beric four of these were brought and handed to the men, who took them with lively satisfaction.

"Could you take us with you to see your chiefs?" Beric asked.

They shook their heads. "No strangers can enter the swamps; but the chiefs will come to see you."

"It is very urgent that no time shall be lost," Beric said, "the Romans may be here very shortly."

"By the time the sun is at its highest the chiefs will be here or we will bring you an answer," they said. "Come with us now, we will show you where to expect them, for they will not leave the edge of our land."

After half an hour's walking through a swampy soil they arrived at the edge of a sluggish stream of water. Here tied to a bush was a boat constructed of basket work covered with hide. In it lay two long poles. The men took their places in the coracle, pushed out into the stream, and using their poles vigorously were soon lost to sight among the thick grove of rush and bushes. Aska and Beric returned to the hamlet.

"Have you any idea of the number of these people?" they asked the headman.

"No," he said, "no one has any idea; the swamps are of a vast extent from here away to the north. We know that long ago when the Iceni endeavoured to penetrate there they were fiercely attacked by great numbers, and most of those who entered perished miserably, but for ages now there has been no trouble. The land was large enough for us, why should we fight to conquer swamps which would be useless to us? We believe that there are large numbers, although they have, from the nature of the country, little dealings with each other; but live scattered in twos and threes over their country, since, living by fishing and fowling, they would not care to dwell in large communities. They never talk much about themselves, but I have heard that they say that parts of the swamps are inhabited by strange monsters, huge serpents and other creatures, and that into these none dare penetrate."

"All the better," Beric said; "we are not afraid of monsters of any kind, and they might therefore let us settle in one of these neighbourhoods where we could clear out these enemies of theirs for them. It strikes me that our greatest difficulty will be to get our cattle across the morasses to firm ground. We shall have to contrive some plan for doing so. It will be no easy matter to feed so large a number as we shall be on fish and wildfowl."

At noon the two chiefs returned to the spot where the men had left them, taking with them Boduoc and another of their followers. A few minutes after they arrived there they heard sounds approaching, and in a short time four boats similar to those they had seen, and each carrying two men in addition to those poling, made their way one after another through the bushes that nearly met across the stream. Most of the men were dressed like the two who had visited the village, but three of them were in attire somewhat similar to that of the Iceni. These were evidently the chiefs. Several of the men were much shorter and darker than those they had first seen, while the chiefs were about the same stature. All carried short bows and quivers of light arrows, and spears with the points hardened in the fire, for the Iceni living near the swamps had been strictly forbidden to trade in arms or metal implements with the Fenmen. The chiefs, however, all carried swords of Iceni make. Before the chiefs stepped ashore their followers landed, and at once, to the surprise of Beric, scattered among the bushes. In two or three minutes they returned and said something in their own language to their chiefs, who then stepped ashore.

"They were afraid of an ambush," Aska muttered, "and have satisfied themselves that no one is hidden near."

The chiefs were all able to speak the language of the Iceni, and a long conversation ensued between them and Beric. They protested at first that it was impossible for them to grant the request made; that for long ages no stranger had penetrated the swamps, and that although the intention of those who addressed them might be friendly, such might not always be the case, and that when the secrets of the paths and ways were once known they would never be free from danger of attack by their neighbours.

"There is more room to the north," they said; "the Fen country is far wider there, there is room for you all, while here the dry lands are occupied by us, and there is no room for so many strangers. We wish you well; we have no quarrel with you. Ages have passed now since you drove our forefathers from the land; that is all forgotten. But as we have lived so long, so will we continue. We have no wants; we have fish and fowl in abundance, and what more we require we obtain in barter from you."

"Swords like those we sent you are useful," Aska said. "They are made by the Romans, and are vastly better than any we have. With one of those you might chop down as many saplings in a day as would build a hut, and could destroy any wild beasts that may lurk in your swamps. The people who are coming now are not like us. We were content with the land we had taken, and you dwelt among us undisturbed for ages; but the Romans are not like us, they want to possess the whole earth, and when they have overrun our country they will never rest content till they have hunted you out also. There are thousands of us who will seek refuge in your swamps. You may oppose us, you may kill numbers of us, but in the end, step by step, we shall find our way in till we reach an island of firm land where we can establish ourselves. It is not that we have any ill will towards you, or that we covet your land, but with the Romans behind us, slaying all they encounter, we shall have no choice but to go forward.

"It will be for your benefit as well as ours. Alone what could you do against men who fight with metal over their heads and bodies that your arrows could not penetrate, and with swords and darts that would cut and pierce you through and through? But with us--who have met and fought them in fair battle, and have once even defeated them with great slaughter--to help you to guard your swamps, it would be different, and even the Romans, brave as they are, would hesitate before they tried to penetrate your land of mud and water. Surely there must be some spots in your morasses that are still uninhabited. I have heard that there are places that are avoided because great serpents and other creatures live there, but so long as the land is dry enough for our cattle to live and for us to dwell we are ready to meet any living thing that may inhabit it."

The chiefs looked awestruck at this offer on the part of the strangers, and then entered into an animated conversation together.

"The matter is settled," Aska said in a low voice to Beric. "There are places they are afraid to penetrate, and I expect that, much as they object to our entering their country, they would rather have us as neighbours than these creatures that they are so much afraid of."

When the chiefs' consultation was finished, the one who had before spoken turned to them and said: "What will you give if we take you to such a place?"

"How far distant is it?" Aska asked.

"It is two days' journey from here," the chief said. "The distance is not great, but the channels are winding and difficult. There is land many feet above the water, but how large I cannot say. Three miles to the west from here is the great river you call the Ouse, it is on the other side of that where we dwell. None of us live on this side of that river. Three hours' walk north from here is a smaller river that runs into the great one. At the point where the two rivers join you will cross the Ouse, and then journey west in boats for a day; that will take you near the land we speak of."

"But how are we to get the boats? We have no time to make them."

"We will take you in our boats. This man," and he pointed to one of those who had been with them in the morning, "will go with you as a guide through the swamps to the river to the north. There we will meet you with twenty boats, and will take a party to the spot we speak of. Then we will sell you the boats--we can build more--and you can take the rest of your party over as you like. What will you give us?"

"We will give you twenty swords like those I sent you, and twenty spearheads, and a hundred copper arrowheads, and twenty cattle."

The chiefs consulted together. "We want grain and we want skins," their spokesman said. "We have need of much grain, for if the Romans take your land and kill your people, where shall we buy grain? And we want skins, for it takes two skins to make a boat, and we shall have to build twenty to take the place of those we give you."

"We can give the skins," Aska said, after a consultation with Beric; "and I doubt not we can give grain. How much do you require?"

"Five boat loads filled to the brim."

"To all your other terms we agree," Aska said; "and you shall have as much grain as we can obtain. If we fall short of that quantity we will give for each boat load that is wanting three swords, six spearheads, and ten arrowheads."

The bargain was closed. The Fenmen had come resolved not to allow the strangers to enter their land, but their offer to occupy any spot, even if tenanted by savage beasts, entirely changed the position. In the recesses of the swamps to the east of the Ouse lay a tract of country which they avoided with a superstitious fear. In the memory of man none had dared to approach that region, for there was a tradition among them that, when they had first fled from the Iceni, a large party had penetrated there, and of these but a few returned, with tales of the destruction of their companions by huge serpents, and monsters of strange shapes, some of which were clothed in armour impenetrable to their heaviest weapons. From that time the spot had been avoided. Legends had multiplied concerning the creatures that dwelt there, and it now seemed to the chiefs that they must be gainers in any case by the bargain.

If the monsters conquered and devoured the Iceni, as no doubt they would do, they would be well rid of them. If the Iceni destroyed the monsters a large tract of country now closed would be open for fishing and fowling. They therefore accepted, without further difficulty, the terms the strangers offered. It was, moreover, agreed that any further parties of Iceni should be free to join the first comers without hindrance, and that guides should be furnished to all who might come to the borders of the swamps to join their countrymen. They were to act in concert in case of any attack by the Romans, binding themselves to assist each other to the utmost of their powers.

"But how are we to convey our cattle over?" Beric asked.

The native shook his head. "It is too far for them to swim, and the ground in most places is a swamp, in which they would sink."

"That must be an after matter, Beric," Aska said. "We will talk that over after we have arrived. Evidently we can do nothing now. The great thing is to get to this place they speak of, and to prepare it to receive the women and other fugitives. When will you have the boats at the place you name?"

"Three hours after daylight tomorrow."

"We will be there. You shall receive half the payments we have agreed upon before we start, the rest shall be paid you when you return with the boats and hand them over for the second detachment to go."

The native nodded, and at once he and his companions took their places in their coracles, leaving the native who was to act as guide behind them.

"They are undersized little wretches," Boduoc said, as they started for the village; "no wonder that our forefathers swept them out of the land without any difficulty. But they are active and sturdy, and, knowing their swamps as they do, could harass an invader terribly. I don't think that at present they like our going into their country, but they will be glad enough of our aid if the Romans come."

When they reached the village they found that the herds had just arrived. The headman was surprised when they told him that the Fenmen had agreed to allow them a shelter in the swamps, and he and eight or ten men who had straggled in since Beric's party arrived, expressed their desire to accompany the party with their families. Other women in the village would likewise have gone, but Aska pointed out to them that they had better go north and take shelter among the Brigantes, as all the women of his tribe had done, except those whose men were with them.

"You will be better off there than among the swamps, and we cannot feed unnecessary mouths; nor have we means of transporting you there. We, too, would shelter in the woods, were it not that we mean to harass the Romans, so we need a place where they cannot find us. But as you go spread the news that Aska has sought refuge in the swamps with two hundred fighting Sarci, and that all capable of bearing arms who choose to join them can do so. They must come to the junction of the two rivers, and there they will hear of us."

As the villagers were unable to take away with them their stores of grain, they disposed of them readily to Beric in exchange for gold ornaments, with which they could purchase cattle or such things as they required from the Brigantes; they also resigned all property in their swine and cattle, which were to be left in the woods, to be fetched as required. Aska and Beric having made these arrangements, sat down to discuss what had best be done, as the twenty boats would only carry sixty, and would be away for two days before they returned for the second party. Boduoc was called into the council, and after some discussion it was agreed that the best plan would be for the whole party to go down together to the junction of the rivers, each taking as large a burden of grain as he could carry, and driving their cattle before them.

They heard from the headman that the whole country near the river was densely covered with bushes, and that the ground was swampy and very difficult to cross. They agreed, therefore, that they would form a strong intrenchment at the spot where they were to embark. It was unlikely in the extreme that the Romans would seek to penetrate such a country, but if they did they were to be opposed as soon as they entered the swamps, and a desperate stand was to be made at the intrenchment, which would be approachable at one or two points only. Six men were to be left at the village to receive the women and children when they arrived. The guide was to return as soon as he had led the main party to the point where the boats were to meet them, and to lead the second party to the same point.

That evening, indeed, the women began to arrive, and said that they believed all would be in on the following day. Among them was Boduoc's mother, who told Beric that her eldest daughter had started with Berenice and Cneius to meet the Romans as soon as the news of the defeat reached them. When day broke, Beric's command, with the women who had arrived, set off laden with as much grain in baskets or cloths as they could carry, and driving the cattle and pigs before them. The country soon became swampy, but their guide knew the ground well, and by a winding path led them dry footed through the bushes, though they could see water among the roots and grass on either side of them. They had, however, great difficulty with the cattle and pigs, but after several attempts to break away, and being nearly lost in the swamps, from which many of them had to be dragged out by sheer force, the whole reached the river. The men of the rear guard in charge of the main body of the swine and cattle did not arrive there until midday.

The spot to which the guide led them was on the river flowing east and west, a mile from its junction with the main stream, as he told them that the swamps were too deep near the junction of the river for them to penetrate there.

Some of the boats were already at the spot. When they reached it Aska and Beric at once began to mark out a semicircle, with a radius of some fifty yards, on the river bank. Ten of the cattle were killed and skinned, and as others of the party came up they were set to work to cut down the trees and undergrowth within the semicircle, and drag them to its edge, casting them down with their heads outwards so as to form a formidable abbatis. Within half an hour of the appointed time the twenty boats had arrived together with as many more, in which the grain, hides, and other articles agreed to be paid were to be carried off. Three of the cattle were cut up, and their flesh divided among the twenty boats, in which a quantity of grain was also placed. The seven remaining carcasses were for the use of the camp, the ten hides, half the grain, swords, spears, and arrowheads agreed upon, were handed over to the natives, and Beric, as an extra gift, presented each of the three chiefs who had come with the boats with one of the Roman shields, picked up on the field of battle.

The chiefs were greatly pleased with the present, and showed more goodwill than they had exhibited at their first interview. Aska had arranged with Beric to remain behind in charge of the encampment. As soon, therefore, as the presents had been handed over, Beric with Boduoc and three men to each boat took their places and pushed from shore. The boats of the Fenmen put off at the same time, and the natives, of whom there was one in each of Beric's boats, poled their way down the sluggish stream until they reached a wide river. The chiefs here shouted an adieu and directed their course up the river, while Beric's party crossed, proceeded down it for two miles, and then turned up a narrow stream running into it. All day they made their way along its windings; other streams came in on either side or quitted it; and, indeed, for some hours they appeared to be traversing a network of water from which rose trees and bushes. The native in Beric's boat, which led, could speak the language of the Iceni, and he explained to Beric that the waters were now high, but that when they subsided the land appeared above them, except in the course of the streams.

"It is always wet and swampy," he said; "and men cannot traverse this part on foot except by means of flat boards fastened to the feet by loops of leather; this prevents them from sinking deeply in."

Late in the afternoon the country became drier, and the land showed itself above the level of the water. The native now showed signs of much perturbation, stopping frequently and listening.

"I have come much farther now," he said, "than I have ever been before, and I dare not have ventured so far were it not that these floods would have driven everything back; but I know from an old man who once ventured to push farther, that this is the beginning of rising ground, and that in a short time you will find it dry enough to land. I advise you to call the other boats up so that in case of danger you can support each other."

The stream they were following was now very narrow, the branches of the trees meeting overhead.

"Can any of the other Fenmen in the boats speak our language?" Beric asked.

The man replied in the negative.

"That is good," he said; "I don't want my men to be frightened with stories about monsters. I don't believe in them myself, though I do not say that in the old time monsters may not have dwelt here. If anything comes we shall know how to fight it; but it is gloomy and dark enough here to make men uncomfortable without anything else to shake their courage."

At last they reached a spot where the bank was two feet above the water, and they could see that it rose further inland. Several of the other Fenmen had been shouting for some time to Beric's boatmen, and their craft had been lagging behind. Beric therefore thought it well to land at once. The boats were accordingly called up, the meat and grain landed, and the men leapt ashore, the boatmen instantly poling their crafts down stream at their utmost speed.

"We will go no farther tonight," Beric said; "but choose a comfortable spot and make a fire. It will be time enough in the morning to explore this place and fix on a spot for a permanent encampment."

A place was soon chosen and cleared of bushes. The men in several of the boats had at starting brought brands with them from the fires. These were carried across each other so as to keep the fire in, and eight or ten of these brands being laid together in the heart of the brushwood and fanned vigorously a bright flame soon shot up. The men's spirits had sunk as they passed through the wild expanse of swamp and water, but they rose now as the fire burned up. Meat was speedily frying in the flames, and this was eaten as soon as it was cooked, nothing being done with the grain, which they had no means of pounding. They had also brought with them several jars of beer from the village, and these were passed round after they had eaten their fill of meat.

"We will place four sentries," Beric said, "there may well be wolves or other wild beasts in these swamps."

After supper was over Boduoc questioned Beric privately as to the monsters of which their boatman had spoken.

"It is folly," Beric said. "You know that we have legends among ourselves, which we learned from the natives who were here before we came, that at one time strange creatures wandered over the country; but if there were such creatures they died long ago. These Fenmen have a story among themselves that such beasts lived in the heart of the swamp here when they first fled before us. It is quite possible that this is true, for although they died ages ago on the land they may have existed long afterwards among the swamps where there were none to disturb them. I have read in some of the Roman writers that there are creatures protected by a coat of scales in a country named Egypt, and that they live hundreds of years. Possibly these creatures, which the legends say were a sort of Dragon, may have lingered here, but as they do not seem to have shown themselves to the Fenmen since their first arrival here, it is not at all likely that there are any of them left; if there are we shall have to do battle with them."

"Do you think they will be very formidable, Beric?"

"I do not suppose so. They might be formidable to one man, but not to sixty well armed as we are; but I have not any belief that we shall meet with them."

The night passed quite quietly, and in the morning the band set out to explore the country. It rose gradually until they were, as Beric judged, from forty to fifty feet above the level of the swamp. Large trees grew here, and the soil was perfectly dry. The ground on the summit was level for about a quarter of a mile, and then gradually sank again. A mile farther they were again at the edge of a swamp.

"Nothing could have suited us better," Beric said. "At the top we can form an encampment which will hold ten thousand men, and there is dry ground a mile all round for the cattle and swine."

Presently there was a shout from some men who had wandered away, and Beric, bidding others follow, ran to the spot. They found men standing looking in wonder at a great number of bones lying in what seemed a confused mass.

"Here is your monster," Beric said; "they are snake bones." This was evident to all, and exclamations of wonder broke from them at their enormous size. One man got hold of a pair of ribs, and placing them upright they came up to his chin. The men looked apprehensively round.

"You need not be afraid," Beric said. "The creature has probably been dead hundreds of years. You see his skin is all decayed away, and it must have been thick and tough indeed. By the way the bones are piled together, he must have curled up here to die. He was probably the last of his race. However, we will search the island thoroughly, keeping together in readiness to encounter anything that we may alight upon."

Great numbers of snakes were found, but none of any extraordinary size.

"No doubt they fled here in the rains," Beric said, "when the water rose and covered the swamps; we shall not be troubled with them when the morasses dry. Anyhow they are quite harmless, and save that they may kill a chicken or two when we get some, they will give us no trouble. The swine will soon clear them off."

It was late in the day before the search was completed, and they then returned to the camping ground of the night before, quite assured that there was no creature of any size upon the island. Just as evening was falling on the following day they heard shouts.

"Are you alive?" a voice, which Beric recognized as that of his boatman, shouted.

"Yes," he exclaimed, "alive and well. There is nothing to be afraid of here."

A few minutes later the twenty boats again came up. The Fenmen this time ventured to land, but Beric's boatman questioned him anxiously about the monsters. Beric, who thought it as well to maintain the evil reputation of the place, told him that they had searched the island and had found no living monsters, but had come across a dead serpent, who must have been seventy or eighty feet long.

"There are no more of them here," he said, "but of course there may be others that have been alarmed at the noises we made and have taken to the swamps. This creature has been dead for a long time, and may have been the last of his race. However, if one were to come we should not be afraid of it with a hundred and twenty fighting men here."

The Fenmen, after a consultation among themselves, agreed that it would be safer to pass the night with the Iceni than to start in the darkness among the swamps. When they left in the morning Beric sent a message to Aska describing the place, and begging him to send up some of the women with the next party with means of grinding the grain. As soon as the boats were started Beric led the party up to the top of the rise, and then work was begun in earnest, and in a couple of days a large number of huts were constructed of saplings and brushwood cleared off from the centre of the encampment. Some women arrived with the next boat loads, and at once took the preparation of food into their hands. Aska sent a message saying that the numbers at his camp were undiminished, as most of the fighting men belonging to the villages round who had survived the battle had joined him at once with their wives, and that fresh men were pouring in every hour. He urged Beric to leave Boduoc in charge of the island, and to return with the empty boats in order that they might have a consultation. This Beric did, and upon his arrival he found that there were over four hundred men in camp, with a proportionate number of women and children. There were several subchiefs among them, and Aska invited them to join in the council.

"It is evident," he said, "that so large a number as this cannot find food in one place in the swamps, at any rate until we have learned to catch fish and snare wildfowl as the Fenmen do. The swine we can take there, but these light boats would not carry cattle in any numbers, though some might be thrown and carried there, with their legs tied together. At present this place is safe from attack. There is only one path, our guide says, by which it can be approached. I propose that we cut wide gaps through this, and throw beams and planks over them. These we can remove in case of attack. When we hear of the Romans' approach we can throw up a high defence of trees and bushes behind each gap."

"That will be excellent," Beric agreed, "and you would doubtless be able to make a long defence against them on the causeway. But you must not depend upon their keeping upon that. They will wade through the swamp waist deep, and, if it be deeper still, will cut down bushes and make faggots and move forward on these. So, though you may check them on the causeway, they will certainly, by one means or other, make their way up to your intrenchment, and you must therefore strengthen this in every way. I should build up a great bank behind it, so that if they break through or fire the defences you can defend the bank. There is one thing that must be done without delay; we must build more boats. There must be here many men from the eastern coast, where they have much larger and stronger craft than these coracles. I should put a strong party to work upon them. Then, in case of an attack, you could, when you see that longer resistance would be vain, take to the boats and join me; or, when the Romans approach, send them off to fetch my party from the island. Besides, we shall want to move bodies of men rapidly so as to attack and harass the enemy when they are not expecting us.

"I should say that we ought to have at least twenty great flatboats able to carry fifty men each. Speed would not be of much consequence, as the Romans will have no boats to follow us; besides, except on the Ouse and one or two of the larger streams, there is no room for rowing, and they must be poled along. Let us keep none but fighting men here. As all the villagers fled north there must be numbers of cattle and swine wandering untended in all the woods, and in many of the hamlets much grain must have been left behind, therefore I should send out parties from time to time to bring them in. When the large boats are built we can transport some of the cattle alive to the island; till then they must be slaughtered here; but with each party a few swine might be sent to the island, where they can range about as they choose. What is the last news you have of the Romans?"

"They are pressing steadily north, burning and slaying. I hear that they spare none, and that the whole land of the Trinobantes, from the Thames to the Stour, has been turned into a waste."

"It was only what we had to expect, Aska. Have any more of my people come in since I left?"

"Only a young girl. She arrived last night. It is she that brought the news that I am giving you. She is a sister of your friend Boduoc, and her mother, who had given her up for lost, almost lost her senses with delight when she returned. The family are fortunate, for another son also came in two or three days ago."

Beric at once went in search of Boduoc's mother, whom he found established with her girls in a little bower.

"I am glad indeed that your daughter has returned safe," he said, as the old woman came out on hearing his voice.

"Yes, I began to think that I should never see her face again, Beric; but I am fortunate indeed, when so many are left friendless, that all my four children should be spared.

"Tell the chief how you fulfilled your mission," she said to the girl.

"It was easy enough," she replied. "Had I been by myself I should have returned here three days since, but the little lady could not make long journeys, and it was three days after we left before we saw any of the Romans. At last we came upon a column of horse. When we saw them the little lady gave me this bracelet, and she put this gold chain into my hand and said, 'Beric.' So I knew that it was for you. Then I ran back and hid myself in the trees while they went forward. When they got near the soldiers on horseback the man lifted up his arms and cried something in a loud voice. Then they rode up to them, and for some time I could see nothing. Then the horsemen rode on again, all but two of them, who went on south. The man rode behind one of them, and the little lady before another. Then I turned and made hither, travelling without stopping, except once for a few hours' sleep. There are many fugitives in the woods, and from them I heard that the land of the Trinobantes was lit up by burning villages, and that the Romans were slaughtering all. Some of those I met in the wood had hid themselves, and had made their way at night, and they saw numbers of dead bodies, women and children as well as men, in the burned hamlets."

"You have done your mission well," Beric said. "Boduoc will be glad when I tell him how you have carried out my wish. We must find a good husband for you some day, and I will take care that you go to him with a good store of cattle and swine. Where is your brother?"

"He is there," she said, "leaning against that tree waiting for you."

"I am glad to see you safe among us," Beric said to the young man. "How did you escape the battle?"

"I was driving the chariot with Parta's attendants, as I had from the day we started. I kept close behind her chariot, and escaped with her when the line of wagons was broken to let the queen pass. When we got far away from the battle your mother stopped her chariot and bade me go north. 'I have no more need of attendants,' she said; 'let them save themselves. Do you find my son if he has escaped the battle, and tell him that I shall share the fate of Boadicea. I have lived a free woman, and will die one. Tell him to fight to the end against the Romans, and that I shall expect him to join me before long in the Happy Island. Bid him not lament for me, but rejoice, as he should, that I have gone to the Land where there are no sorrows.' Then I turned my chariot and drove to your home to await your coming there if you should have escaped. It was but a few hours after that the messengers brought the news that you were safe, and that the survivors of your band were to join you at Soto with such men as might have escaped. As Parta's orders were to take the women with me to the north, I drove them two days farther, taking with me a lad, the brother of one of them. Then I handed over the chariot to him, to convey them to the land of the Brigantes, and started hither on foot to join you."

"You shall go on with me tomorrow, you and your mother and sisters. Boduoc will be rejoiced to see you all. We have found a place where even the Romans will hardly reach us.

CHAPTER IX
THE STRUGGLE IN THE SWAMP

That evening Beric had a long talk with Aska and four or five men from the coast accustomed to the building of large boats. The matter would be easy enough, they said, as the boats would not be required to withstand the strain of the sea, and needed only to be put together with flat bottoms and sides. With so large a number of men they could hew down trees of suitable size, and thin them down until they obtained a plank from each. They would then be fastened together by strong pegs and dried moss driven in between the crevices. Pitch, however, would be required to stop up the seams, and of this they had none.

"Then," Beric said, "we must make some pitch. There is no great difficulty about that. There are plenty of fir trees growing near the edges of the swamps, and from the roots of these we can get tar."

The men were all acquainted with the process, which was a simple one. A deep hole was dug in the ground. The bottom of this was lined with clay, hollowed out into a sort of bowl. The hole was then filled with the roots of fir closely packed together. When it was full a fire was lit above it. As soon as this had made its way down earth was piled over it and beaten down hard, a small orifice being left in the centre. In this way the wood was slowly converted into charcoal, and the resin and tar, as they oosed out under the heat, trickled down into the bowl of clay at the bottom. As little or no smoke escaped after the fire was first lighted, the work could be carried on without fear of attracting the attention of any bodies of the enemy who might be searching the country.

Two months passed. By the end of that time the intrenchment on the river bank had been made so strong that it could resist any attack save by a very large body of men. That on the island had also been completed, and strong banks thrown up at the only three points where a landing could be effected from boats.

The swamps had been thoroughly explored in the neighbourhood, and another island discovered, and on this three hundred men had been established, while four hundred remained on the great island, and as many in the camp on the river. There were over a thousand women and children distributed among the three stations. Three hundred men had laboured incessantly at the boats, and these were now finished. While all this work had been going on considerable numbers of fish and wildfowl had been obtained by barter from the Fenmen, with whom they had before had dealings, and from other communities living among the swamps to the north. Many of the

Iceni, who came from the marshy districts of the eastern rivers, were also accustomed to fishing and fowling, and, as soon as the work on the defences was finished and the tortuous channels through the swamps became known to them, they began to lay nets, woven by the women, across the streams, and to make decoys and snares of all sorts for the wildfowl.

The framework for many coracles had been woven of withies by the women, and the skins of all the cattle killed were utilized as coverings, so that by the end of the two months they had quite a fleet of little craft of this kind. As fast as the larger boats were finished they were used for carrying cattle to the islands, and a large quantity of swine were also taken over.

During this time the Romans had traversed the whole country of the Iceni. The hamlets were fired, and all persons who fell into their hands put to death; but the number of these was comparatively small, as the greater part of the population had either moved north or taken to the woods, which were so extensive that comparatively few of the fugitives were killed by the search parties of the Romans. From the few prisoners that the Romans took they heard reports that many of the Iceni had taken refuge in the swamps, and several strong bodies had moved along the edge of the marsh country without attempting to penetrate it.

Aska and Beric had agreed that so long as they were undisturbed they would remain quiet, confining themselves to their borders, except when they sent parties to search for cattle in the woods or to gather up grain that might have escaped destruction in the hamlets, and that they would avoid any collision with the Romans until their present vigilance abated or they attempted to plant settlers in their neighbourhood.

Circumstances, however, defeated this intention. They learned from the Fenmen that numerous fugitives had taken refuge in the southern swamps, and that these sallying out had fallen upon parties of Romans near Huntingdon, and had cut them to pieces. The Romans had in consequence sent a considerable force to avenge this attack. These had penetrated some distance into the swamps, but had there been attacked and driven back with much slaughter. But a fortnight later a legion had marched to Huntingdon, and crossing the river there had established a camp opposite, which they called Godmancastra, and, having collected a number of natives from the west, were engaged in building boats in which they intended to penetrate the swamp country and root out the fugitives.

"It was sure to come sooner or later," Aska said to Beric. "Nor should we wish it otherwise. We came here not to pass our lives as lurking fugitives, but to gather a force and avenge ourselves on the Romans. If you like I will go up the river and see our friends there, and ascertain their strength and means of resistance. Would it be well, think you, to tell them of our strong place here and offer to send our boats to bring them down, so that we may make a great stand here?"

"No, I think not," Beric said. "Nothing would suit the Romans better than to catch us all together, so as to destroy us at one blow. We know that in the west they stormed the intrenchments of Cassivellaunus, and that no native fort has ever withstood their assault. I should say that it ought to be a war of small fights. We should attack them constantly, enticing them into the deepest parts of the morass, and falling upon them at spots where our activity will avail against their heavily weighted men. We should pour volleys of arrows into their boats as they pass along through the narrow creeks, show ourselves at points where the ground is firm enough for them to land, and then falling back to deep morasses tempt them to pursue us there, and then turn upon them. We should give them no rest night or day, and wear them out with constant fighting and watching. The fens are broad and long, stretching from Huntingdon to the sea; and if they are contested foot by foot, we may tire out even the power of Rome."

"You are right, Beric; but at any rate it will be well to see how our brethren are prepared. They may have no boats, and may urgently need help."

"I quite agree with you, and I think it would be as well for you to go. You could offer to bring all their women and children to our islands here, and then we would send down a strong force to help them. We should begin to contest strongly the Roman advance from the very first."

Accordingly Aska started up the Ouse in one of the large boats with twelve men to pole it along, and three days afterwards returned with the news that there were some two thousand men with twice that many women and children scattered among the upper swamps.

"They have only a few small boats," he said, "and are in sore straits for provisions. They drove at first a good many cattle in with them, but most of these were lost in the morasses, and as there have been bodies of horse moving about near Huntingdon, they have not been able to venture out as we have done to drive in more."

"Have they any chief with them?" Beric asked.

"None of any importance. All the men are fugitives from the battle, who were joined on their way north by the women of the villages. They are broken up into groups, and have no leader to form any general plan. I spoke to the principal men among them, and told them that we had strongly fortified several places here, had built a fleet of boats, and were prepared for warfare; they will all gladly accept you as their leader. They urgently prayed that we would send our boats down for the women and children, and I promised them that you would do so, and would also send down some provisions for the fighting men."

The next morning the twenty large boats, each carrying thirty men and a supply of meat and grain, started up the river, Beric himself going with them, and taking Boduoc as his lieutenant. Aska remained in command at the river fort, where the force was maintained at its full strength, the boat party being drawn entirely from the two islands. Four miles below Huntingdon they landed at a spot where the greater part of the Iceni there were gathered. Fires were at once lighted, and a portion of the meat cooked, for the fugitives were weak with hunger. As soon as this was satisfied, orders were issued for half the women and children to be brought in.

These were crowded into the boats, which, in charge of four men in each, then dropped down the stream, Beric having given orders that the boats were to return as soon as the women were landed on the island. He spent the next two days in traversing the swamps in a coracle, ascertaining where there was firm ground, and where the morasses were impassable. He learned all the particulars he could gather about the exact position of the Roman camp, and the spot where the boats were being constructed--the Iceni were already familiar with several paths leading out of the morasses in that neighbourhood--and then drew out a plan for an attack upon the Romans.

He had brought with him half the Sarci who had retired with him from the battle. These he would himself command. A force of four hundred men, led by Boduoc, were to travel by different paths through the swamp; they were then to unite and to march round the Roman camp, and attack it suddenly on three sides at once.

The camp was in the form of a horseshoe, and its ends resting on the river, and it was here that the boats were being built. Beric himself with his own hundred men and fifty others were to embark in four boats. As soon as they were fairly beyond the swamp, they were to land on the Huntingdon side, and to tow their boats along until within two or three hundred yards of the Roman camp, when they were to await the sound of Boduoc's horn. Boduoc's instructions were that he was to attack the camp fiercely on all sides. The Roman sentries were known to be so vigilant that there was but slight prospect of his entering the camp by surprise, or of his being able to scale the palisades at the top of the bank of earth. The attack, however, was to be made as if in earnest, and was to be maintained until Beric's horn gave the signal for them to draw off, when they were to break up into parties as before, and to retire into the heart of the swamp by the paths by which they had left it.

The most absolute silence was to be observed until the challenge of the Roman sentries showed that they were discovered, when they were to raise their war shouts to the utmost so as to alarm and confuse the enemy.

The night was a dark one and a strong wind was blowing, so that Beric's party reached their station unheard by the sentries on the walls of the camp. It was an hour before they heard a distant shout, followed instantly by the winding of a horn, and the loud war cry of the Iceni. At the same moment the trumpets in the Roman intrenchments sounded, and immediately a tumult of confused shouting arose around and within the camp. Beric remained quiet for five minutes till the roar of battle was at its highest, and he knew that the attention of the Romans would be entirely occupied with the attack. Then the boats were again towed along until opposite the centre of the horseshoe; the men took their places in them again and poled them across the river.

The fifty men who accompanied the Sarci carried bundles of rushes dipped in pitch, and in each boat were burning brands which had been covered with raw hides to prevent the light being seen. They were nearly across the river when some sentries there, whose attention had hitherto been directed entirely to the walls, suddenly shouted an alarm. As soon as the boats touched the shore, Beric and his men leapt out, passed through the half built boats and the piles of timber collected beside them, and formed up to repel an attack. At the same moment the others lighted their bundles of rushes at the brands, and jumping ashore set fire to the boats and wood piles. Astonished at this outburst of flame within their camp, while engaged in defending the walls from the desperate attacks of the Iceni, the Romans hesitated, and then some of them came running down to meet the unexpected attack.

But the Sarci had already pressed quickly on, followed by some of the torch bearers, and were in the midst of the Roman tents before the legionaries gathered in sufficient force to meet them. The torches were applied to the tents, and fanned by the breeze, the flames spread rapidly from one to another. Beric blew the signal for retreat, and his men in a solid body, with their spears outward, fell back. The Romans, as they arrived at the spot, rushed furiously upon them; but discipline was this time on the side of the Sarci, who beat off all attacks till they reached the river bank. Then in good order they took their places in the boats, Beric with a small body covering the movement till the last; then they made a rush to the boats; the men, standing with their poles ready, instantly pushed the craft into the stream, and in two minutes they were safe on the other side.

The boats and piles of timber were already blazing fiercely, while the Roman camp, in the centre of the intrenchment, was in a mass of flames, lighting up the helmets and armour of the soldiers ranged along the wall, and engaged in repelling the attacks of the Iceni. As soon as the Sarci were across, they leapt ashore and towed the boat along by the bank. A few arrows fell among them, but as soon as they had pushed off from the shore most of the Romans had run back to aid in the defence of the walls. Beric's horn now gave the signal that the work was done, and in a short time the shouts of the Iceni began to subside, the din of the battle grew fainter, and in a few minutes all was quiet round the Roman camp.

There was great rejoicing when the parties of the Iceni met again in the swamp. They had struck a blow that would greatly inconvenience the Romans for some time, would retard their attack, and show them that the spirit of the Britons was still high. The loss of the Iceni had been very small, only some five or six of Beric's party had fallen, and twenty or thirty of the assailants of the wall; they believed that the Romans had suffered much more, for they could be seen above their defences by the light of the flames behind them, while the Iceni were in darkness. Thus the darts and javelins of the defenders had been cast almost at random, while they themselves had been conspicuous marks for the missiles of the assailants.

In Beric's eyes the most important point of the encounter was that it had given confidence to the fugitives, had taught them the advantage of fighting with a plan, and of acting methodically and in order. There was a consultation next morning. Beric pointed out to the leaders that although it was necessary sometimes with an important object in view to take the offensive, they must as a rule stand on the defensive, and depend upon the depth of their morasses and their knowledge of the paths across them to baffle the attempts of the Romans to penetrate.

"I should recommend," he said, "that you break up into parties of fifteens and twenties, and scatter widely over the Fen country, and yet be near enough to each other to hear the sound of the horn. Each party must learn every foot of the ground and water in the neighbourhood round them. In that way you will be able to assemble when you hear the signal announcing the coming of the Romans, you will know the paths by which you can attack or retreat, and the spots where you can make your way across, but where the Romans cannot follow you. Each party must earn its sustenance by fishing and fowling; and in making up your parties, there should be two or three men in each accustomed to this work. Each party must provide itself with coracles; I will send up a boat load of hides. Beyond that you must search for cattle and swine in the woods, when by sending spies on shore you find there are no parties of Romans about.

"The parties nearest to Huntingdon should be always vigilant, and day and night keep men at the edge of the swamp to watch the doings of the

Romans, and should send notice to me every day or two as to what the enemy are doing, and when they are likely to advance. Should they come suddenly, remember that it is of no use to try to oppose their passage down the river. Their boats will be far stronger than ours, and we should but throw away our lives by fighting them there. They may go right down to the sea if they please, but directly they land or attempt to thrust their boats up the channels through the swamp, then every foot must be contested. They must be shot down from the bushes, enticed into swamps, and overwhelmed with missiles. Let each man make himself a powerful bow and a great sheath of arrows pointed with flints or flakes of stone, which must be fetched from the dry land, although even without these they will fly straight enough if shot from the bushes at a few yards' distance.

"Let the men practice with these, and remember that they must aim at the legs of the Romans. It is useless to shoot at either shields or armour. Besides, let each man make himself a spear, strong, heavy, and fully eighteen feet long, with the point hardened in the fire, and rely upon these rather than upon your swords to check their progress. Whenever you find broad paths of firm ground across the swamps, cut down trees and bushes to form stout barriers.

"Make friends with the Fenmen. Be liberal to them with gifts, and do not attempt to plant parties near them, for this would disturb their wildfowl and lead to jealousy and quarrels. However well you may learn the swamps, they know them better, and were they hostile might lead the Romans into our midst. In some parts you may not find dry land on which to build huts; in that case choose spots where the trees are stout, lash saplings between these and build your huts upon them so as to be three or four feet above the wet soil. Some of my people who know the swamps by the eastern rivers tell me that this is the best way to avoid the fen fevers."

Having seen that everything was arranged, Beric and his party returned to their camp. For some time the reports from the upper river stated that the Romans were doing little beyond sending out strong parties to cut timber. Then came the news that a whole legion had arrived, and that small forts containing some two hundred men each were being erected, three or four miles apart, on both sides of the Fen.

"That shows that all resistance must have ceased elsewhere," Aska said, "or they would never be able to spare so great a force as a legion and a half against us. I suppose that these forts are being built to prevent our obtaining cattle, and that they hope to starve us out. They will hardly succeed in that, for the rivers and channels swarm with fish, and now that winter is coming on they will abound with wildfowl."

"I am afraid of the winter," Beric said, "for then they will be able to traverse the swamps, where now they would sink over their heads."

"Unless the frosts are very severe, Beric, the ground will not harden much, for every foot is covered with trees and bushes. As to grain we can do without it, but we shall be able to fetch some at least down from the north. Indeed, it would need ten legions to form a line along both sides of the Fen country right down to the sea and to pen us in completely."

By this time the Iceni had become familiar with the channels through the swamps for long distances from their fastness, and had even established a trade with the people lying to the northwest of the Fen country. They learnt that the Romans boasted they had well nigh annihilated the Trinobantes and Iceni; but that towards the other tribes that had taken part in the great rising they had shown more leniency, though some of their principal towns had been destroyed and the inhabitants put to the sword.

A month later a fleet of boats laden with Roman soldiers started from Huntingdon and proceeded down the Ouse. Dead silence reigned round them, and although they proceeded nearly to the sea they saw no signs of a foe, and so turning they rowed back to Huntingdon. But in their absence the Iceni had not been idle. The spies from the swamps had discovered when the expedition was preparing to start, and had found too that a strong body of troops was to march along the edges of the swamps in order to cut off the Iceni should they endeavour to make their escape.

The alarm had been sounded from post to post, and in accordance with the orders of Beric the whole of the fighting men at once began to move south, some in boats, some in their little coracles, which were able to thread their way through the network of channels. The night after the Romans started, the whole of the fighting force of the Britons was gathered in the southern swamps, and two hours before daybreak issued out. Some five hundred, led by Aska, followed the western bank of the river towards Huntingdon, which had for the time been converted into a Roman city, inhabited by the artisans who had constructed the boats and the settlers who supplied the army; it had been garrisoned by five hundred legionaries, of whom three hundred had gone away in the boats.

The main body advanced against the Roman camp on the opposite bank, in which, as their spies had learnt, three hundred men had been left as a garrison. By Beric's orders a great number of ladders had been constructed. As upon the previous occasion the camp was surrounded before they advanced against it, and when the first shout of a sentry showed that they were discovered Beric's horn gave the signal, and with a mighty shout the Britons rushed on from all sides. Dashing down the ditch, and climbing the steep bank behind it the Iceni planted their ladders against the palisade, and swarming over it poured into the camp before the Romans had time to gather to oppose them. Beric had led his own band of two hundred trained men against the point where the wall of the camp touched the river, and as soon as they were over formed them up and led them in a compact body against the Romans.

In spite of the suddenness of the attack, the discipline of the legionaries was unshaken, and as soon as their officers found that the walls were already lost they formed their men in a solid body to resist the attack. Before Beric with his band reached the spot the Romans were already engaged in a fierce struggle with the Britons, who poured volleys of darts and arrows among them, and desperately strove, sword in hand, to break their solid formation. This they were unable to do, until Beric's band six deep with their hedge of spears before them came up, and with a loud shout threw themselves upon the Romans. The weight and impetus of the charge was irresistible. The Roman cohort was broken, and a deadly hand to hand struggle commenced. But here the numbers and the greatly superior height and strength of the Britons were decisive, and before many minutes had passed the last Roman had been cut down, the scene of the battle being lighted up by the flames of Huntingdon.

A shout of triumph from the Britons announced that all resistance had ceased. Beric at once blew his horn, and, as had been previously arranged, four hundred of the island men immediately started under Boduoc to oppose the garrison at the nearest fort, should they meet these hastening to the assistance of their comrades. Then a systematic search for plunder commenced. One of the storehouses was emptied of its contents and fired, and by its light the arms and armour of the Roman soldiers were collected, the huts and tents rifled of everything of value, the storehouses emptied of their stores of grain and provisions, and of the tools that had been used for the building of boats. Everything that could be of use to the defenders was taken, and fire was then applied to the buildings and tents. Morning broke before this was accomplished, and laden down with spoil the Iceni returned to their swamps, Boduoc's and Aska's parties rejoining them there.

The former had met the Romans hurrying from the nearest fort to aid the garrison of the camp. Beric's orders had been that Boduoc was if possible to avoid a fight, as in the open the discipline of the Romans would probably prevail over British valour. The Iceni, therefore, set up a great shouting in front and in the rear of the Romans, shooting their missiles among them, and being unable in the dark to perceive the number of their assailants, and fearful that they had fallen into an ambush, the Romans fell back to their fort. Aska's party had also returned laden with plunder, and as soon as the whole were united a division of this was made. The provisions, clothing, and arms were divided equally among the men, while the stores of rope, metal, canvas, and other articles that would be useful to the community were set aside to be taken to the island. Thither also the shields, armour, and helmets of the Roman soldiers were to be conveyed, to be broken up and melted into spear and arrow heads.

As the Roman boats returned two days later from their useless passage down the river, they were astonished and enraged by outbursts of mocking laughter from the tangle of bushes fringing the river. Not a foe was to be seen, but for miles these sounds of derisive laughter assailed them from both sides of the stream. The veterans ground their teeth with rage, and would have rowed towards the banks had not their officers, believing that it was the intention of the Britons to induce them to land, and then to lead them into an ambush, ordered them to keep on their way. On passing beyond the region of the swamp a cry of dismay burst from the crowded boats, as it was perceived that the town of Huntingdon had entirely disappeared. As they neared the camp, however, the sight of numerous sentries on the walls relieved them of part of their anxiety; but upon landing they learnt the whole truth, that the five hundred Roman soldiers in the camp and at Huntingdon had fallen to a man, and that the whole of the stores collected had been carried away or destroyed.

The news had been sent rapidly along the chain of forts on either side of the swamp, and fifty men from each had been despatched to repair and reoccupy the camp, which was now held by a thousand men, who had already begun to repair the palisades that had been fired by the Britons.

This disaster at once depressed and infuriated the Roman soldiers, while it showed to the general commanding them that the task he had been appointed to perform was vastly more serious than he had expected. Already, as he had traversed mile after mile of the silent river, he had been impressed with the enormous difficulty there would be in penetrating the pathless morasses, extending as he knew in some places thirty or forty miles in width. The proof now afforded of the numbers, determination, and courage of the men lurking there still further impressed him with the gravity of the undertaking. Messengers were at once sent off to Suetonius, who was at Camalodunum, which he was occupied in rebuilding, to inform him of the reverse, and to ask for orders, and the general with five hundred men immediately set out for the camp of Godman.

Suetonius at once proceeded to examine for himself the extent of the Fen country, riding with a body of horsemen along the eastern boundary as far as the sea, and then, returning to the camp, followed up the western margin until he again reached the sea. He saw at once that the whole of the Roman army in Britain would be insufficient to guard so extensive a line, and that it would be hopeless to endeavour to starve out men who could at all times make raids over the country around them. The first step to be taken must be to endeavour to circumscribe their limits. Orders were at once sent to the British tribes in south and midlands to send all their available men, and as these arrived they were set to work to clear away by axe and fire the trees and bush on the eastern side of the river Ouse.

As soon as the intentions of the Romans were understood, the British camp at the junction of the rivers was abandoned, as with so large a force of workmen the Romans could have made wide roads up to it, and although it might have resisted for some time, it must eventually fall, while the Romans, by sending their flotilla of boats down, could cut off the retreat of the garrison. For two months thirty thousand workmen laboured under the eyes of strong parties of Roman soldiers, and the work of denuding the swamps east of the Ouse was accomplished.

Winter had now set in, but the season was a wet one, and although the Romans made repeated attempts to fire the brushwood from the south and west, they failed to do so. Severe frost accompanied by heavy snow set in late, and as soon as the ground was hard enough the Romans entered the swamps near Huntingdon, and began their advance northwards. The Britons were expecting them, and the whole of their fighting force had gathered to oppose them. Beric and Aska set them to work as soon as the Roman army crossed the river and marched north, and as the Romans advanced slowly and carefully through the tangled bushes, they heard a strange confused noise far ahead of them, and after marching for two miles came upon a channel, where the ice had been broken into fragments.

They at once set to work to cut down bushes and form them into faggots to fill up the gaps, but as they approached the channel with these they were assailed by volleys of arrows from the bushes on the opposite side. The light armed troops were brought up, and the work of damming the channel at a dozen points, was covered by a shower of javelins and arrows. The Britons, however, had during the past month made shields of strong wicker work of Roman pattern, but long enough to cover them from the eyes down to the ankles, and the wicker work was protected by a double coating of ox hide. Boys collected the javelins as fast as they were thrown, and handed them to the men. As soon as the road across the channel was completed the Romans poured over, believing that now they should scatter their invisible foes; but they were mistaken, for the Britons with levelled spears, their bodies covered with their bucklers, burst down upon them as they crossed, while a storm of darts and javelins poured in from behind the fighting line.

Again and again they were driven back, until after suffering great loss they made good their footing at several points, when, at the sound of a horn, resistance at once ceased, and the Britons disappeared as if by magic.

Advancing cautiously the Romans found that the ice in all the channels had been broken up, and they were soon involved in a perfect network of sluggish streams. Across these the Britons had felled trees to form bridges for their retreat, and these they dragged after them as soon as they crossed. Every one of these streams was desperately defended, and as the line of swamp grew wider the Roman front became more and more scattered.

Late in the afternoon a sudden and furious attack was made upon them from the rear, Beric having taken a strong force round their flank. Numbers of the Romans were killed before they could assemble to make head against the attack, and as soon as they did so their assailants as usual drew off. After a long day's fighting the Romans had gained scarce a mile from the point where resistance had commenced, and this at a cost of over three hundred men. Suetonius himself had commanded the attack, and when the troops halted for the night at the edge of an unusually wide channel, he felt that the task he had undertaken was beyond his powers. He summoned the commanders of the two legions to the hut that had been hastily raised for him.

"What think you?" he asked. "This is a warfare even more terrible than that we waged with the Goths in their forests. This Beric, who is their leader, has indeed profited by the lessons he learned at Camalodunum. No Roman general could have handled his men better. He is full of resources, and we did not reckon upon his breaking up the ice upon all these channels. If we have had so much trouble in forcing our way where the swamps are but two miles across, and that with a frost to help us, the task will be a terrible one when we get into the heart of the morasses, where they are twenty miles wide. Yet we cannot leave them untouched. There would never be peace and quiet as long as these bands, under so enterprising a leader, remained unsubdued. Can you think of any other plan by which we may advance with less loss?"

The two officers were silent. "The resistance may weaken," one said after a long pause. "We have learnt from the natives that they have not in all much above three thousand fighting men, and they must have lost as heavily as we have."

Suetonius shook his head. "I marked as we advanced," he said, "that there was not one British corpse to four Romans. We shoot at random, while they from their bushes can see us, and even when they charge us our archers can aid but little, seeing that the fighting takes place among the bushes. However, we will press on for a time. The natives behind us must clear the ground as fast as we advance, and every foot gained is gained for good."

Three times during the night the British attacked the Romans, once by passing up the river in their coracles and landing behind them, once by marching out into the country round their left flank, and once by pouring out through cross channels in their boats and landing in front. All night, too, their shouts kept the Romans awake in expectation of attack.

For four days the fighting continued, and the Romans, at the cost of over a thousand men, won their way eight miles farther. By the end of that time they were utterly exhausted with toil and want of sleep; the swamps each day became wider, and the channels larger and deeper. Then the Roman leaders agreed that no more could be done. Twelve miles had been won and cleared, but this was the mere tongue of the Fenland, and to add to their difficulties that day the weather had suddenly changed, and in the evening rain set in. It was therefore determined to retreat while the ground was yet hard, and having lighted their fires, and left a party to keep these burning and to deceive the British, the Romans drew off and marched away, bearing to the left so as to get out on to the plain, and to leave the ground, encumbered with the sharp stumps of the bushes and its network of channels, behind them as soon as possible.

CHAPTER X
BETRAYED

The Britons soon discovered that the Romans had retreated, but made no movement in pursuit. They knew that the legionaries once in open ground were more than their match, and they were well content with the success they had gained. They had lost in all but four hundred men, while they were certain that the Romans had suffered much more heavily, and that there was but little chance of the attack being renewed in the same manner, for if their progress was so slow when they had frost to aid them, what chance would they have when there was scarce a foot of land that could bear their weight? The winter passed, indeed, without any further movement. The Britons suffered to some extent from the damps; but as the whole country was undrained, and for the most part covered with forest, they were accustomed to a damp laden atmosphere, and so supported the fogs of the Fens far better than they would otherwise have done.

In the spring, grain, which had been carefully preserved for the purpose, was sown in many places where the land was above the level of the swamps. A number of large boats had been built during the winter, as Beric and Aska were convinced that the next attack would be made by water, having learned from the country people to the west that a vast number of flat bottomed boats had been built by the Romans.

Early in the spring fighting again began. A great flotilla of boats descended from Huntingdon, and turning off the side channels entered the swamp. But the Britons were prepared. They were now well provided with tools, and numbers of trees had been felled across the channels, completely blocking the passage. As soon as the boats left the main river, they were assailed with a storm of javelins from the bushes, and the Romans, when they attempted to land, found their movements impeded by the deep swamp in which they often sank up to the waist, while their foes in their swamp pattens traversed them easily, and inflicted heavy losses upon them, driving them back into their boats again. At the points where the channels were obstructed desperate struggles took place. The Romans, from their boats, in vain endeavoured, under the storm of missiles from their invisible foes, to remove the obstacles, and as soon as they landed to attempt to do so they were attacked with such fury that they were forced to fall back.

Several times they found their way of retreat blocked by boats that had come down through side channels, and had to fight their way back with great loss and difficulty. After maintaining the struggle for four days, and suffering a loss even greater than that they had incurred in their first attack, the Romans again drew off and ascended the river. The Fenmen had joined the Iceni in repelling the attack. The portion of the swamp they inhabited was not far away, and they felt that they too were threatened by the Roman advance. They had therefore rejoined the Iceni, although for some time they had kept themselves aloof from them, owing to quarrels that had arisen because, as they asserted, some of the Iceni had entered their district and carried off the birds from their traps. Beric had done all in his power to allay this feeling, recompensing them for the losses they declared they had suffered, and bestowing many presents upon them. He and Aska often talked the matter over, and agreed that their greatest danger was from the Fenmen.

"They view us as intruders in their country," Aska said, "and doubtless consider that in time we shall become their masters. Should they turn against us they could lead the Romans direct to our islands, and if these were lost all would be lost."

"If you fear that, Aska," Boduoc, who was present, said, "we had better kill the little wretches at once."

"No, no Boduoc," Beric said. "We have nothing against them at present, and we should be undeserving of the protection of the gods were we to act towards them as the Romans act towards us. Moreover, such an attempt would only bring about what we fear. Some of them, knowing their way as they do through the marshes, would be sure to make their escape, and these would bring the Romans down upon us. Even did we slay all this tribe here, the Fenmen in the north would seek to avenge their kinsmen, and would invite the Romans to their aid. No, we must speak the Fenmen fair, avoid all cause of quarrel, do all we can to win their goodwill, and show them that they have nothing to fear from us. Still, we must always be on guard against treachery. Night and day a watch must be set at the mouths of all the channels by which they might penetrate in this direction."

Another month passed. The Romans still remained in their forts round the Fens. The natives had now been brought round to the western side, and under the protection of strong bodies of soldiers were occupied in clearing the swamp on that side. They made but little progress, however, for the Britons made frequent eruptions among them, and the depth of the morasses in this direction rendered it well nigh impossible for them to advance, and progress could only be made by binding the bush into bundles and forming roads as they went on. From their kinsmen in the northwest, Beric learned that a new propraetor had arrived to replace Suetonius, for it was reported that the wholesale severity of the latter was greatly disapproved of in Rome, so that his successor had come out with orders to pursue a milder policy, and to desist from the work of extirpation that Suetonius was carrying on. It was known that at any rate the newcomer had issued a proclamation, saying that Rome wished neither to destroy nor enslave the people of Britain, and that all fugitives were invited to return to their homes, adding a promise that no molestation should be offered to them, and that an amnesty was granted to all for their share in the late troubles.

"What do you think, Aska?" Beric asked when they heard the news.

"It may be true or it may not," Aska said. "For myself, after the treatment of Boadicea, and the seizure of all her husband's property, I have no faith in Roman promises. However, all this is but a rumour. It will be time enough to consider it when they send in a flag of truce and offer us terms of surrender. Besides, supposing the proclamation has been rightly reported, the amnesty is promised only for the past troubles. The new general must have heard of the heavy losses we inflicted on the Romans as soon as he landed, and had he meant his proclamation to apply to us he would have said so. However, I sincerely trust that it is true, even if we are not included, and are to be hunted down like wild beasts. Rome cannot wish to conquer a desert, and you have told me she generally treats the natives of conquered provinces well after all resistance has ceased. It may well be that the Romans disapprove of the harshness of Suetonius, although the rising was not due to him so much as to the villain Decianus. Still he was harsh in the extreme, and his massacre of the Druids enlisted every Briton against him. Other measures may now be tried; the ground must be cultivated, or it is useless to Rome. There are at present many tribes still unsubdued, and were men like Suetonius and Decianus to continue to scourge the land by their cruelties, they might provoke another rising as formidable as ours, and bring fresh disaster upon Rome. But whether the amnesty applies to us or not, I shall be glad to hear that Suetonius has left. We know that three days ago at any rate he was at their camp opposite Huntingdon, and he may well wish to strike a blow before he leaves, in order that he may return with the credit of having crushed out the last resistance."

Two nights later, an hour before daybreak, a man covered with wounds, breathless and exhausted, made his way up to the intrenchment on the principal island.

"To arms!" he shouted. "The Romans are upon us!" One of the sentries ran with the news to Beric's hut. Springing from his couch Beric sounded his horn, and the band, who were at all times kept to the strength of four hundred, rushed to the line of defences.

"What is it? What is your news?" Beric asked the messenger.

"It is treachery, Beric. With two comrades I was on watch at the point where the principal channel hence runs into the river. Suddenly we thought we heard the sound of oars on the river above us. We could not be sure. It was a faint confused sound, and we stood at the edge of the bank listening, when suddenly from behind us sprang out a dozen men, and before we had time to draw a sword we were cut down. They hewed at us till they thought us dead, and for a time I knew nothing more. When I came to myself I saw a procession of Roman boats turning in at the channel. For a time I was too faint to move; but at last I crawled down a yard or two to the water and had a drink. Then my strength gradually returned and I struggled to my feet.

"To proceed by land through the marshes at night was impossible, but I found my coracle, which we had hidden under the bushes, and poled up the channel after the Romans, who were now some distance ahead. The danger gave me strength, and I gained upon them. When I could hear their oars ahead I turned off by a cross channel so as to strike another leading direct hither. What was my horror when I reached it to see another flotilla of Roman boats passing along. Then I guessed that not only we but the watchers at all the other channels must have been surprised and killed by the treacherous Fenmen. I followed the boats till I reached a spot where I knew there was a track through the marshes to the island.

"For hours I struggled on, often losing the path in the darkness and falling into swamps, where I was nearly overwhelmed; but at last I approached the island. The Romans were already near. I tried each avenue by which our boats approached, but all were held by them. But at last I made my way through by one of the deepest marshes, where at any other time I would not have set foot, even in broad daylight, and so have arrived in time to warn you."

"You have done well. Your warning comes not, I fear, in time to save us, but it will enable us at least to die like men, with arms in our hands."

Parties of men were at once sent down to hold the intrenchments erected to cover the approaches. Some of those who knew the swamps best were sent out singly, but they found the Romans everywhere. They had formed a complete circle round the island, all the channels being occupied by the boats, while parties had been landed upon planks thrown across the soft ground between the channels to prevent any from passing on foot.

"They will not attack until broad daylight," Aska said, when all the men who had been sent out had returned with a similar tale. "They must fight under the disadvantage of not knowing the ground, and would fear that in the darkness some of us would slip away."

Contrary to expectation the next day passed without any movement by the Romans, and Beric and Aska agreed that most likely the greater portion of the boats had gone back to bring up more troops.

"They will not risk another defeat," Aska said, "and they must be sure that, hemmed in as we are, we shall fight to the last."

The practicability of throwing the whole force against the Romans at one point, and of so forcing their way through was discussed; but in that case the women and children, over a thousand in number, must be left behind, and the idea was therefore abandoned. Another day of suspense passed. During the evening loud shouts were heard in the swamp, and the Britons had no doubt that the boats had returned with reinforcements. There were three points where boats could come up to the shore of the island. Aska, Boduoc, and another chief, each with a hundred men, took their posts in the intrenchments there, while Beric, with a hundred of the Sarci, remained in the great intrenchment on the summit, in readiness to bear down upon any point where aid was required. Soon after daybreak next morning the battle began, the Romans advancing in their flat bottomed boats and springing on shore. In spite of a hail of missiles they advanced against the intrenchments; but these were strongly built in imitation of the Roman works, having a steep bank of earth surmounted by a solid palisade breast high, and constructed of massive timber.

For some hours the conflict raged, fifty of the defenders at each intrenchment thrusting down with their long spears the assailants as they strove to scale the bank, while the other fifty rained arrows and javelins upon them; and whenever they succeeded in getting up to the palisade through the circle of the spears, threw down their bows and opposed them sword in hand. Again and again the Romans were repulsed with great slaughter, the cries of exultation from the women who lined the upper intrenchment rose loud and shrill.

Beric divided his force into three bodies. The first was to move down instantly if they saw the defenders of the lower intrenchment hard pressed; the others were to hold their position until summoned by Beric to move down and join in the fray. He himself paced round and round the intrenchment, occupied less with the three desperate fights going on below than with the edge of the bushes between those points. He knew that the morasses were so deep that even an active and unarmed man could scarce make his way through them and that only by springing from bush to bush. But he feared that the Romans might form paths by throwing down faggots, and so gain the island at some undefended point.

Until noon he saw nothing to justify his anxiety; everything seemed still in the swamp. But he knew that this silence was deceptive, and the canopy of marsh loving trees completely hid the bushes and undergrowth from his sight. It was just noon when a Roman trumpet sounded, and at once at six different points a line of Roman soldiers issued from the bushes. Beric raised his horn to his lips and blew the signal for retreat. At its sound the defenders of the three lower intrenchments instantly left their posts and dashed at full speed up the hill, gaining it long before the Romans, who, as they issued out, formed up in order to repel any attack that might be made upon them.

"So they have made paths across the swamp," Aska said bitterly, as he joined Beric. "They would never have made their way in by fair fighting."

"Well," Beric said, "there is one more struggle, and a stout one, and then we go to join our friends who have gone before us in the Happy Island in the far west. We need not be ashamed to meet them. They will welcome us as men who have struggled to the last for liberty against the oppressor, and who have nobly upheld the honour of the Iceni. We shall meet with a great welcome."

Not until the Romans had landed the whole of the force they had brought up, which Beric estimated as exceeding two thousand men, did they advance to the attack, pressing forward against all points of the intrenchment. The Iceni were too few for the proper defence of so long a circuit of intrenchments, but the women and boys took their places beside them armed with hatchets, clubs, and knives. The struggle was for a long time uncertain, so desperately did the defenders fight; and it was not until suffering the loss of a third of their number, from the missiles and weapons of the British, that the Romans at last broke through the intrenchment. Even then the British fought to the last. None thought of asking for quarter, but each died contented if he could kill but one Roman. The women flung themselves on the spears of the assailants, preferring death infinitely to falling into the hands of the Romans; and soon the only survivors of the Britons were a group of some thirty men gathered on a little knoll in the centre of the camp.

Beric had successfully defended the chief entrance to the camp until the Romans burst in at other places, and then, blowing his horn, he had tried to rally his men in the centre for a final stand. Aska had already fallen, pierced by a Roman javelin; but Boduoc and a small body of the Sarci had rallied round Beric, and had for a time beaten off the assaults of the Romans. But soon they were reduced to half their number, and were on the point of being overwhelmed by the crowds surrounding them, when a Roman trumpet sounded and their assailants fell back. An officer made his way towards them and addressed Beric.

"Suetonius bids me say that he honours bravery, and that your lives will be spared if you lay down your arms."

"Tell Suetonius that we scorn his mercy," Beric said, "and will die as we have lived, free men."

The Roman bade his men stand to their weapons, and not move until his return. It was a few minutes before he came back again. Behind him were a number of soldiers, who had laid aside their arms and provided themselves with billets of wood and long poles. Before Beric could understand what was intended, he and his companions were struck to the ground by the discharge of the wooden missiles or knocked down by the poles. Then the Romans threw themselves upon them and bound them hand and foot, the camp was plundered, fire applied to the huts, and the palisades beaten down. Then the captives were carried down to the boats, and the Romans rowed away through the marshes. They had little to congratulate themselves upon. They had captured the leader of the Iceni, had destroyed his stronghold and slain four hundred of his followers, but it had cost them double that number of men, and a large portion of the remainder bore wounds more or less severe.

Boduoc and the other prisoners were furious at their capture. The Britons had no fear whatever of death, but capture was regarded as a disgrace; and that they alone should have been preserved when their comrades had all been killed and the women and children massacred, was to them a terrible misfortune. They considered that they had been captured by an unworthy ruse, for had they known what was intended they would have slain each other, or stabbed themselves, rather than become captives.

Beric's feelings were more mixed. Although he would have preferred death to captivity, his ideas had been much modified by his residence among the Romans, and he saw nothing disgraceful in what he could not avoid. He would never have surrendered; would never have voluntarily accepted life; but as he had been taken captive against his will and in fair fight, he saw no disgrace in it. He wondered why he and his companions had been spared. It might be that they were to be put to death publicly, as a warning to their countrymen; but he thought it more likely that Suetonius had preserved them to carry them back to Rome as a proof that he had, before giving up the command, crushed out the last resistance of the Britons to Roman rule. As the captives had been distributed among the boats, he had no opportunity of speaking to his companions until, about midnight, the flotilla arrived at Godmancastra. Then they were laid on the ground together, a guard of six men taking post beside them. Boduoc at once broke out in a torrent of execrations against the Romans.

"They had a right to kill us," he said, "but they had no right to dishonour us. We had a right to die with the others. We fought them fairly, and refused to surrender. It is a shameful tyranny thus to disgrace us by making us captives. I would not have refused death to my most hated foe; but they shall not exult over us long. If they will not give me a weapon with which to put an end to my life, I will starve myself."

There was an exclamation of fierce assent from the other captives.

"They have not meant to dishonour us, Boduoc, but to do us honour," Beric said. "The Romans do not view these things in the same light that we do. It is because, in their opinion, we are brave men, whom it was an honour to them to subdue, that they have thus taken us. You see they slew all others, even the women and children. We were captured not from pity, not because they wished to inflict disgrace upon us, but simply as trophies of their own valour; just as they would take a standard. We may deem ourselves aggrieved because we have not, like the rest, died fighting to the last, and so departed for the Happy Island; but it is the will of the gods that we should not make the journey for a time. It is really an honour to us that they have deemed us worthy of the trouble of capture, instead of slaying us. Like you, I would rather a thousand times have died; but since the gods have decreed it otherwise, it is for us to show that not even captivity can break our spirit, but that we are able to bear ourselves as brave men who, having done all that men could do against vastly superior force, still preserve their own esteem, and give way neither to unmanly repinings nor to a sullen struggle against fate.

"Nothing would please the Romans better than for us to act like wild beasts caught in a snare, gnashing our teeth vainly when we can no longer strike, and either sulkily protesting against our lot, or seeking to escape the pains of death or servitude by flying from life. Let us preserve a front haughty and unabashed. We have inflicted heavy defeats upon Rome, and are proud of it. Let them see that the chains on our bodies have not bound our spirit, and that, though captives, we still hold ourselves as free men, fearless of what they can do to us. In such a way we shall win at least their respect, and they will say these are men whom we are proud of having overcome."

"By the sacred oak, Beric, you speak rightly," Boduoc exclaimed. "Such was the bearing of Caractacus, as I have heard, when he fell into their hands, and no one can say that Caractacus was dishonoured. No man can control his fate; but, as you say, we may show that we are above fate. What say you, my friends, has Beric spoken well?"

A murmur of hearty assent came from the other captives, and then the Roman sergeant of the guard, uneasy at this animated colloquy among the captives, gruffly ordered silence.

Beric translated the order. "Best sleep, if we can," he added. "We shall be stronger tomorrow."

Few, however, slept, for all were suffering from wounds more or less severe. The following morning their bonds were unloosed, and their wounds carefully attended to by a leech. Then water and food were offered to them, and of these, following Beric's example, they partook heartily. An hour later they were placed in the centre of a strong guard, and then fell in with the troops who were formed up to escort Suetonius to Camalodunum.

"What are they going to do to us, think you?" Boduoc asked Beric.

"They are either going to put us to death publicly at Camalodunum, as a warning against resistance, or they are going to take us to Rome. I think the latter. Had Suetonius been going to remain here, he might be taking us to public execution; but as he has, as we have heard, been ordered home, he would not, I think, have troubled himself to have made us prisoners simply that his successor might benefit by the example of our execution. It is far more likely, I think, that he will carry us to Rome in order to show us as proofs that he has, before leaving Britain, succeeded in crushing out all resistance here."

"And what will they do with us at Rome?"

"That I know not, Boduoc; possibly they will put us to death there, but that is not their usual custom. Suetonius has gained no triumph. A terrible disaster has fallen upon the Romans during his command here; and though he may have avenged their defeat, he certainly does not return home in triumph. After a triumph the chief of the captives is always put to death, sacrificed to their gods. But as this will be no triumph, we shall, I should say, be treated as ordinary prisoners of war. Some of these are sold as slaves; some are employed on public works. Of some they make gladiators--men who fight and kill each other in the arena for the amusement of the people of Rome, who gather to see these struggles just as we do when two warriors who have quarrelled decide their differences by combat."

"The choice does not appear a pleasing one," Boduoc said, "to be a private or public slave, or to be killed for the amusement of the Romans."

"Well, the latter is the shortest way out of it, anyhow, and the one I should choose; but it must be terrible to have to fight with a man with whom one has had no quarrel," Beric said.

"Well, I don't know, Beric. If he is a captive like yourself, he must be just as tired of life as you are. So, if he kills you he is doing you a service; if you kill him, you have greatly obliged him. So, looking at it in that way, it does not much matter which way it goes; for if you do him this service one day, someone else may do you a like good turn the next."

"I had not looked at it in that way, Boduoc," Beric said, laughing. "Well, there is one thing, I do not suppose the choice will be given us. At any rate I shall be glad to see Rome. I have always wished to do so, though I never thought that it would be as a captive. Still, it will be something even in this evil that has befallen us to see so great a city with all its wonders. Camalodunum was but as a little hamlet beside it."

On the evening of the second day after leaving Godmancastra they arrived at Camalodunum, which in the year that had passed since its destruction, had already been partially rebuilt and settled by Gaulish traders from the mainland, Roman officials with their families and attendants, officers engaged in the civil service and the army, friends and associates of the procurator, who had been sent out to succeed Catus Decianus, priests and servants of the temples. Suetonius had already sent to inform the new propraetor, Petronius Turpillianus, of the success which he had gained, and a crowd assembled as the procession was seen approaching, while all eyes were directed upon the little party of British captives who followed the chariot of Suetonius.

Many of the newcomers had as yet scarcely seen a native, so complete had been the destruction of the Trinobantes, and they looked with surprise and admiration at these men, towering a full head above their guards, and carrying themselves, in spite of their bonds, with an air of fearless dignity. Most of all they were surprised when they learned that the youth--for Beric was as yet but eighteen--who walked at their head was the noted chief, who had during the past year inflicted such heavy losses upon the troops of Rome, and who had now only been captured by treachery. As yet he lacked some inches of the height of his companions, but he bade fair in another two or three years to rival the tallest among them in strength and vigour. The procession halted before the building which had been erected from the ruins of the old city as a residence for the propraetor. Petronius, surrounded by a number of officials, came out to meet Suetonius.

"I congratulate you on your success, Suetonius," he said. "It will make my task all the easier in carrying out my orders to deal mildly with the people."

"And it will make my return to Rome all the more pleasant, Petronius, and I thank you again for having permitted me to continue in command of my troops until I had revenged the losses we have suffered at the hands of these barbarians. It is, of course, for you to decide upon the fate of Beric and his companions; assuredly they deserve death, but I should like to take them with me as captives to Rome."

"I should prefer your doing so, Suetonius. I could hardly pardon men who have so withstood us, but, upon the other hand, I should grieve to commence my rule by an act of severity; besides, I hope through them to persuade the others--for, as you told me in your letter, it is but a fraction of these outlaws that you have subdued--to lay down their arms. It is well, indeed, that you have taken their chief, and that he, as I hear, has partly been brought up among us and speaks our language."

"Yes, he lived here for some five years as a hostage for his tribe. He was under the charge of Caius Muro, who returned to Rome after our defeat of the Britons. I made inquiries about him, when I learned that he was chief of the insurgents, and heard that he was tractable and studious when among us, and that Caius thought very highly of his intelligence."

"They are noble looking men," Petronius said, surveying the group of captives; "it is an honour to conquer such men. I will speak with their chief presently."

"I shall make no longer delay," Suetonius said. "Ships have been lying at the port in readiness for my departure for the last two weeks, and I would fain sail tomorrow or next day. Glad I shall be to leave this island, where I have had nothing but fighting and hardships since I landed."

"And you have done well," Petronius said courteously. "It was but half conquered when you landed, it is wholly subdued now. It is for me only to gather the fruit of your victories."

"Never was there such an obstinate race," Suetonius replied angrily. "Look at those men, they bear themselves as if they were conquerors instead of conquered."

"They are good for something better than to be killed, Suetonius; if we could mate all our Roman women with these fair giants, what a race we should raise!"

"You would admire them less if you saw them pouring down on you shouting like demons," Suetonius said sullenly.

"Perhaps so, Suetonius; but I will endeavour to utilize their strength in our service, and not to call it into the field against us. Now, let us enter the house. Varo," he said to one of his officers, "take charge of the captives until Suetonius sails. Guard them strongly, but treat them well. Place them in the house, where they will not be stared at by the crowd. If their chief will give you his word that they will not attempt to escape, their bonds can be removed; if not, they must remain bound."

Varo at once called a centurion of the legion in garrison at Camalodunum, and bade him bring up his company. These on their arrival surrounded the captives and marched with them to a guardhouse near. When they entered Varo said to Beric:

"The orders of the propraetor are, that you shall all be released from your bonds if you will give your oath that you will not try to escape."

Beric turned to the others and asked if they were willing to give the promise. "In no case could we escape," he said, "you may be sure we shall be guarded too strictly for that. It were better that we should remain bound by our own promise than by fetters." As they all consented, Beric, in their name, took an oath that they would not attempt to escape, so that the ropes that bound their arms were at once taken off, and in a short time a meal was sent to them from the house of Petronius.

Soon after they had finished an officer came in and requested Beric to accompany him to the propraetor.

"I will bring two of my followers with me," Beric said. "I would not say aught to the Roman governor that my tribesmen should not hear."

The officer assented, and Beric with Boduoc and another subchief followed him to the house of the propraetor. Petronius was seated with Suetonius at his side, while a number of officers and officials stood behind him.

"How is it, Beric," he asked, "that, as I hear, you, who speak our language and have lived for years amongst us, come to be a leader of those who have warred against us?"

"It is, perhaps, because I studied Roman books, and learned how you value freedom and independence," Beric replied, "and how you revolt against tyranny. Had Rome been conquered by a more powerful nation, every Roman would have risen in arms had one tenth of the tyranny been practised against them which Catus Decianus exercised against us. We have been treated worse than the beasts of the field; our lives, our properties, and the honour of our women were sacrificed at his will. Death was a thousand times better than such treatment. I read that Rome has elsewhere been a worthy conqueror, respecting the religion of the tribes it subdued, and treating them leniently and well. Had we been so treated we should have been, if not contented, patient under our lot, but being men we rose against the infamous treatment to which we were subject; and although we have been conquered and well nigh exterminated, there are Britons still remaining, and if such be the treatment to which they are subjected it is not till the last Briton is exterminated that you will rule this island."

A murmur of surprise at the boldness with which the young captive spoke ran round the circle.

"Have you inquired since you arrived," Beric went on, "of the infamous deeds of Decianus? How he seized, without the shadow of excuse, the property of Boadicea? and how, when she came here for justice for herself and her insulted daughters, he ordered her to be scourged? Should we, a free born people, submit to such an indignity to our queen? I knew from the first that our enterprise was hopeless, and that without order or discipline we must in the end be conquered; but it was better a thousand times to die than to live subject to treatment worse than that which you give to your slaves."

"I believe that there is justice in your complaints, Beric," Petronius said calmly, "and it is to lessen these grievances that Rome has sent me hither. Vengeance has been fully taken for your rebellion, it is time that the sword was laid aside. I have already issued a proclamation granting an amnesty to all who then rose against us. Your case was different, you have still continued in arms and have resisted our power, but I trust that with your capture this will end. You and your companions will go to Rome with Suetonius; but there are many of your followers still in arms, with these I would treat, not as a conqueror with the conquered, but as a soldier with brave foes. If they will lay down their arms they shall share the amnesty, and be free to return every man to his own land, to dwell there and cultivate it free from all penalty or interruption. Their surrender would benefit not only themselves but all the Britons. So long as they stand in arms and defy our power we must rule the land with the sword, but when they surrender there will be peace throughout the island, and I trust that the Britons in time will come to look upon us as friends."

"If Rome had so acted before," Beric said, "no troubles would have arisen, and she might now be ruling over a contented people instead of over a desert."

"There are still many of your tribesmen in the Fens?"

"There is an army," Beric replied. "You have taken one stronghold, and that by surprise, but the lesson will not be lost upon them. There will be no traitors to guide your next expedition; by this time the last Fenman in the southern swamps will have been killed. There will be a heavy vengeance taken by my countrymen."

"I would fain put a stop to it all," Petronius said. "Upon what terms, think you, would your countrymen surrender?"

"They will not surrender at all," Beric said; "there is not a man there but will die rather than yield. But if you will solemnly take oath that those who leave the Fens and return to their villages shall live unmolested, save that they shall--when their homes are rebuilt and their herds again grazing around them--pay a tribute such as they are able to bear, they will, I believe, gladly leave the Fens and return to their villages, and the fugitives who have fled north will also come back again."

"I am ready to take such an oath at the altar," Petronius said. "I have come to bring peace to the land. I am ready to do all in my power to bring it about; but how are they to know what I have done?"

"I would say, Petronius, let us, your captives, be present when you take the oath. Release four of my band; choose those most sorely wounded, and who are the least able to support the journey to Rome. I will send them with my bracelet to the Fens. I will tell them what you have said, and they will testify to having seen you swear before your gods; and I will send my last injunctions to them to return again to their land, to send for the fugitives to return from the north, and to say from me that they will return as free men, not as slaves, and that there is no dishonour in accepting such terms as you offer."

"I will do as you say," the Roman agreed. "Suetonius, you can spare four of your captives, especially as there are assuredly some among them who could ill support the fatigues of the journey. Return now to your friends, Beric; tomorrow morning you shall meet me at the temple, and there I will take an oath of peace with Britain."

CHAPTER XI
A PRISONER

On leaving the propraetor Beric further informed his comrades of the offer that Petronius had made.

"And you think he will keep his oath?" Boduoc asked.

"I am sure of it," Beric said; "he has been sent out by Rome to undo the mischief Suetonius and Decianus have caused. His face is an honest one, and a Roman would not lie to his gods any more than we would."

"But you ought to have made terms with them, Beric," Boduoc said. "You ought to have made a condition that you should be allowed to stay. It matters not for us, but you are the chief of all the Iceni who are left."

"In the first place, Boduoc, I was not in a position to make terms, seeing that I am a captive and at their mercy; and in the next place, I would not if I could. Think you that the tribesmen would then accept my counsels to leave the Fens and return to their homes? They would say that I had purchased my life and freedom from the Romans, and had agreed to betray them into their hands."

"No one would venture to say that of you, Beric."

"You may think not, Boduoc; but if not now, in the future it would be said that, as before I was brought up among the Romans, so now I had gone back to them. No, even if they offered to all of us our liberty, I would say, let those go who will, but I remain a captive. Had the message come to us when I was free in the Fens I would have accepted it, for I knew that, although we might struggle long, we should be finally overpowered. Moreover, the marsh fevers were as deadly as Roman swords, and though for a year we have supported them, we should in time, perhaps this year when the summer heats come, have lost our strength and have melted away. Thus, had I believed that the Romans were sincere in their wish for peace, and that they desired to see the land tilled, I would have accepted their terms, because we were in arms and free, and could still have resisted; but as a captive, and conquered, I scorn to accept mercy from Rome."

By this time they had arrived at the house where the other captives were guarded, and Beric repeated the terms that Petronius had offered.

"They will not benefit us," he said. "We are the captives of Suetonius, and being taken with arms in our hands warring against Rome, we must pay the penalty; but, for the sake of our brethren, I rejoice. Our land may yet be peopled again by the Iceni, and we shall have the consolation that, whatever may befall us, it is partly our valour that has won such terms from Rome. There are still fifteen hundred fighting men in the swamps, and twice as many women and children. There may be many more lurking in the Fens to the north, for great numbers, especially from our northern districts, must have taken refuge with the Brigantes. Thus, then, there will, when all have returned, be a goodly number, and it is our defence of the Fenlands that has won their freedom for them. We may be captives and slaves, but we are not dishonoured. For months we have held Suetonius at bay, and two Romans have fallen for every Briton; and even at last it was by treachery we were captured.

"None of us have begged our lives of Rome. We fought to the last, and showed front when we were but twenty against two thousand. It was not our fault that we did not die on the field, and we can hold our heads as high now when we are captives as we did when we were free men. We know not what may be our fate at Rome, but whatever it be, it will be a consolation to us to know that our people again wander in the old woods; that our women are spinning by their hearthstones; that the Iceni are again a tribe; and that it is we who have won this for them."

An enthusiastic assent greeted Beric's words.

"Now," he said, "we must choose the four who shall carry the message. I said those most sorely wounded, but since four are to go they can care little who are chosen. Most of us have lost those we love, but there are some whose wives may have been elsewhere when the attack was made. Let these stay, and let those who have no ties save that of country go to Rome."

Only two men were found whose families had not been on the island when it was attacked. These and the two most seriously wounded were at once chosen as the messengers. The next morning the whole of the captives were escorted to the temple, which was but a small building in comparison with the great edifice that had been destroyed at the capture of Camalodunum. Here Petronius and all the principal officers and officials were assembled. Sacrifice was offered, and then Petronius, laying his hand on the altar, declared a solemn peace with the Britons, and swore that, so long as they remained peaceable subjects of Rome, no man should interfere with them, but all should be free to settle in their villages, to till their land, and to tend their herds free from any molestation whatever. Beric translated the words of the oath to the Britons. Petronius then bade the four men who had been chosen stand forward, and told them to carry his message to their countrymen.

"Enough blood has been shed on both sides," he said. "It is time for peace. You have proved yourselves worthy and valiant enemies; let us now lay aside the sword and live together in friendship. I sent orders last night for the legions to leave their forts by the Fenland and to return hither, so that the way is now open to your own land. We can settle the terms of the tribute hereafter, but it shall not be onerous."

After leaving the temple Beric gave his messages to the men, and they at once started under an escort for the camp, the officer in charge of them being ordered to provide them with a boat, in which they were to proceed alone to their countrymen.

That evening Petronius sent for Beric, and received him alone. "I am sorry," he said, "that I cannot restore you and your companions to your tribe, but in this I am powerless, as Suetonius has captured you, and to him you belong. I have begged him, as a personal favour, to hand you over to me, but he has refused, and placed as we are I can do no more. I have, however, written to friends in Rome concerning you, and have said that you have done all in your power to bring about a pacification of the land, and have begged them to represent to Nero and the senate that if a report reach this island that you have been put to death, it will undo the work of pacification, and perhaps light up a fresh flame of war."

There had, indeed, been an angry dispute between Suetonius and his successor. The former, although well pleased to return to Rome, was jealous of Petronius, and was angry at seeing that he was determined to govern Britain upon principles the very reverse of those he himself had adopted. Moreover, he regarded the possession of the captives as important, and deemed that their appearance in his train, as proofs that before leaving he had completely stamped out the insurrection, would create a favourable impression, and would go far to restore him to popular opinion. This was, as he had heard from friends in Rome, strongly adverse to him, in consequence of the serious disasters and heavy losses which had befallen the Roman arms during his propraetorship, and he had therefore refused with some heat to grant the request of Petronius.

The next morning the captives were mustered, and were marched down to the river and placed on board a ship. There were six vessels lying in readiness, as Suetonius was accompanied not only by his own household, but by several officers and officials attached to him personally, and by two hundred soldiers whose time of service had expired, and who were to form his escort to Rome. To Beric, from his residence in Camalodunum, large ships were no novelty, but the Britons with him were struck with astonishment at craft so vastly exceeding anything that they had before seen.

"Could we sail in these ships to Rome?" Boduoc asked.

"You could do so, but it would be a very long and stormy voyage passing through the straits between two mountains which the Romans call the Pillars of Hercules. Our voyage will be but a short one. If the wind is favourable we shall reach the coast of Gaul in two days, and thence we shall travel on foot."

Fortunately the weather was fine, and on the third day after setting sail they reached one of the northern ports of Gaul. When it was known that Suetonius was on board, he was received with much pomp, and was lodged in the house of the Roman magistrate. As he had no desire to impress the inhabitants of the place, the captives were left unbound and marched through the streets under a guard of the Roman spearmen. Gaul had long been completely subdued, but the inhabitants looked at the captives with pitying eyes. When these reached the house in which they were to be confined, the natives brought them presents of food, bribing the Roman guards to allow them to deliver them.

As the language of the two peoples was almost identical, the Gauls had no difficulty in making themselves understood by the captives, and asked many questions relating to the state of affairs in Britain. They had heard of the chief, Beric, who had for a year successfully opposed the forces of Rome, and great was their surprise when they found that the youngest of the party was the noted leader. Two days later they started on their long march.

Inured as the Britons were to fatigue, the daily journeys were nothing to them. They found the country flourishing. Villages occurred at frequent intervals, and they passed through several large towns with temples, handsome villas, and other Roman erections similar to those that they had sacked at the capture of Camalodunum.

"The people here do not seem to suffer under the Roman rule at any rate," Boduoc remarked; "they appear to have adopted the Roman dress and tongue, but for all that they are slaves."

"Not slaves, Boduoc, though they cannot be said to be free; however, they have become so accustomed to the Roman dominion that doubtless they have ceased to fret under it; they are, indeed, to all intents and purposes Roman. They furnish large bodies of troops to the Roman armies, and rise to positions of command and importance among them. In time, no doubt, unless misfortunes fall upon Rome, they will become as one people, and such no doubt in the far distance will be the case with Britain. We shall adopt many of the Roman customs, and retain many of our own. There is one advantage, you see, in Roman dominion--there are no more tribal wars, no more massacres and slaughters, each man possesses his land in peace and quiet."

"But what do they do with themselves?" Boduoc asked, puzzled. "In such a country as this there can be few wild beasts. If men can neither fight nor hunt, how are they to employ their time? They must become a nation of women."

"It would seem so to us, Boduoc, for we have had nothing else to employ our thoughts; but when we look at what the Romans have done, how great an empire they have formed, how wonderful are their arts, how good their laws, and what learning and wisdom they have stored up, one sees that there are other things to live for; and you see, though the Romans have learned all these things, they can still fight. If they once turn so much to the arts of peace as to forget the virtues of war, their empire will fall to pieces more rapidly than it has been built up."

Boduoc shook his head, "These things are well enough for you, Beric, who have lived among the Romans and learned many of their ways. Give me a life in which a man is a man; when we can live in the open air, hunt the wolf and the bear, meet our enemies face to face, die as men should, and go to the Happy Island without bothering our brains about such things as the arts and luxuries that the Romans put such value on. A bed on the fallen leaves under an oak tree, with the stars shining through the leaves, is better than the finest chamber in Rome covered with paintings."

"Well, Boduoc," Beric said good temperedly, "we are much more likely to sleep under the stars in Rome than in a grand apartment covered with paintings; but though the one may be very nice, as you say, in summer, I could very well put up with the other when the snow lies deep and the north wind is howling."

They did not, as Beric had hoped, cross the tremendous mountains, over which, as he had read in Polybius, Hannibal had led his troops against Rome. Hannibal had been his hero. His dauntless bravery, his wonderful resources, his cheerfulness under hardships, and the manner in which, cut off for years from all assistance from home, he had yet supported the struggle and held Rome at bay, had filled him with the greatest admiration, and unconsciously he had made the great Carthaginian his model. He was therefore much disappointed when he heard from the conversation of his guards that they were to traverse Gaul to Massilia, and thence take ship to Rome.

The Roman guards were fond of talking to their young captive. Their thoughts were all of Rome, from which they had been so long absent, and Beric was eager to learn every detail about the imperial city; the days' marches therefore passed pleasantly. At night they were still guarded, but they were otherwise allowed much liberty, and when they stopped for two or three days at a place they were free to wander about as they chose, their great stature, fair hair, and blue eyes exciting more and more surprise as they went farther south, where the natives were much shorter and swarthier than those of northern Gaul.

One of the young officers with Suetonius had taken a great fancy to Beric, and frequently invited him to spend the evening with him at their halting places. When they approached Massilia he said, "I have some relations in the city, and I will obtain leave for you to stay with me at their house while we remain in the town, which may be for some little time, as we must wait for shipping. My uncle is a magistrate, and a very learned man. He is engaged in writing a book upon the religions of the world, and he seldom remains long at any post. He has very powerful friends in Rome, and so is able to get transferred from one post to another. He has been in almost every province of the empire in order to learn from the people themselves their religions and beliefs. I stayed with him for a month here two years since on my way to Britain, and he was talking of getting himself transferred there, after he had been among the Gauls for a year or two; but his wife was averse to the idea, protesting that she had been dragged nearly all over the world by him, and was determined not to go to its furthest boundaries. But I should think that after the events of the last year he has given up that idea. I know it will give him the greatest possible pleasure to converse with one who can tell him all about the religions and customs of the Britons in his own language."

Massilia was by far the largest city that the Britons had entered, and they were greatly surprised at its magnitude, and at the varieties of people who crowded its streets. Even Boduoc, who professed a profound indifference for everything Roman, was stupefied when he saw a negro walking in the train of a Roman lady of rank.

"Is it a human being, think you," he murmured in Beric's ear, "or a wild creature they have tamed? He has not hair, but his head is covered with wool like a black sheep."

"He is a man," Beric replied. "Across the sea to the south there are brown men many shades darker than the people here, and beyond these like lands inhabited by black men. Look at him showing his teeth and the whites of his eyes. He is as much surprised at our appearance, Boduoc, as we are at his. We shall see many like him in Rome, for Pollio tells me that they are held in high estimation as slaves, being good tempered and obedient."

"He is hideous, Beric; look at his thick lips. But the creature looks good tempered. I wonder that any woman could have such an one about the house. Can they talk?"

"Oh, yes, they talk. They are men just the same as we are, except for their colour."

"But what makes them so black, Beric?"

"That is unknown; but it is supposed that the heat of the sun, for the country they inhabit is terribly hot, has in time darkened them. You see, as we have gone south, the people have got darker and darker."

"But are they born that colour, Beric?"

"Certainly they are."

"If a wife of mine bore me a child of that colour," Boduoc said, "I would strangle it. And think you that it is the heat of the sun that has curled up their hair so tightly?"

"That I cannot say--they are all like that."

"Well, they are horrible," Boduoc said positively. "I did not think that the earth contained such monsters."

Soon after the captives were lodged in a prison, Pollio came to see Beric, and told him that he had obtained permission for him to lodge at his uncle's house, he himself being guarantee for his safe custody there; accordingly they at once started together.

The house was a large one; for, as Pollio had told Beric by the way, his uncle was a man of great wealth, and it was a matter of constant complaint on the part of his wife that he did not settle down in Rome. Passing straight through the atrium, where he was respectfully greeted by the servants and slaves, Pollio passed into the tablinum, where his uncle was sitting writing.

"This is the guest I told you I should bring, uncle," he said. "He is a great chief, young as he looks, and has given us a world of trouble. He speaks Latin perfectly, and you will be able to learn from him all about the Britons without troubling yourself and my aunt to make a journey to his country."

Norbanus was an elderly man, short in figure, with a keen but kindly face. He greeted Beric cordially.

"Welcome, young chief," he said. "I will try to make your stay here comfortable, and I shall be glad indeed to learn from you about your people, of whom, unfortunately, I have had no opportunity hitherto of learning anything, save that when I journeyed up last year to the northwest of Gaul, I found a people calling themselves by the same name as you. They told me that they were a kindred race, and that your religion was similar to theirs."

"That may well be," Beric said. "We are Gauls, though it is long since we left that country and settled in Britain. It may well be that in some of the wars in the south of the island a tribe, finding themselves overpowered, may have crossed to Gaul, with which country we were always in communication until it was conquered by you. We certainly did not come thence, for all our traditions say that the Iceni came by ship from a land lying due east from us, and that we were an offshoot of the Belgae, whose country lay to the northwest of Gaul."

"The people I speak of," the magistrate said, "have vast temples constructed of huge stones placed in circles, which appear to me to have, like the great pyramids of Egypt, an astronomical signification, for I found that the stones round the sacrificial altars were so placed that the sun at its rising threw its rays upon the stone only upon the longest day of summer."

"It is so with our great temples," Beric said; "and upon that day sacrifices are offered. What the signification of the stones and their arrangements is I cannot say. These mysteries are known only to the Druids, and they are strictly preserved from the knowledge of those outside the priestly rank."

"Spare him for today, uncle," Pollio said laughing. "We are like, I hear, to be a fortnight here before we sail; so you will have abundant time to learn everything that Beric can tell you. I will take him up now, with your permission, and introduce him to my aunt and cousins."

"You will find them in the garden, Pollio. Supper will be served in half an hour. Tomorrow, Beric, we will, after breakfast, renew this conversation that my feather brained young nephew has cut so short."

"My Aunt Lesbia will be greatly surprised when she sees you," Pollio laughed as they issued out into the garden. "I did not see her until after I had spoken to my uncle, and I horrified her by telling her that the noted British chief Beric, who had defeated our best troops several times with terrible slaughter, was coming here to remain under my charge until we sail for Rome. She was shocked, considering that you must be a monster of ferocity; and even my pretty cousins were terrified at the prospect. I had half a mind to get you to attire yourself in Roman fashion, but I thought that you would not consent. However, we shall surprise them sufficiently as it is."

Lesbia was seated with her two daughters on couches placed under the shade of some trees. Two or three slave girls stood behind them with fans. A dalmatian bore hound lay on the ground in front of them. Another slave girl was singing, accompanying herself on an instrument resembling a small harp, while a negro stood near in readiness to start upon errands, or to fetch anything that his mistress might for the moment fancy. Lesbia half rose from her reclining position when she saw Pollio approaching, accompanied by a tall figure with hair of a golden colour clustering closely round his head. The Britons generally wore their hair flowing over their shoulders; but the Iceni had found such inconvenience from this in making their way through the close thickets of the swamps, that many of them--Beric among the number--had cut their hair close to the head. With him it was but a recurrence to a former usage, as while living among the Romans his hair had been cut short in their fashion. The two girls, who were fifteen and sixteen years old, uttered an exclamation of surprise as Beric came near, and Lesbia exclaimed angrily:

"You have been jesting with us, Pollio. You told me that you were going to bring Beric the fierce British chief here, and this young giant is but a beardless lad."

Pollio burst into a fit of laughter, which was increased at the expression of astonishment in Lesbia's face when Beric said, in excellent Latin,--"Pollio has not deceived you, lady. My name is Beric, I was the chief of the Britons, and my followers gave some trouble even to Suetonius."

"But you are not the Beric whom we have heard of as leading the insurgent Britons?"

"There is no other chief of my name," Beric said. "Therefore, if you heard aught of good or evil concerning Beric the Briton, it must relate to me."

"This is Beric, aunt," Pollio said, "and you must not judge him by his looks. I was with Suetonius in his battles against him, and I can tell you that we held him in high respect, as we had good cause for doing, considering that in all it cost the lives of some twelve hundred legionaries before we could overcome him, and we took him by treachery rather than force."

"But how is it that he speaks our language?" Lesbia asked.

"I was a hostage for five years among the Romans," Beric said, "and any knowledge I may have of the art of war was learned from the pages of Caesar, Polybius, and other Roman writers. The Romans taught me how to fight them."

"And now," Pollio broke in, "I must introduce you in proper form. This is my Aunt Lesbia, as you see; these are my cousins Aemilia and Ennia. Do you know, girls, that these Britons, big and strong as they are, are ruled by their women. These take part in their councils, and are queens and chieftainesses, and when it is necessary they will fight as bravely as the men. They are held by them in far higher respect than with us, and I cannot say that they do not deserve it, for they think of other things than attiring themselves and spending their time in visits and pleasure."

"You are not complimentary, Pollio," Aemilia said; "and as to attire, the young Romans think as much of it as we do, and that without the same excuse, for we are cut off from public life, and have none save home pursuits. If you treat us as you say the Britons treat their women, I doubt not that we should show ourselves as worthy of it."

"Now I ask you fairly, Aemilia, can you fancy yourself encouraging the legionaries in the heat of battle, and seizing spear and shield and rushing down into the thick of the fight as I have seen the British women do?"

"No, I cannot imagine that," Aemilia said laughing. "I could not bear the weight of a shield and spear, much less use them in battle. But if the British women are as much bigger and stronger than I am, as Beric is bigger and stronger than you are, I can imagine their fighting. I wondered how the Britons could withstand our troops, but now that I see one of them there is no difficulty in comprehending it, and yet you do not look fierce, Beric."

"I do not think that I am fierce," Beric said smiling; "but even the most peaceful animal will try and defend itself when it is attacked."

"Have you seen Norbanus?" Lesbia asked.

"He has seen him," Pollio replied; "and if it had not been for me he would be with him still, for my uncle wished to engage him at once in a discourse upon the religion and customs of his people; I carried Beric away almost forcibly."

Lesbia sighed impatiently. The interest of her husband in these matters was to her a perpetual source of annoyance. It was owing to this that she so frequently travelled from one province to another, instead of enjoying herself at the court in Rome. But although in all other matters Norbanus gave way to her wishes, in this he was immovable, and she was forced to pass her life in what she considered exile. She ceased to take any further interest in the conversation, but reclined languidly on her couch, while Pollio gave his cousins a description of his life in Britain, and Beric answered their numerous questions as to his people. Their conversation was interrupted by a slave announcing that supper was ready, and Lesbia was relieved at finding that Beric thoroughly understood Roman fashions, and comported himself at table as any other guest would have done. The girls sat down at the meal, although this was contrary to usual custom; but Norbanus insisted that his family should take their meals with him, save upon occasions of a set banquet.

"It seems wonderful," Ennia said to her sister later on, "that we should have been dining with the fierce chief of whom we have heard so much, and that he should be as courteous and pleasant and well mannered as any young Roman."

"A good deal more pleasant than most of them," Aemilia said, "for he puts on no airs, and is just like a merry, good tempered lad, while if a young Roman had done but a tithe of the deeds he has he would be insufferable. We must get Pollio to take us tomorrow to see the other Britons. They must be giants indeed, when Beric, who says he is but little more than eighteen years, could take Pollio under his arm and walk away with him."

In the morning, accordingly, Pollio started with his two cousins to the prison, while Beric sat down for a long talk with Norbanus in his study. Beric soon saw that the Roman viewed all the matters on which he spoke from the standpoint of a philosopher without prejudices.

After listening to all that Beric could tell him about the religion of the Britons, he said, "It is remarkable that all people appear to think that they have private deities of their own, who interest themselves specially on their behalf, and aid them to fight their battles. I have found no exception to this rule, and the more primitive the people the more obstinate is this belief. In Rome at present the learned no longer believe in Jupiter and Mars and the rest of the deities, though they still attend the state ceremonies at the temples, holding that a state religion is necessary. The lower class still believe, but then they cannot be said to reason. In Greece scepticism is universal among the upper class, and the same may now be said of Egypt. Our Roman belief is the more unaccountable since we have simply borrowed the religion of the Greeks, the gods and their attributes being the same, with only a change of name; and yet we fancy that these Greek gods are the special patrons of Rome.

"Your religion seems to me the most reasonable of any I have studied, and approaches more nearly than any other to the highest speculations of the Greek philosophers. You believe in one God, who is invisible and impersonal, who pervades all nature; but having formed so lofty an idea of him, you belittle him by making him a special god of your own country, while if he pervades all nature he must surely be universal. The Jews, too, believe in a single God, and in this respect they resemble you in their religion, which is far more reasonable than that of nations who worship a multiplicity of deities; but they too consider that their God confines His attention simply to them, and rules over only the little tract they call their own--a province about a hundred miles long, by thirty or forty wide. From them another religion has sprung. This has made many converts, even in Rome, but has made no way whatever among the learned, seeing that it is more strange and extravagant than any other. It has, however, the advantage that the new God is, they believe, universal, and has an equal interest in all people. I have naturally studied the tenets of this new sect, and they are singularly lofty and pure. They teach among other things that all men are equal in the sight of God--a doctrine which naturally gains for them the approval of slaves and the lower people, but, upon the other hand, brings them into disfavour with those in power.

"They are a peaceful sect, and would harm no one; but as they preach that fighting is wrong, I fear that they will before long come into collision with the state, for, were their doctrines to spread, there would soon be a lack of soldiers. To me it appears that their views are impracticable on this subject. In other respects they would make good citizens, since their religion prescribes respect to the authorities and fair dealing in all respects with other men. They are, too, distinguished by charity and kindness towards each other. One peculiarity of this new religion is, that although springing up in Judaea, it has made less progress among the Jews than elsewhere, for these people, who are of all others the most obstinate and intolerant, accused the Founder of the religion, one Christus, before the Roman courts, and He was put to death, in my opinion most unjustly, seeing that there was no crime whatever alleged against Him, save that He perverted the religion of the Jews, which was in no way a concern of ours, as we are tolerant of the religions of all people."

"But Suetonius attacked our sacred island and slew the priests on the altars," Beric objected.

"That is quite true," Norbanus said, "but this had nothing whatever to do with the religion, but was simply because the priests stirred up insurrection against us. We have temples in Rome to the deities of almost every nation we have subdued, and have suffered without objection the preachers of this new doctrine to make converts. The persecutions that have already begun against the sect are not because they believe in this Christus, but because they refuse to perform the duties incumbent upon all Roman citizens. Two of my slaves belong to the sect. They know well that I care not to what religion they belong, and indeed, for my part, I should be glad to see all my slaves join them, for the moral teaching is high, and these slaves would not steal from me, however good the opportunity. That is more than I can say of the others. Doubtless, had I been fixed in Rome, the fact that they belonged to these people would have been kept a secret, but in the provinces no one troubles his head about such matters. These are, to my mind, matters of private opinion, and they have leave from me to go on their meeting days to the place where they assemble, for even here there are enough of them to form a gathering.

"So long as this is done quietly it is an offence to no one. The matter was discussed the other day among us, for orders against Christians came from Rome; but when the thing was spoken of I said that, as I believed members of the sect were chiefly slaves, who were not called upon to perform military duties, I could not deem that the order applied to them, and that as these were harmless people, and their religion taught them to discharge their duty in all matters save that of carrying arms, I could not see why they should be interfered with. Moreover, did we move in the matter, and did these people remain obstinate in their Faith, we might all of us lose some valuable slaves. After that no more was said of the matter. Now tell me about your institution of the bards, of which I have heard. These men seem not only to be the depositors of your traditions and the reciters of the deeds of your forefathers, but to hold something of a sacred position intermediate between the Druids and the people."

For some hours Beric and his host conversed on these subjects, Beric learning more than he taught, and wondering much at the wide knowledge possessed by Norbanus. It was not until dinner was announced that the Roman rose.

"I thank you much, Beric, for what you have told me, and I marvel at the interest that you, who have for the last two years been leading men to battle, evince in these matters. After five minutes of such talk my nephew Pollio would begin to weary."

"I was fond of learning when I was in the household of Caius Muro, but my time was chiefly occupied by the study of military works and in military exercises; still I found time to read all the manuscripts in Muro's library. But I think I learned more from the talk of Cneius Nepo, his secretary, who was my instructor, than from the books, for he had travelled much with Muro, and had studied Greek literature."

Pollio had returned some time before with his cousins.

"I would have come in before to carry you away," he whispered to Beric as they proceeded to the dinner table, "but it would have put out my uncle terribly, and as I knew you would have to go through it all I thought it as well that you should finish with it at once."

"I am glad you did not," Beric replied. "It has been a great pleasure to me to listen to your uncle's conversation, from which I have learned a good deal."

Pollio glanced up to see if Beric was joking. Seeing that he spoke in perfect good faith, he said:

"Truly, Beric, you Britons are strange fellows. I would rather go through another day's fighting in your swamps than have to listen to uncle for a whole morning."

As they sat down he went on:

"The girls are delighted with your Britons, Beric. They declare they are not only the biggest but the handsomest men they ever saw, and I believe that if your lieutenant Boduoc had asked either of them to return with him and share his hut in the swamps they would have jumped at the offer."

The girls both laughed.

"But they are wonderful, Beric," Aemilia said. "When you told us that you were not yet full grown I thought you were jesting, but I see now that truly these men are bigger even than you are. I wish I had such golden hair as most of them have, and such a white skin. Golden hair is fashionable in

Rome, you know, but it is scarce, except in a few whose mothers were Gauls who have married with Romans."

"It is the nature of man to admire the opposite to himself," Norbanus said. "You admire the Britons because they are fair, while to them, doubtless, Roman women would appear beautiful because their hair and their eyes are dark."

"But Beric has not said so, father," Aemilia said laughing.

"I am not accustomed to pay compliments," Beric said with a smile, "but assuredly your father is right. I have been accustomed for the last two years to see British maidens only. These are fair and tall, some of them well nigh as tall as I, and as they live a life of active exercise, they are healthy and strong."

"That they are," Pollio broke in. "I would as soon meet a soldier of the Goths as one of these maidens Beric speaks of, when her blood is up. I have seen our soldiers shrink from their attack, when, with flashing eyes and hair streaming behind them, they rush down upon us, armed with only stones and billets of wood that they had snatched up. What they may be in their gentler moments I know not, and I should hesitate to pay my court to one, for, if she liked it not, she would make small difficulty in throwing me outside the door of her hut."

"You are too quick, Pollio," Aemilia said. "Beric was about to compare us with them."

"The comparison is difficult," Beric said; "but you must not imagine our women as being always in the mood in which Pollio has seen them. They were fighting, not for their lives, but in order to be killed rather than fall into the hands of your soldiers. Ordinarily they are gentle and kind. They seemed to Pollio to be giantesses, but they bear the same proportion to our height as you do to the height of the Roman men."

"I meant not to say aught against them," Pollio broke in hastily. "I meant but to show my cousins how impossible it was for you to make any comparison between our women and yours. All who know them speak well of the British women, and admire their devotion to their husbands and children, their virtue, and bravery. You might as well compare a Libyan lioness with a Persian cat as the British women with these little cousins of mine."

"But the Persian cat has, doubtless, its lovable qualities," Beric said smiling. "It is softer and gentler and better mannered than the lioness, though, perhaps, the lion might not think so. But truly your Roman ladies are beyond comparison with ours. Ours live a life of usefulness, discharging their duties as mistress of the household, intent upon domestic cares, and yet interested as ourselves in all public affairs, and taking a share in their decision. Your ladies live a life of luxury. They are shielded from all trouble. They are like delicate plants by the side of strong saplings. No rough air has blown upon them. They are dainty with adornments gathered from the whole world, and nature and art have combined alike to make them beautiful."

"All of which means, Aemilia," Pollio laughed, "that, in Beric's opinion, you are pretty to look at, but good for nothing else."

"I meant not that," Beric said eagerly, "only that the things you are good for are not the things which British women are good for. You have no occasion to be good housewives, because you have slaves who order everything for you. But you excel in many things of which a British woman never so much as heard. There is the same difference that there is between a cultured Roman and one of my tribesmen."

"Human nature is the same everywhere," Norbanus said, "fair or dark, great or small. It is modified by climate, by education, by custom, and by civilization, but at bottom it is identical. And now, Pollio, I think you had better take Beric down to the port, the sight of the trade and shipping will be new to him."

CHAPTER XII
A SCHOOL FOR GLADIATORS

As the vessels carrying Suetonius, his suite, and captives sailed up the Tiber it was met by a galley bearing the orders of the senate that Suetonius was not to traverse the streets with an armed suite and captives in his train, but was to land as a private person; that the soldiers were to march to the barracks on the Capitoline, where they would receive their arrears of pay and be disbanded; and that the captives were to be handed over to a centurion, who with his company would be at the landing place to receive them. Pollio took the news to Beric, who was on board the same ship, the rest of the captives being with the soldiers in the vessel which followed.

"I am rejoiced, indeed," he said, "for although I knew that the general would not receive a triumph, I feared that if he made a public entry it was possible there might be a public outcry for your life, which would, by our custom, have been forfeited had there been a triumph. I doubt not that the hand of Petronius is in this; his messengers would have arrived here weeks ago, and it may be that letters despatched as much as a month after we left have preceded us. Doubtless he would have stated that his clemency had had the desired effect, and that all trouble was at an end; he may probably have added that this was partly due to your influence, and warned them that were you put to death it would have a deplorable effect among your people and might cause a renewal of trouble. Suetonius is furious, for he has hoped much from the effect his entry with captives in his train would have produced. He has powerful enemies here; scarce a noble family but has lost a connection during the troubles in Britain, and Suetonius is of course blamed for it. You and I know that, although he has borne himself harshly towards the Britons, the rising was due to Catus rather than to him, but as Catus is a creature of Nero the blame falls upon Suetonius."

"It was the deeds of Catus that caused the explosion," Beric said; "but it would have come sooner or later. It was the long grinding tyranny that had well nigh maddened us, that drove Caractacus first to take up arms, that raised the western tribes, and made all feel that the Roman yoke was intolerable. The news of the massacre of the Druids and the overthrow of our altars converted the sullen discontent into a burning desire for revenge, and the insult to Boadicea was the signal rather than the cause of the rising. It is to the rule of Suetonius that it is due that hundreds of thousands of Britons, Romans, and their allies have perished."

"The fault of Suetonius," Pollio said, "was that he was too much of a soldier. He thought of military glory, and left all other matters, save the leading of his troops, in the hands of his civilians. Petronius is a general, but he has distinguished himself more in civil matters. Two generals have been sent out with him, to lead the troops if necessary, but he has been chosen as an administrator."

"They should have sent him out ten years ago," Beric said, "and there then would have been no occasion for generals."

They were now approaching Rome, and Beric's attention was entirely occupied by the magnificent scene before him, and with the sight of the temples and palaces rising thickly upon the seven hills. Massilia had surprised him by its size and splendour, but beside Rome it was only a village. "Rome would do well," he said to Pollio, "to bring the chiefs of every conquered country hither; the sight would do more than twenty legions to convince them of the madness of any efforts to shake off the Roman yoke."

"I will see you tomorrow," Pollio said as they neared the landing place. "I shall see many of my friends today, and get them to interest themselves in your behalf. I will find out for you where Caius Muro is at present; doubtless he too will do what he can for you, seeing that you lived so long in his charge;" for Beric had not mentioned to his friend aught of the manner in which he had saved Muro's daughter at the sack of Camalodunum.

As soon as the centurion came on board Pollio recommended Beric to his care, saying that he was the chief of the party of British captives, and that during the journey he had formed a close friendship with him.

"I shall not be in charge of him long," the centurion said. "I have but to hand him over to the governor of the prison, but I will tell him what you have said to me. He must now go on board the other ship and join his companions, for my orders are that they are not to be landed until after dark." Pollio nodded to Beric; this was another proof that it was determined the populace should not be excited in favour of Suetonius by the passage of the captives through the streets.

Beric rejoined his companions. "Well, Boduoc, what think you of Rome?"

"I have been thinking how mad our enterprise was, Beric. You told me about the greatness of Rome and from the first predicted failure, but I thought this was because you had been infected by your Roman training; I see now that you were right. Well, and what do you think is going to be done with us?"

"It is evident there is going to be no public display of us, Boduoc. Suetonius is at present in disgrace, and we shall be either sent into the school for gladiators, or set to work at some of the palaces Nero is building."

"They may do what they like," Boduoc said, "but I will not fight for their amusement. They may train me if they like and send me into the arena, but if they do I will not lift sword, but will bid my opponent slay me at once."

There was a murmur of assent from some of the others; but another who said, "Well, I would rather die fighting anyway than work as a slave at Roman palaces," found a response from several.

The next day they were marched up to Nero's palace.

Surprised as they might be by the splendour of the streets they traversed, and by the grandeur and magnificence of the palace, they betrayed no sign whatever of their feelings, but marched through the vast halls with their wealth of marble and adornments with calm and unmoved faces. At last they reached the audience hall, where the emperor was seated with a throng of courtiers behind him.

Nero was five-and-twenty, but looked older, for his dissolute habits had already left their marks upon his features. He had an air of good temper, and a rough frankness of manner that rendered him popular among the mass of the people, whom he courted by every means in his power, distributing with lavish hand the wealth he gained by confiscation and spoliation of the rich. The Britons bowed deeply before him and then stood upright and fearless.

"By Hercules," the emperor said to the councillor standing next to him, "but these are grand men! No wonder Suetonius has had such trouble in subduing them. And this young man is their chief? Truly, as Petronius said in his letter, he is but a lad. You speak our language too?" he went on, addressing Beric.

"I was brought up as a hostage among the Romans," he replied, "and was instructed in their language and literature."

"Then you should have known better than to rise against us, young chief."

"Two years ago I was but a boy, Caesar," Beric replied, "scarce deemed old enough to fight, much less to give an opinion in the presence of my elders. I was well aware that the struggle must end in our defeat; but when the chiefs of my nation decided for war, I had nought to do but to go with them."

"But how is it, then, that you came to command so many, and became in time the leader of so large a band?"

"It was because I had studied your military books, and knew that only by an irregular warfare could we hope to prolong our existence. It was no longer an insurrection; we were simply fugitives trying to sell our lives dearly. If Suetonius had offered us terms we would gladly have laid down our arms, but as he simply strove to destroy us we had, like animals brought to bay, to fight for our own lives. The moment Petronius offered to allow my people to return to their homes and pay tribute to Rome I advised them to submit."

"So Petronius tells me, and he has said much to excuse your conduct.

"I would I could enlist this band as my bodyguard," Nero said in a low voice, turning to his councillor, "but the praetorian guards are jealous of their privileges, and none save a Roman can be enrolled in their ranks."

"It would be dangerous, Caesar; the praetorians are well affected to your majesty, and in these days when there are so many ambitious generals at the head of armies it would be unwise to anger them."

"Then we will send them to the schools to be trained. Send this lad with the four best of the others to Scopus, and divide the rest among three other schools. The Romans have never seen such men as these in the arena. We must not spoil it by matching them at present with men whose skill more than makes up for their want of strength. Two years in the schools will make marvels of them. The lad will want more than that before he gains his full bulk and strength, but he will some day turn out such a gladiator as Rome has never seen; and if after a time we can find no champion to withstand him, we can match him against the lions. I will myself give Scopus orders concerning him."

So saying he waved his hand. The guards closed round the captives and they were led away.

"What is it all about, Beric?" Boduoc asked.

"We are to go to the school for gladiators," Beric said; "but as the emperor considers that you will all need two years' training at the exercises before you will be fit to appear in the ring, we shall have time to think matters over. Much may happen before that. Nero may be liked by the mass of the people, but he is hated and feared, as I hear, by the upper classes. He may be assassinated or overthrown before that."

"I don't see that it will make much difference to us," Boduoc grumbled.

"I don't know that it would. At any rate we have time before us. We shall be well taken care of, well fed, and have plenty of exercise. Before now the gladiators have shaken Rome to its centre. What has happened once may happen again."

As they passed along the streets of Rome the news that a party of fair haired giants were being escorted under a guard spread rapidly, and a crowd soon filled the streets. Windows opened and ladies looked curiously down at the procession. Beric marched at the head of his party, who followed four abreast, and their air of calmness and self possession, their proud bearing, and the massive strength of their figures roused the admiration of the multitude, who, on learning from the guards that the captives were Britons, greeted them with shouts of approval. So thick became the crowd before they reached their destination, that the Roman soldiers had difficulty in forcing their way through. As they turned into the street in which stood the great school of Scopus the crowd at once guessed the destination of the captives.

"By all the gods!" one of the lookers on said, "these fellows will furnish us with grand sport in the arena."

"It is a shame to turn such grand looking men into gladiators," a woman said.

"What, would you like to pick a husband out among them, dame?" the first speaker laughed.

"I would not mind. At any rate, I would prefer any of them to such an ill looking scarecrow as you," she retorted. "It is bad enough when they kill off some of those Gauls, who are far too good for such work; but the best of them I have seen in the arena lacks six inches, both in height and breadth of shoulder, of these Britons."

"Ah!" the man grumbled, "that is always the way with women; they think of nothing but strength."

"Why shouldn't we? Men think of nothing but beauty."

And so, amid a chorus of remarks, for the most part complimentary, the Britons strode along, surrounded by their escort, until they reached the entrance to the school of Scopus. The master, attracted by the noise in the street, was standing at the entrance. He was a broad built man, but without an ounce of superfluous flesh, with muscles and sinews standing up in knots and ridges, and evidently possessed of extreme activity as well as strength.

"Nero has sent you five fresh scholars, Scopus."

"By Hercules," Scopus said, "they are splendid barbarians! Whence come they?"

"They are Britons."

"Ah! Yes, Claudius brought back a few with him, but that was before I was here. I would they were all a few years younger. They are in their prime now; and to make a man first class, one should begin with him young. This youngster here is just the age. I warrant me there will not be many who can hold their own against him when I have trained him."

"He is their chief," the centurion said, "and speaks our language as well as you do."

"That is good. I can speak a little Gaulish; but there is always trouble with newcomers from out of the way countries when we have no one who speaks their language."

"Well, I will leave them with you; they are in your charge. I have the other fifteen to divide among three other schools."

"I will take care of them," Scopus said. "There is good feeding and good drinking here, and no one runs away. There is nowhere to run to, that is one thing. Still, what could a man want more than to be well housed, well fed, and have the companionship of plenty of good fellows? Don't you think so?" and he turned to Beric.

"It is of no use asking for more if one is not likely to get it; certainly we might do worse."

"Well, follow me," Scopus said. "I will introduce you to your comrades."

Beric and his companions took a hearty farewell of the others, Beric telling them that doubtless they would have frequent occasions of meeting; he then followed Scopus into a large hall. Here some forty or fifty men were assembled. Some were swinging weights round their heads, others were engaged at gymnastic exercises. Two men, under the direction of an instructor, were fighting with blunted swords; one great fellow, armed with sword and shield, was hotly pursuing an active man of little over half his weight, carrying a trident in one hand and a net in the other, amid the laughter of a group watching them.

At the entrance of Scopus and his companions the proceedings were arrested.

"Here are some fresh hands," Scopus said, "who have come to fill up the vacancies made in the games ten days since. They are Britons, and I should imagine will require a lot of training before they are fit for the arena. One of them talks Latin. The rest, I fancy, will have, for the present, to content themselves with the companionship of you Gauls, who are, as I believe, of kindred race, though it seems to me that either you must have fallen off in size, or they have increased since you separated."

Some seven or eight Gauls stepped forward and addressed the Britons, and the latter, glad to find men who could speak their language, responded heartily. The gladiators were of many races. Besides the Gauls there were four or five Goths; some Iberians, lean swarthy men; Numidians, fleet of foot, lithe and active--these were used more often for contests with wild beasts than in the gladiatorial conflicts, for which they lacked strength and weight--

Parthians and Scythians, together with a score of natives of Italy, Romans and others, who had taken to the profession of gladiator as they might have done to any other calling.

"Now," Scopus said to Beric, "you are free of the place; there are no prisoners here. There are regular hours and exercises; but beyond that your time is your own, to walk in the city, to see the shows, or to remain here. As you see, all here dress somewhat after Roman fashion, so that as they go abroad they may not be stared at. There is no obligation that way, but it is more comfortable. There are upwards of a hundred schools in Rome. Some are larger than mine, and some smaller, but there is not one that stands higher. When one of my men enters the ring the audience know that they are going to see good sport."

"Do we have to fight against each other, or against strangers?"

"Against strangers," Scopus said. "When there is going to be a show day, so many schools are warned to send three or four men, as the case may be, and the master of ceremonies matches them against each other. Sometimes there may be ten couples, sometimes forty or fifty, it depends whether it is a great occasion or not; and of course each school hopes to see its champions win. That fellow you saw running with a net, he is a Scythian, and so quick and nimble that he always gets away, and is ready for a throw again before his opponent can overtake him. He is a great favourite of the public, for he has been in the arena twelve times and has always conquered."

"What do you consider to be the best weapon--the trident or the sword?"

"If a man is active without being strong, I should make a retiarius of him," Scopus said. "If he is strong without being active, he would naturally fight with sword and buckler. Then there is the caestus, but the Romans do not care for that, though, to my mind, it is the finest of all the exercises; for that both strength and activity are required, but it is not bloody enough for the Romans. Perhaps the thing that demands the greatest skill and nerve and strength at the same time is to fight wild beasts. However, we settle none of these things at first. After a few months' training we see what a man's capabilities are, and what he himself has a fancy for. I always let a man choose, if he has any very strong wish in the matter, for he is sure to succeed best in that. There are many who, even with all my care, never turn out first class. These are reserved to fight in what may be called general contests, which have become popular lately, ten against ten, or fifty against fifty. On two or three grand occasions there have been as many as a thousand engaged. For these no particular skill is required; it is one side against the other. Lastly, there are a few who turn out so useless that it would be a waste of pains to try to make anything of them. These are sent to the galleys, or to the public works."

"You never find any unwilling to learn?" Beric said.

"Not one," the man said carelessly. "A man has to defend himself, and even with blunt swords he will get awkward cracks if he cannot protect his head. Besides, in the arena a man's life depends upon his skill, and the conquered is sure to have no mercy shown him unless he has borne himself well. Therefore, each man is anxious to learn. I have had a few obstinate fellows, for the most part Goths, who would do nothing. I simply send them down to the galleys, and I warrant me that they are not long in finding out what fools they have been, and would give a good deal to exchange their beds of hard boards and their coarse food for a life of pleasure and freedom here."

"As long as it lasts," Beric said.

"Yes, as long as it lasts. But with all its dangers it is likely to last as long as that of a galley slave. What with bad food and hardship and toil and the taskmaster's whip and the burning sun, a galley slave's life is a short one; while a skilful gladiator may live for many years, and in time save money enough to set up a school as I have done."

"Were you a gladiator once?" Beric asked.

"Certainly I was; and so were all the masters of the schools, except, perhaps, a few Greeks, whose methods differ from ours.

"I was ten years in the arena, and fought thirty-five battles. In thirty I was victorious, in the other five I was defeated; but as I was a favourite, and always made a good fight, the thumbs were turned up, which, as you may know, is the signal for mercy."

"Are you a Roman?"

"No, I am a Thessalian. I took to it young, having got into trouble at home. We have blood feuds there, and having killed the chief of a house with which my people had a quarrel I had to fly, and so made to Pola. Thence I crossed to Brundusium. I worked there in the dockyard for a year or two; but I was never fond of hard work of that sort, so I came on here and entered a school. Now, as you see, I am master of one. A gladiator who distinguishes himself gets many presents, and I did well. The life is not a bad one after all."

"It must be hateful having to fight with men with whom you have no quarrel," Beric said.

"You don't feel that after the first minute or two," Scopus laughed. "There is a man standing opposite to you with a sword or a trident, and you know very well that if you do not kill him, he is going to kill you. It makes very little difference, after you once face each other, whether there was any quarrel between him and you beforehand or not; the moment the fighting begins, there is an end of all nonsense of that sort.

"What is an enemy? A man who wants to do you harm. This man facing you is going to kill you, unless you kill him. There cannot be a worse enemy than that. After all, it is just the same with soldiers in a battle. They have no particular quarrel with the men facing them; but directly the arrows begin to fly, and a storm of javelins come singing through the air, you think of nothing but of trying to kill the men who are trying to kill you. I thought as you do before I entered the arena the first time, but I never felt so afterwards. All these things are matters of usage, and the gladiator, after his first combat, enters the ring with just the same feeling as a soldier marches to meet an enemy."

Beric was silent. He had no doubt that there was some truth in what Scopus said; his own experience in battle had shown him this. But he was still determined in his mind that, come what would, he would not fight for the amusement of the Romans. But it was of no use to say this now; it might be a long time before he was required to enter the arena, and until then he might as well apply himself to gaining strength and science in arms. It did not seem to him that there was any possibility of escape, but he might at least take to the woods, and stand at bay there, and be killed in a fair open fight. The next morning the exercises began. They were at first of a moderate character, and were only intended to strengthen the muscles and add to the endurance. For the first six months they were told that their work would consist only of gymnastic exercises--lifting weights, wielding heavy clubs, climbing ropes, wrestling, and running on foot. Their food was simple but plentiful. All adopted the Roman costume, in order to avoid observation when they went abroad. Being a strong body, and individually formidable, they were free from the rough jokes generally played upon newcomers, and when, after six hours of exercise, they sat down to a hearty dinner, the general feeling among them was that things were better than they expected, and the life of a gladiator, with the exception of his appearances in the arena, was by no means a bad one. Pollio called in the afternoon, as he had promised, and had a long talk with Beric.

"In the first place, I have some bad news for you, Beric. Caius Muro remained here but a month after his return from Britain, and was then sent to command the legion in the north of Syria."

"That is bad news indeed, Pollio. I had looked forward to seeing him. I had made sure that I should find one friend at least in Rome."

"It is unfortunate indeed, Beric, for he would have spoken for you, and might have obtained a better lot for you. I hate seeing you here," he said passionately, "but it is better than being executed at once, which is the lot that generally befalls the chief of captives taken in war. Scopus is not a bad fellow when things go well, but they say that he is a fiend when his blood is up. He is one of the finest fighters we ever had in the arena, though he left it before I was old enough to go there. I know him well, however, for I used to come here with my elder brother, who was killed four years ago in Africa. It is quite the fashion among the young Romans to go the round of the schools and see the gladiators practising, and then when the sports come on they bet on the men they consider the most skilful."

"A fine sport," Beric said sarcastically.

"Well, you see, Beric, we have been bred up to it, and we wager upon it just as you Britons do on your fights between cocks. I never felt any hesitation about it before, because I had no particular personal interest in any of the combatants. After all, you know, life is dull in Rome for those who take no part in politics, who have no ambition to rise at the court, and who do not care overmuch for luxury. We have none of the hunting with which you harden your muscles and pass your time in Britain. Therefore it is that the sports of the arena are so popular with our class as well as with that below it. You must remember, too, that the greater portion of the gladiators are captives taken in war, and would have been put to death at once had they not been kept for this."

"I do not say they have anything to complain of, Pollio, but I am sure that most of them would much rather perish in battle than be killed in the arena."

"Yes, but it is not a question of being killed in battle, Beric; it is a question of being captured in battle and put to death afterwards. It may be the fashion some day or other to treat captives taken in war with generosity and honour, but it certainly is not so at present, either with us or with any other nation that I know of. I don't think that your people differ from the rest, for every soul who fell into their hands was slain."

"I quite admit that," Beric said; "and should have had no cause for complaint had I been slain as soon as I was captured. But there is something nobler in being killed as a victim of hate by a victorious enemy than to have to fight to the death as a holiday amusement."

"I admit that," Pollio said, "and though, since Nero came to the throne, there has been an increase in these gladiatorial displays, methinks there are fewer now than in the days before the Empire, when Spartacus led twenty thousand gladiators against Rome. There is one thing, if the creed of those Jews of whom Norbanus was speaking to you ever comes to be the dominant religion, there will be an end to the arena, for so averse are these people to fighting, that when placed in the arena they will not make even an effort to defend themselves. They do not, as do the Goths sometimes, lower their swords and fall on the points. Suicide they consider wrong, and simply wait calmly like sheep to be killed. I have been talking with some friends over the persecutions of two years ago, just after I left for Britain, and they say it was wonderful to see the calmness with which the Christians meet death. They say the persecution was given up simply because the people became sick of spectacles in which there was no interest or excitement. Well, Beric, are you ready to go out with me?"

"You will not be ashamed to walk through the streets with a gladiator, Pollio?"

"Ashamed! on the contrary, you must know that gladiators are in fashion at present, Beric. The emperor prides himself on his skill, and consorts greatly with gladiators, and has even himself fought in the arena, and therefore it is the thing with all who are about the court to affect the society of gladiators. But as yet you are not one of them although you may have commenced your training for the arena. But fashion or not, it would have made no difference to me, you are my friend whatever evil fortune may have done for you. The only difference is that whereas, had you not been in fashion, I should have taken you with me only to the houses of intimate friends, as I did at Massilia, now you will be welcome everywhere. Besides, Beric, even in Rome a chief who has kept Suetonius at bay for a year, and who is, moreover, a Latin scholar accustomed to Roman society, is recognized as being an object of great interest, especially when he is young and good looking. I am glad to see that you have adopted clothes of our fashion; they set you off to much better advantage than does the British garb, besides attracting less attention."

"I hope that you are not going to take me today to meet any people, Pollio; I want to see the temples and public buildings."

"It shall be just as you wish, Beric."

For hours Beric wandered about Rome with Pollio, so interested in all he saw that he was scarce conscious of the attention he himself attracted. From time to time they met acquaintances of Pollio, who introduced them to Beric as "my friend the chief of the Iceni, who cost us a year's hard work and some twelve hundred men before we captured him. Petronius has written so strongly to Nero in his favour that his life has been spared, and he has been placed in the school of Scopus;" and the languid young Romans, looking at Beric's height and proportions, no longer wondered at the trouble that the Roman legions had had in overcoming the resistance of a mere handful of barbarians. Beric on his part was by no means surprised at the appearance of these young courtiers. He had seen many of the same type at Camalodunum, and had heard Caius lament the effeminacy of the rising generation; but he knew that these scented young nobles could, if necessary, buckle on armour and fight as valiantly as the roughest soldier; though why they should choose to waste their lives at present in idleness, when there was so much work to be done in every corner of the vast empire, was altogether beyond his comprehension.

"Why is there a crowd gathered round that large building?" he asked Pollio.

"That is one of the public granaries. Corn is brought here in vast quantities from Sardinia and Sicily, from Spain and Africa, and since Nero came to the throne it is distributed gratis to all who choose to apply for it. No wonder Nero is popular among the people; he feeds them and gives them shows--they want nothing more. It is nothing to them, the cruelties he exercises upon the rich."

"But it must encourage the people in lazy habits," Beric said.

Pollio shrugged his shoulders. "They think because they are citizens of the capital of the world they have a right to live in idleness, and that others should work for them. At any rate it keeps them in a good temper. There have been great tumults in Rome in past times, but by drawing the tribute in corn and distributing it freely here Nero keeps them in a high state of contentment."

"You don't like Nero, Pollio?"

"I hate him," Pollio said. "He is a tyrant--greedy, cruel, and licentious. He had his own mother murdered because she opposed his plans, and some of our best and noblest citizens have been put to death, either because Nero was jealous of their popularity, or because he desired to grasp their possessions. It is horrible that Rome, which has conquered the world, should lie prostrate at the feet of a creature like this. It was because my father feared that some spy among the slaves might report what I said about Nero that caused him to send me out to Suetonius, who is a connection of our family, and he will ere long obtain for me some other employment away from the capital. I shall be glad to be gone, the atmosphere here seems to stifle one. Nero's spies are everywhere, and a man is afraid of speaking his thoughts even in his own house. I like to take life easily, but I would rather be battling with your people in the swamps than living in idleness in Rome."

"I thought you were glad to return, Pollio?"

"I thought I should be, Beric, but I suppose the active life in Britain has spoilt me. I used to scent my hair and lounge in the baths, and frequent the shows, and lead just such a life as the young men we have spoken to this afternoon, and I was contented with it. I wonder at myself now, but I cannot take up the old life where I left it. I have been back for twenty-four hours, and I am restless already and am longing to be doing something."

"I should think," Beric said with a smile, "that you might well put up with Rome for a few weeks. It seems to me that it will take years to know all its wonders. There are the great libraries, too, filled with the manuscripts, and as you understand Greek you could study the writings of the sages and philosophers."

"I would rather row in the galleys," Pollio said. "I don't mind an hour or two now and then with the historians, but the philosophers are too deep for my shallow brain. Would you like to look into a library now?"

Beric assented eagerly, and they entered one of these buildings. It consisted of a great hall with innumerable couches and benches for readers. Round the walls were pigeonholes, in which the manuscripts were deposited, and numerous attendants moved to and fro among the readers, supplying them with such manuscripts as they desired, and taking away those they had done with. Leaving the hall they passed through a series of large apartments, in which hundreds of men were at work copying manuscripts.

"These are scribes," Pollio said. "Very many of them are slaves whom the owners allow to work here, sharing with them their earnings; others are freedmen who have either purchased their liberty from their savings, or have been manumitted by their owners. You see many of the most popular writings, such as those of Caesar, Tacitus, Livy, or the poets Horace, Virgil, and Ovid, are constantly in demand, and scores of copies must be kept on hand. Then again many of the Greek authors are greatly in request. The manuscripts wear out and must be replaced, so that at the various libraries there are some thousands of scribes always kept employed. You see among the scribes men of many nationalities. Those men, for instance, are Egyptians. You see the rolls they are copying, they are made of papyrus, which is got, as I have heard my uncle say, from the leaf of a sort of water plant. Some of them are copying these writings on to vellum for the use of those who understand the Egyptian language, others are translating them into Latin. Those men are Persians, and those at the tables near them are Jews. They are making translations of their sacred books, which are much read at present, partly owing to the fact that the people are troublesome, and probably an army will have to be sent against them, partly because of the Christian sect, whose doctrines are founded upon the Jewish sacred books, and are supported, as they claim, by various prognostications of their augurs, or, as they call them, prophets. The books, therefore, are of interest to the learned, and it may be that some who come here to read them are secretly disciples of the sect."

"Can I come here and read?" Beric asked eagerly.

"Certainly you can, these libraries are open to all. So are the baths, at least the greater portion of them; everything is free here. But it is nearly time for us now to be going home."

Beric availed himself at once of the advantages offered by the public libraries. It was only thus that men of moderate means could in those days obtain access to books, for the cost of manuscripts was considerable, and libraries were only to be found in the houses of the wealthy. His taste for reading was a matter of astonishment among the gladiators, and was the subject of a good deal of jesting. This, however, was for the most part of a good natured kind, but upon the part of one named Lupus it was sneering and offensive.

This man, who was a professional gladiator, that is one of those who had taken to it as a trade, was a Roman of unusual stature and strength. He had been a worker in iron, and from making arms took to their use. He had won many victories in the arena, and was considered the champion of the school of Scopus, the only man who approached him in the number of victories being Porus, the Scythian, whose strong point, however, lay in his activity and his dexterity in throwing the net rather than in strength. Lupus had, from the first day of the Britons' arrival at the ludus, viewed them with aversion, his hostility to Beric being especially marked, and he particularly objected to the slight deference shown to him by his companions, in spite of the protests of Beric himself, who in vain pointed out to them that he was now no longer their chief, and that they were in all respects comrades and equals.

Lupus had carefully abstained from any remarks that would bring him into collision with the other Britons. Mortified as he was that his strength and stature, of which he was very proud, had been thrown into the shade by that of the newcomers, he felt that in a quarrel their rough strength might render them more than his match. Beric, however, he considered as but a youth, and though doubtless powerful, deemed that his muscles would be no match for his own seasoned strength. As yet he had not seen Beric tried with any arms, and thought that the young barbarian could know nothing of the management of weapons. At first his annoyance only took the form of addressing him with an affected deference as "my lord Beric;" but the discovery that, while he himself was unable to read or write, the young Briton was fond of study, and spent his spare time in the public libraries, afforded him opportunities for constant sneers.

These Beric took in good part, but Boduoc, who had now picked up enough Latin to understand the gist of his remarks, one day intervened, and seizing Lupus by the shoulder dashed him to the ground. The Roman sprang to his feet, caught up a knife from the table, and rushed at Boduoc. Scopus, however, who was present, with an angry growl sprang upon him, seizing him by the throat with so vigorous a grasp that his face became purple, his eyes stared, and he in vain gasped for breath. Then he flung him down into a corner of the room with such force that he lay half stunned.

"You dog," he exclaimed, "how dare you take a knife? I will have no quarrels here, as you know; and if you again venture on a disturbance I will bid your comrades tie you up, and will flay the skin off your back with the lash. The Briton was perfectly right. Why can't you leave his friend alone? I have marked your ill natured jests before, and am glad that he punished you."

Lupus rose slowly to his feet with an angry glare in his eyes. He knew, however, that Scopus had in his time been unrivalled in the arena, and that, moreover, the rest, who had been offended by his airs of superiority, would side with the lanista against him.

"I said nothing to the Briton," he said; "it was the boy I addressed. If it was an offence, why did he not take it up? Is he a coward that others have to fight his battles? If he is offended, why does he not challenge me to fight, as is customary in all the ludi?"

"Because he is as yet but a pupil, and will not be fit to enter the arena for three or four years," Scopus said. "A fight can only be between trained gladiators. You don't suppose that a fresh joined youth is going to fight with one who has won a score of times in the arena?"

"Excuse me, Scopus," Beric said quietly, "I am perfectly ready to fight with this braggadocio, and challenge him to a contest; a few hard knocks will do neither of us any harm, therefore let us go into the school and have it out. It is much better so than to have perpetual quarrelling."

Scopus would have objected, but the gladiators broke into shouts of "A fight! a fight!" and, as it was according to the rules of all the ludi that quarrels should be fought out with wooden swords without interference by the lanistae, he simply shrugged his shoulders.

"Well, as he has challenged you, Lupus, I have nothing to say to it;" and the whole of those present at once adjourned to the school.

The combatants were armed with bucklers and with swords of the same weight to those ordinarily used, but with square edges with the corners rounded off, so that though they would give a heavy blow they would not cut.

Lupus, confident in his skill, and furious at the humiliation he had just suffered, at once sprang upon Beric, but the latter as nimbly leaped back, catching the blow on his buckler, and at the same time bringing his own with such force and weight upon the Roman's left shoulder that it brought him for a moment on his knee. A shout of astonishment and applause burst from the lookers on. Lupus would have instantly renewed the fight, but Beric stepped back and lowered his sword.

"Your left arm is disabled," he said. "You had best wait till you can use your buckler again; it would not be a fair match now."

Furious as he was, Lupus felt the truth of what his opponent said, and though the burst of applause at Beric's magnanimity angered him even more than before, he drew back a step or two. At the order of Scopus two of the others came forward with some oil, with which for some minutes they kneaded his shoulder.

"I am ready again," he said at last, and the gladiators drew back, and the opponents faced each other. Lupus had learned that Beric was not, as he had supposed, entirely untaught; but although he attributed the blow he had received solely to his own rashness, he renewed the conflict with the same care and prudence he would have shown had he been fighting with edged weapons in the arena. He soon found, however, that he had met with an opponent differing widely from those he had hitherto fought. Beric had had excellent teachers among the veteran legionaries at Camalodunum, and to skill in the sword he added a prodigious activity. Instead of fighting in the ordinary Roman method, standing firm, with the body bent forward and the buckler stretched out at the level of the shoulder in front of him, he stood lightly poised on his feet, ready to spring forward or back, and with his shield across his body.

In vain Lupus tried to get to close quarters. His cramped attitude prevented rapid movement, and he could not get even within striking distance of his opponent save when the latter sprang in to deliver a blow. These, however, fell vainly, for Lupus was fighting now calmly and warily, and with sword or shield guarded every blow aimed at him. Beric soon felt that he should but exhaust himself did he continue to attack in this fashion, and presently desisted, and standing his ground awaited the attack of Lupus. The blows fell fast and heavy now. Then Beric purposely lowered his buckler a moment; Lupus instantly struck, springing a pace forward. Beric sharply threw up his left arm, striking up the hand of Lupus as it fell, and at the same moment brought his weapon with tremendous force down upon the head of his antagonist, who fell as if killed.

"Habet, habet!" shouted the gladiators, alike exultant and astonished at the defeat of the bully of the school.

"By the gods, Beric," Scopus said, "you have given him a lesson. I talked abut four years' training, but even now I would send you into the arena without fear. Why, there are but one or two gladiators who are considered the superior of Lupus with the sword, and he had from the first no chance with you."

"It was simply because he did not understand my way of fighting," Beric said quietly. "No, Scopus, I will have the four years' training before I fight. I have chanced to overcome Lupus this time, but I am not going to match myself against men until I have my full strength."

Scopus laughed. "That looks as if there was strength enough in your arm, Beric," he said pointing to the prostrate figure. "However, I know from what you have said that you wish to put off your entry into the arena as long as possible, and doubtless practice and teaching will render you a far better swordsman than you are now. Take him away," he said to the others, pointing to Lupus. "Dash cold water over him till he comes round, and then bandage his head. I doubt if his skull be not broken. One of you had better go for a leech to examine him; and mind, let not a word be breathed outside the school as to this contest. We will keep it silent until it is time for Beric to enter the arena, and then we shall be dull indeed if we do not lay bets enough on him to keep us in wine for a year. There is no fear of Lupus himself saying a word about it. You may be sure that, roughly shaken as his conceit may be, he will hold his tongue as to the fact that he has found his master in what he was pleased to call a boy. Mind, if I ever hear a word spoken outside the school on the subject, I will make it my business to find out who spread the report, and it will be very bad for the man who did it when I bring it home to him."

It was upwards of a week before Lupus was able to enter the gymnasium again. Beric had particularly requested the others to make no allusion to his discomfiture, but from that time the superiority of Lupus was gone, and Beric's position in the school was fully established.

CHAPTER XIII
A CHRISTIAN

While Beric thus spent his time between his exercises and the schools and one or other of the libraries, varied occasionally by paying a visit with Pollio, Boduoc and his companions were not ill contented with their life. Most of them had, during the long journey through Gaul, picked up a few words of Latin from their guards, and as it was the language of the gymnasium, and was the only medium by which the men of the various nationalities could communicate with each other, they now rapidly increased their knowledge of it, Beric strongly urging them to become acquainted with it as soon as possible, as it might be most useful and important to them. None of the others besides Boduoc were, Scopus thought, ever likely to be a credit to him in the more serious contests in the ring, but all showed an aptitude for wrestling and boxing, and the lanista was well content with this, as the games in the arena frequently commenced with these comparatively harmless sports, and in many of the provincial cities wrestlers and boxers were in great request.

Beric was much pleased when he heard from the master that he intended to confine his teaching to these two exercises only with regard to his companions; for although men were sometimes seriously hurt by blows given by the masses of leather and lead, which, wound round the fist, were used to give weight to the blows, a final termination to the contests was rare. In the exercises the men practised with many wrappings of wadding and cotton wound round the caestus, answering the purpose of the modern boxing glove. Beric himself was very partial to the exercise, and as it strengthened the muscles, and gave quickness and activity to the limbs, Scopus encouraged him in it.

"I do not see the use of the caestus," Beric said one day. "One could hit and guard much more quickly without it. It is good, no doubt, for exercise, as it strengthens the muscles, but surely for fighting it would be better to lay it aside. What is the advantage of it? With the bare fist one can knock an opponent down, and with a very few blows strike him senseless. What more can you want than that?"

"Yes, for men like you Britons that would do, for a straight blow from any one of you would well nigh break in the bones of the face of an ordinary man, and, as you say, you could strike much more quickly without the weight on your hands, but with smaller men a contest might last for hours without the caestus, and the spectators would get tired of it; but I will try the experiment some day, and put up one of the Britons against Asthor the Gaul, hands against the caestus, and see what comes of it. At present he is more skilful than any of your people, but they are getting on fast, and when one of them is fairly his match in point of skill I will try it. If the Briton wins, I will, when they first go into the arena, match them against the champions of the other schools with bare hands against armed ones, and they will get great credit if they win under those conditions. Both at that and at wrestling you Britons are likely to carry all before you. I should like to train you all only for that."

"I wish you would," Beric said earnestly.

"There is less honour in winning at wrestling and boxing than in the other contests," Scopus said.

"For that I care nothing whatever, Scopus; besides, you would get more credit from my winning in those games than from my being killed in the others. Strength and height count for much in them, while against an active retiarius strength goes for very little."

"But you are active as well as strong, Beric, and so is Boduoc. Moreover, when Caesar sent you to me to be prepared for the ring, he meant that you should take part in the principal contests, and he would be furious if, on some great occasion, when he expected to see you stand up against a famous champion, it turned out that you were only a wrestler."

"I am ready and willing to learn all the exercises, Scopus--I should like to excel in them all--but you might put me up as a wrestler and boxer; then if Nero insisted on my betaking myself to other weapons, I could do so without discredit to you. But my opinion is that every man should do what he can do best. Were we to fight with clubs, I think that we need have no fear of any antagonists; but our strength is for the most part thrown away at sword play, at which any active man with but half our strength is our match. You have told me that Nero often looks in at your school, and doubtless he will do so when he comes back from Greece. You could then tell him that you had found that all the Britons were likely to excel rather in wrestling and boxing, where their strength and height came into play, than in the other exercises, and that you therefore were instructing them chiefly in them."

"I will see what I can do," Scopus said. "I like you Britons, you are good tempered, and give me no trouble. I will tell you what I will do, I will send to Greece for the best instructor in wrestling I can get hold of, they are better at that than we are, and wrestling has always ranked very high in their sports. Most of you already are nearly a match for Decius; but you are all worth taking pains about, for there are rich prizes to be won in the provincial arenas, as well as at Rome; and in Greece, where they do not care for the serious contests, there is high honour paid to the winners in the wrestling games."

As time went on Beric had little leisure to spend in libraries, for the exercises increased in severity, and as, instead of confining himself, as most of the others did, to one particular branch, he worked at them all, the day was almost entirely given up to exercises of one kind or another. His muscles, and those of his companions, had increased vastly under the training they received. All had been accustomed to active exercise, but under their steady training every ounce of superfluous flesh disappeared, their limbs became more firmly knit, and the muscles showed out through the clear skin in massive ridges.

"We should astonish them at home, Beric," Boduoc said one day. "It is strange that people like the Romans, who compared to us are weakly by nature, should have so studied the art of training men in exercises requiring strength. I used to wonder that the Roman soldiers could wield such heavy spears and swords. Now I quite understand it. We were just as nature made us, they are men built up by art. Why, when we began, my arms used to ache in a short time with those heavy clubs, now I feel them no more than if they were willow wands."

Pollio had remained but two months in Rome, and had then gone out with a newly appointed general to Syria. Beric had missed his light hearted friend much, but he was not sorry to give up the visits with him to the houses of his friends. He felt that in these houses he was regarded as a sort of show, and that the captured British chief, who was acquainted with the Latin tongue and with Roman manners, was regarded with something of the same curiosity and interest as a tamed tiger might be. Besides, however much gladiators might be the fashion in Rome, he felt a degradation in the calling, although he quite appreciated the advantage that the training would be to him should he ever return to Britain. He was pleased to learn from Pollio, on the day before he started, that he had heard that his uncle would ere long return to Rome.

"I believe," he said, "that it is entirely my aunt's doing. You know how she hates what she calls her exile, and I hear that she has been quietly using all her family influence to obtain his recall and his appointment as a magistrate here. I learn she is likely to succeed, and that my uncle will be one of these fine days astounded at receiving the news that he is appointed a magistrate here. I don't suppose he will ever learn my aunt's share in the matter, and will regard what others would take as a piece of supreme good luck as a cruel blow of fortune. However, if he did discover it, my aunt would maintain stoutly that she did it for the sake of the girls, whom she did not wish to see married to some provincial officer, and condemned, as she had been, to perpetual exile; and as she would have the support of all her relations, and even of my father, who is also convinced that it is the greatest of all earthly happiness for a Roman to reside at Rome, my uncle for once will have to give in. Aemilia, too, will be glad to return to Rome, though I know that Ennia is of a different opinion. I believe, from what she let drop one day, that she has a leaning towards the new sect, of which she has heard from the old slave who was her nurse. It will be a great misfortune if she has, for it would cause terrible trouble at home, and if any fresh persecution breaks out, she might be involved. I am sure my aunt has no suspicion of it, for if she had the slave would be flogged to death or thrown to the fishes, and Ennia's life would be made a burden to her till she consented to abandon the absurd ideas she had taken up."

But if Norbanus had returned with his family to Rome, Beric had heard nothing of it. Had Pollio been at Rome he would at once have taken him to see them on their return, but now that he had gone there was no one from whom he would hear of their movements, and Norbanus himself would be so much occupied with his new duties, and with the society with which Lesbia would fill the house, that he would have no time to inquire about the British captive he had received as his guest at Massilia.

One evening, when the rest of the gladiators were engaged in a hot discussion as to the merits of some of those who were to appear at the games given in celebration of the funeral obsequies of a wealthy senator, Beric asked Boduoc to accompany him for a walk.

"One gets sick of all that talk about fighting," he said as they went out. "How men can sit indoors in a hot room heavy with the smoke of the lamps, when they can go out on such a lovely night as this, I cannot understand. We do not have such nights as this at home, Boduoc."

"No," Boduoc assented reluctantly, for it was seldom that he would allow anything Roman to be superior to what he was accustomed to in Britain; "the nights are certainly fine here, and so they need be when it is so hot all day that one can scarcely breathe outside the house. It seems to me that the heat takes all the strength out of my limbs."

Beric laughed. "It did not seem so, Boduoc, when today you threw Borthon, who is as heavy and well nigh as strong as yourself, full five yards through the air. Let us turn out from these busy streets and get among the hills--not those on which the palaces stand, but away from houses and people."

"What a night it would be for wolf hunting!" Boduoc said suddenly, when they had walked along for some distance in silence.

"Yes, that was fine sport, Boduoc; and when we slew we knew we were ridding the land of fierce beasts."

"Well, many of the gladiators are not much better, Beric. There is Porus, who may be likened to a panther; there is Chresimus, who is like a savage bull; Gripus, who, when not at work, is for ever trying to stir up strife. Truly, I used to think, Beric, that I could not slay a man unless he was an enemy, but I scarce feel that now. The captives in war are like ourselves, and I would not, if I could help it, lift sword against them. But many of the men are malefactors, who have been sentenced to death as gladiators rather than to death by the executioner, and who, by the terms of the sentence, must be killed within the course of a year. Well, there is no objection to killing these; if you do not do it, someone else will. Then there are the Romans, these are the roughest and most brutal of all; they are men who have been the bullies of their quarters, who fight for money only, and boast that it is a disappointment to them when, by the vote of the spectators, they have to spare an antagonist they have conquered. It is at least as good a work to kill one of these men as to slay a wolf at home. Then there are the patricians, who fight to gain popular applause, and kill as a matter of fashion; for them I have assuredly no pity.

"No, I hope I shall never have to stand up against a captive like myself but against all others I can draw my sword without any of the scruples I used to feel. I hear that if one of us can but hold his own for three years, in most cases he is given his liberty. I do not mean that he would be allowed to go home, but he is free from the arena."

They were now near the summit of one of the hills, where a clear sweep had been made of all the houses standing there in order that a stately temple should be erected on the site. Suddenly they heard a scream in a female voice.

"There is some villainy going on, Boduoc, let us break in upon the game." They ran at the top of their speed in the direction from which they had heard the cry, and came upon a group of seven or eight men, belonging, as they could see by the light of the moon, to the dregs of the city. A female was lying on the ground, another was clinging to her, and two men with coarse jeers and laughter were dragging her from her hold when the two Britons ran up.

Beric struck one of the men to the ground with a terrible blow, while Boduoc seizing the other hurled him through the air, and he fell head foremost among a heap of the masonry of a demolished building. The other men drew their knives, but as Beric and his companion turned upon them there was a cry, "They are gladiators," and the whole of them without a moment's hesitation took to their heels.

Beric then turned towards the females, and as the light of the moon fell full on his face the one with whom the men had been struggling exclaimed, "Why, it is surely Beric!"

Beric looked at her in surprise. "It is the lady Ennia!" he exclaimed. "Why, what are you doing at this time of night in so lonely a place, and without other attendants than this woman?"

"It is my nurse," Ennia said; "I was on my way with her, Beric, to a secret meeting of Christians held in an underground room of one of the villas that stood here. I have been there several times before and we have not been molested, but, as I gathered from what the men said, they noticed the light fall upon my necklace and bracelet as I passed by a lamp, and so followed us. Happily they overtook us before we reached the place of meeting. Had they followed us farther they might have come upon us there, and then much more harm would have been done. They came up and roughly demanded who we were, and bade me hand over my jewels. Lycoris answered them, and they struck her down. I threw myself down on her and clung to her, but they would soon have plundered and perhaps killed me had not you arrived."

"Do not you think, Ennia, that it is foolish and wrong of you thus to go out unprotected at night to such a place as this, and, as I suppose, without the knowledge of your father and mother?"

"They do not know," she said, "but it is my duty to go. It is the only opportunity I have for hearing the Word preached."

"I cannot think, Ennia, that it is your duty," Beric said gravely. "The first duty of a young woman is to obey her parents, and I think that you, being as yet scarce a woman, are not able to judge between one religion and another. I know nothing of the doctrines of this sect save what your father told me; but he said that they were good and pure, and, being so, I am sure that they cannot countenance disobedience to parents."

"The words are 'Forsake all, and follow Me,'" Ennia said firmly.

"That could not have been said to one of your age, Ennia. I was reading the Jewish sacred book the other day, and one of the chief commandments is to honour your father and mother. Well, I think, at any rate, that it were best not to go there tonight. These men may return, and at any rate I will not allow you thus to wander about at night unprotected. Boduoc and I will escort you to your house. When you get there I trust that you will think this over, and that you will see that such midnight excursions are altogether wrong, whatever the motive may be; but at any rate, if you must go, I must obtain your promise that you will write to me at the school of Scopus the gladiator, to tell me at what hour you start. I shall not intrude my presence upon you, nor accompany you, for this would be to make myself an accomplice in what I consider your folly; but I shall always be near you, and if you are again disturbed on your way Boduoc and I will be at hand to punish those who meddle with you."

The old nurse by this time had regained her feet.

"You are the nurse of this young lady," Beric said to her sternly, "and should know better than to bring her into danger. If Norbanus knew what you have done he would have you cut in pieces."

"It is not the fault of Lycoris. She begged and entreated me not to come, but I would not listen to her. You are angry with me, Beric, but you would not be angry if you knew what it was to me. Younger than I have died for the Faith, and I would die too if it were necessary."

Beric made no reply, he was indeed deeply vexed at what he considered an act of mad folly. The daughters of Norbanus had been very friendly and kind to him at Massilia, and he felt a debt of gratitude to their father; and this escapade on the part of Ennia, who was as yet scarce sixteen, vexed him exceedingly. He was not sure, indeed, but that he ought to go straight to Norbanus and tell him what had happened, yet he feared that in such a case the anger of the magistrate would be so great that Ennia would be forced by him into becoming one of the vestal virgins, or be shut up in strict imprisonment. Scarce a word was spoken as they passed down the hill and into the streets, now almost deserted. At last Ennia stopped at the entrance used by the slaves to her father's house.

"Will you give me your promise," he asked, "about going out at night again? I implore you, I beseech you do not again leave the house of your father at night unknown to him. You cannot tell the dangers you run by so doing, or the misery you may bring, not only on yourself, but on your parents."

"I promise you," Ennia said. "I owe you so great a debt of gratitude that even your harsh words do not anger me. I will think over what you have said, and try to do what may seem to me my duty."

"That is all I ask," Beric said more gently; and then turning walked away with Boduoc, who had but faintly understood what was being said, but was surprised at the recognition between Beric and this girl, whom he had not particularly noticed when at Massilia.

"That is Pollio's cousin, the younger daughter of the magistrate I stayed with at Massilia. It was well for her that it was not Pollio who came to her rescue instead of us."

"I should say so," Boduoc said dryly. "Pollio would scarcely be a match for eight cutthroats."

"I did not mean that, Boduoc. I meant that he would have rated her soundly."

"It seemed to me that you were rating her somewhat soundly, Beric. I scarce ever heard you speak so harshly before, and I wondered the more as you are neither kith nor kin to her, while by the heartiness with which you scolded her you might have been her own brother."

"I did not think whether I had a right to scold her or not, Boduoc. I liked both the maiden and her sister, and their father was very kind to me. Moreover, after all Pollio has done for us, the least I could do was to look after his cousin. But even if I had known nothing whatever of her or her friends, I should have spoken just as I did. The idea of a young girl like that wandering about at night with no one but an old slave to protect her in an unfrequented quarter of Rome! It is unheard of."

"But what were they doing there, Beric?"

"They were going to a meeting place of a new religion there is in Rome. The people who belong to it are persecuted and obliged to meet in secret. The old woman belongs to it, and has, I suppose, taught Ennia. I have heard that the sect is spreading, and that although most of those who adhere to it are slaves, or belong to the poorer class, there are many of good family who have also joined it."

"Well, I should have thought," Boduoc said, "that the Romans had no cause to be dissatisfied with their gods. They have given them victory, and dominion, and power, and wealth. What more could they want of them? I could understand that we, whose god did nothing to assist us in our fight against the Romans, should seek other gods who might do more for us. But that a Roman should have been discontented with his gods is more than I can understand. But what is that sudden flash of light?"

"It is a fire, and in these narrow streets, with a brisk wind blowing, it may well spread. There, do you hear the watchmen's trumpets giving the alarm? Let us get back quickly, Boduoc. It may be that we shall be all turned out to fight the fire if it spreads."

They were not far from the school now, and a few minutes' run took them there. The house was quiet, but a few oil lamps burning here and there enabled them to make their way to the broad planks, arranged like a modern guard bed, on which they slept with their three comrades.

"Is that you, Beric?" Scopus, who slept in a cubicule leading off the great room, asked.

"Yes it is; Boduoc and I."

"You are very late," he growled. "Late hours are bad for the health. Are you sober?"

Beric laughed.

"No, I need not ask you," Scopus went on. "If it had been some of the others who had been out so late, I should have been sure they would have come home as drunk as hogs; but that is not your way."

"There is a fire not very far off, Scopus, and the wind is blowing strongly."

Scopus was at once on his feet and came out into the room. "I don't like fires," he said uneasily. "Let us go up on the roof and see what it is like."

Short as the time had been since Beric first saw the flash of light the fire had already spread, and a broad sheet of flame was shooting up into the air. "It is down there in the most crowded quarter, and the wind is blowing strongly. It is likely to be a big fire. Listen to the din."

A chorus of shouts, the shrieks of women, and the tramp of many feet running, mingled with the sounding of the watchmen's horns.

"The soldiers will soon be there to keep order," Scopus said. "As every household is obliged to keep a bucket in readiness, and there is an abundance of water; they will cope with it. At any rate the wind is not blowing in this direction. It is half a mile away fully."

"Can we go down and see if we can be of any assistance?" Beric asked. "We might help in removing goods from the houses, and in carrying off the aged and sick."

"You can if you like, Beric. I would not say as much for those who are training hard, for the loss of a night's rest is serious; but as it will be some months before you Britons are ready for the arena, it will do you no harm."

Beric went below, aroused his countrymen, and went with them and Boduoc. The streets were alive. Men were running in the direction of the fire carrying buckets; women were standing at the doors inquiring of the passersby if they knew what street was on fire, and whether it was likely to spread. The sound of military trumpets calling the soldiers to arms rose in various parts of the city, and mingled with the hoarse sound of the watchmen's horns. As they approached the fire the crowd became thicker.

Beric admired the coolness shown and the order that already reigned. The prefect of the 7th Cohort of the Night Guard, always on duty to guard the streets from thieves or fire, was already on the spot, and under his directions, and those of several inferior officials, the men, as fast as they arrived, were set to pass buckets along from the fountains and conduits.

"Who are you?" the magistrate asked, as the five tall figures came up the street in the light of the fire.

"We belong to the school of Scopus," Beric said. "We have come down to see if we can be of assistance. We are strong, and can move goods from houses threatened, or carry off the sick should there be any; or we can throw water on the flames."

"The soldiers will do that," the magistrate said, "that is their business; but, as you say, you may be of use in helping clear the houses outside their lines. The flames are spreading. Come with me, I will take you to the centurion commanding a company of the Night Guard here, for if he saw you coming out of the house with goods he might take you for plunderers."

The centurion, who was hard at work with his men, nodded an assent.

"It were well to get some more stout fellows like these," he said to the magistrate. "In spite of our efforts the fire is making headway, and the sooner the houses in its path are stripped the better."

A strong body of volunteers for the work was soon organized, and an official placed in charge of it. All night they worked without intermission, Beric and his comrades keeping together and astonishing those who were working with them by the strength and activity they displayed. But fast as they worked the flames advanced faster. They were half suffocated by smoke, and the sparks fell thickly round them. The workers carried the goods out of the houses into the street, where other parties conveyed them to open spaces. Lines of men down all the streets leading to the scene of the fire passed along buckets of water. These the soldiers carried up on to the roofs, which they deluged, while others wetted the hangings and furniture that had not been removed.

Parties of troops strove to pull down the houses in the path of the flames, while others again marched up and down preserving order. The Night Guard entered the houses, compelled all to leave, and saw that none were left behind; while sentries kept guard over the goods piled high in the open spaces. When morning broke, Beric gave up the work to a fresh party and returned with his companions to the school. They found it deserted, save by the slaves, the others having, as they learned, gone to the fire an hour before with Scopus.

"We will have a bath to get rid of the dust and sweat," Beric said. "But first we will go up to the roof and have a look at the fire. We had no time when we were working to think much of it; but as we were always being driven back by it, it must have spread a good deal."

An exclamation of surprise broke from them when they gained the roof. Smoke and flames were rising over a large area. A dense canopy overhung the town, a confused din filled the air, while momentarily deep heavy sounds told of falling roofs and walls.

"This is terrible, Boduoc."

"Why terrible, Beric? For my part I should like to see Rome utterly destroyed, as she has destroyed so many other towns."

"The Romans would build it up again more magnificent than before, Boduoc. No, it would be a misfortune to the world if Rome were destroyed; but there is little chance of that. They have had many fires before now; this is a large one certainly, but by this time all the troops in the city must be there, and if the wind drops they will soon arrest the progress of the flames."

The other Britons quite agreed with Boduoc, and though ready to work their hardest to aid in saving the property of individuals, they looked on with undisguised satisfaction at the great conflagration. On such a point as this Beric knew that it would be useless to argue with them.

"You had better come down from the roof, Boduoc. There are others watching the fire besides ourselves; and if it were reported that some of the gladiators from the school were seen making exulting gestures, there would be a popular tumult, and it is likely as not we should be charged with being the authors of the fire. Let us go down, get some food, and then have a bath and sleep for a while. There is little chance of the fire being checked at present. At any rate, we have done our share of work."

After a few hours' sleep Beric again went up to the roof. The fire had made great progress, and, as he could see, was not only travelling with the wind, but working up against it. It was already much nearer to the school than it had been. As to the width of the area of the conflagration the smoke prevented him from forming any opinion; but he judged that the length was fully a mile. It was evident that the progress of the fire was causing great dismay. Groups were gathered on the housetops everywhere, while the streets were crowded with fugitives laden with household goods, making their way towards the thinly populated portions of the hills. After eating some bread and fruit, Beric again sallied out with his four companions. On their way down they met Scopus with several of the gladiators returning.

"What is being done, Scopus?"

"As far as stopping the fire nothing is being done. It has been given up. What can be done when the fire is sweeping along a mile broad, and the heat is so great that there is no standing within a hundred yards of it? All the soldiers are there, and the magistrates and the guards, and all the rest of them, but all that can be done is to prevent the scum of the city from sacking and plundering. Scores of men have been scourged and some beheaded, but it is no easy matter to keep down the mob. There are parties of guards in every street. The whole of the Praetorians are under arms, but the terror and confusion is so great and spread over so wide a space that it is well nigh impossible to preserve order. Proclamations have just been issued by the senate calling upon all citizens to gather at their places of assembly in arms, enjoining them to preserve order, and authorizing the slaying of all robbers caught in the act of plundering. All persons within a certain distance of the fire are recommended to send their wives and families, with their jewels and all portable wealth, to the public gardens, where strong guards of the Praetorians will be posted."

"It seems to me that the fire is advancing in this direction, also, Scopus."

"It is spreading everywhere," Scopus said gloomily. "The heat seems to draw the air in from all directions, and the flames surge sometimes one way and sometimes another. You had better not go far away, Beric; if the flames crawl up much nearer we shall have to prepare for a move. We have no jewels to lose, nor is the furniture of much value, but the arms and armour, our apparatus, clothes, and other things must be carried off."

The scene as Beric went forward was pitiful in the extreme. Weeping women carrying heavy burdens and with their children clinging to their dress came along. Some searched up and down frantically for members of the family who had been lost in the crowd. Old men and women were being helped along by their relations. The sick were being borne past upon doors or the tops of tables.

Among the fugitives were groups of men from the poorest districts by the river, who were only restrained from snatching at the ornaments and caskets of the women by the presence of the soldiers, standing at short intervals along the street and at the doors of the principal houses. In spite of the vigilance of the guard, however, such thefts occasionally took place, and the screams that from time to time rose in the side streets told of the work of plunder going on there.

"I should like to turn down here and give a lesson to some of these villains," Boduoc said.

"I should like nothing better, Boduoc, but it would not do to get into a fray at present. It would only bring up the guard, and they would not be likely to ask many questions as to who was in fault, but would probably assume at once that we, being gladiators, were there for the purpose of robbery, and that the row had arisen over the division of spoil. Look, there is a centurion taking a party of men down the street where we heard those screams. Let us move back a few paces and see what is going to happen. Yes, there is another party of soldiers coming in at the other end. The women are running out of the houses to tell their grievances."

Small parties of soldiers entered the houses. Shouts and yells could be heard even above the surrounding din. Men jumped from windows or ran out into the street only to be cut down by the troops there, and so each body of soldiers continued to advance until they met in the centre of the street, and then, after a few words between the officers, each party returned by the way it had come. They had done their work, and the street had been completely cleared of the plunderers.

"You see, Boduoc, had we run down there when we heard the cries it would have gone hard with us. The troops certainly spent no time in questioning; the women might have told them, perhaps, that we had come to their assistance; still it is just as well that we keep clear of the matter."

Beric's party skirted along the fire for some distance. At some points to windward of the flames efforts were still being made to prevent their spread, large numbers of men being employed in pulling down houses under the supervision of the fire guard. Bodies of troops guarded the entrances to all the streets, and kept back the crowd of sightseers, who had assembled from all parts of the city. Fearing that they might be impressed for the work of demolition, the Britons returned to the school. The familia, as the members of any school of this kind were called, were all assembled. Scopus was walking moodily up and down the gymnasium, but it was evident by the countenances of most of the men that they felt a deep satisfaction at the misfortune that had befallen Rome. From time to time Scopus ascended to the roof, or sent one of the men out to gather news, but it was always to the same effect, the fire was still spreading, and assuming every hour more serious proportions. Towards evening the flames had approached so closely, that Scopus gave orders for the men to take up the bundles that had already been made up, containing everything of any value in the school.

"You had better not wait any longer," he said; "at any moment there may be orders for all schools to go down to help the troops, and then we should lose everything."

Accordingly the heavy packets were lifted by the men on to their heads or shoulders, and they started for the Palatine, which was the nearest hill. Here were many of the houses of the wealthy, and the owners of most of these had already thrown open their gardens for the use of the fugitives. In one of these the gladiators deposited their goods. Two of the party having been left to guard them the rest went out to view the fire.

There was little sleep in Rome that night. It was now evident to all that this was no local conflagration, but that, if the wind continued to blow, it threatened the entire destruction of a considerable portion of the town. Every space and vantage ground from which a view of the fire could be obtained was crowded with spectators.

"There were great fires when we destroyed Camalodunum, Verulamium, and London," Boduoc said, "but this is already larger than any of those, and it is ever spreading; even at this distance we can hear the roar of the flames, the crash of the falling houses, and the shouts of the workers."

"It is a terrible sight, indeed, Boduoc. It looks like a sea of fire. So far the part involved is one of the oldest and poorest in the city, but if it goes on like this the better quarters will soon be threatened. If we get no special orders tomorrow, we will go down to the house of Norbanus and give what help we can in the removal of his goods. His library is a very valuable one, and its loss would be a terrible blow to him. I remember that at Camalodunum there was nothing I regretted so much as the destruction of the books."

"It is all a matter of taste," Boduoc said. "I would rather have a good suit of armour and arms than all the books in Rome. Why some people should worry their brains to make those little black marks on paper, and others should trouble to make out what they mean, is more than I can understand. However, we shall be glad to help you to carry off the goods of Norbanus."

CHAPTER XIV
ROME IN FLAMES

All night the gladiators watched the ever widening area of fire. In the morning proclamations were found posted in every street, ordering all citizens to be under arms, as if expecting the attack of an enemy; each district was to be patrolled regularly, and all evildoers found attempting to plunder were to be instantly put to death, the laws being suspended in face of the common danger. All persons not enrolled in the lists of the city guards were exhorted to lend their aid in transporting goods from the neighbourhood of the fire to a place of safety in the public gardens, and the masters of the schools of gladiators were enjoined to see that their scholars gave their aid in this work.

"Well, we may as well set to work," Scopus said. "There are some of my patrons to whom we may do a good service."

"Will you let me go with my comrades first to aid Norbanus, a magistrate who has done me service?" Beric said. "After I have helped to move his things I will join you wherever you may appoint."

Scopus nodded. "Very well, Beric. I shall go first to the house of Gallus the praetor, he is one of my best friends. After we are done there we will go to the aid of Lysimachus the senator; so, if you don't find us at the house of Gallus, you will find us there."

Beric at once started with the four Britons to the house where he had left Ennia. It was distant but half a mile from the point the fire had now reached, and from many of the houses round the slaves were already bearing goods. Here, however, all was quiet. The door keeper, knowing Beric, permitted him and his companions to enter without question. Norbanus was already in his study. He looked up as Beric approached him. "Why, it is Beric!" he said in surprise. "I heard that you were in one of the ludi and was coming to see you, but I have been full of business since I came here. I am glad that you have come to visit me."

"It is not a visit of ceremony," Beric said; "it is the fire that has brought me here."

"Lesbia tells me that it is still blazing," Norbanus said indifferently. "She has been worrying about it all night. I tell her I am not praetor of the fire guard, and that it does not come within my scope of duty. I went down yesterday afternoon, but the soldiers and citizens are all doing their work under their officers, and doubtless it will soon be extinguished."

"It is ever growing, Norbanus. It is within half a mile of your house now, and travelling fast."

"Why, it was treble that distance last night," Norbanus said in surprise. "Think you that there is really danger of its coming this way?"

"Unless a change takes place," Beric said, "it will assuredly be here by noon; even now sparks and burning flakes are falling in the street. The neighbours are already moving, and I would urge you to lose not a moment's time, but summon your slaves, choose all your most valuable goods, and have them carried up to a place of safety. If you come up to the roof you will see for yourself how pressing is the danger."

Norbanus, still incredulous, ascended the stairs, but directly he looked round he saw that Beric had not exaggerated the state of things.

"I have brought four of my tribesmen with me," Beric said, "and we are all capable of carrying good loads. There ought to be time to make three journeys at least up to the gardens on the hill, where they will be safe. I should say, let half your slaves aid us in carrying up your library and the valuables that come at once to hand, and then you can direct the others to pack up the goods you prize most so that they shall be ready by our return."

"That shall be done," Norbanus said, "and I am thankful to you, Beric, for your aid."

Descending, Norbanus at once gave the orders, and then going up to the women's apartments told Lesbia to bid the female slaves pack at once all the dresses, ornaments, and valuables. The cases containing the books were then brought out into the atrium, and there stacked in five piles. They were then bound together with sacking and cords.

"But what are you going to do with these great piles?" Norbanus said as he came down from above, where Lesbia was raging at the news that much of their belongings would have to be abandoned. "Why, each of them is a wagon load."

"They are large to look at, but not heavy. At any rate we can carry them. Is there anyone to whom we shall specially take them, or shall we place a guard over them?"

"My cousin Lucius, the senator, will, I am sure, take them for me. His house is surrounded by gardens, and quite beyond reach of fire. His wife is Lesbia's sister, and Aemilia shall go up with you."

The Britons helped each other up with the huge packets, four slaves with difficulty raising the last and placing it on Beric's head.

"The weight is nothing now it is up," he said, "though I wish it were a solid packet instead of being composed of so many of these book boxes."

The cases in which the Romans usually kept their books were about the size and shape of hat boxes, but of far stronger make, and each holding from six to ten rolls of vellum. A dozen slaves under the superintendence of the steward, and carrying valuable articles of furniture, followed the Britons, and behind them came Aemilia, with four or five female slaves carrying on their heads great packages of the ladies' clothing. The house of Lucius was but half a mile away from that of Norbanus. Even among the crowd of frightened men and women hurrying up the hill the sight of the five Britons, with their prodigious burdens created lively astonishment and admiration.

"Twenty such men as those," one said, "would carry off a senator's villa bodily, if there was room for it in the road."

"They are the Titans come to life again," another remarked. "It would take six Romans to carry the weight that one of them bears."

When they neared the villa of Lucius, Aemilia hurried on ahead with the female slaves, and was standing at the door with the senator when the Britons approached. The senator uttered an exclamation of astonishment.

"Whence have you got these wonderful porters, Aemilia?"

"I know not," the girl said. "We were dressing, when our father called out that we were to hurry and to put our best garments together, for that we were to depart instantly, as the fire was approaching. For a few minutes there was terrible confusion. The slaves were packing up our things, all talking together, and in an extreme terror. Our mother was terribly upset, and I think she made things worse by giving fresh orders every minute. In the middle of it my father shouted to me to come down at once, and the slaves were to bring down such things as were ready. When I got down I was astonished at seeing these great men quite hidden under the burdens they carried, but I had no time to ask questions. My father said, 'Go with them to my cousin Lucius, and ask him to take in our goods,' and I came."

By this time the party had reached the house.

"Follow me," Lucius said, leading the way along the front of the house, and round to the storehouses in its rear. Aemilia accompanied him. The slaves deposited their burdens on the ground, and then aided the Britons to lower theirs. Aemilia gave an exclamation of astonishment as Beric turned round.

"Why, it is Beric the Briton!" she exclaimed.

"You did not recognize me, then?" Beric said smiling.

"I should have done so had I looked at you closely," she said, "in spite of your Roman garb; but what with the crowd, and the smoke, and the fright, I did not think anything about it after my first wonder at seeing you so loaded. Where did you come from so suddenly to our aid? Are these your countrymen? Ennia and I have asked our father almost every day since we came to Rome to go and find you, and bring you to us. He always said he would, but what with his business and his books he was never able to. How good of you to come to our aid! I am sure the books would never have been saved if it had not been for you, and father would never have got over their loss."

"I knew where your house was," Beric said, "and was glad to be able to do something in gratitude for your father's kindness at Massilia. But I must not lose a moment talking; I hope to make two or three more trips before the fire reaches your house. Your slaves have orders to return with us. Will you tell your steward to guide us back by a less frequented road than that we came by, and then we can keep together and shall not lose time forcing our way through the crowd."

By the time they reached the house of Norbanus the slaves left behind had packed up everything of value.

"I will go up," Norbanus said, "with all the slaves, male and female, if you will remain here to guard the rest of the things till we return. Several parties of ill favoured looking men have entered by the door, evidently in the hopes of plunder, but left when they saw we were still here. The ladies' apartments have been completely stripped, and their belongings will go up this time, so that there will be no occasion for them to return. If the flames approach too closely before we come back, do not stay, Beric, nor trouble about the goods that remain. I have saved my library and my own manuscripts, which is all I care for. My wife and daughters have saved all their dresses and jewels. All the most valuable of my goods will now be carried up by my slaves, and if the rest is lost it will be no great matter."

Beric and his companions seated themselves on the carved benches of the atrium and waited quietly. Parties of marauders once or twice entered, for the area of the fire was now so vast that even the troops and armed citizens were unable properly to guard the whole neighbourhood beyond its limits; but upon seeing these five formidable figures they hastily retired, to look for booty where it could be obtained at less risk.

The fire was but a few hundred yards away, and clouds of sparks and blazing fragments were falling round the house when Norbanus and his slaves returned. These were sufficient to carry up the remaining parcels of goods without assistance from the Britons, who, however, acted as an escort to them on their way back. Their throats were dry and parched by the hot air, and they were glad of a long draught of the good wine that Lucius had in readiness for their arrival. Beric at first refused other refreshment, being anxious to hasten away to join Scopus, but the senator insisted upon their sitting down to a meal.

"You do not know when you may eat another," he said; "there will be little food cooked in this part of Rome today."

As Beric saw it was indeed improbable that they would obtain other food if they neglected this opportunity, he and the others sat down and ate a good, though hasty, meal.

"You will come and see us directly the fire is over," Norbanus said as they rose to leave. "Remember, I shall not know where to find you, and I have had no time to thank you worthily for the service that you have rendered me. Many of the volumes you have saved were unique, and although my own manuscripts may be of little value to the world, they represent the labour of many years."

Hurrying down to the rendezvous Scopus had given him, Beric found that both villas had already been swept away by the fire. He then went up to the spot where their goods were deposited, but the two gladiators in charge said that they had seen nothing whatever of Scopus.

"Then we will go down and do what we can," Beric said. "Should Scopus return, tell him that we will be here at nightfall."

For another two days the conflagration raged, spreading wider and wider, and when at last the wind dropped and the fury of the flames abated, more than the half of Rome lay in ashes. Of the fourteen districts of the city three were absolutely destroyed, and in seven others scarce a house had escaped. Nero, who had been absent, reached Rome on the third day of the fire. The accusation that he had caused it to be lighted, brought against him by his enemies years afterwards, was absurd. There had been occasional fires in Rome for centuries, just as there had been in London before the one that destroyed it, and the strong wind that was blowing was responsible for the magnitude of the fire.

There can, however, be little doubt that the misfortune which appeared so terrible to the citizens was regarded by Nero in a different light. Nero was prouder of being an artist than of being an emperor. Up to this time Rome, although embellished with innumerable temples and palaces, was yet the Rome of the Tarquins. The streets were narrow, and the houses huddled together. Mean cottages stood next to palaces. There was an absence of anything like a general plan. Rome had spread as its population had increased, but it was a collection of houses rather than a capital city.

Nero saw at once how vast was the opportunity. In place of the rambling tortuous streets and crowded rookeries, a city should rise stately, regular, and well ordered, with broad streets and noble thoroughfares, while in its midst should be a palace unequalled in the world, surrounded by gardens, lakes, and parks. There was ample room on the seven hills, and across the Tiber, for all the population, with breathing space for everyone. What glory would there not be to him who thus transformed Rome, and made it a worthy capital of the world! First, however, the people must be attended to and kept in good humour, and accordingly orders were at once issued that the gardens of the emperor's palaces should be thrown open, and the fugitives allowed to encamp there. Such magazines as had escaped the fire were thrown open, and food distributed to all, while ships were sent at once to Sicily and Sardinia for large supplies of grain for the multitude.

While the ruins were still smoking the emperor was engaged with the best architects in Rome in drawing out plans for laying out the new city on a superb scale, and in making preparations for the commencement of work. The claims of owners of ground were at once wiped out by an edict saying, that for the public advantage it was necessary that the whole of the ground should be treated as public property, but that on claims being sent in other sites would be given elsewhere. Summonses were sent to every town and district of the countries under the Roman sway calling for contributions towards the rebuilding of the capital. So heavy was the drain, and so continuous the exactions to raise the enormous sums required to pay for the rebuilding of the city and the superb palaces for the emperor, that the wealth of the known world scarce sufficed for it, and the Roman Empire was for many years impoverished by the tremendous drain upon its resources.

The great mass of the Roman population benefited by the fire. There was work for everyone, from the roughest labourer to the most skilled artisan and artist. Crowds of workmen were brought from all parts. Greece sent her most skilful architects and decorators, her sculptors and painters. Money was abundant, and Rome rose again from her ruins with a rapidity which was astonishing.

The people were housed far better than they had ever been before; the rich had now space and convenience for the construction of their houses, and although most of them had lost the greater portion of their valuables in the fire, they were yet gainers by it. All shared in the pride excited by the new city, with its broad streets and magnificent buildings, and the groans of the provincials, at whose cost it was raised, troubled them not at all. It was true that Nero, in his need for money, seized many of the wealthier citizens, and, upon one pretext or other, put them to death and confiscated their property; but this mattered little to the crowd, and disturbed none save those whose wealth exposed them to the risk of the same fate.

Beric saw nothing of these things, for upon the very day after the fire died out Scopus started with his scholars to a villa on the Alban Hills that had been placed at his disposal by one of his patrons. There were several other schools in the neighbourhood, as the air of the hills was considered to be far healthier and more strengthening than that of Rome. In spite of the public calamity Nero continued to give games for the amusement of the populace, other rich men followed his example, and the sports of the amphitheatre were carried on on an even more extensive scale than before.

Scopus took six of his best pupils to the first games that were given after the fire. Four of them returned victorious, two were sorely wounded and defeated. Their lives had, however, been spared, partly on account of their skill and bravery, partly because the emperor was in an excellent humour, and the mass of the spectators, on whom the decision of life or death rested, saw that the signal for mercy would be acceptable to him.

The Britons greatly preferred their life on the Alban Hills to that in Rome; for, their exercises done, they could wander about without being stared at and commented upon.

The pure air of the hills was invigorating after that of the great city; and here, too, they met ten of their comrades whose ludi had been all along established on the hills. Plans of escape were sometimes talked over, but though they could not resist the pleasure of discussing them, they all knew that it was hopeless. Though altogether unwatched and free to do as they liked after the work of the day was over, they were as much prisoners as if immured in the strongest dungeons. The arm of Rome stretched everywhere; they would be at once followed and hunted down wherever they went. Their height and complexion rendered disguise impossible, and even if they reached the mountains of Calabria, or traversed the length of Italy successfully and reached the Alps--an almost hopeless prospect--they would find none to give them shelter, and would ere long be hunted down. At times they talked of making their way to a seaport, seizing a small craft, and setting sail in her; but none of them knew aught of navigation, and the task of traversing the Mediterranean, passing through the Pillars of Hercules, and navigating the stormy seas beyond until they reached Britain, would have been impossible for them.

News came daily from the city, and they heard that Nero had accused the new sect of being the authors of the conflagration, that the most rigid edicts had been issued against them, and that all who refused to abjure their religion were to be sent to the wild beasts in the arena.

Beric had not seen Norbanus since the day when he had saved his library from the fire; but a few days after they had established themselves in the hills he received a letter from him saying that he had, after much inquiry, learned where Scopus had established his ludus; he greatly regretted Beric had left Rome without his seeing him, and hoped he would call as soon as he returned. His family was already established in a house near that of Lucius. After that Beric occasionally received letters from Aemilia, who wrote sometimes in her father's name and sometimes in her own. She gave him the gossip of Rome, described the wonderful work that was being done, and sent him letters from Pollio to read.

One day a letter, instead of coming by the ordinary post, was brought by one of the household slaves.

"We are all in terrible distress, Beric," she said. "I have told you about the severe persecution that has set in of the Christians. A terrible thing has happened. You know that our old nurse belonged to that sect. She often talked to me about it, but it did not seem to me that what she said could be true; I knew that Ennia, who is graver in her disposition than I am, thought much of it, but I did not think for a moment that she had joined the sect. Two nights ago some spies reported to one of the praetors that some persons, believed to be Christians, were in the habit of assembling one or two nights a week at a lonely house belonging to a freedman. A guard was set and the house surrounded, and fifty people were found there. Some of them were slaves, some freedmen, some of them belonged to noble families, and among them was Ennia.

"She had gone accompanied by that wretched old woman. All who had been questioned boldly avowed themselves to be Christians, and they were taken down and thrown into prison. Imagine our alarm in the morning when we found that Ennia was missing from the house, and our terrible grief when, an hour later, a messenger came from the governor of the prison to say that Ennia was in his charge. My father is quite broken down by the blow. He does not seem to care about Ennia having joined the new sect--you know it is his opinion that everyone should choose their own religion--but he is chiefly grieved at the thought that she should have gone out at night attended only by her nurse, and that she should have done this secretly and without his knowledge. My mother, on the other hand, is most of all shocked that Ennia should have given up the gods of Rome for a religion of slaves, and that, being the daughter of a noble house, she should have consorted with people beneath her.

"I don't think much of any of these things. Ennia may have done wrong, but that is nothing to me. I only think of her as in terrible danger of her life, for they say that Nero will spare none of the Christians, whether of high or low degree. My father has gone out this morning to see the heads of our family and of those allied to us by kinship, to try to get them to use all their influence to obtain Ennia's pardon. My mother does nothing but bemoan herself on the disgrace that has fallen upon us. I am beside myself with grief, and so, as I can do nothing else, I write to tell you of the trouble that has befallen us. I will write often and tell you the news."

Beric's first emotion was that of anger that Ennia should, after the promise she had given him, have again gone alone to the Christian gathering. Then he reflected that as he was away from Rome, she was, of course, unable to keep that promise. He had not seen her since that night, for she had passed straight through the atrium with her mother while he was assisting the slaves to take up their burdens.

He could not help feeling an admiration for her steadfastness in this new Faith that she had taken up. By the side of her livelier sister he had regarded her as a quiet and retiring girl, and was sure that to her these midnight outings by stealth must have been very terrible, and that only from the very strongest sense of duty would she have undertaken them. Now her open avowal of Christianity, when she must have known what were the penalties that the confession entailed, seemed to him heroic.

"It must be a strange religion that could thus influence a timid girl," he said to himself. "My mother killed herself because she would not survive the disaster that had fallen upon her people and her gods; but her death was deemed by all Britons to be honourable. Besides, my mother was a Briton, strong and firm, and capable of heroic actions. This child is courting a death that all who belong to her will deem most dishonourable. There is nothing of the heroine in her disposition; it can only be her Faith in her religion that sustains her. As soon as I return to Rome I will inquire more into it."

It was now ten months since Beric had entered the school of Scopus. He was nearly twenty years old, and his constant and severe exercises had broadened him and brought him to well nigh his full strength. Scopus regarded him with pride, for in all the various exercises of the arena he was already ahead of the other gladiators. His activity was as remarkable as his strength, and he was equally formidable with the trident and net as with sword and buckler; while in wrestling and with the caestus none of the others could stand up against him. He had been carefully instructed in the most terrible contest of all, that against wild beasts, for Scopus deemed that, being a captive of rank and importance, he might be selected for such a display.

A Libyan, who had often hunted the lion in its native wilds, had described to him over and over again the nature of the animal's attack, and the spring with which it hurls itself upon its opponent, and Scopus having obtained a skin of one of the animals killed in the arena, the Libyan had stuffed it with outstretched paws; and Scopus obtained a balista, by which it was hurled through the air as if in the act of springing. Against this Beric frequently practised.

"You must remember," the Libyan said, "that the lion is like a great cat, and as it springs it strikes, so that you must avoid not only its direct spring, but its paws stretched to their full extent as it passes you in the air. You must be as quick as the animal itself, and must not swerve till it is in the air. Then you must leap aside like lightning, and, turning as you leap, be ready to drive your spear through it as it touches the ground. The inert mass, although it may pass through the air as rapidly as the wild beast, but poorly represents the force and fierceness of the lion's spring. We Libyans meet the charge standing closely together, with our spears in advance for it to spring on, and even then it is rarely we kill it without one or two being struck down before it dies. Bulls are thought by some to be more formidable than lions; but as you are quick, you can easily evade their rush. The bears are ugly customers. They seem slow and clumsy, but they are not so, and they are very hard to kill. One blow from their forepaws will strip off the flesh as readily as the blow of a tiger. They will snap a spear shaft as easily as if it were a reed. They are all ugly beasts to fight, and more than a fair match for a single man. Better by far fight the most skilled gladiator in the ring than have anything to do with these creatures. Yet it is well to know how to meet them, so that if ill fortune places you in front of them, you may know how to do your best."

Accounts came almost daily to the hills of the scenes in the arena, and the Romans, accustomed though they were to the fortitude with which the gladiators met the death stroke, were yet astonished at the undaunted bearing of the Christians--old men and girls, slaves and men of noble family, calmly facing death, and even seeming to rejoice in it.

One evening a slave brought a note from Aemilia to Beric. It contained but a few words:

"Our efforts are vain; Ennia is condemned, and will be handed to the lions tomorrow in the arena. We have received orders to be present, as a punishment for not having kept a closer watch over her. I think I shall die."

Beric went to Scopus at once.

"You advised me several times to go to the arena, Scopus, in order to learn something from the conflicts. I want to be present tomorrow. Porus and Lupus are both to fight."

"I am going myself, Beric, and will take you with me. I shall start two hours before daybreak, so as to be there in good time. As their lanista I shall enter the arena with them. I cannot take you there, but I know all the attendants, and can arrange for you to be down at the level of the arena. It may not be long before you have to play your part there, and I should like you to get accustomed to the scene, the wall of faces and the roar of applause, for these things are apt to shake the nerves of one unaccustomed to them."

Beric smiled. "After meeting the Romans twenty times in battle, Scopus, the noise of a crowd would no more affect me than the roar of the wind over the treetops. Still I want to see it; and more, I want to see how the people of this new sect face death. British women do not fear to die, and often slay themselves rather than fall into the hands of the Romans, knowing well that they will go straight to the Happy Island and have no more trouble. Are these Christians as brave?"

Scopus shrugged his shoulders. "Yes, they die bravely enough. But who fears death? Among all the peoples Rome has conquered where has she met with cowards? Everywhere the women are found ready to fall by their husbands' swords rather than become captives; to leap from precipices, or cast themselves into blazing pyres. Is man anywhere lower than the wild beast, who will face his assailants till the last? I have seen men of every tribe and people fight in the arena. If conquered, they raise their hand in order to live to conquer another day; but not once, when the thumbs have been turned down, have I seen one flinch from the fatal stroke."

"That is true enough," Beric said; "but methinks it is one thing to court death in the hour of defeat, when all your friends have fallen round you, and all hope is lost, and quite another to stand alone and friendless with the eyes of a multitude fixed on you. Still I would see it."

The next day Beric stood beside Scopus among a group of guards and attendants of the arena at one of the doors leading from it. Above, every seat of the vast circle was crowded with spectators. In the centre of the lower tier sat the emperor; near him were the members of his council and court. The lower tiers round the arena were filled by the senators and equities, with their wives and daughters. Above these were the seats of officials and others having a right to special seats, and then came, tier above tier to the uppermost seats, the vast concourse of people. When the great door of the arena opened a procession entered, headed by Cneius Spado, the senator at whose expense the games were given. Then, two and two, marched the gladiators who were to take part in it, accompanied by their lanistae or teachers. Scopus, after seeing Beric well placed, had left him to accompany Porus and Lupus.

The gladiators were variously armed. There were the hoplomachi, who fought in complete suits of armour; the laqueatores, who used a noose to catch their adversaries; the retiarii, with their net and trident, and wearing neither armour nor helmet; the mirmillones, armed like the Gauls; the Samni, with oblong shields; and the Thracians, with round ones. With the exception of the retiarii all wore helmets, and their right arms were covered with armour, the left being protected by the shield. The gladiators saluted the emperor and people, and the procession then left the arena, the first two matched against each other again entering, each accompanied by his lanista.

Both the gladiators were novices, the men who had frequently fought and conquered being reserved for the later contests, as the excitement of the audience became roused. One of the combatants was armed as a Gaul, the other as a Thracian.

The combat was not a long one. The men fought for a short time cautiously, and then closing exchanged fierce and rapid blows until one fell mortally wounded. A murmur of discontent rose from the spectators, there had not been a sufficient exhibition of skill to satisfy them. Eight or ten pairs of gladiators fought one after the other, the excitement of the audience rising with each conflict, as men of noted skill now contended. The victors were hailed with shouts of applause, and the vanquished were spared, a proof that the spectators were in a good temper and satisfied with the entertainment. Beric looked on with interest. In the age in which he lived feelings of compassion scarcely existed. War was the normal state of existence. Tribal wars were of constant occurrence, and the vanquished were either slain or enslaved. Men fought out their private quarrels to the death; and Beric, being by birth Briton and by education Roman, felt no more compunction at the sight of blood than did either Briton or Roman.

To him the only unnatural feature in the contest was that there existed neither personal nor tribal hostility between the combatants, and that they fought solely for the amusement of the spectators. Otherwise he was no more moved by the scenes that passed before his eyes than is a Briton of the present day by a friendly boxing match. He was more interested when Porus entered the arena, accompanied by Scopus. He liked Porus, who, although quick and fiery in temper, was good natured and not given to brawling. He had often practised against him, and knew exactly his strength and skill. He was clever in the management of his net, but failed sometimes from his eagerness to use his trident. He was received with loud applause when he entered, and justified the good opinion of the spectators by defeating his antagonist, who was armed as a Samnite, the spectators expressing their dissatisfaction at the clumsiness of the latter by giving the hostile signal, when the Gaul--for the vanquished belonged to that nationality--instead of waiting for the approach of Porus, at once stabbed himself with his own sword.

The last pair to fight were Lupus and one of the Britons. He had not been trained in the school of Scopus, but in one of the other ludi, and as he was the first of those brought over by Suetonius to appear in the arena, he was greeted with acclamation as loud as those with which Lupus was received. Tall as Lupus was, the Briton far exceeded him in stature, and the interest of the spectators was aroused by the question whether the strength of the newcomer would render him a fair match for the well known skill of Lupus. A buzz went round the amphitheatre as bets were made on the result. Beric felt a thrill of excitement, for the Briton was one of the youngest and most active of his followers, and had often fought side by side with him against the Romans.

How well he had been trained Beric knew not, but as he knew that he himself was superior in swordmanship to Lupus, he felt that his countryman's chances of success were good. It was not long, however, before he saw that the teaching the Briton had received had been very inferior to that given at the school of Scopus, and although he twice nearly beat Lupus to the ground by the sheer weight of his blows, the latter thrice wounded him without himself receiving a scratch. Warned, however, of the superior strength of the Briton Lupus still fought cautiously, avoiding his blows, and trying to tire him out. For a long time the conflict continued, then, thinking that his opponent was now weakened by his exertions and by loss of blood, Lupus took the offensive and hotly pressed his antagonist, and presently inflicted a fourth and more severe wound than those previously given.

A shout rose from the spectators, "Lupus wins!" when the Briton, with a sudden spring, threw himself upon his opponent. Their shields clashed together as they stood breast to breast. Lupus shortened his sword to thrust it in below the Briton's buckler, when the latter smote with the hilt of his sword with all his strength full upon his assailant's helmet, and so tremendous was the blow that Lupus fell an inert mass upon the ground, while a tremendous shout rose from the audience at this unexpected termination of the contest. Scopus leaned over the fallen man. He was insensible but breathed, being simply stunned by the weight of the blow. Scopus held up his own hand, and the unanimous upturning of the thumbs showed that the spectators were well satisfied with the skill and courage with which Lupus had fought.

CHAPTER XV
THE CHRISTIANS TO THE LIONS

After the contest in which Lupus had been defeated there was a pause. The gladiatorial part of the show was now over, but there was greater excitement still awaiting the audience, for they knew Nero had ordered that some of the Christians were to be given to the lions. There was a hush of expectation as the door was opened, and a procession, consisting of a priest of Jupiter and several attendants of the temple, followed by four guards conducting an elderly man with his two sons, lads of seventeen or eighteen, entered. They made their way across the arena and stopped before the emperor. The priest approached the prisoners, holding out a small image of the god, and offered them their lives if they would pay the customary honours to it. All refused. They were then conducted back to the centre of the arena, and the rest, leaving them there, filed out through the door. The old man laid his hands on the shoulders of his sons and began singing a hymn, in which they both joined. Their voices rose loud and clear in the silence of the amphitheatre, and there was neither pause nor waver in the tone as the entrance to one of the cages at the other end of the arena was opened, and a lion and a lioness appeared. The animals stood hesitating as they looked round at the sea of faces, then, encouraged by the silence, they stepped out, and side by side made the circuit of the arena, stopping and uttering a loud roar as they came upon the track along which the bleeding bodies of those who had fallen had been dragged. When they had completed the circle they again paused, and now for the first time turned their attention to the three figures standing in its centre. For a minute they stood irresolute, and then crouching low crawled towards them.

Beric turned his head. He could view without emotion a contest of armed men, but he could not, like the population of Rome, see unarmed and unresisting men pulled down by wild beasts. There was a dead stillness in the crowded amphitheatre, then there was a low sound as of gasping breath. One voice alone continued the hymn, and soon that too ceased suddenly. The tragedy was over, and the buzz of conversation and comment again broke out among the spectators. Certainly these Christians knew how to die. They were bad citizens, they had doubtless assisted to burn Rome, but they knew how to die.

A strong body of guards provided with torches now entered. The lions were driven back to their dens, the bodies being left lying where they had fallen. Four batches of prisoners who were brought out one after another met with a similar fate. Then there was another pause. It was known that a girl of noble family was to be the last victim, and all eyes were turned to

Norbanus, who, with his wife and Aemilia, sat in the front row near Nero, with two Praetorian guards standing beside them. Norbanus was deadly pale, but the pride of noble blood, the stoicism of the philosopher, and the knowledge of his own utter helplessness combined to prevent his showing any other sign of emotion. Lesbia sat upright and immovable herself. She was not one to show her emotion before the gaze of the common people.

Aemilia, half insensible, would have fallen had not the guard beside her supported her. She had seen nothing of what had passed in the arena, but had sat frozen with horror beside her mother. Again the doors opened, a priest of Diana, followed by a procession of white robed attendants, and six virgins from the temple of Diana, entered, followed by Ennia between the attendants of the temple, while a band of lictors brought up the rear. Even the hardened hearts of the spectators were moved by the youth and beauty of the young girl, who, dressed in white, advanced calmly between her guards, with a gentle modest expression on her features. When the procession formed up before the emperor, she saluted him. The priest and the virgins surrounded her, and urged her to pay reverence to the statue of Diana.

Pointing to her parents, they implored her for their sake to recant. Pale as death, and with tears streaming down her cheeks, she shook her head quietly. "I cannot deny the Lord who died for me," she said.

Nero himself rose from his seat. "Maiden," he said, "if not for your own sake, for the sake of those who love you, I pray you to cease from your obstinacy. How can a child like you know more than the wisest heads of Rome? How can you deny the gods who have protected and given victory to your country? I would fain spare you."

"I am but a child, as you say, Caesar," Ennia replied. "I have no strength of my own, but I am strong in the strength of Him I worship. He gave His life for me--it is not much that I should give mine for Him."

Nero sank back on his seat with an angry wave of his hand. He saw that the sympathy of the audience was with the prisoner, and would willingly have gained their approval by extending his clemency towards her. The procession now returned to the centre of the arena, where the girls, weeping, took leave of Ennia, who soon stood alone a slight helpless figure in the sight of the great silent multitude. Nero had spoken in a low tone to one of his attendants. The door of another cage was opened, and a lion, larger in bulk than any that had previously appeared, entered the arena, saluting the audience with a deep roar. As it did so a tall figure, naked to the waist, sprang forward from the group of attendants behind a strong barrier at the other end of the arena. He was armed only with a sword which he had snatched from a soldier standing next to him. Deep murmurs of surprise rose from the spectators. The master of ceremonies exchanged a few words with the emperor, and a body of men with torches and trumpets ran forward and drove the lion back into its den. Then Beric, who had been standing in front of Ennia, advanced towards the emperor.

"Who are you?" Nero asked.

"I am Beric, once chief of the Iceni, now a British captive. I received great kindness on my way hither from Norbanus, the father of this maid. As we Britons are not ungrateful I am ready to defend her to the death, and I crave as a boon, Caesar, that you will permit me to battle against the lion with such arms as you may decide."

"Are you a Christian?" the emperor asked coldly.

"I am not. I am of the religion of my nation, and Rome has always permitted the people that have been subdued to worship in their own fashion. I know nought of the Christian doctrines, but I know that this damsel at least can have had nought to do with the burning of Rome, and that though she may have forsaken the gods of Rome, in this only can she have offended. I pray you, and I pray this assembly, to let me stand as her champion against the beasts."

A burst of applause rose from the spectators. This was a novelty, and an excitement beyond what they had bargained for. They had been moved by the youth of the victim, and now the prospects of something even more exciting than the rending to pieces of a defenceless girl enlisted them in favour of the applicant. Moreover the Romans intensely admired feats of bravery, and that this captive should offer to face single handed an animal that was known to be one of the most powerful of those in the amphitheatre filled them with admiration. Accustomed as they were to gaze at athletes, they were struck with the physique and strength of this young Briton, with the muscles standing up massive and knotted through the white skin.

"Granted, granted!" they shouted; "let him fight."

Nero waited till the acclamation ceased, and then said: "The people have spoken, let their will be done. But we must not be unfair to the lion; as the maiden was unarmed so shall you stand unarmed before the lion."

The decision was received in silence by the spectators. It was a sentence of death to the young Briton, and the silence was succeeded by a low murmur of disapproval. Beric turned a little pale, but he showed no other sign of emotion.

"Thanks, Caesar, for so much of a boon," he said in a loud, steady voice; "I accept the conditions, it being understood that should the gods of my country, and of this maiden, defend me against the lion, the damsel shall be free from all pain and penalty, and shall be restored to her parents."

"That is understood," Nero replied.

With an inclination of his head to the emperor and a wave of his hand to the audience in general, Beric turned and walked across the arena to the barrier. Scopus was standing there.

"You are mad, Beric. I grieve for you. You were my favourite pupil, and I looked for great things from you, and now it has come to this, and all is over."

"All is not quite over yet, Scopus. I will try to do credit to your training; give me my cloak." He wrapped himself in its ample folds, and then walked quietly back to the centre of the arena. A murmur of surprise rose from the spectators. Why should the Briton cumber his limbs with this garment?

On reaching his position Beric again threw off the cloak, and stood in the short skirt reaching scarce to the knees. "I am unarmed," he cried in a loud voice. "You see I have not as much as a dagger." Then he tore off two broad strips from the edge of the garment and twisted them into ropes, forming a running noose in each, threw the cloak, which was composed of the stout cloth used by the common people, over his arm, and signed to the attendants at the cage to open the door.

"Oh, Beric, why have you thrown away your life in a useless attempt to save mine?" Ennia said as he stood before her.

"It may not be useless, Ennia. My god has protected me through many dangers, and your God will surely assist me now. Do you pray to Him for aid."

Then as the door of the den opened he stepped a few paces towards it. A roar of applause rose from the vast audience. They had appreciated his action in making the ropes, and guessed that he meant to use his cloak as a retiarius used his net; there would then be a contest and not a massacre. Enraged at its former treatment the lion dashed out of its den with a sudden spring, made three or four leaps forward, and then paused with its eyes fixed on the man standing in front of it, still immovable, in an easy pose, ready for instant action. Then it sank till its belly nearly touched the ground, and began to crawl with a stealthy gliding motion towards him. More and more slowly it went, till it paused at a distance of some ten yards.

For a few seconds it crouched motionless, save for a slow waving motion of its tail; then with a sharp roar it sprang through the air. With a motion as quick Beric leaped aside, and as it touched the ground he sprang across its loins, at the same moment wrapping his cloak in many folds round its head, and knotting the ends tightly. Then as the lion, recovering from its first surprise, sprang to its feet with a roar of anger and disgust, Beric was on his feet beside it.

For a moment it strove to tear away the strange substance which enveloped its head, but Beric dropped the end of a noose over one of its forepaws, drew it tight, and with a sudden pull jerked the animal over on its back. As it sprang up again the other forepaw was noosed, and it was again thrown over. This time, as it sprang to its feet, Beric struck it a tremendous blow on the nose. The unexpected assault for a moment brought it down, but mad with rage it sprang up and struck out in all directions at its invisible foe, leaping and bounding hither and thither. Beric easily avoided the onslaught, and taking every opportunity struck it three or four times with all his force on the ear, each time rolling it over and over. The last of these blows seemed almost to stun it, and it lay for a moment immovable.

Again Beric leaped upon it, coming down astride of its loins with all his weight, and seizing at once the two ropes. The lion uttered a roar of dismay and pain, and struck at him first with one paw and then with the other. By his coolness and quickness, however, he escaped all the blows, and then, when the lion seemed exhausted, he jerked tightly the cords, twisting them behind the lion's back and with rapid turns fastening them together. The lion was helpless now. Had Beric attempted to pull the cords in any other position it would have snapped them like pack thread, but in this position it had no strength, the pads of the feet being fastened together and the limbs almost dislocated. As the animal rolled over and over uttering roars of vain fury, Beric snatched the cloth from its head, tore off another strip, twisted it, and without difficulty bound its hind legs together. Then he again wrapped it round the lion's head, and standing up bowed to the spectators.

A mighty shout shook the building. Never had such a feat been seen in the arena before, and men and women alike standing up waved their hands with frantic enthusiasm. Beric had not escaped altogether unhurt, for as the lion struck out at him it had torn away a piece of flesh from his side, and the blood was streaming down over his white skirt. Then he went up to Ennia, who was standing with closed eyes and hands clasped in prayer. She had seen nothing of the conflict, and had believed that Beric's death and her own were inevitable.

"Ennia," he said, "our gods have saved me; the lion is helpless." Then she sank down insensible. He raised her on his shoulder, walked across the arena, passed the barrier, and, ascending the steps, walked along before the first row of spectators and handed her over to her mother. Then he descended again, and bowed deeply, first to the emperor and then to the still shouting people.

The giver of the games advanced and placed on his head a crown of bay leaves, and handed to him a heavy purse of gold, which Beric placed in his girdle, and, again saluting the audience, rejoined Scopus, who was in a state of enthusiastic delight at the prowess of his pupil.

"You have proved yourself the first gladiator in Rome," he said. "Henceforth the school of Scopus is ahead of all its rivals. Now we must get your side dressed. Another inch or two, Beric, and the conflict would not have ended as it did."

"Yes, if the lion had not been in such a hurry to strike, and had stretched its paw to the fullest, it would have fared badly with me," Beric said; "but it was out of breath and spiteful, and had not recovered from the blow and from the shock of my jumping on it, which must have pretty nearly broken its back. I knew it was a risk, but it was my only chance of getting its paws in that position, and in no other would my ropes have been strong enough to hold them."

"But how came you to think of fighting in that way?" Scopus asked, after the leech, who was always in attendance to dress the wounds of the gladiators, had bandaged up his side.

"I never expected to have to fight the beasts unarmed," Beric said, "but I had sometimes thought what should be done in such a case, and I thought that if one could but wrap one's cloak round a lion's head the beast would be at one's mercy. Had I had but a caestus I could have beaten its skull in, but without that I saw that the only plan was to noose its limbs. Surely a man ought to be able to overcome a blinded beast."

"I would not try it for all the gold in Rome, Beric, even now that I have seen you do it. Did you mark Caesar? There is no one appreciates valiant deeds more than he does. At first his countenance was cold--I marked him narrowly--but he half rose to his feet and his countenance changed when you first threw yourself on the lion, and none applauded more warmly than he did when your victory was gained. Listen to them; they are shouting for you again. You must go. Never before did I know them to linger after a show was over. They will give you presents."

"I care not for them," Beric said.

"You must take them," Scopus said, "or you will undo the favourable impression you have made, which will be useful to you should you ever enter the arena again and be conquered. Go, go!"

Beric again entered the arena, and the attendants led him up to the emperor, who presented him with a gold bracelet, saying:

"I will speak to you again, Beric. I had wondered that you and your people should have resisted Suetonius so long, but I wonder no longer."

Then Beric was led round the arena. Ladies threw down rings and bracelets to him. These were gathered up by the attendants and handed to him as he bowed to the givers. Norbanus, his wife, and daughter had already left their seats, surrounded by friends congratulating them, and bearing with them the still insensible girl. Having made the tour of the arena Beric again saluted the audience and retired. One of the imperial attendants met them as they left the building.

"The emperor bids me say, Scopus, that when Beric is recovered from his wound he is to attend at the palace."

"I thought the emperor meant well towards you," Scopus said. "You will in any case fight no more in the arena."

"How is that?" Beric asked in surprise.

"Did you not hear the shouts of the people the last time you entered, Beric?"

"I heard a great confused roar, but in truth I was feeling somewhat faint from loss of blood, and did not catch any particular sounds."

"They shouted that you were free from the arena henceforth. It is their custom when a gladiator greatly distinguishes himself to declare him free, though I have never known one before freed on his first appearance. The rule is that a gladiator remains for two years in the ring, but that period is shortened should the people deem that he has earned his life by his courage and skill. For a moment I was sorry when I heard it, but perhaps it is better as it is. Did you remain for two years, and fight and conquer at every show, you could gain no more honour than you have done. Now I will get a lectica and have you carried out to the hills. You are not fit to walk."

They were joined outside by Porus and Lupus. The former was warm in his congratulation.

"By the gods, Beric, though I knew well that you would gain a great triumph in the arena when your time came, I never thought to see you thus fighting with the beasts unarmed. Why, Milo himself was not stronger, and he won thirteen times at the Olympian and Pythian games. He would have won more, but no one would venture to enter against him. Why, were you to go on practising for another five years, you would be as strong as he was, and as you are as skilful as you are strong it would go hard with any that met you. I congratulated myself, I can tell you, when I heard the people shout that you were free of the arena, for if by any chance we had been drawn against each other, I might as well have laid down my net and asked you to finish me at once without trouble."

"It was but a happy thought, Porus: if a man could be caught in a net, why not a lion blinded in a cloak? That once done the rest was easy."

"Well, I don't want any easy jobs of that sort," Porus said. "But let us go into a wine shop; a glass will bring the colour again to your cheeks."

"No, no, Porus," Scopus said. "Do you and Lupus drink, and I will drink with you, but no wine for Beric. I will get him a cup of hot ass's milk; that will give him strength without fevering his blood. Here is a place where they sell it. I will go in with him first, and then join you there; but take not too much. You have a long walk back, and I guess, Lupus, that your head already hums from the blow that Briton gave it. By Bacchus, these Britons are fine men! I thought you had got an easy thing of it, when boom! and there you were stretched out like a dead man."

"It was a trick," Lupus said angrily, "a base trick."

"Not at all," Scopus replied. "You fought as if in war; and in war if you had an opponent at close quarters, and could not use your sword's point, you would strike him down with the hilt if you could. As I have told you over and over again, you are a good swordsman, but you don't know everything yet by a long way, and you are so conceited that you never will. I hoped that drubbing Beric gave you a few days after he joined us would have done you good, but I don't see that it has. There are some men who never seem to learn. If it had not been for you our ludus would have triumphed all round today; but when one sees a man we put forward as one of our best swordsmen defeated by a raw Briton, people may well say, 'Scopus has got one or two good men; there is Beric, he is a marvel; and Porus is good with the net; but as for the rest, I don't value them a straw.'"

The enraged gladiator sprang upon Scopus, but the latter seized him by the waist and hurled him down with such force that he was unable to rise until Porus assisted him to his feet. As to Scopus, he paid him no farther attention, but putting his hand on Beric's shoulder led him into the shop. A long draught of hot milk did wonders for Beric, and he proposed walking, but Scopus would not hear of it.

"Sit down here for five minutes," he said, "till I have a cup of wine with the others. I should think Lupus must need it pretty badly, what with the knock on the head and the tumble I have just given him. I am not sorry that he was beaten by your countryman, for since he has had the luck to win two or three times in the arena, his head has been quite turned. He would never have dared to lay his hand on me had he not been half mad, for he knows well enough that I could strangle him with one hand. The worst of him is, that the fellow bears malice. He has never forgiven you the thrashing you administered to him. Now I suppose he will be sulky for weeks; but if he does it will be worse for him, for I will cut off his wine, and that will soon bring him to his senses."

Scopus had gone but a few minutes when he returned with a lectica, which was a sort of palanquin, carried by four stout countrymen.

"Really, Scopus, it is ridiculous that I should be carried along the streets like a woman."

"Men are carried as well as women, Beric, and as you are a wounded man you have a double right to be carried. Here is a bag with all those ornaments you got. It is quite heavy to lift."

The bearers protested loudly at the weight of their burden when they lifted the lectica, but the promise of a little extra pay silenced their complaints. They were scarcely beyond the city when Beric, who was weaker from loss of blood than he imagined, dozed off to sleep, and did not wake till the lectica was set down in the atrium of the house on the Alban Hills.

Next morning he was extremely stiff, and found himself obliged to continue on his couch.

"It is of no use your trying to get up," Scopus said; "the muscles of your flank are badly torn, and you must remain quiet."

An hour later a rheda or four wheeled carriage drove up to the door, and in another minute Norbanus entered Beric's cubicle. There were tears in his eyes as he held out both hands to him. "Ah, my friend," he said, "how happy you must be in the happiness you caused to us! Who could have thought, when I entertained, as a passing guest, the friend of Pollio, that he would be the saviour of my family? You must have thought poorly of us yesterday that I was not at the exit from the amphitheatre to meet and thank you. But I hurried home with Ennia, and having left her in charge of her mother and sister came back to find you, but you had left, and I could learn no news of you. I searched for some time, and then guessing that you had been brought home by Scopus, I went back to the child, who is sorely ill. I fear that the strain has been too much for her, and that we shall lose her. But how different from what it would have been! To die is the lot of us all, and though I shall mourn my child, it will be a different thing indeed from seeing her torn to pieces before my eyes by the lion. She has recovered from her faint, but she lies still and quiet, and scarce seems to hear what is said to her. Her eyes are open, she has a happy smile on her lips, and I believe that she is well content now that she has done what she deems her duty to her God. She smiled when I told her this morning that I was coming over to see you, and said in a whisper, 'I shall see him again, father.'"

"Would she like to see me now?" Beric said, making an effort to rise.

"No, not now, Beric. I don't think somehow that she meant that. The leech said that she must be kept perfectly quiet; but I will send a slave with a letter to you daily. Oh, what a day was yesterday! The woes of a lifetime seemed centred in an hour. I know not how I lived as I sat there and waited for the fatal moment. All the blood in my veins seemed to freeze up as she was left alone in the arena. A mist came over my eyes. I tried to close them, but could not. I saw nothing of the amphitheatre, nothing of the spectators, nothing but her, till, at the sudden shout from the crowd, I roused myself with a start. When I saw you beside her I thought at first that I dreamed; but Aemilia suddenly clasped my arm and said, 'It is Beric!' Then I hoped something, I know not what, until Nero said that you must meet the lion unarmed.

"Then I thought all was over--that two victims were to die instead of one. I tried to rise to cry to you to go, for that I would die by Ennia, but my limbs refused to support me; and though I tried to shout I did but whisper. What followed was too quick for me to mark. I saw the beast spring at you; I saw a confused struggle; but not until I saw you rise and bow, while the lion rolled over and over, bound and helpless, did I realize that what seemed impossible had indeed come to pass, and that you, unarmed and alone, had truly vanquished the terrible beast.

"I hear that all Rome is talking of nothing else. My friends, who poured in all the evening to congratulate us, told me so, and that no such feat had ever been seen in the arena."

"It does not seem much to me, Norbanus," Beric said. "It needed only some coolness and strength, though truly I myself doubted, when Nero gave the order to fight without weapons, if it could be done. I cannot but think that Ennia's God and mine aided me."

"It is strange," Norbanus said, "that one so young and weak as Ennia should have shown no fear, and that the other Christians should all have met their fate with so wonderful a calm. As you know, I have thought that all religions were alike, each tribe and nation having its own. But methinks there must be something more in this when its votaries are ready so to die for it."

"Do not linger with me," Beric said. "You must be longing to be with your child. Pray, go at once. She must be glad to have you by her, even if she says little. I thank you for your promise to send news to me daily. If she should express any desire to see me, I will get Scopus to provide a vehicle to carry me to Rome; but in a few days I hope to be about."

"Your first visit must be to Caesar, when you are well enough to walk," Norbanus said. "They tell me he bade you come to see him, and he would be jealous did he know that he was not the first in your thoughts."

Norbanus returned to Rome, and each day a letter came to Beric. The news was always the same; there was no change in Ennia's condition.

Beric's wound healed rapidly. Hard work and simple living had so toughened his frame that a wound that might have been serious affected him only locally, and mended with surprising rapidity. In a week he was up and about, and three days later he felt well enough to go to Rome.

"You would have been better for a few days more rest," Scopus said, "but Nero is not fond of being kept waiting; and if he really wishes to see you it would be well that you present yourself as soon as possible."

"I care nothing for Nero," Beric said; "but I should be glad, for the sake of Norbanus, to see his daughter. It may be that my presence might rouse her and do her good. I want none of Nero's favours; they are dangerous at best. His liking is fatal. He has now murdered Britannicus, his wife Octavia, and his mother Agrippina. He has banished Seneca, and every other adviser he had he has either executed or driven into exile."

"That is all true enough, Beric, though it is better not said. Still, you must remember you have no choice. There is no thwarting Nero; if he designs to bestow favours upon you, you must accept them. I agree with you that they are dangerous; but you know how to guard yourself. A man who has fought a lion with naked hands may well manage to escape even the clutches of Nero. He has struck down the greatest and richest; but it is easier for one who is neither great nor rich to escape. At any rate, Beric, I have a faith in your fortune. You have gone through so much, that I think surely some god protects you. By the way, what are you going to do with that basketful of women's ornaments that I have locked up in my coffer?"

"I thought no more about them, Scopus."

"I should advise you to sell them. In themselves they are useless to you. But once turned into money they may some day stand you in good stead. They are worth a large sum, I can tell you, and I don't care about keeping them here. None of my school are condemned malefactors. I would never take such men, even to please the wealthiest patron. But there is no use in placing temptation before any, and Porus and Lupus will have told how the Roman ladies flung their bracelets to you. I will take them down to a goldsmith who works for some of my patrons, and get him to value them, if you will."

"Thank you, Scopus, I shall be glad to get rid of them. How would you dress for waiting on Caesar?"

"I have been thinking it over," Scopus said. "I should say well, and yet not too well. You are a free man, for although Nero disposed of you as if you had been slaves, you were not enslaved nor did you bear the mark of slavery, therefore you have always dressed like a free man. Again, you are a chief among your own people; therefore, as I say, I should dress well but quietly. Nero has many freedmen about him, and though some of these provoke derision by vying with the wealthiest, this I know would never be done by you, even did you bask in the favour of Nero. A white tunic and a paenula of fine white cloth or a lacerna, both being long and ample so as to fall in becoming folds, would be the best. As I shall ride into Rome with you, you can there get one before going to see Nero."

On arriving at Rome Beric was soon fitted with a cloak of fine white stuff, the folds of which showed off his figure to advantage. Scopus accompanied him to Nero's palace.

"I know several of his attendants," he said, "and can get you passed in to the emperor, which will save you waiting hours, perhaps, before you can obtain an audience."

Taking him through numerous courts and along many passages they reached a chamber where several officials of the palace were walking and talking, waiting in readiness should they be required by Nero. Scopus went up to one with whom he was well acquainted. After the usual greetings he explained to him that he had, in accordance with Nero's order, brought the young Briton, Beric, who had conquered the lion in the arena, and begged him to ask the emperor whether he would choose to give him audience at present.

"I will acquaint his chief chamberlain at once, Scopus, and will ask him, for your sake, to choose his moment for telling Nero. It may make a great difference in the fortunes of the young man whether Caesar is in a good temper or not when he receives him. It is not often at present that he is in bad humour. Since the fire his mind has been filled with great ideas, and he thinks of little but making the city in all respects magnificent, and as he loves art in every way this is a high delight to him; therefore, unless aught has gone wrong with him, he will be found accessible. I will go to the chamberlain at once, my Scopus."

It was half an hour before he returned. "The chamberlain said that there could not be a better time for your gladiator to see Caesar, and therefore he has spoken to him at once, and Nero has ordered the Briton to be brought to him. These two officials will conduct him at once to his presence."

Beric was taken in charge by the two ushers, and was led along several passages, in each of which a guard was on duty, until they reached a massive door. Here two soldiers were stationed. The ushers knocked. Another official presented himself at the door, and, beckoning to Beric to follow him, pushed aside some rich hangings heavy with gold embroidery. They were now in a small apartment, the walls of which were of the purest white marble, and the furniture completely covered with gold. Crossing this he drew another set of hangings aside, entered with Beric, bowed deeply, and saying, "This is the Briton, Caesar," retired, leaving Beric standing before the emperor.

The apartment was of moderate size, exquisitely decorated in Greek fashion. One end was open to a garden, where plants and shrubs of the most graceful foliage, brought from many parts of the world, threw a delicious shade. Statues of white marble gleamed among them, and fountains of perfumed waters filled the air with sweet odours. Nero sat in a simple white tunic upon a couch, while a black slave, of stature rivalling that of Beric, knelt in front of him holding out a great sheet of parchment with designs of some of the decorations of his new palace. Nero waved his hand, and the slave, rolling up the parchment, took his stand behind the emperor's couch. The latter looked long and steadily at him before speaking, as if to read his disposition.

"Beric," he said, "I have seen you risk your life for one who was but little to you, for I have spoken to Norbanus, and have learned from him the nature of your acquaintance with him, and found that you have seen but little of this young maiden for whom you were ready to risk what seemed certain death. Moreover, she was but a young girl, and her life can have had no special value in your eyes; therefore, it seems to me that you are one who would be a true and faithful friend indeed to a man who on his part was a friend to you. You have the other qualities of bravery and skill and strength. Moreover, you belong to no party in Rome. I have inquired concerning you, and find that although Pollio, the nephew of Norbanus, introduced you to many of his friends, you have gone but little among them, but have spent your time much, when not in the ludus, in the public libraries. Being myself a lover of books, the report inclines me the more toward you. I feel that I could rely upon you, and you would find in me not a master but a friend. Of those around me I can trust but few. They serve from interest, and if their interest lay the other way they would desert me. I have many enemies, and though the people love me, the great families, whose connections and relations are everywhere, think only of their private aims and ends, and many deem themselves to have reasons for hatred against me. I need one like you, brave, single minded, resolute, and faithful to me, who would be as simple and as true when raised to wealth and honour as you have shown yourself when but a simple gladiator. Wilt thou be such a one to me?"

"I am but ill fitted for such a post, Caesar," Beric said gravely. "I have been a chief and leader of my own people, and my tongue would never bring itself to utter the flattering words used by those who surround an imperial throne. Monarchs love not the truth, and my blunt speech would speedily offend you. A faithful guard to your majesty I might be, more than that I fear I never could be, for even to please you, Nero, I could not say aught except what I thought."

"I should expect and wish for no more," Nero said. "It is good to hear the truth sometimes. I heard it from Seneca; but, alas! I did not value it then as I should have done. I am older and wiser now. Besides, Seneca was a Roman, and necessarily mixed up in the intrigues that are ever on foot, and connected with half the great families in Rome. You stand alone, and I should know that whatever you said the words would be your own, and would not have been put in your mouth by others, and even when your opinions ran counter to mine I should respect them. Well, what do you say?"

"It is not for me to bargain with the master of Rome," Beric said. "I am ready to be your man, Caesar, to lay down my life in your defence, to be your guard as a faithful hound might be; only, I pray you, take me not in any way into your confidence as to state affairs, for of these I am wholly ignorant. My ideas are those of a simple British chief. Rome and its ways are too complicated for me to understand, and were you to speak to me on such matters I should soon forfeit your favour. For we in Britain are, as it were, people of another world--simple and straightforward in our thoughts and ways, and with no ideas of state expediency. Therefore, I pray you, let me stand aloof from all such matters, and regard me simply as one ready to strike and die in your defence, and as having no more interest or knowledge of state affairs and state intrigues than those statues in the garden there."

"So be it," Nero said. "You are modest, Beric, and modesty is a virtue rare in Rome; but I appreciate your honesty, and feel sure that I can rely upon you for faithful service. Let me see, to what office shall I appoint you? I cannot call you my bodyguard, for this would excite the jealousy of the Praetorians." He sat in thought for a minute. "Ah!" he exclaimed, "you are fond of books, I will appoint you my private librarian. My libraries are vast, but I will have a chamber close to mine own fitted up with the choicest books, so that I can have ready at hand any that I may require. This will be an excuse for having you always about my person."

"I do not speak Greek, Caesar."

"You shall have under you a Greek freedman, one Chiton, who is now in my library. He will take charge of the rolls, for I do not intend that you should remain shut up there. It is but a pretext for your presence here."

He touched a bell and a servant entered. "Tell Phaon to come to me." A minute later Phaon, a freedman who stood very high in the confidence of Nero, entered.

"Phaon," the emperor said, "this is Beric the Briton, he has entered my service, and will have all my trust and confidence even as you have. Prepare for him apartments close to mine, and appoint slaves for his service. See that he has everything in accordance with his position as a high official of the palace. Let one of the rooms be furnished with sets of books, of which I will give you a list, from my library. Chiton is to be in charge of it under him. Beric is to be called my private librarian. I wish him to be at all times within call of me. You will be friends with Beric, Phaon, for he is as honest as you are, and will be, like you, a friend of mine, and, as you may perceive, is one capable of taking part of a friend in case of need."

Phaon bowed deeply and signed to Beric to follow him; the latter bowed to Nero, who nodded to him pleasantly, and left the room with Phaon. The freedman took him to his private apartment.

"Nero has chosen well this time, methinks," he said after a close scrutiny of the newcomer. "It is no easy post on which you have entered, Beric. Nero is changeable in his moods, but you carry your heart in your face, and even he can have no suspicions of you. Take my advice, make friends with no man, for one who stands high in court favour today may be an exile or condemned tomorrow, and then all connected with him in any way are apt to share his fate; therefore, it is best to stand quite alone. By tomorrow morning you will find everything in readiness for you here."

CHAPTER XVI
IN NERO'S PALACE

Upon leaving Phaon, Beric was conducted to the room where he had left Scopus. The latter at once joined him, and without asking any questions left the palace with him.

"I would ask nothing until you were outside," Scopus said. "They were wondering there at the long audience you have had with Nero. Judging by the gravity of your face, things have not gone well with you."

"They have gone well in one sense," Beric said, "though I would vastly rather that they had gone otherwise. I feel very much more fear now than when I stood awaiting the attack of the lion."

And he then related to Scopus the conversation he had had with Nero. The lanista inclined himself humbly to the ground.

"You are a great man now, Beric, though, as you say, the place is not without its dangers. I guessed when Caesar sent for you that he purposed to use your strength and courage in his service. Your face is one that invites trust, and Nero was wise enough to see that if he were to trust you he must trust you altogether. He has acted wisely. He deemed that, having no friends and connections in Rome, he could rely upon you as he could rely upon no one who is a native here. You will be a great man, for a time at any rate."

"I would rather have remained at your ludus, Scopus. I shall feel like a little dog I saw the other day in a cage of one of the lions. The beast seemed fond of it, but the little creature knew well that at any moment the lion might stretch out its paw and crush it."

Scopus nodded.

"That is true enough, Beric, though there are tens of thousands in Rome who would gladly run the risk for the sake of the honour and profit. Still, as I said to you before we started, I have faith in your good fortune and quickness, and believe that you may escape from the bars where another would lose his skin. Tell to none but myself what Caesar has said to you. The world will soon guess that your post as private librarian is but a pretext for Caesar to have you near him. It is not by such a post that the victor of the arena would be rewarded." They now went together to a goldsmith.

"Ah! Scopus, I have been expecting you. I saw you in the arena with your two gladiators. Afterwards I saw this tall young Briton fight the lion, and when I heard that he was at your ludus I said to myself, 'Scopus will be bringing him to me to dispose of some of the jewelry to which the ladies were so prodigal.'"

"That is our errand, Rufus. Here is the bag."

The goldsmith opened it.

"You don't expect me to name a price for all these articles, Scopus? It will take me a day to examine and appraise them; and, indeed, I shall have to go to a friend or two for money, for there is enough here to stock a shop. Never did I know our ladies so liberal of their gifts."

"Ah!" Scopus said, "and you don't often see gifts so well deserved; but, mind you, if it had been I who had fought the lion--I, who have nothing to recommend me in the way of either stature or looks--it would have been a very different thing. Youth and stature and good looks go for a great deal even in the arena, I can tell you. Well, Beric will call in a day or two. Here is the inventory of the jewels; I have got a copy at home. Do you put the price you will give against each, and then he can sell or not as he pleases. He is not going to sacrifice them, Rufus, for he has no need of money; Caesar has just appointed him to his household."

The manner of the jeweller changed at once.

"The list shall be ready for you in two days," he said to Beric respectfully. "If you have need of money on account now I can let you have as much as you will." Beric shook his head.

"I have all that I require," he said. "I will return it may be in two days, it may be more--I know not precisely how much my duties may occupy me."

"You will get full value for your goods," Scopus said when they left the shop--"that was why I mentioned that you had entered Nero's household, for it is a great thing to have a friend at court."

"And how about yourself, Scopus? You have kept me and trained me for months. Now you are going to lose my services just when you might begin to get a return. Moreover, I may tell you that I shall as soon as possible get Boduoc with me. So you must name a sum which will amply recompense you for the trouble and expense that you have had with us."

"I shall be no loser, Beric. When captives in war are sent to be trained in a ludus the lanista is paid for a year's keep and tuition for them. After that he makes what he can from those who give entertainments. Therefore I received from the imperial treasury the regular amount for you and your comrades. Moreover, the senator who gave the performances sent me a very handsome sum--more than he had agreed to give me for Porus and Lupus together-- saying that, although he had not engaged you, your deeds in the arena had delighted the people beyond measure, and that as his show would be talked about for years, it was but fair he should pay your lanista a sum worthy of the performance. And now farewell! You know that I and your comrades at the ludus will always be glad to see you. We shall be back in Rome as soon as my place is rebuilt."

"You may be sure that I will come, Scopus. You have shown me much kindness, and if in any way I can repay you I will do so. Tell Boduoc I hope very shortly to have him with me, and that maybe I shall be able to find means of withdrawing the others from the arena."

As soon as they separated Beric walked rapidly to the house where Norbanus had taken up his abode. As he reached the door he paused, for he heard within the sounds of wailing, and felt that he had come too late.

"Tell Norbanus," he said to the slave at the door, "that Beric is here, but that unless he wishes to see me I will leave him undisturbed, as I fear by the cries that the Lady Ennia is dead."

"She died early this morning," the slave said. "I will tell my master that you are here."

He returned almost directly.

"Norbanus prays you to enter," he said, and led the way to the magistrate's study.

"Ah, my friend," the Roman said, "it is over! Ennia died this morning. She passed away as if in sleep. It is a terrible grief to me. Thanks to the gods I can bear that as becomes a Roman; but how would it have been had I seen her torn to pieces under my eyes? Ah, Beric you know not from what you have saved us! We could never have lifted up our heads again had she died so. Now we shall grieve for her as all men grieve for those they love; but it will be a grief without pain, for assuredly she died happy. She spoke of you once or twice, and each time she said, 'I shall see him again.' I think she was speaking her belief, that she should meet you after death. The Christian belief in a future state is like yours, you know, Beric, rather than like ours."

"She was a gentle creature," Beric said, "and as she dared even death by the lions for her God, assuredly she will go to the Happy Island, though it may not be the same that the Druids tell us Britons of. And how are the Ladies Lesbia and Aemilia?"

"My wife is well," the magistrate said. "She has not the consolations of philosophy as I have, but I think that she feels it is better for the child herself that she should have so died. Ennia would always have remained a Christian, and fresh troubles and persecutions would have come. Besides, her religion would have put her apart from her mother and her family. To me, of course, it would have made no difference, holding the views that I do as to the religions of the world; but my wife sees things in a different light. Aemilia is worn out with watching and grief, but I know that she will see you presently, that is, if you are not compelled to return at once to the hills."

"I return there no more. I have seen Nero today, and he has appointed me an official in his household. It will seem ridiculous to you when I say that I am to be his private librarian. That, of course, is but a pretext to keep me near his person, deeming that I am strong enough to be a useful guard to him, and being a stranger am not likely to be engaged in any intrigue that may be going on. I would rather have remained at the ludus for a time; but there is no refusing the offers of an emperor, and he spoke to me fairly, and I answered him as one man should do another, frankly and openly."

"Nero has done wisely," Norbanus said warmly, "though for you the promotion is perilous. To be Nero's friend is to be condemned beforehand to death, though for a time he may shower favours upon you. He is fickle and inconstant, and you have not learned to cringe and flatter, and are as likely as not to anger him by your outspoken utterances."

"I shall assuredly say what I think if he questions me," Beric said quietly; "but if he values me as a guard, he will scarce question me when he knows that I should express an opinion contrary to his own."

"When do you enter his service, Beric?"

"I am to present myself tomorrow morning."

"Then you will stay with us tonight, Beric. This is a house of mourning, but you are as one of ourselves. You must excuse ceremony, for I have many arrangements to make, as Ennia will be buried tomorrow."

"I will go out into the garden," Beric said.

"Do so. I will send up word to Aemilia that you are there. Doubtless she would rather meet you there than before the slaves."

Beric had been sitting in the shade for half an hour when he saw Aemilia coming towards him. Her face was swollen with crying, and the tears were still streaming down her cheeks. Beric took her hand, and would have bent over it, when she grasped his with both of hers and pressed it to her lips.

"Oh, Beric," she cried, "what have you not done for us, and how much do we not owe you! Had it not been for you, I should be mourning now, not for Ennia who lies with a smile on her face in her chamber, but for Ennia torn to pieces and devoured by the lion. It seemed to me that I too should die, when suddenly you stood between her and the fierce beast, seeming to my eyes as if a god had come down to save her; and when all the people gave you up as lost, standing there unarmed and calmly waiting the lion's attack, I felt that you would conquer. Truly Ennia's God and yours must have stood beside you, though I saw them not. How else could you have been so strong and fearless? Ennia thought so too. She told me so one night when the house was asleep, and I only watching beside her. 'My God was with him,' she said. 'None other could have given him the strength to battle with the lion. He will bring him to Himself in good time, and I shall meet him again.' She said something about your knowing that she was a Christian. But, of course, you could not have known that."

"I did know it, Aemilia;" and Beric then told her of his meeting with Ennia and the old slave when they were attacked by the plunderers on the way home from their place of meeting. "She promised me not to go again," he said, "without letting me know, in which case I should have escorted her and protected her from harm. But just after that there was the fire, and I had to go away with Scopus to the Alban Hills; and so, as she knew that I could not escort her, I never heard from her. I would that I had been with her that night she was arrested, then she might not have fallen into the hands of the guard. Indeed, had I been here I would have gone gladly, for it seemed to me there must be something strange in the religion that would induce a quiet gentle girl like her to go out at night unknown to her parents. Now I desire even more to learn about it. Her God must surely have given her the strength and courage that she showed when she chose death by lions rather than deny Him."

"I, too, should like to know something about it," Aemilia said. "By the way Ennia spoke, when she said you knew that she was a Christian, it seemed to me that, if you did know, which I thought was impossible, she thought you were angry with her for becoming a Christian."

"I was angry with her not for being a Christian, but for going out without your father's knowledge, and I told her so frankly. If it had been you I should not have been so much surprised, because you have high spirits and are fearless in disposition; but for her to do so seemed so strange and unnatural, that I deemed this religion of hers must be bad in that it taught a girl to deceive her parents."

"What did she say, Beric?"

"I could see that she considered it her duty beyond all other duties, and so said no more, knowing nothing of her religion beyond what your father told me."

"I wish Pollio had been here," the girl said; "he would have thought as I do about the loss of Ennia. My father has his philosophy, and considers it rather a good thing to be out of the world. My mother was so horrified when she heard that Ennia was a Christian, that I am sure she is relieved at her death. I am not a philosopher, and it was nothing to me whether Ennia took up with this new sect or not. So you see I have no one who can sympathize with me. You can't think how dreadful the thought is that I shall be alone in future."

"We grow accustomed to all things," Beric said. "I have lost all my relations, my country, and everything, and I am here a stranger and little better than a slave, and yet life seems not so unpleasant to me. In time this grief will be healed, and you will be happy again."

"I am sure I should never have been happy, Beric, if she had died in the arena. I should always have had it before my eyes--I should have dreamt of it. But why do you say that until today you have been almost a slave? Why is it different today?"

Beric told her of his new position.

"If I could take your position, and have your strength but for one night," Aemilia said passionately, "I would slay the tyrant. He is a monster. It is to him that Ennia's death is due. He has committed unheard of crimes; and he will kill you, too, Beric. He kills all those whom he once favours."

"I shall be on my guard, Aemilia; besides, my danger will not be great, for he will have nothing to gain by my death. I shall keep aloof from all intrigues, and he will have no reason to suspect me. The danger, if danger there be, will come from my refusing to carry out any of his cruel orders. I am ready to be a guard, but not an executioner."

"I know how it will end," the girl sighed; "but I shall hope always. You conquered the lion, maybe you will conquer Nero."

"Who is a very much less imposing creature," Beric smiled. A slave girl at this moment summoned Aemilia into the house. She waited a moment.

"Remember, Beric," she said, "that if trouble and danger come upon you, any such poor aid as I can give will be yours. I am a Roman girl. I have not the strength to fight as you have, but have the courage to die; and as, at the risk of your life, you saved Ennia for us, so would I risk my life to save yours. Remember that a woman can plot and scheme, and that in dealing with Nero cunning goes for as much as strength. We have many relatives and friends here, too, and Ennia's death in the arena would have been viewed as a disgrace upon the whole family; so that I can rely upon help from them if need be. Remember that, should the occasion arise, I shall feel your refusal of my help much more bitterly than any misfortune your acceptance of it could bring upon me." Then turning, the girl went up to the house.

On arriving at Nero's palace the next morning, and asking for Phaon, Beric was at once conducted to his chamber.

"That is well," the freedman said as he entered. "Nero is in council with his architects at present. I will show you to your chamber at once, so that you will be in readiness."

The apartment to which Phaon led Beric was a charming one. It had no windows in the walls, which were covered with exquisitely painted designs, but light was given by an opening in the ceiling, under which, in the centre of the room, was the shallow basin into which the rain that penetrated through the opening fell. There were several elegantly carved couches round the room. Some bronze statues stood on plinths, and some pots of tall aquatic plants stood in the basin; heavy hangings covered the entrance.

"Here," Phaon said, drawing one of them aside, "is your cubicule, and here, next to it, is another. It is meant for a friend of the occupant of the room; but I should not advise you to have anyone sleep here. Nero would not sleep well did he know that any stranger was so close to his apartment. This, and the entrance at the other end of the room, lead into passages, while this," and he drew back another curtain, "is the library."

This room was about the same size as that allotted to Beric, being some twenty-five feet square. Short as the notice had been, a wooden framework of cedar wood, divided into partitions fifteen inches each way, had been erected round, and in each of these stood a wooden case containing rolls of manuscripts, the name of the work being indicated by a label affixed to the box. Seated at a table in one of the angles was the Greek Chiton, who saluted Beric.

"We shall be good friends, I hope," Beric said, "for I shall have to rely upon you entirely for the Greek books, and it is you who will be the real librarian."

Chiton was a man of some thirty years of age, with a pale Greek face; and looking at him earnestly Beric thought that it looked an honest one. He had anticipated that the man Nero had chosen would be placed as a spy over him; but he now concluded this was not so, and that Nero at present trusted him entirely.

"This passage," Phaon said, "leads direct to Caesar's private apartment, a few steps only separate them. The passage on this side of your room also leads there, so that either from here or from it you can be summoned at once. Now let us return to your room. It is from there you will generally go to Nero when he summons you. That door at the end of the short passage will not be kept locked, while this one from the library cannot be opened from your side. Three strokes of Nero's bell will be the signal that he requires you. If after the three have sounded there is another struck smartly, you will snatch up your sword and rush in instantly by night or day."

"What are my duties to be?" Beric asked when they had returned to his room, "for Chiton can discharge those of librarian infinitely better than I can do."

"You will sit and read here, or pass the time as you like, until nine o'clock, at which hour Nero goes to the baths. At eleven he goes out to inspect the works or to take part in public ceremonies. At three he sups, and the meal lasts sometimes till seven or eight, sometimes until midnight. Your duties in the library will end when he goes to the baths, and after that you will be free, unless he summons you to attend him abroad, until supper is concluded. At night you will draw back the curtains between the passage and your room and that of your cubicule, so that you may hear his summons, or even his voice if loudly raised. You will lie down with your sword ready at hand. I should say your duties will begin at six in the morning, and it is only between that hour and nine that you will be a prisoner in the library."

"I shall not find it an imprisonment," Beric said. "Three hours is little enough to study, with all that wealth of books ready at hand. How about Chiton?"

"He will be on duty whenever the emperor is in the palace; beyond that he is free to go where he likes, so that he be ready at all times to produce any book that Nero may call for. Your meals will be brought up to you by your attendant from the imperial kitchen. There are, you know, baths in the palace for the use of the officials. You will find in this chest a supply of garments of all kinds suitable for different occasions, and here, in the cubicule, ready to hand, are a sword and dagger, with a helmet, breastplate, and shield, to be worn only when Caesar desires you to accompany him armed. If there is anything else that you require, you have but to give the order to your attendant, who will obtain it from the steward of the palace."

At this moment a slave drew aside the hanging: "Caesar expects you, Beric."

Nero was standing at the top of the steps into the garden when Beric entered.

"Walk with me, Beric," he said. "For three hours I have been going into the affairs of the city, and hearing letters read from the governors of the provinces. It will be a change to talk of other things. Tell me about this Britain of yours. I know about your wars, tell me of your life at home."

Beric at once complied. He saw that it was not information about religion and customs that the emperor desired to hear, but talk about simple matters that would distract his thoughts from the cares of state. He talked, then, of his native village, of his mother with her maids at work around her, of hunting expeditions as a boy with Boduoc, and how both had had a narrow escape of being devoured by wolves. Nero listened in silence as they strolled under the deep shade of the trees. At times he hardly seemed to be listening, but occasionally he asked a question that showed he was following what Beric said.

"Your talk is like a breath from the snow clad mountains," he said at last, "or a cup of cold water to a thirsty traveller. The word Romans never occurred in it, and yet it was in our tongue. You were brought up among us, as I heard. Tell me of that."

Briefly Beric described his life at Camalodunum.

"It is a strange mixture," Nero said; "the cultivated Roman and the wild Briton. I understand now better than I did before, your risking your life for the Christian girl in the arena. You did not love her?"

"No, Caesar; we Britons do not think of marriage until we are at least five-and-twenty. We hold that young marriages deteriorate a race. Ennia was little more than a child, according to our notions. She was scarce sixteen, and when I saw her before, for a few days only, she was a year younger; but I think that I should have done the same had I never seen her before. We Britons, like the Gauls, hold women in high respect, and I think that few of my people would hesitate to risk their lives to save a helpless woman."

"I think we are all for self here," Nero said; "but we can admire what we should not think of imitating. I like you, Beric, because you are so different from myself and from all around me. We are products of Rome, you of the forest; every man here sighs for power or wealth, or lives for pleasure--I as much as any. We suffer none to stand in our way, but trample down remorselessly all who hinder us. As to risking our lives for the sake of a woman, and that woman almost a stranger, such an idea would never so much as occur to us. This is not the only girl you have saved. I received a letter from Caius Muro some months ago, saying that the news had come to him in Syria that Beric, the young chief of the Iceni, who had so long withstood Suetonius, had been brought a prisoner to Rome, and he besought me, should Beric still be alive, to show favour to him, as he had saved his little daughter, when all others had been slain, at the sack of Camalodunum, and that he had hidden her away until after the defeat of Boadicea, and had then sent her safe and unharmed back to the Romans. The matter escaped my mind till now, though, in truth, I bade my secretary write to him to say that I would befriend you. But it is strange that, having so much life and spirit in that great body of yours, you should yet hold life so cheaply. It was the way with our forefathers, but it is not so now, perhaps because our life is more pleasant than theirs was. Tell me, has Phaon done all to make you comfortable? Is there aught else that you would wish? if so, speak freely."

"There is one thing I should like, Caesar; I should like to have with me my follower Boduoc, he who was the companion of my boyhood, who fought with me in that hut against the wolves, and was ever by my side in the struggle among our fens. I ask this partly for my own sake, and partly that I may the better do the duty you have set me of acting as your guard. The air of palaces is heavy, and men wake not from sleep as when they lie down in the forest and carry their lives in their hands. I might not hear your call; but with him with me we could keep alternate watch through the night, and the slightest sounds would reach our ears. We could even take post close to the hangings of your chamber, just as the Praetorians guard all the avenues on the other side. I might even go further. There were twenty of my countrymen brought hither with me. All are picked men, not one but in strength and courage is my equal. I would say, place them in offices in the palace; make them door keepers, or place some of them here as labourers under your gardeners, then at all times you would have under your orders a body of twenty devoted men, who would escort you in safety though half Rome were in tumult. They would sleep together among the slaves, where I could instantly summon them. I can answer for their fidelity, they would follow me to the death against any foe I bade them attack."

"It is an excellent idea, Beric, and shall be carried out. They were all sent to the ludi, if I mistake not, and will have skill as well as strength and courage. I will bid my secretary send an order for their discharge, and that they present themselves to Phaon tomorrow. He will find occupations for them, and I will myself bid him so dispose of them that they shall be well satisfied with their appointments. Truly, as you say, a guard of twenty gladiators of your strength and courage might well defend me against a host. Now it is time that I went to my bath."

Upon the following day the British captives were all disposed as door keepers in the palace. Beric was present when they presented themselves before Phaon, and had afterwards a private interview with them. They were delighted at finding that they were again under his leadership. All hated as much as ever the occupation of gladiator, although only the man who had defeated Lupus had as yet appeared in the arena.

"Your duties will be simple and easy," Beric said. "You will only have to see that no strangers pass you without authority. Each of you will have one or more attendants with you, who will take the names of those who present themselves to those whom they wish to see, and will, on bringing an authorization for them to pass, escort them to the person with whom they have business. Of course the orders will be different at different posts, but these you will receive from the officials of the chamberlain. You will be on duty, as I learn, for six hours each day, and will for the rest of the time be free to go where you please. I suppose by this time all of you have learned sufficient Latin to converse freely. Remember that at nine o'clock in the evening you must all be in the palace. Phaon has arranged for an apartment that you will occupy together. There you will keep your arms, and be always ready, when you receive a message from me, to attend prepared for fighting. There is one thing more: do not mingle with the Romans more than you can help; listen to no tales relating to the emperor, and let no man discuss with you any question of state. Everything that is done in the palace is known, and were you seen talking with any man who afterwards fell under the suspicion of Nero it might cost you your lives. Remember that, whatever may be the duties assigned to you here, we are really assembled as a sort of special bodyguard to him; he is our general. It is no business of ours what his private acts may be. It may be that he is cruel to the powerful and wealthy, but on the other hand he spends his money lavishly on the people of Rome, and is beloved by them. If they as Romans do not resent his acts towards senators and patricians it is no business of ours, strangers and foreigners here, to meddle in the matter. It may be that in time, if we do our duty well, Nero may permit us to return to Britain."

There was a murmur of approval.

"Nero may cut off the head of every man in Rome for what I care," Boduoc said. "I owe nothing to the Romans. They are all our enemies, from the highest to the lowest; and if Nero is disposed to be our friend he can do what he likes with them. But I do wish he had given us something more to do than to hang about his palace."

Six months passed. Beric stood high in favour with Nero. Two or three times, in order to test the vigilance of his guard, he had sounded his bell. On each occasion an armed figure had instantly entered his room, only to retire when he waved his hand; so that the slave who slept at the other door found Nero alone when he entered, and brought him a cooling drink, or performed some other little office that served as an excuse for his summons, the emperor being well aware how great would be the jealousy of the Praetorian guard, were report to reach them that Caesar had guards save themselves.

Beric often followed in the train of the emperor when he went abroad; and as it speedily became known that he was a favourite of Nero, his friendship was eagerly sought by those who frequented the court, and his good offices solicited by those who had requests to make of the emperor. Large sums of money had been sometimes offered him for his good offices, but he steadily refused to accept any presents whatever, or to mingle in the affairs of others, except in very occasional cases, where it seemed to him that those who sought his aid had been cruelly and unfairly dealt with by officials or venal magistrates.

The sale of his jewels had brought him in a large sum of money, which he had placed in the hands of Norbanus; and the handsome appointments Nero had assigned to his office were very much more than sufficient for his wants. He was always a welcome guest at the house of Norbanus, and now that he was an official high in favour with Nero, even Lesbia received him with marked courtesy. The conversation always turned, when the ladies were present, upon general topics--the gossip of society in Rome, news from the provinces, and other similar matters, for Beric begged them not to speak of the serious events of the day.

"I am one of Nero's guards, and I do not want to have to hate my work, or to wish well to those from whom I am bound to protect him. To me he is kind and friendly. At times when I am with him in the garden or alone in his room he talks to me as an equal, of books and art, the condition of the people, and other topics.

"It seems to me that there are two Neros: the one a man such as he was when he ascended the throne--gentle; inclined to clemency; desirous of the good of his people, and of popularity; a lover of beautiful things; passionately devoted to art in all its branches; taking far greater pleasure in the society of a few intimate friends than in state pageants and ceremonies. There is another Nero; of him I will not talk. I desire, above all things, not to know of him. I believe that he has been driven to this war upon many of the best and worthiest in Rome, by timidity. He is suspicious. Possibly he has reason for his suspicions; possibly they are unfounded. I do not wish to defend him. All this is a matter for you Romans, and not for me. I wish to know nothing about it; to leave all public matters to those they may concern; to shut my eyes and my ears as much as I can to all that goes on around me. It is for that reason that I go so little to other houses save this. I meet those about the court at the baths, the gymnasium, and in the streets. But at these places men speak not of public affairs, they know not who may be listening; and certainly they would not speak before me. Happily, as I am known to stand high in Caesar's favour, I am the last person to whom they would say aught in his blame. Thus it is that, though sometimes I come, from chance words let fall, to know that proscriptions, accusations, confiscations, and executions take place; that the Christians are still exposed to horrible persecutions and tortures; that a gloom hangs over society, and that no man of wealth and high station can regard himself as safe, it is only a vague rumour of these things that I hear; and by keeping my ears sealed and refusing to learn particulars, to listen to private griefs and individual suffering, I am still able to feel that I can do my duty to Caesar."

Norbanus and Lesbia alike agreed with Beric's reasoning; the former, indeed, himself took but comparatively little interest in what passed around him. The latter was, on the other hand, absorbed in the politics of the hour. She was connected with many noble families, and knew that a member of these might fall at any moment under Nero's displeasure. To have a friend, then, high in the favour of Nero was a matter of great importance; and she therefore impressed upon all her intimates that when they found Beric at her house they should scrupulously avoid all discussion of public affairs.

CHAPTER XVII
BETROTHAL

Nero had, within a short time of Beric's establishment in the palace, spoken to him of his apprehension of the increasing power of the party who, having reverted to the opinions of the Stoic philosophers, were ever denouncing the luxury and extravagance of modern ways, and endeavouring, both by example and precept, to reintroduce the simplicity and severity of former times.

"All this," Nero said angrily, "is of course but a cloak under which to attack me. Piso and Plautus, Seneca and Lucan, do but assume this severity of manners. They have plotted and intrigued against me. I shall never be safe while they live."

"Caesar," Beric said gravely, "I am but a soldier, but born a free Briton and a chief. I cannot sell my service, but must give it loyally and heartily. You honour me with your favour and confidence; I believe that I am worthy of it. I do not serve you for money. Already I have begged you not to heap presents upon me. Wealth would be useless to me did I desire it. Not only have you offered to bestow estates upon me, but I have learned already that there are many others who, seeing that I am favoured by you, would purchase my friendship or my advocacy by large sums. I should despise myself if I cared for money. You would, I know honour me not only with your trust that I can be relied upon to do my duty as your guard, but by treating me as one in your confidence in other matters. At the risk, then, of exciting your displeasure and forfeiting your favour, I must again pray you not to burden me with state matters. Of these I know nothing, and wish to know nothing. Save that of Seneca, I scarce know the names of the others of whom you have spoken. I am wholly ignorant of the intrigues of court life, and I seek to know nothing of them, and am therefore in no position to give any opinion on these matters; and did I speak from only partial knowledge I should do these men great wrong.

"In the next place, Caesar, I am not one who has a double face, and if you ask my opinion of a matter in which I thought that others had ill advised you, I should frankly say that I thought you were wrong; and the truth is never palatable to the great. I try, therefore, to shut my ears to everything that is going on around me, for did I take note of rumours my loyalty to you might be shaken."

"Perhaps you are right," Nero said, after a long pause. "But tell me, once and for all, what you do think on general matters. It is good to have the opinion of one whom I know to be honest."

"On one subject only are my convictions strong, Caesar. I think that the terrible persecution of the Christians is in itself horrible, and contrary to all the traditions of Rome. These are harmless people. They make no disturbances; they do injury to no one; they are guilty of no act that would justify in any way the tortures inflicted upon them. I am not a Christian, I know nothing of their doctrines; but I am unable to understand how one naturally clement and kind hearted as you are can give way to the clamour of the populace against these people. As to those of whom you speak, and others, I have no opinions; but were I Caesar, strong in the support of the Praetorian guards, and in the affection of the people at large, I would simply despise plotters. The people may vaguely admire the doctrines of the Stoics, but they themselves love pleasure and amusements and spectacles, and live upon your bounty and generosity. There can then be nothing to fear from open force. Should there be conspirators who would attempt to compass their ends by assassination, you have your guards to protect you. You have myself and my little band of countrymen ready to watch over you unceasingly."

"No care and caution will avail against the knife of the assassin," Nero said gloomily. "It is only by striking down conspirators and assassins that one can guard one's self against their weapons. Julius Caesar was killed when surrounded by men whom he deemed his friends."

Beric could not deny the truth of Nero's words. "That is true, Caesar, and therefore I do not presume to criticise or even to have an opinion upon acts of state policy. These are matters utterly beyond me. I know nothing of the history of the families of Rome. I know not who may, with or without reason, deem that they have cause of complaint against you, or who may be hostile to you either from private grievances or personal ambitions, and knowing nothing I wish to know nothing. I desire, as I said when you first spoke to me, to be regarded as a watchdog, to be attached to you by personal kindness, and to guard you night and day against conspirators and assassins. I beseech you not to expect more from me, or to deem it possible that a Briton can be qualified to give any opinion whatever as to a matter so alien to him as the intrigues and conspiracies of an imperial city. Did I agree with you, you would soon doubt my honesty; did I differ from you, I should incur your displeasure."

Nero looked up at the frank countenance of the young Briton.

"Enough," he said smiling, "you shall be my watchdog and nothing more."

As time went on Nero's confidence in his British guard steadily increased. He had his spies, and knew how entirely Beric kept himself aloof from intimate acquaintanceship with any save the family of Norbanus, and learned, too, that he had refused many large bribes from suitors. For a time, although he knew it not, Beric was constantly watched. His footsteps were followed when he went abroad, his conversations with others in the baths, which formed the great centres of meeting, and stood to the Romans in the place of modern clubs, were listened to and noted. It was observed that he seldom went to convivial gatherings, and that at any place when the conversation turned on public affairs he speedily withdrew; that he avoided all display of wealth, dressed as quietly as it was possible for one in the court circle to do, and bore himself as simply as when he had been training in the ludus of Scopus. There he still went very frequently, practising constantly in arms with his former companions, preferring this to the more formal exercises of the gymnasium. Thus, after a time, Nero became confirmed in his opinion of Beric's straightforward honesty, and felt that there was no fear of his being tampered with by his enemies.

One result of this increased confidence was that Beric's hours of leisure became much restricted, for Nero came to require his attendance whenever he appeared in public. With Beric and Boduoc among the group of courtiers that followed him, the emperor felt assured there was no occasion to fear the knife of the assassin; and it was only when he was at the baths, where only his most chosen friends were admitted, or during the long carousals that followed the suppers, that Beric was at liberty, and in the latter case Boduoc was always near at hand in case of need.

Nero's precautions were redoubled after the detection of the conspiracy of Piso. That this plot was a real one, and not a mere invention of Nero to justify his designs upon those he hated and feared, is undoubted. The hour for the attempt at assassination had been fixed, the chief actor was prepared and the knife sharpened. But the executions that followed embraced many who had no knowledge whatever of the plot. Seneca was among the victims against whom there was no shadow of proof.

After the discovery of this plot Beric found his position more and more irksome in spite of the favour Nero showed him. Do what he would he could not close his ears to what was public talk in Rome. The fabulous extravagances of Nero, the public and unbounded profligacy of himself and his court, the open defiance of decency, the stupendous waste of public money on the new and most sumptuous palace into which he had now removed, were matters that scandalized even the population of Rome. Senators, patricians, grave councillors, noble matrons were alike willingly or unwillingly obliged to join in the saturnalia that prevailed. The provinces were ruined to minister to the luxury of Rome. The wealth of the noblest families was sequestrated to the state. All law, order, and decency were set at defiance.

To the Britons, simple in their tastes and habits, this profusion of luxury, this universal profligacy seemed absolutely monstrous. When they met together and talked of their former life in their rude huts, it seemed that the vengeance of the gods must surely fall upon a people who seemed to have lost all sense of virtue, all respect for things human and divine. To Beric the only bearable portions of his existence were the mornings he spent in reading, and in the study of Greek with Chiton, and in the house of Norbanus. Of Lesbia he saw little. She spent her life in a whirl of dissipation and gaiety, accompanying members of her family to all the fetes in defiance of the wishes of Norbanus, whose authority in this matter she absolutely set at naught.

"The emperor's invitations override the authority of one who makes himself absurd by his presumption of philosophy. I live as do other Roman ladies of good family. Divorce me if you like; I have the fortune I brought you, and should prefer vastly to go my own way."

This step Norbanus would have taken but for the sake of Aemilia. By his orders the latter never went abroad with her mother or attended any of the public entertainments, but lived in the quiet society of the personal friends of Norbanus. Lesbia had yielded the point, for she did not care to be accompanied by a daughter of marriageable age, as by dint of cosmetics and paint she posed as still a young woman. Aemilia had long since recovered her spirits, and was again the merry girl Beric had known at Massilia.

One day when Beric called he saw that Norbanus, who was seldom put out by any passing circumstance, was disturbed in mind.

"I am troubled indeed," he said, in answer to Beric's inquiry. "Lesbia has been proposing to me the marriage of Rufinus Sulla, a connection of hers, and, as you know, one of Nero's intimates, with Aemilia."

Beric uttered an exclamation of anger.

"He is one of the worst of profligates," he exclaimed. "I would slay him with my own hand rather than that Aemilia should be sacrificed to him."

"And I would slay her first," Norbanus said calmly; "but, as Lesbia threatened when I indignantly refused the proposal, Rufinus has but to ask Nero's approval, and before his orders my authority as a father goes for nothing. I see but one way. It has seemed to me for a long time, Beric, that you yourself felt more warmly towards Aemilia than a mere friend. Putting aside our obligations to you for having risked your life in defence of Ennia, there is no one to whom I would more willingly give her. Have I been mistaken in your thoughts of her?"

"By no means," Beric said. "I love your daughter Aemilia, but I have never spoken of it to you for two reasons. In the first place I shall not be for some years of the age at which we Britons marry, and in the second I am but a captive. At present I stand high in the favour of Nero, but that favour may fail me at any day, and my life at the palace is becoming unbearable; but besides, it is impossible that this orgy of crime and debauchery can continue. The vengeance of heaven cannot be much longer delayed. The legions in the provinces are utterly discontented and well nigh mutinous, and even if Rome continues to support Nero the time cannot be far off when the legions proclaim either Galba, or Vespasian, or some other general, as emperor, and then the downfall of Nero must come. How then could I ask you for the hand of Aemilia, a maiden of noble family, when the future is all so dark and troubled and my own lot so uncertain?

"I cannot raise my sword against Caesar, for, however foul his crimes, he has treated me well. Had it not been for that I would have made for Praeneste, when the gladiators rose there the other day, and for the same reason I can do nothing to prepare the way for a rising here. I know the ludus of Scopus would join to a man. There is great discontent among the other schools, for the people have become so accustomed to bloodshed that they seem steeled to all pity, and invariably give the signal for the despatch of the conquered. As to your offer, Norbanus, I thank you with all my heart; but were it not for this danger that threatens from Rufinus, I would say that at the present time I dare not link her lot to mine. The danger is too great, the future too dark. It seems to me that the city and all in it are seized with madness, and above all, at the present time, I would not for worlds take her to the palace of Nero. But if Aemilia will consent to a betrothal to me, putting off the period of marriage until the times are changed, I will, with delight, accept the offer of her hand, if she too is willing, for in Briton, as in Gaul, our maidens have a voice in their own disposal."

Norbanus smiled. "Methinks, Beric, you need not fear on that score. Since the day when you fought the lion in the arena you have been her hero and the lord of her heart. Even I, although but short sighted as to matters unconnected with my work, could mark that, and I believe it is because her mother sees and fears it that she has determined to marry her to Rufinus. I will call her down to find out whether she is ready to obey my wishes."

In a minute or two Aemilia came down from the women's apartments above.

"My child," Norbanus said, "I have offered you in marriage to Beric. He has accepted, saving only that you must come to him not in obedience to my orders but of your own free will, since it is the custom of his country that both parties should be equally free of choice. What do you say, my child?"

Aemilia had flushed with a sudden glow of colour as her father began, and stood with downcast eyes until he had finished.

"One moment before you decide, Aemilia," Beric said. "You know how I am situated, and that at any moment I may be involved in peril or death; that life with me can scarcely be one of ease or luxury, and that even at the best you may be an exile for ever from Rome."

She looked up now. "I love you, Beric," she said. "I would rather live in a cottage with you for my lord and master than in a palace with any other. I would die with you were there need. Your wishes shall always be my law."

"That is not the way in Britain," Beric said, as he drew her to him and kissed her. "The husband is not the lord of his wife, they are friends and equals, and such will we be. There is honour and respect on both sides."

"It will be but your betrothal at present," Norbanus said. "Neither Beric nor I would like to see you in the palace of Caesar; but the sponsalia shall take place today, and then he can claim you when he will. Come again this evening, Beric. I will have the conditions drawn up, and some friends shall be here to witness the form of betrothal. This haste, child, is in order to give Beric power to protect you. Were you free, Rufinus might obtain an order from Nero for me to give you to him, but once the conditions are signed they cannot be broken save by your mutual consent; and moreover, Beric can use his influence with the emperor on behalf of his betrothed wife, while so long as you remain under my authority he could scarcely interfere did Nero give his promise to Rufinus."

"Will my mother be here?"

"She will not, nor do I desire her presence," Norbanus said decidedly. "She has defied my authority and has gone her own path, and it is only for your sake that I have not divorced her. She comes and she goes as she chooses, but her home is with her family, not here. She has no right by law to a voice in your marriage. You are under my authority and mine alone. It is but right that a good mother should have an influence and a voice as to her daughter's marriage; but a woman who frequents the saturnalia of Nero has forfeited her mother's rights. It will be time enough for her to hear of it when it is too late for her to cause trouble. Now do you two go into the garden together, for I have arrangements to make."

At six o'clock Beric returned to the house. In the atrium were gathered a number of guests; some were members of the family of Norbanus, others were his colleagues in office--all were men of standing and family. Beric was already known to most of them, having met them at suppers at the house. When all were assembled Norbanus left the room, and presently returned leading Aemilia by the hand.

"My friends," he said, "you already know why you are assembled here, namely to be witnesses to the betrothal of my daughter to Beric the Briton. Vitrio, the notary, will read the conditions under which they are betrothed."

The document was a formal one, and stated that Norbanus gave up his potestas or authority over his daughter Aemilia to Beric, and that he bound himself to complete the further ceremony of marriage either by the religious or civil form as Beric might select whenever the latter should demand it, and that further he agreed to give her on her marriage the sum of three thousand denarii, and to leave the whole of his property to her at his death; while Beric on his part bound himself to complete the ceremonies of marriage whenever called upon by Norbanus to do so, and to pay him at the present time one thousand denarii on the consideration of his signing the present agreement, and on his delivering up to him his authority over his daughter.

"You have heard this document read, Norbanus," the notary said, when he had concluded the reading. "Do you assent to it? And are you ready to affix your signature to the contract?"

"I am ready," Norbanus said.

"And you, Beric?"

"I am also ready," Beric replied.

"Then do you both write your signatures here."

Both signed, and four of the guests affixed their signatures as witnesses. Norbanus then placed Aemilia's hand in Beric's. "You are now betrothed man and wife," he said. "I transfer to you, Beric, my authority over my daughter; henceforth she is your property to claim as you will."

A minute later there was a sudden movement at the door, and Lesbia entered in haste. "News has just been brought to me of your intention, Norbanus, and I am here to say that I will not permit this betrothal."

"You have no voice or authority in the matter," Norbanus said calmly. "Legal right to interfere you never had. Your moral right you have forfeited. The conditions have been signed. Aemilia is betrothed to Beric."

Lesbia broke out into passionate reproaches and threats, but Norbanus advanced a step or two towards her, and said with quiet dignity, "I have borne with you for her sake, Lesbia. Now that she belongs to Beric and not to me, I need not restrain my just indignation longer. I return your property to your hands."

Lesbia stepped back as if struck. The words were the well known formula by which a Roman divorced his wife. She had not dreamed that Norbanus would summon up resolution to put this disgrace upon her, and to bring upon himself the hostility of her family. Her pride quickly came to her aid.

"Thanks for the release," she said sarcastically; "far too much of my life has already been wasted on a dotard, and my family will see that the restitution of my property is full and complete: but beware, Norbanus, I am not to be outraged with impunity, and you will learn to your cost that a woman of my family knows how to revenge herself."

Then turning she passed out of the door, entered her lectica and was carried away.

"I must apologize to you, my friends," Norbanus said calmly, "for having brought you to be present at an unpleasant family scene, but I had not expected it, and know not through whom Lesbia obtained the news of what was doing here. I suppose one of the slaves carried it to her. But these things trouble not a philosopher; for myself I marvel at my long patience, and feel rejoiced that at last I shall be free to live my own life."

"You have done well, Norbanus," one of his colleagues said, "though I know not what Nero will say when he hears of it, for severity among husbands is not popular at present in Rome."

"I can open my veins as Seneca did," Norbanus said calmly; "neither death nor exile have any terrors for me. Rome has gone mad, and life for a reasoning being is worthless here."

"I shall represent the matter to Nero," Beric said, "and as it is seldom that I ask aught of him, I doubt not he will listen to me. When he is not personally concerned, Nero desires to act justly, and moreover, I think that he can weigh the advantages of the friendship of a faithful guard against that of his boon companions. I will speak to him the first thing in the morning. He frequently comes into the library and reads for an hour. At any rate there is no chance of Lesbia being beforehand with me. It is too late for her to see Rufinus and get him to approach Nero tonight."

"Let us talk of other matters," Norbanus said, "all these things are but transitory." He then began to talk on his favourite topic--the religions of the world, while Beric drew Aemilia, who had been weeping since the scene between her parents, into the tablinum.

"It is unlucky to weep on the day of your betrothal, Aemilia."

"Who could help it, Beric? Besides, as it is not for my own troubles the omen will have no avail. But it is all so strange and so rapid. This morning I was in trouble, alarmed at what my mother told me of her intentions, fearful that my father, who has so long yielded to her, would permit her to have her own way in this also. Then came the great joy when he told me that he would give me to you--that you, who of all men I thought most of, was henceforth to be my lord. Then, just when my happiness was complete, and I was formally bound to you, came my mother. Ennia and I always loved our father most, he was ever thoughtful and kind to us, while even as children our mother did not care for us. As we grew up she cared still less, thinking only of her own pleasures and friends, and leaving us almost wholly in charge of the slaves; but it was not until Ennia was seized as a Christian that I knew how little she loved us. Then she raved and stormed, lamented and wept, not because of the fate of Ennia, not because of the terrible death that awaited her, but because of the disgrace it brought upon herself. Even after she was brought here she scarce came in to see her, and loudly said that it would be best for her to die. Lately, as you know, I have seen little of her; she spends all her time abroad, has defied my father's authority; and brought grief and trouble upon him. Still, to a daughter it is terrible that her mother should be divorced."

"Let us not think of it now, Aemilia. Your father has acted, as he always does, rightly and well. I know much more of what is going on than you do, and I can tell you that Lesbia, who was so jealous of the honour of her name when Ennia was concerned, is bringing far greater dishonour upon her name by her own actions. And now let us talk of ourselves. The act you have just done, dear, may bring all sorts of sacrifices upon you. At any moment I may be a fugitive, and, as you know, the families of those who incur Nero's wrath share in their disgrace; and if I am forced to fly, you too may be obliged to become a fugitive."

She looked up brightly. "I shall not mind any hardships I suffer for your sake, Beric. Rome is hateful to me since Ennia stood in the arena. I would rather share a hut with you among the savage mountains of the north than a palace here."

"I trust that trouble is still far distant, but I shall, as soon as I can, find a retreat where, in case I fall under Nero's displeasure, you can lie hid until I can send for you."

"I have such a retreat, Beric. Since Ennia's death I have seen a good deal of the Christians. Lycoris, you know, was captured at the same time as Ennia, and was put to death by fire; but her daughter, married to a freedman who had purchased her liberty from my father, managed to escape with her husband when the place was surrounded. I have met her several times since. She and her husband are living hidden in the catacombs, where she tells me many of their sect have taken refuge from the persecutions.

"The last time I saw her she said to me, 'No one's life is safe in this terrible city, and none, however high in station, can say that they may not require refuge. Should you need an asylum, Aemilia, go to the house of a freedman, one Mincius, living in the third house on the right of a street known as the Narrow one, close behind the amphitheatre at the foot of the Palatine Hill, and knock thrice at the door. When they open, say, 'In the name of Christ,' then they will take you in. Tell them that you desire to see me, and that you are the sister of Ennia, the daughter of Norbanus, and they will lead you to us. There is an entrance to the catacombs under the house. As the sister of Ennia you will be warmly received by all there, even although you yourself may not belong to us. The galleries and passages are of a vast extent and known only to us. There is no fear of pursuit there.'"

"That is good news, Aemilia; it is sad that, but an hour betrothed, we are forced to think of refuges, but it will be happiness to me to know that if danger threatens, you have a place of retreat. You see this ring; Nero himself gave it me; mark it well, so that you may know it again. It is a figure of Mercury carved on an amethyst. When you receive it, by night or day, tarry not a moment, but wrap yourself in a sombre mantle like that of a slave, and hie you to this refuge you speak of; but first see your father, tell him where you are going and why, so that he may fly too, if he choose."

"He will not do that," Aemilia said, "and how can I leave him?"

"You must leave him because you belong to me, Aemilia, and because you are acting on my orders. The danger to you is far greater than to him. You are my wife, he only my father in law, and they would strike at me first through you. Besides, there are other reasons. Your father is a Roman of the old type, and like Seneca and Plautus, and others of the same school, will deem it no loss when the time comes to quit life. However, you will tell him of the danger, and he must make his own choice. I shall beg him to hand to you at once the money which I placed in his care now a year ago. Do you hand it over to the woman you speak of, and ask her to hide it away in the caves till you ask for it again; these Christians are to be trusted. I have much money besides, for Nero is lavishly generous, and it would anger him to refuse his bounty. This money I have placed in several hands, some in Rome, some elsewhere, so that if forced to fly I can at any rate obtain some of my store without having to run into danger."

"One more question, Beric. Should I ever have to take refuge among the Christians, and like Ennia come to love their doctrines, would you be angered if I joined their sect? If you would I will not listen to them, but will tell them that I cannot talk or think of these things without my husband's consent."

"You are free to do as you like, Aemilia. Since Ennia died I have resolved upon the first opportunity to study the doctrines of these people, for truly it must be a wonderful religion that enables those who profess it to meet a cruel death not only without fear but with joy. You know Ennia said we should meet again, and I think she meant that I, too, should become a Christian. Ask the woman if I also, as a last resource, may take refuge among them."

"I will ask her, Beric; but I am sure they will gladly receive you. Have you not already risked your life to save a Christian?"

The other guests having now left, Norbanus joined them, and Beric told him of the arrangements they had made in case of danger. He warmly approved of them.

"It will be a relief to me as to you, Beric, to know that Aemilia's safety is provided for. As for myself, fate has no terrors for me; but for you and her it is different. She is yours now, for although but betrothed she is virtually your wife. You have but to take her by the hand and to declare her your wife in the presence of witnesses, and all is done. There is, it is true, a religious ceremony in use only among the wealthier classes, but this is rather an occasion for pomp and feasting, and is by no means needful, especially as you have no faith in the Roman gods. What are the rites among your own people, Beric?"

"We simply take a woman by the hand and declare her our wife. Then there is feasting, and the bride is carried home, and there is the semblance of a fight, the members of her family making a show of preventing us; but this is no part of the actual rite, which is merely public assent on both sides. And now I must be going. Nero will be feasting for a long time yet; but Boduoc has been on guard for many hours and I must relieve him. Farewell, Norbanus; we have been preparing for the worst, but I trust we shall escape misfortune. Farewell, my Aemilia!" and kissing her tenderly Beric strode away to the palace of Nero.

He had not seen Boduoc since early morning, and the latter, standing on guard outside the private entrance to Nero's apartments, greeted his arrival, "Why, Beric, I began to fear that some harm had befallen you. I came in this morning after the bath and found you had gone out. I returned again at six and found your chamber again empty, but saw that you had returned during my absence; I went on guard, and here have I been for four hours listening to all that foolish singing and laughter inside. How Caesar, who has the world at his command, can spend his time with actors and buffoons, is more than I can understand. But what has kept you?"

As there was no fear of his voice being heard through the heavy hangings, Beric, to Boduoc's intense surprise, related the events of the day.

"So you have married a Roman girl, Beric! Well, I suspected what would come of it when you spent half your time at the house of Norbanus. I would rather that you had married one of our own maidens; but as I see no chance of our return to Britain for years, if ever, one could hardly expect you to wait for that. At any rate she is the best of the Roman maidens I have seen. She neither dyes her hair nor paints her face, and although she lacks stature, she is comely, and is always bright and pleasant when I have accompanied you there. I am inclined to feel half jealous that you have another to love you besides myself, but I will try and not grudge her a share of your affection."

"Well, hand me your sword, Boduoc, and betake yourself to your bed. I will remain on guard for the next four hours, or until the feasting is over. Nero often opens the hangings the last thing to see if we are watchful, and he likes to see me at my post. I wish to find him in a good temper in the morning."

The next morning, to Beric's satisfaction, Nero came into the library early. Chiton, as was his custom, retired at once.

"I was inspired last night, Beric," the emperor said. "Listen to these verses I composed at the table;" and he recited some stanzas in praise of wine.

"I am no great judge of these matters, Caesar," Beric said; "but they seem to me to be admirable indeed. How could it be otherwise, when even the Greeks awarded you the crown for your recitations at their contests? Yesterday was a fortunate day for me, also, Caesar, for Norbanus betrothed his daughter to me."

The emperor's face clouded, and Beric hastened to say:

"There is no talk of marriage at present, Caesar, for marriage would interfere with my duties to you. Therefore it is only when you have no longer an occasion for my services that the betrothal will be converted into marriage. My first duty is to you, and I shall allow nothing to interfere with that."

Nero's face cleared. "That is right," he said graciously. "You might have married better, seeing that you enjoy my favour; but perhaps it is as well as it is. Norbanus is a worthy man and a good official, although his ideas are old fashioned; but it is reported of him that he thinks of nothing but his work, and mixes himself up in no way in politics, living the life almost of a recluse. It was one of his daughters you championed in the arena. She died soon afterwards, I heard. Has he other children?"

"Only the maiden I am betrothed to, Caesar. He is now alone, for his wife has long been altogether separated from him, being devoted to gaiety and belonging to a family richer and more powerful than his, and looking down upon her husband as a mere bookworm. He has borne with her neglect and disobedience to his wishes for a long time, and has shown, as it seemed to me, far too great a weakness in exerting his authority; but his patience has at last failed, and when yesterday, in defiance of him, she would have interfered to prevent my betrothal to his daughter, he divorced her."

"Divorce is the fashion," Nero said carelessly. "I know his wife Lesbia, she has frequently been present with members of her family at my entertainments. She is a fine woman, and I wonder not that she and the recluse her husband did not get on well together. She will soon be consoled."

"I have mentioned it to you, Caesar, because she is a revengeful woman, and might cause rumours unfavourable to her husband to be reported to you. He is the most simple and single minded of men, and his thoughts are entirely occupied, as you say, with the duties of his office and with the learned book upon which he has long been engaged; but although a philosopher in his habits he holds aloof from all parties, and even in his own family never discusses public affairs. Had it been otherwise, you may be sure that I, your majesty's attendant and guard, should have abstained from visiting his house."

"I know this to be the case, Beric. Naturally, when I first placed you near my person, I was interested in knowing who were your intimates, and caused strict inquiries to be made as to the household of Norbanus and his associates; all that I heard was favourable to him, and convinced me that he was in no way a dangerous person."

Nero left the room, and returned shortly bearing a casket. "Give these jewels to your betrothed, Beric, as a present from Caesar to the wife of his faithful guard."

Beric thanked the emperor in becoming terms, and in the afternoon carried the jewels, which were of great value, to Aemilia.

"They are a fortune in themselves," he said; "in case of danger, take them from the casket and conceal them in your garments. No one could have been more cordial than Nero was this morning; but he is fickle as the wind, and when Rufinus and others of his boon companions obtain his ear his mood may change altogether."

CHAPTER XVIII
THE OUTBREAK

It was not long, indeed, before Beric found that hostile influences were at work. Nero was not less friendly in his manner, but he more than once spoke to him about Aemilia.

"I hear," he said one day, "that your betrothed is very beautiful Beric."

"She is very fair, Caesar," Beric replied coldly.

"I know not how it is that I have not seen her at court," Nero continued.

"Her tastes are like those of her father," Beric said. "She goes but seldom abroad, and has long had the principal care of her father's household."

"But you should bring her now," Nero persisted. "The wife of one of the officials of the palace should have a place at our entertainments."

"She is not at present my wife, Caesar, she is but my betrothed; and as you have yourself excused me from attendance at all entertainments, it would be unseemly for her, a Roman maiden, though betrothed to me, to appear there."

"There are plenty of other Roman maidens who appear there," Nero said pettishly. Beric made no reply, and the subject was not again alluded to at that time; but the emperor returned to it on other occasions, and Beric at last was driven to refuse point blank.

"I am your majesty's guard," he said. "I watch you at night as well as by day, and, as I have told your majesty, I cannot perform my duties properly if I have to be present at your entertainments. I should not permit my wife or my betrothed to be present in public unless I were by her side. Your majesty took me for what I was, a simple Briton, who could be relied upon as a guard, because I had neither friends nor family in Rome, and was content to live a simple and quiet life. I am willing to abstain from marriage in order that I may still do my service as heretofore; but if I have to attend entertainments, you cannot rely upon my constant vigilance. It is for you to choose, Caesar, whether you most require vigilant guards, who could be trusted as standing aloof from all, or the addition of two persons to the crowds you entertain. I am sure, Caesar," he went on as the emperor made no reply, "it is not yourself who is now speaking to me; it is Rufinus, formerly a suitor for the hand of the daughter of Norbanus, who has been whispering into your ear and abusing the favour you show him. He dare not show his animosity to me openly, for one who has conquered a lion would make but short work of him. Your majesty, I pray you, let not the word of men like this come between yourself and one you know to be faithful to you."

"You are right, Beric," Nero said. "I will press you no farther; it was but a passing thought. I had heard of the beauty of your betrothed, and though I would see if she were as fair as report makes her; but since you do not wish it to be so, it shall not be spoken of again."

But Beric knew enough of Nero to be aware that, like most weak men, he was obstinate, and that Rufinus and his friends would not allow the matter to drop. Every preparation was therefore made for sudden flight. Aemilia was warned on no account to trust any message she might receive purporting to be from him, and the Britons in the palace, who were heartily sick of their monotonous duty, were told to hold themselves in readiness for action. Beric knew that he could depend on the slave who had been assigned to him as an attendant. He was not the man who had at first served him, and who, as Beric doubted not, had acted as a spy upon him. When it was found that there was nothing to discover this man had been removed for other work, and a slave boy of some seventeen years old had taken his place. To him Beric had behaved with great kindness, and the lad was deeply attached to him. He had several times taken notes and messages to the house of Norbanus, and Beric told Aemilia that when it became necessary to send her the ring, he should probably intrust it to him.

A week later Boduoc was on guard at ten in the evening. In the distant banqueting hall he could hear sounds of laughter and revelry, and knowing the nature of these feasts he muttered angrily to himself that he, a Briton, should be standing there while such things were being done within. Suddenly he heard a step approaching the hangings. They were drawn back, and one of the court attendants said, "Caesar requires the attendance of Beric the Briton in the banqueting hall."

"I will tell him," Boduoc said. "He will come directly." Beric was sitting reading when Boduoc entered and gave the message.

"This means mischief, Boduoc," he said. "I have never been sent for before to one of these foul carousals. Philo, come hither!"

The lad, who was lying on a mat by the door, rose. "Philo, take this ring. Follow me to the door of the banqueting room, and stand behind the hangings. If I say 'Run, Philo!' carry out the orders that I have before given you. Speed first to the room where the Britons sleep, and tell them to arm and come up by the private stairs to my room instantly. They know the way. They are then to pass on through the passage and the next room and wait behind the hangings, when Boduoc will give them orders. Directly you have given my message speed to the house of Norbanus, and demand in my name to see the lady Aemilia. If she has retired to her room she must be roused. If the slaves make difficulty, appeal to Norbanus himself. He will fetch her down to you. Give her this ring, and say the time has come."

"I will do it, my lord. Where am I to join you afterwards?"

"I shall take the road to the Alban Hills first; I think that if you are speedy, you may be on the Alban road before me. Now follow me. Boduoc, do you come as far as the hangings of the banqueting room, and stand there with Philo. You will be able to hear what passes within. Do not enter unless I call you. Bring my sword with you."

Beric passed through two or three large apartments and then entered the banqueting room. It was ablaze with lights. A dozen men and as many women, in the scantiest costumes, lay on couches along each side of the table. All were crowned with chaplets of flowers, and were half covered with roses, of which showers had fallen from above upon them. Nero lay on a couch at the end of the table; his features were flushed with wine. Beric repressed the exclamation of indignant disgust that rose to his lips, and walking calmly up to Nero said coldly, "I am told that you want me, Caesar."

"I do, my fighter of lions," Nero said unsteadily. "I would see this paragon of whom Rufinus tells me, whom you guard so jealously from my eyes. Send and fetch her hither. She will be a worthy queen of our revels."

"It is an honour to me to obey your majesty's commands in all matters that regard myself," Beric said; "but in regard to my promised wife, no! This is no place for a Roman lady; and even at the risk of your displeasure, Caesar, I refuse to dishonour her by bringing her into such an assembly."

"I told you he would refuse, Caesar," Rufinus, who was lying on the couch next to Nero, laughed.

Nero was speechless with surprise and anger at Beric's calm refusal to obey his orders. "Do I understand," he said at last, "that you refuse to obey me?"

"I do, Caesar. It is not a lawful command, and I distinctly refuse to obey it."

"Then, by the gods, your life is forfeit!" Nero said, rising to his feet.

"You may thank your gods, Caesar, that I have more sense of honour than you. Were it otherwise, I would strike you dead at my feet. But a British chief disdains to fight an unarmed foe, and I who have eaten your bread and taken your wages am doubly bound not to lift my hand against you." Then he lifted his voice and cried, "Run, Philo!"

The revellers by this time had all started to their feet. Nero, shrinking backwards behind them, called loudly for help. Rufinus, who had shown bravery in the wars, drew a dagger from beneath his toga and sprang at Beric. The latter caught his uplifted wrist, and with a sharp wrench forced him to drop the weapon; then he seized him in his grasp. "You shall do no more mischief, Rufinus," he said, and raising him in his arms hurled him with tremendous force against a marble pillar, where he fell inert and lifeless, his skull being completely beaten in by the blow.

The hall rang with the shrieks of women and the shouts of men. There was a sound of heavy footsteps, and eight of the Praetorian guards, with drawn swords, ran in on the other side of the chamber. "Boduoc!" Beric shouted; and in a moment his follower stood beside him and handed him his sword and buckler.

"Kill him!" Nero shouted frantically. "The traitor would have slain me."

Beric and Boduoc stepped back to the door by which they had entered, and awaited the onset of the Praetorians. For a moment these hesitated, for Beric's figure was well known in the palace, and not one of them but had heard of his encounter with the lion. The emperor's shouts, however, overcame their reluctance, and shoulder to shoulder they rushed forward to the attack. Two fell instantly, helmet and head cloven by the swords of the Britons, who at once took the offensive and drove the others before them, slaying three more and putting the others to flight. But the success was temporary, for now a great body of the guard poured into the room.

"Step back through the doorway, Boduoc," Beric said; "their numbers will not avail them then."

The doors were ten feet in width. This gave room to but three men to enter at once and use their arms to advantage, and for two or three minutes the Britons kept the Praetorians at bay, eight of them having fallen beneath their blows; then there was a shout, and the Roman soldiers came running in at a door at the end of the chamber. "Fall back to the next door," Beric said; but as he spoke there was a rush behind, and nineteen Britons ran into the room, and uttering the war cry of the Iceni flung themselves upon the Roman soldiers. These, taken by surprise at the sudden appearance of these tall warriors, and ignorant of what further reinforcements might be coming up, gave ground, and were speedily beaten back, a score of them falling beneath the Britons' swords.

"Now retreat!" Beric cried as the room was cleared; "retreat at full speed. Show them the way, Boduoc, by the staircase down into the garden. Quick! there is not a moment to lose. I will guard the rear."

They ran down the passage, through Beric's room, down a long corridor, and then by stairs leading thence into the garden, which was indeed a park of considerable size, with lakes, shrubberies, and winding walks. The uproar in the palace was no longer heard by the time they were halfway across the park; but they ran at full speed until they reached a door in the wall. Of this Beric had some time before obtained a key from the head gardener, and always carried this about with him. As they stopped they looked back towards the palace. Distant shouts could be heard, and the lights of numbers of torches could be seen spreading out in all directions.

Beric opened the door and locked it behind him when all had passed out. "Now," he said to his companions, "make your way down to the road leading out to the Alban Hills. Break up and go singly, so that you may not be noticed. It will be a good half hour before the news of what has occurred is known beyond the palace. Do not pass through the frequented streets, but move along the dark lanes as much as possible. When half a mile beyond the city we will reunite."

An hour later the whole party were gathered beyond the city. All were delighted to escape from what they considered slavery, and the fact that they had again bucklers on their arms and swords by their sides made them feel as if their freedom were already obtained.

"This puts one in mind of old times," Boduoc said joyously; "one might think we were about to start on an expedition in the fens. Well, they have taught us all somewhat more than we knew before, and we will show them that the air of Rome has robbed us of none of our strength. Where go we now, Beric?"

"First to the ludus of Scopus; I learned a week since that he had taken his band out again to the Alban Hills for the hot season. I believe that most of his men will join us, if not all. As soon as the news is spread that we are in arms we could, if we wished it, be joined by scores of gladiators from the other schools. There are hundreds who would, if the standard of revolt were raised, prefer dying fighting in the open to being slain to gratify a Roman mob."

"Ay, that there are," put in another of the band. "I have never ceased to lament that I did not fall that day on our island in the fens."

"Think you there will be pursuit, Beric?" another asked.

"No; the first thought of Nero will be to assemble all the Praetorians for his protection; they will search the palace and the park, expecting attack rather than thinking of pursuit. In the morning, when they find that all is quiet, and that it is indeed only us with whom there is trouble, they will doubtless send parties of searchers over the country; but long before that we shall be a day's march ahead. My wish is to gain the mountains. I do not want to head a great rebellion against Rome--disaster would surely come of it at last, and I should have only led men to their death. A hundred men is the outside number I will take. With that number we may live as outlaws among the mountains to the south; we could move so rapidly that large forces could not follow us, and be strong enough to repulse small ones. There is plenty of game among the hills, and we should live as we did at home, chiefly by hunting."

Just as they were approaching the hills a quick step was heard behind them, and the lad Philo ran up.

"Ah, you have overtaken us, Philo! 'tis well, lad, for your life would have been forfeited had you stayed in Rome.

"Well," he asked, drawing him aside, "you saw the lady Aemilia. What said she?"

"She said, 'Tell my lord that I obey, but that I pray him to let me join him and share his dangers if it be possible; but be it tomorrow or five years hence, he will find me waiting for him at the place he knows of.' Norbanus was present when she spoke. I told him what I had heard in the banqueting room, and he said 'Beric has done rightly. Tell him that he has acted as a Roman should do, but as Romans no longer act, caring less for their honour than do the meanest slaves, and that I thank him for having thus defended my daughter against indignity.' He was glad, he said, that his life would end now, for it was a burden to him under such conditions. He gave me this bag of gold to bring to you, saying that he should have no farther need for it, and that, leaving in such haste, you would not have time to furnish yourself with money. It is heavy," the boy said. "I should have caught you some time earlier, but twenty or more pounds' weight makes a deal of difference in a long run."

On arriving at the house of Scopus Beric bade the others wait without, and stepping over the slaves lying at the entrance, he went quietly to the sleeping chamber of the lanista.

"Who is this?" Scopus asked as he entered.

"It is I, Beric; throw your mantle on and come outside with me, Scopus. I would speak with you alone, and do not wish that all should know that I have been here."

"In trouble?" Scopus asked as they left the house. "Ay, lad, I expected it, and knew that sooner or later it would come. What is it?"

"Nero ordered me to fetch Aemilia to his foul carousal. I refused. Rufinus, at whose instigation he acted, attacked me. I hurled him against a pillar, and methinks he was killed, and then Nero, in alarm for his life, called in the Praetorians. Boduoc and my countrymen joined me, and we slew some thirty of them, and then made our escape, and are taking to the mountains."

"And you have come to ask my gladiators to join?" Scopus said shortly.

"No," Beric replied; "when I started I thought of so doing, but as I walked hither I decided otherwise. It would not be fair to you. Did I ask them some would join, I know, others might not. The loss of their services I could make up to you; but if it were known that we had been here, and that some of your band had joined me, Nero's vengeance would fall on you all."

"I thank you, Beric; if some went I must go myself, for I dare not remain, and though I wish you well, and hate the tyrant, I am well off and comfortable, and have no desire to throw away my life."

"There is one I should like to take with me--Porus; we were good friends when I was here, and I know that he hates this life and longs to be free from it. He would have run away and joined the gladiators when they rose at Praeneste had I not dissuaded him. He could leave without the others knowing it, and in the morning you might affect a belief that he has run away, and give notice to the magistrate here and have him sought for. In that way there would be no suspicion of his having joined us. I know that he is valuable to you, being, I think, the best of your troop, but I will pay you whatever price you place his services at."

"No, no," Scopus said, "I will give him to you, Beric, for the sake of our friendship, and for your consideration for me in not taking the rest with you. I have done well by you and him. Stay here and I will fetch him out to you; it may be that many will desert both from me and the other lanistae when they hear that you have taken to the mountains, but for that I cannot be blamed. You have come far out of your way to come hither."

"Yes, 'tis a long detour, but it will matter little. We shall skirt round the foot of the hills, cross the Lyris below Praeneste, and then make straight to the mountains. They will not search for us in that direction, and we will take shelter in a wood when day breaks, and gain the mountains tomorrow night. Once there we shall be safe, and shall move farther south to the wild hills between Apulia and Campania, or if it is too hot for us there, down into Bruttium, whence we can, if it be needed, cross into Sicily. I am not thinking of making war with Rome. We intend to live and die as free men, and methinks that in the mountains we may laugh at the whole strength of Rome."

"You will find plenty of others in the same condition there, Beric; escaped slaves and gladiators constantly make for the hills, and there have been many expeditions against the bands there, who are often strong enough to be a danger to the towns near the foot of the mountains."

"We are not going to turn brigands," Beric said; "there is game on the hills, and we are all hunters, and I have money enough to pay for all else we require did we live there for years. But fetch me Porus. We must be far from here by daylight."

Porus soon came out, much surprised at being suddenly roused from sleep, and silently brought out of the house by Scopus. As soon as Beric explained to him what had happened, he joyfully agreed to join him, and stole in and fetched his arms. Then with a hearty adieu to Scopus Beric placed himself at the head of his band and struck off by the road to Praeneste. Walking fast they arrived at the bank of the Lyris before daybreak, crossed the river in a fisherman's boat they found on the bank, and just as daylight showed in the sky entered an extensive grove, having walked over forty miles since leaving Rome. They slept during the day, taking it by turns to watch at the edge of the wood, and when it was again dark started afresh, and were, when morning broke, high up on the slopes of the Apennines.

"I feel a free man again now," Boduoc said. "It does not seem to me that I have drawn a breath of fresh air since I entered Rome; but fresh air, good as it is, Beric, is not altogether satisfying, and I begin to feel that I have eaten nothing since I supped the day before yesterday."

"We will push on for another hour," Beric said, "and then we shall be fairly beyond the range of cultivation. At the last house we come to we will go in and purchase food. Flour is the principal thing we need; we shall have no difficulty in getting goats from the herdsmen who pasture their animals among the hills."

An hour later Beric, with Boduoc and two of his followers, went up to a farm house. The farmer and his servants ran into the house, raising cries of alarm at the sight of the four tall armed figures.

"Do not fear," Beric said when he reached the door, "we are not brigands, but honest men, who desire to pay for what we need."

Somewhat reassured, the farmer came out. "What does my lord require?" he asked, impressed by a nearer view of Beric's dress and arms.

"How much flour have you in the house?" Beric asked, "and what is the price of it?"

The farmer had three sacks of flour. "I will take them all," Beric said, "and three skins of wine if you have them. I would also buy two sheep if you name me a fair price for the whole."

The farmer named a price not much above that which he would have obtained in the market, and Beric also bought of him a number of small bags capable of containing some fifteen or twenty pounds of flour each. Then one of the men fetched up the rest of the band; the flour was divided and packed in the small bags; the sheep were killed and cut up; three of the men lifted the wine skins on to their shoulders; the rest took the flour and meat, and they marched away, leaving the farmer and his family astounded at the appearance of these strange men with fair hair and blue eyes, and of stature that appeared to them gigantic.

Still ascending the mountain the band halted in a forest. Wood was soon collected and a fire lighted. The contents of one of the bags was made into dough at a stream hard by, divided into cakes and placed on red hot ashes, while the meat was cut up and hung over the fire.

"We have forgotten drinking horns," Beric said, "but your steel cap, Porus, will serve us for a drinking cup for today."

After a hearty meal they lay down for some hours to sleep, and then resumed their march. They were getting well into the heart of the mountains when a figure suddenly appeared on a crag above them.

"Who are you?" he shouted, "and what do you here in the mountains?"

"We are fugitives from the tyranny of Rome," Beric replied. "We mean harm to no man, but those who would meddle with us are likely to regret it."

"You swear that you are fugitives," the man called back.

"I swear," Beric said, holding up his hand.

The man turned round and spoke to someone behind him, and a moment later a party of fifteen men appeared on the crag and began to descend into the ravine up which Beric's band were making their way.

"It is the Britons," the leader exclaimed as he neared them. "Why, Beric, is it you, tired already of the dignities of Rome? How fares it with you, Boduoc?"

Beric recognized at once a Gaul, one of the gladiators of Scopus, who had some months before fled from the ludus. In a minute the two bands met. Most of the newcomers were Gauls, and, like their leader, escaped gladiators, and as Beric's name was well known to all they saluted him with acclamations. Both parties were pleased at the meeting, for, akin by race and speaking dialects of the same language, they regarded each other as natural allies.

"The life of an outlaw will be a change to you after Nero's palace, Beric," Gatho, their leader, said.

"A pleasant change," Beric replied. "I have no taste for gilded chains. How do you fare here, Gatho?"

"There are plenty of wild boars among the mountains, and we can always get a goat when they are lacking. There are plenty of them wild all over the hills, escaped captives like ourselves. As for wine and flour, we have occasionally to make a raid on the villages."

"I do not propose to do that," Beric said; "I have money to buy what we require; and if we set the villagers against us, sooner or later they will lead the troops after us up the mountains."

"I would gladly do that too, but the means are lacking. We owe the peasants no ill will, but one must live, you know."

"Have you any place you make your headquarters?"

"An hour's march from hence; I will lead you to it."

The united bands continued to climb the hills, and on emerging from the ravine Gatho led them for some distance along the upper edge of a forest, and then turned up a narrow gorge in the hillside with a little rivulet running down it. The ravine widened out as they went up it, till they reached a spot where it formed a circular area of some hundred and fifty feet in diameter, surrounded on all sides by perpendicular rocks, with a tiny cascade a hundred feet in height falling into it at the farther end. Some rough huts of boughs of trees were erected near the centre.

"A good hiding place," Beric said, "but I see no mode of retreat, and if a peasant were to lead a party of Romans to the entrance you would be caught in a trap."

"We have only been here ten days," Gatho said, "and never stop long in one place; but it has the disadvantage you speak of. However, we have always one or two men posted lower down, at points where they can see any bodies of men ascending the hills. They brought us notice of your coming when you were far below, so you see we are not likely to be taken by surprise, and the Roman soldiers are not fond of night marches among the mountains."

As it was some hours since the Britons had partaken of their meal they were quite ready to join the Gauls in another, and the carcass of a wild boar hanging up near the huts was soon cut up and roasting over a fire, the Britons contributing wine and flour to the meal. After it was over there was a long talk, and after consulting together Gatho and his band unanimously agreed in asking Beric to take command of the whole party.

"We all know you, Beric," Gatho said. "None could like you have fought a lion barehanded, and I know that there was no one in the ludus who was your match with the sword, while Boduoc and the other five were infinitely superior to any of us in strength. Besides, you are well versed in Roman ways, and have led an army against them, therefore we all are ready to accept you as our leader and to obey your orders if you will take us."

"I will do so willingly, Gatho. I do not wish to have more than fifty men with me, for it would be difficult to find subsistence for a larger number. A hundred is the outside number, and doubtless we shall be able to gather other recruits should we choose to raise the band to that number; but all who follow me must obey me as implicitly as did my own tribesmen in our struggle with the Romans, and must swear to do no harm to innocent people, and to abstain from all violence and robbery. I am ready to be a leader of outlaws but not of brigands. I desire only to live a free life among the mountains. If the Romans come against us we will fight against them, and the spoil we may take from them is lawful booty, to be used in exchange for such things as we may require. But with the peasants we will make friends, and if we treat them well they will bring us news of any expeditions that may be on foot for our capture. As I said I have money enough to buy everything we want at present, and can obtain more if necessary, so that there is no reason for us to rob these poor people of their goods. Here we are too near Rome for them to be disaffected, but further south we shall find them not unwilling to aid us, for the provinces are ground into the dust by the exactions necessary to pay for the cost of the rebuilding of Rome and to support the extravagance of Nero."

The Gauls cheerfully took the required oath.

"You, Gatho, will continue to act as my lieutenant with your Gauls, Boduoc commands the Britons under me. It may be necessary at times for the band to divide, as when game is scarce we may find a difficulty in keeping together, especially if we recruit our band up to a hundred. I am determined to have no malefactors who have fled from justice nor riotous men among us. I should prefer that they should be chiefly your countrymen, but we will not refuse gladiators of other nations who have been captured as prisoners of war. We want no escaped slaves among us. A man who has once been a slave might try to buy his pardon and freedom by betraying us. We will be free men all, asking only to live in freedom among the mountains, injuring none, but determined to fight and die in defence of that freedom."

These sentiments were warmly welcomed by the Gauls. The next day the number of men on the lookout was increased, and the band, breaking up into small parties, scattered among the mountains in pursuit of wild boars and goats. Some were to return, successful or not, at night to the encampment, and on the following day to take the place of those on watch, and relays were provided so that during the week each would take a turn at that duty.

Never did men enjoy a week's hunting with greater zest than the Britons. To them life seemed to begin anew, and although the skies were bluer and the mountains higher and rougher than those of Britain, it seemed to them that they were once again enjoying their native air, and of an evening rude chants of Gaul and Britain echoed among the rocks.

Porus, the Syrian, stood somewhat apart from the rest, not understanding the tongue of the others, and he therefore became naturally the special companion of Beric; for having been six years in Rome he spoke Latin fluently.

"It is I who must go down to get you news, Beric," he said one day. "You Britons could not disguise yourselves, for even if you stained your cheeks and dyed your hair your blue eyes and your height would betray you at once. The Gauls, too, though shorter than you, are still much taller and broader men than the Romans, and there are none of them who speak the language well enough to ask a question without their foreign tongue being detected. I am about the height of the Romans, and am swarthier than the Gauls, and could, if I borrowed the dress of one of the goatherds, pass among them without notice. It would certainly be well, as you were saying, to know what is being done below, and whether there is any idea of sending troops up into the mountains to search for us.

"You may be sure that after the scare you gave Nero, and the defeat of his guards, the matter will not be allowed to drop, and that they will search all Italy for you. I should think that, at first, they will seek for you in the north, thinking that you would be likely, after taking to the hills--which you would be sure to do, for such a party could never hope to traverse the plains unnoticed--to keep along the chain to the north, cross the Cisalpine plains, and try the passage of the great mountains."

"At any rate it will be well, Porus, to know what they are doing. If they are at present confining their search to the northern range we can stay where we are with confidence. I should be sorry to move, for we are well placed here; there is good water and game is abundant. We certainly shall soon lack wine, but for everything else we can manage. We have meat in abundance, and have flour to last for some time, for both we and the Gauls eat but little bread; besides, if pushed, we can do as the peasants do, pound up acorns and beechnuts and make a sort of bread of them."

"Very well, Beric, I will go down tomorrow."

Early in the morning, however, two of the men on sentry came in and said that they observed the glitter of the sun on spearhead and armour far down the hillside.

"If they are after us," Beric said, "as I expect they are, they have doubtless learned that we are somewhere in this part of the mountains from the man of whom we bought the wine and flour. I don't suppose he intended to do us harm, but when he went down to purchase fresh supplies he may well have mentioned that a party of strong men of unusual height, and with fair hair, had bought up his stock, paying for it honestly, which would perhaps surprise him more than anything. If the news had come to the ears of any of the officials, they, knowing the hue and cry which was being made for us, would have sent word at once to Praeneste or Rome. We must at once recall those who are away. Philo, take a couple of brands and go and light the signal fire."

A pile of dry wood had been placed in readiness upon a projecting rock a mile away and standing in position where it was visible from a considerable extent of the hillside. It had been settled that the parties of hunters who did not return at nightfall should occasionally send one of their number to a point whence he could get a view of the beacon.

"Directly the pile is well alight, Philo, pluck up green bushes and tufts of grass and throw upon it, so as to make as much smoke as possible."

There were eighteen men in the encampment, and four out on guard. Boduoc and Gatho were both away, and as soon as Philo had started with the brands Beric and Porus set out with the two scouts.

"That was where we saw them," one of them said, pointing far down the hillside, "but by this time they will no doubt have entered the wooded belt."

"We must find out something about their numbers," Beric said. "Not that I wish to fight; for were we to inflict losses upon them they would more than ever make efforts to overtake us. Still, it will be as well to know what force they may think sufficient to capture us."

"I will go down through the forest," Porus said, "doubtless they will have some light armed troops with the spearmen; but they must be fleet indeed if they overtake me after all my training."

"Do not let them see you if you can help it, Porus, or they will follow close behind you, although they might not overtake you, and that might bring on a fight."

"I will be careful;" and leaving his buckler behind him, Porus started on his way down the mountain.

In an hour and a half he returned. "I have had a good view of them," he said; "they have halted at the place where we got the flour. There are a hundred heavy armed troops and a hundred archers and slingers."

"They have come in strength," Beric said; "it shows that they do not hold the Britons cheaply. We will return at once to the camp. By this time the hunters should be back."

Sending one of the men to call in the other sentries, they returned to the huts. Boduoc, with a party of ten men, had already come in, and said that they had seen Gatho's party making their way down from a point high up in the mountains.

"We will pause no longer," Beric said, "we shall meet them as they descend; take the flour and what little wine remains, and let us be going. Scatter the fire and extinguish the brands; unless they have found some goatherd who has marked us coming and going, they may not find this place. I hope they will not do so, as it would encourage them by the thought that they had nearly captured us."

The party had ascended the mountain half a mile when they met Gatho returning.

"I like not to retreat without fighting," he said, when he had heard from Beric of the coming of the Romans and their force; "but I agree with you that it is better not to anger them farther."

"I want three of the fleetest footed of your men, Gatho, to stay behind with Porus and watch them, themselves unseen. We will cross over the crest of the hills to the eastern side, Porus. Do you mark that tall craig near the summit; you will find one of us there, and he will lead you to our camping place. I want to know whether the Romans, after spending the day searching the hills, go back through the forest, or whether they encamp here. In the one case we can return, in the other it will be better to move south at once. We could laugh at their heavy armed spearmen, but their archers and slingers carry no more weight than we do, and would harass us sorely with their missiles, which we have no means of returning."

As soon as the men to remain with Porus were chosen, the rest of the band proceeded on their way.

CHAPTER XIX
OUTLAWS

It was late at night before Porus with the three Gauls joined the rest of the band in their new encampment on the eastern slope of the hills.

"As soon as the moon rises, Beric, we must be up and moving. The Romans are in earnest. When they came through the forest they ascended for some little distance, and then the spearmen halted and the light armed troops scattered in parties of four searching the country like dogs after game. They were not very long before they discovered signs of us, whether footmarks or broken twigs I know not, but following them they soon came upon the entrance of the ravine. No doubt our marks were plain enough there, for the spearmen were brought down. What happened then I know not; no doubt they entered and found that we had gone. At any rate, in a short time they set out briskly up the mountain, the spearmen as before keeping together, and the light armed men scattering.

"All day they searched, and it was well that you crossed the crest. They halted for the night halfway between the forest and the summit, and I determined to learn something of their intentions. So after it was dark I laid aside my arms and crawled into the camp. The ground was broken and rough, and there was no great difficulty in getting close to their fires. I learned that the whole of the legion at Praeneste had been sent into the mountains, and that there were twenty parties of equal force; they were but a mile and a half apart, and considered that they could search every foot of the ground for thirty miles along, and would assuredly discover us if we were still in this part. More than that, troops from Corfinium and Marrubium had started to search the eastern slopes, and between them they made sure that they should catch you, now that they had found, by the heat of the earth where our fire had been, that we must have been there but an hour or so before their arrival."

"If that is the case we must make our way to the south at once," Beric said. "It is well indeed that we decided to retreat without fighting, for had we retired, closely pursued by their archers, their shouts would certainly have been heard by some of the other parties. It is fortunate we did not light a fire; had we done so it might have brought some of the troops from Marrubium, which cannot be far distant from here, upon us. The moon will not be up for three hours yet, and it is useless to try to make our way among these mountains until we have her light, therefore let all lie down to sleep; I will keep guard and will rouse you when it is time to move."

Beric sat listening intently for any sound that would tell of the approach of foemen. He had, however, but small fear that the Romans were moving at present. It would be even more difficult for them than for his men to make their way about in the darkness; besides, the day must have been an extremely fatiguing one for them. They had, doubtless, started long before dawn, had had to climb the mountains, and had been all day on their feet. They would scarcely recommence the search before morning. Easy on this score, his thoughts turned to Rome. That Aemilia had gained the shelter of the Catacombs he had no doubt, and he wondered how she fared there among the Christian fugitives. As to Norbanus he had but slight hopes of ever seeing him alive. Nero's vengeance always extended to the families of those who offended him, and Norbanus would certainly be held responsible for the flight of Aemilia. He thought it indeed probable that as soon as Aemilia left, Norbanus would have called his friends together, and, having opened his veins, would die as Piso had done discussing philosophy with them.

As soon as the moon was fairly up he aroused his companions and they started along the hillside. It was difficult work making their way on, now descending into a deep ravine, now climbing a rugged slope, now passing along a bare shoulder. There was no pause until day broke, when they descended into a gorge and lay down among some clumps of bushes, one man being sent half a mile down while two others were posted on each side of the ravine. They had good reason for hope, however, that they had got beyond the point to which the searching parties would extend on the eastern side of the hill. The day passed without alarms, although the sentries above more than once heard the sounds of distant trumpets. As soon as the sun set they continued their way, halting again until the moon rose, and then keeping south until daybreak.

They were sure now that they were far beyond the parties of Romans, but after a few hours' sleep they again pressed on, and at night lighted their fires and prepared for a longer stay. But the orders of Nero were so imperative that the troops, having thoroughly searched the mountains at the point where they had ascended them, united, and also moved south in a long line extending from the summit of the hills to the lower edge of the forest; and after two days' halt the fugitives again moved south, and continued their journey until they found themselves among the wild and lofty hills of Bruttium.

But their numbers had swollen as they went, for the other fugitive bands among the hills were also driven south by the advance of the Romans, and it was a miscellaneous body of gladiators, escaped slaves, and malefactors, in all over five hundred strong, that crossed the mountains into Bruttium. There was a general wish among them that Beric should take the command of the whole. This, however, he absolutely declined to do, upon the ground that it was impossible for so large a body of men to keep together, as there would be no means of feeding them. Scattered about they would find an ample supply of meat from the wild goats, boars and semi-wild swine, but together, they would soon scare away the game. From among the gladiators, however, he picked out sufficient men to raise his own force to a hundred strong, and separating from the rest he led them, guided by a charcoal burner, to one of the wildest and most inaccessible points in the promontory.

Here they were safe from pursuit. Bruttium, now called Calabria, is a chain of rugged hills, at that time thickly covered with wood, and although it was possible fairly to search the Apennines in the centre of Italy with six or seven thousand men, a large army would fail to find a band of fugitives in the recesses of the mountains of the south. On the evening of their arrival at the spot they determined to make their headquarters, Beric held a sort of council of war, the whole of the band, as was the custom both in Gaul and Britain, joining in the deliberations.

"So far," Beric began, "we have retreated without fighting; Rome cannot complain that we have been in insurrection against her, we have simply acted as fugitives; but as there is nowhere else whither we can retire, we must turn upon them if they again pursue us. We must then regard this as our abode for a long time, and make ourselves as comfortable as we can. Huts we can erect of the branches of trees, the skins of the goats we kill will provide us with bedding, and if needs be with clothing. Meat will not fail us, for should game become scarce we can buy goats and sheep from the shepherds who come up with their flocks and herds from the villages by the sea. But besides this we need many things for comfort. We must have utensils for cooking, and drinking cups, and shall need flour and wine; we must therefore open communications with one of the towns by the sea. This is the great difficulty, because of all things I fear treachery; for nigh a year we fought the Romans at home, and could have fought them for twenty more had we not been betrayed and surrounded.

"Of that there will always be a danger. I have gold, and shall always pay for what we require; but the other bands among these hills will not be so scrupulous, and as, indeed, they will be forced to take food, they will set the inhabitants against us, and the Romans will have no difficulty in finding guides among them. So long as we keep ourselves far apart from the rest we are comparatively safe; but none of the natives must know of our hiding place. Can anyone propose a good plan for obtaining supplies?"

There was silence for some time. These men were all good for fighting, but few of them had heads to plan. At last Porus said:

"We are, as our guide tells me, but two hours' journey from the hills whence we may look down upon the gulf dividing Bruttium from Sicily. The lower slopes of these hills are, he says, closely cultivated. There are many small villages some distance up on their sides, and solitary farms well nigh up to the crest. It seems to me that we should use one of these farmers as our agent. He must be a man with a wife and family, and these would be hostages. If we told him that if he did our bidding he would be well rewarded, while if unfaithful we would destroy his farmhouse and slay his wife and children, I think we might trust him. Two or three of us could go down with him to the town on the seashore, dressed as men working under him, and help bring up the goods he purchases. The quantity might excite suspicion did he always go to the same place for them, but he need not always do this. If we found it impossible to get enough by means of one man, we might carry out this plan with three or four of them. None of these men need know the direction of our camp; it would suffice that the wine and flour were brought to their houses. We could always send a strong party to fetch them thence as we require them."

"I do not think we can hit on any better plan, Porus;" and as there was a murmur of assent he continued: "I propose, my friends, that we appoint Porus the head of our victualling department, and leave the arrangements to him entirely."

This point was settled. The next morning Porus, taking three of the gladiators who most resembled the natives in appearance, started on his mission. He was completely successful. The farmers on the upper slopes of the hills lived in terror of the banditti among the mountains, and one was readily induced, by the offer of a reward for his service, and of freedom from all molestation, to undertake the business of getting up corn and wine. Henceforth supplies of these articles were obtained regularly. Huts were soon erected; the men were divided into hunting parties, and the life of the fugitives passed quietly, and for a time without incident.

The persons with whom Beric had deposited his money had all been chosen for him by Norbanus. He himself had been too long away from Italy to be acquainted with any outside the walls of Rome; but among his friends there were several who were able to recommend men of property and character to whom the money could be committed with the certainty that it would be forthcoming whenever demanded. At present Beric was amply supplied with funds, for the money that Norbanus had sent to him would last for at least a year; but, four months after reaching Bruttium, he thought it would be as well to warn those in whose charge his own stores had been placed, to hold it in readiness by them in case it should be suddenly asked for. Philo seemed to him the only person he could send on such a mission, and upon the more important one of going to Rome and communicating with Aemilia. He was certain of the fidelity of the lad, and, properly disguised, he was less likely to be recognized in Rome than Porus would be. Clothes such as would be worn by the son of a well to do cultivator were obtained for him, and he was directed to take the road along the coast to Rome, putting up at inns in the towns, and giving out that he was on his way to the capital to arrange for the purchase of a farm adjoining that of his father.

Letters were given him to the persons holding Beric's money; and one for the goldsmith in Rome, with whom a portion of the money he had given for the jewellery that Beric had received at the games was still deposited. This letter was not to be delivered until he had been to the catacombs and seen Aemilia; as, although Scopus had spoken very highly of the man, it was possible that he might, to gain favour with Nero, hand over Beric's messenger to him. Beric fully impressed upon Philo the risks he would run, and told him to make all his calls after nightfall, and to be prepared for instant flight if he mistrusted the manner of any of the men he visited.

"Do not be afraid, Beric," Philo said; "I will not be taken alive. I know that they would torture me to force me to lead them to your hiding place, and I would rather die a thousand times first. I was but a slave when I was allotted to you in the palace of Nero. You have been kind to me, and trusted me. You have allowed me to go with you, and have behaved to me as if I had been free and one of your own people. I have my dagger, and if I see that evil is intended me I will not wait until they lay hands on me, for then my blow might fail, but will make sure. But before I start give me full instructions what I am to say to the Lady Aemilia; for however fully you may write, she will be sure to want to know more, and, above all, instruct me what to do if she demands to join you, and commands me to bring her here. This, methinks, she is sure to do, and I must have your instructions in the matter."

"I shall tell her in my letter, Philo, that this is no place for her, and that I cannot possibly have her here, among rough men, where, at any moment, we may be called upon to make distant and toilsome journeys, and even to fight for our lives."

"That is all very well, my lord; but suppose she says to me it is only because Beric thinks that I cannot support fatigue and hardship that he does not send for me; but I am willing and ready to do so, and I charge you, therefore, to take me to him."

This was a point that Beric had many times thought over deeply. He, too, felt sure that Aemilia would choose to be with him; and accustomed as the Britons were for their wives to share their perils, and to journey with them when they went on warlike expeditions, it seemed to him that she had almost a right to be with him. Then, too, her life must be dreary in the extreme, shut up in caverns where the light of day never penetrated, in ignorance of his fate, and cut off from all kinsfolk and friends. The question so puzzled him that he finally took Porus into his confidence, having a high idea of his good sense.

"She cannot come here," Porus agreed; "but I do not see why you should not bring her from that dismal place where you say she is, and establish her near at hand, either at one of the upper farmhouses, or in a town by the sea. Let me think it over. In an hour I will tell you what seems to me the best plan. My counsel is this," he said, after he had been absent for an hour from the hut, "I myself will go with the lad to fetch her. A Roman lady, even though a fugitive, should not be travelling about the country under the protection of a lad. I dare not go into Rome. I am known to too many of the gladiators, and, disguise myself as I might, I should be recognized before I had been there an hour. I will obtain a dress such as would suit a respectable merchant; I will go down to one of the ports below and take passage in a trading craft bound for Ostia. There I will take lodgings, and giving out that my daughter, who has been staying with friends for her education in Rome, is about to return to Messina with me, will purchase two or three female slaves. When she arrives with Philo, who can pass as her brother and my son, we will take ship and come down hither. I can then bring her up and place her in the house of one of the farmers; or can, if you like, take a house in the town, or lodge her there with people to whom one of the farmers might recommend her. But, at any rate, she could come up to one of the farm houses first, to see you, and then you could arrange matters between you. She would really run no danger. You say she went out but little in Rome, and it would be ill luck indeed were there anyone on this coast who met her there. If it were not for your preposterous height, your yellow hair and blue eyes, there would be no difficulty about the matter at all, for you would have but to cross the straits into Sicily, to buy a small property there, and to settle down quietly; but it is impossible with your appearance to pass as one of the Latin race."

"Besides," Beric said, "I could not desert my comrades. Whatever their lot may be, mine must be also. If we are ever to escape, we must escape together; but for the rest, I think your plan is a good one, Porus, and thank you heartily. When you get to Ostia you will learn all that is going on in Rome, what has befallen Norbanus, and other matters. If Norbanus is alive, Aemilia will certainly be in communication with him by means of the Christians, and will, of course, be guided by his advice."

The next day Porus and Philo set out together. Three weeks passed, and then one morning Philo entered the camp.

"All has gone well, my lord, the Lady Aemilia is at the house of the farmer Cornelius, with whom Porus arranged to receive her on the morning we left you. She has sent no letter, for there were no writing materials in the house, but she awaits your coming."

Beric hastened away at once, accompanied by the lad, who by the way gave an account of his journey.

"It was as I thought," he said. "When I came to the house you told me of, I knocked as you instructed me, gave the ring to the man within and begged him to take it to the Lady Aemilia. He at first pretended that he knew nothing of such a person; but at last, on my showing him the letter addressed to her, he said that some friends of his might know where she was, and that if I called again, two hours before midnight, he might have news of her. When I came back the Lady Aemilia was there. She asked many questions about your health before she opened your letter, the one that you first wrote to her. When she had read it she said, 'My lord bids me stay here, Philo, and I am, above all things, bound to obey him; but he says that he bids me remain, because the hardships would be too great for me. But I know that I could support any hardships; and kind as they are to me here, I would rather go through anything with my husband than remain here; the darkness and the silence are more trying than any hardships. So you see that my lord's orders were given under a misapprehension, and as I am sure he would not have given them had he known that I was not afraid of hardships, and desired above all things to be with him, I shall disobey them, and he, when I join him, must decide whether I have done wrong, and, if he thinks so, send me away from him.'

"Then, my lord, seeing that it was so, I gave her your second letter, in which you said that if she wished to join you you had made arrangements for her doing so. Then she kissed the letter and cried over it, and said that she was ready to depart when I came to fetch her. Then she told me that Norbanus had opened his veins that night after she had left, and that the soldiers of Nero arrived just too late to trouble him; that all his property had been confiscated, and that she had no friends in the world but you.

"It took a week for Porus to obtain two suitable slaves--the one an elderly woman and the other a young servant.

"The goldsmith handed over your money to me at once, saying, 'I am glad to hear that Beric is alive. Tell him that he did badly in not slaying the tyrant when he had him at his mercy. Tell him, too, there are rumours of deep discontent among the legions in the provinces, and a general hope among the better class of Romans that they will ere long proclaim a new emperor and overthrow Nero. Tell him also to be on his guard. There is a talk of an expedition on a large scale, to root out those who are gathered in the mountains of Bruttium. It is said that it is to be commanded by Caius Muro, who but a week ago returned from Syria.'"

"Is it so?" Beric exclaimed. "I know him well, having lived in his house for years. I should be sorry indeed that we should meet as enemies. Heard you aught of his daughter?"

"Not from the goldsmith, but afterwards. She is married, I hear, to Pollio, who is of the family of Norbanus."

"I am indeed glad to hear it, Philo. He also was a great friend of mine, and as he knew Muro in Britain, would doubtless have sought him out in Syria, where he, too, held an office. 'Tis strange indeed that he should have married Berenice, whom I last saw as a girl, now fully four years back. And all went well on the voyage?"

"Well indeed, my lord. I took the Lady Aemilia down to Ostia in a carriage with closed curtains. She stayed two days in the place Porus had hired, and none suspected on the voyage that she was other than his daughter."

"And how is she looking, Philo?"

"At first, my lord, she was looking strangely white, and I feared that her health had suffered; but she said that it was dwelling in the darkness that had so whitened her, and indeed the sun during the voyage has brought the colour back to her cheeks, and she is now looking as she used to do when I carried letters to the house from Nero's palace."

Once arrived at the brow of the hill, looking down upon the Straits of Messina, Beric's impatience could be no longer restrained, and he descended the slope with leaps and bounds that left Philo far behind. Porus was at the door of the farm; Beric grasped his hand.

"She is in there," he said, pointing to a door, and a moment later Aemilia fell into his arms.

In half an hour the door opened.

"Come in, Porus and Philo," Beric called. "I must first thank you, both in my own name and that of my betrothed, for the great service you have rendered us, and the care and kindness with which you have watched over her. We have settled nothing yet about the future, except that tomorrow I shall complete the betrothal, and she will become my wife. It should be done today, but my faithful Boduoc must be here as a witness. It would be a disappointment indeed to him were he not to be present at my marriage. For the present, at any rate, my wife will remain here.

"She would fain go up into the mountains, but that cannot be. Not only is our life too rough for her, but her presence there would greatly add to my anxieties. Here she will be safe, and you, Philo, will remain with her. I am convinced that I can trust Cornelius. You have told me, Porus, that you are assured of his honesty, and as I can pay him well, and he can have no idea that the Romans would be glad to pay a far higher sum for my capture, he has no temptation to be unfaithful to us; besides, his face is a frank and open one. I shall charge him that, while Aemilia remains here, none of his men are to accompany him when he goes down to the port, for, without meaning harm, they might talk to people there of what is going on, and the matter might come to the ears of the authorities."

"I think," Porus said, "it would be well, Beric, that I and the three men who go down with me to bring up goods should take up our residence here. There is an out house which is unused, and which we can occupy. In this way we can keep an eye upon the two men on the farm, and one can be always on the watch to see that no party of armed men is coming up from the port. I believe in the good faith of the farmer, but it is always better to take precautions."

"Far better, Porus. The plan you suggest is an excellent one. We must try and make this chamber a little more fitting for Aemilia's abode."

"That will soon be done," Porus said. "Knowing what your wishes would be in such a matter, I purchased at Ostia sufficient stuff to cover these bare walls, with rugs and such furniture as was requisite. These I brought up in a cart as far as the road extends, and I will now go down with Philo and the two men and bring them up here and help the slaves get the room in order."

Before sunset Beric returned alone to the camp, and the next morning came back to the farm with Boduoc.

"There is one thing I must tell you, Beric," Aemilia said when he went in alone to see her, "I have become a Christian."

"I thought it was likely you would do so, Aemilia," he said; "living among these people, and knowing how Ennia had embraced their religion, it could hardly be otherwise. You shall tell me about it afterwards. I know but little of its tenets, but I know how those who held them faced death, and there must be much indeed in a religion which teaches men so to die."

"You told me that you would not object, Beric, or I would have abstained from attending their assemblies. Still, it was right I should tell you before I became your wife."

Porus and his companion had spent the morning in gathering flowers. These the slaves had made into wreaths and had decorated the room, which was completely changed in appearance since Beric left it on the afternoon before. The roughly built walls were hidden by rich hangings. The floor was covered with matting, on which were placed thick rugs woven in the East. Two or three carved couches were placed against the walls, and as many small tables on tripod legs stood beside them. The farmer and his wife were called in, and in their presence and that of his three followers Beric performed the simple ceremony of a Roman marriage, consisting only of taking Aemilia's hand in his and declaring that, in conformity with the conditions of the pact before made and signed, and with the full consent and authorization of her father, he took her to be his wife.

Beric remained three days down at the cottage, and then rejoined his band. A few days later a messenger came in from one of the bands at the other side of the promontory of Bruttium, saying they had obtained news that preparations were being made at Sybaris for the landing of a very large body of troops, and that it was said to be the intention of the Romans to make a great expedition through the mountains and entirely exterminate the outlaws.

"They would have left us alone," Beric said bitterly, "if it had not been that you made yourselves scourges to the country, pillaging and ravaging the villages among the hills and slaying innocent people."

"We were obliged to live," the man said. "Rome has driven us into the mountains, and we must feed at the expense of Rome."

Beric was silent. He felt that had he himself not had means his own bands would have also taken to pillage. The men who took to the hills regarded themselves as at war with Rome. Rome sent her soldiers against them, and slew every man captured. She hunted them like wild beasts, and as wild beasts they had to live at her expense. Beric was not in advance of the spirit of his time. It was the custom in war to burn, destroy, and slay.

That as Rome warred with them they should war with Rome seemed natural to every fugitive in the hills, and they regarded their leader's action in purchasing what he could have taken by force simply as an act of policy. Their own people had been slain by the Romans, they themselves doomed to risk their lives for the amusement of the Roman mob. If recaptured they would, like the followers of Spartacus, be doubtless put to death by crucifixion. That, under these circumstances, they should be in the slightest degree influenced by any feeling of pity or humanity towards Romans would, if suggested to them, have appeared supremely ridiculous.

Beric felt, then, that for him to say any further word of blame would only have the effect of causing him to be regarded with suspicion and dislike, and would lessen his own influence among the mountain bands.

He therefore said, "That you should take what is necessary is not blamable, against it I have nothing to say; but it was to the interest of all of us that nothing more should be taken. Rome would not have been stirred to send an army against us merely by the complaints of peasants that some of their goats and sheep had been driven off or their granaries emptied; but when it comes to burning villages and slaughtering their inhabitants, and carrying fire and sword down to the seashore, Rome was roused. She felt her majesty insulted, and now we are going to have a veritable army invade the mountains. It is no longer viewed as an affair of brigands, but as an insurrection. However, there is no more to be said, the mischief is done, and we have now only to do our best to repel the invasion. Tell your leaders that tomorrow morning I will set out and join them, and will with them examine the country, mark the lines by which the enemy are likely to advance, decide where obstacles had best be erected, and where the first stand should be made. It may be weeks yet before they come. Roman armies are not moved as quickly as a tribe of mountaineers."

The following day Beric, taking with him the greater portion of his band, marched across the hills under the guidance of the charcoal burner, who had now enrolled himself regularly in its ranks, and had taken the oath of obedience. Their course lay to the northeast, as it was in the Bay of Tarentum that rumour reported that the Romans would land. As, after two days' marching, they neared the spot fixed upon for the rendezvous, they came upon other bands journeying in the same direction; and when these united on a shoulder of the hill commanding a view of the great bay, some eight hundred men were assembled. Fires had been already lighted, and a number of sheep killed and roasted. The leaders withdrew from the rest as soon as they had finished their meal, and seating themselves at a point whence they could see the plains stretching away from the foot of the hills to the gulf, began their consultation.

"I wonder why they are coming round here?" one of the chiefs said; "they might have landed at Rhegium in the straits, and thence marched straight up into the hills. From where your camp is, Beric, you should know what is going on there, for the town stands almost below you. Is nought said there about military preparations?"

"Nothing whatever," Beric replied; "nor do I think it likely that they will attack from that point, for if they advanced thence, we should simply retire through the mountains to the north just as we retired south when they before attacked us. It is clear what their object is: they will sail up that river and will disembark at Cosenza; the hills narrow there, and it is but a short distance across them to the Western Sea. Ascending them they will at once cut us off from any retreat north. They will have their magazines close at hand. A thousand men stationed in a chain across the mountains will suffice to bar our way, while the rest will move south, penning us up as they go, until they drive us down to the very edge of the promontory, where, joined perhaps by a force coming up from Rhegium, they will have us altogether in their grip."

An expression of dismay spread round the circle. They had thought that the Romans would but march straight through the mountains, in which case it would be easy to evade them, but they saw at once that by the erection of a chain of permanent posts across the hill from Cosenza they would be completely hemmed in, and must sooner or later be hunted down.

"Then you think that our only chance is to move to the mountains north of Cosenza before they land, Beric?"

"I do not say that," Beric replied. "To begin with, we are not going to remain passive and allow ourselves to be driven like a flock of sheep into the hurdles. Did they bring against us only heavy armed troops we could laugh at them, for we can march two miles to their one, and move easily among the rocks where they could find no footing. It is only their light armed soldiers we have to fear, but even these must move at the same rate as the hoplites, for if they ventured far away from the protection of the spearmen we should make short work of them. We have over a thousand fighting men in these mountains, and each one of us in close conflict is a match for at least three of their light armed men. In the plains, of course, we should suffer greatly from their missiles before we came to a close conflict; but among these woods and precipices we could fall on them suddenly, and be in their midst before they have time to lay arrow to bow. Therefore, you see, the Romans can move but slowly among the hills, and we will soon teach them that they dare not scatter, and even twelve thousand men do not go for much among these mountains, extending some seventy miles from Cosenza to Rhegium, and from ten to twenty miles across.

"How about food?" one of the others asked.

"In that respect we shall be far better off than they would. We shall really have no difficulty about food. It would need twenty legions to form a cordon along the slopes of these hills on both sides, and we can, while opposing the Romans, always detach parties to make forays down into the plain and drive off sheep, goats, and cattle. Besides, among the lower forests there are herds of swine pasturing, which will be available for our use. The question of food will be of no trouble to us, but on the other hand, it will be a vast trouble to the Romans. Every foot that they advance from their magazines at Cosenza their difficulties will increase. They must make roads as they go, and their convoys will always be exposed to our attacks. Very large bodies of men must otherwise be employed in escorting them. They may form depots at the foot of the hills as they advance, but even then their difficulties will be prodigious.

"I should propose to fight them as we fought them in the swamps of my native land--to harass them night and day, to wear them out with false alarms, to oppose them in the defiles, to hurl down the rocks on them from precipices, to cut off their convoys, and fall upon their camps at night, until they lose all confidence in themselves, and dare only move hither and thither in a solid body. Not until they have destroyed the whole of the forests between Cosenza and Rhegium, and made roads everywhere across the mountains, ought they be able to overcome us. It will be time enough to think of retiring then. By descending the western slopes a long night march would take us north of Cosenza, and we could then take to the hills again; or we could descend upon the coast near Rhegium at night, seize a fishing village, embark in its boats and cross the strait, and before morning be among the mountains of Sicily, which are so vast and far stretching that operations which, though possible, are difficult here, could not probably be carried on against us."

Beric's words were received with enthusiastic approval. Before all had felt dispirited, and though ready to fight to the last, had deemed that the resistance could be but short and their fate certain. Now they saw before them a veritable war, in which they could hope to defend themselves successfully, and if beaten here escape to renew it elsewhere, and which promised them an abundant opportunity for encountering the Romans. This was what they most longed for. Not one there but hated Rome with a bitter hatred, as the author of unnumbered woes to their tribes, their families and themselves. Death had no terrors whatever to these men, so that they could die fighting with Romans. Rising to their feet they returned with exulting shouts to their comrades.

CHAPTER XX
MOUNTAIN WARFARE

The gladiators sprang to their feet as their leaders returned to them, and eagerly questioned them as to the news that had so reanimated them. But they only replied, "Beric will tell you," and Beric was obliged to mount a rock near the spot where they had been feasting, and to repeat to the whole of the assembly his plan for the campaign against the Romans. Loud shouts greeted his speech, the Gauls and Britons clashing their swords against their shields as was their custom, and the others signified their approval each after the manner of his country.

"Beric is our leader! Beric is our leader!" they shouted. "We will follow him to the death." When the tumult had subsided, Beric raised his hand for silence.

"I am willing to accept the leadership," he said; "but if I must lead I must be obeyed. In a warfare like this everything depends upon the orders of him who commands being carried out promptly and without question. I only accept the command because, although younger than most of you, I have already fought the Romans often and successfully. Each of you will remain under your respective chiefs, who will act as my lieutenants, and all must be ready to sacrifice their own wishes and their own opinions to the general welfare. Those whom I order to fight will fight, I know; those whom I tell off to fell trees, to raise obstacles, or to pile stones on the edge of precipices, must labour with equal zeal; while those who are despatched to drive up cattle, or to guard them until needed in the forest, will know that their turn for active fighting will come in good time. The man who disobeys me dies.

"It is only by acting as one man and under one leader that we can hope to resist successfully. You are free men, and may consider it humiliating thus to obey the orders of another; but the Romans are free men too, and yet they submit to the severest discipline, and without the slightest question obey the orders of their general. So it must be here. If all are disposed thus to follow me I accept the command. Let those who cannot so submit themselves withdraw and fight in their own fashion. They shall be free to depart, none harming them."

A great shout followed the conclusion of Beric's speech, and the whole of those present lifted up their hands and swore implicit obedience to him. The next few days were spent in making a careful examination of the mountains above Cosenza, and fixing upon the points where an active resistance could be best made.

"We must have missiles," Beric said one day when his lieutenants were gathered round him. "We will not begin the war until the Romans do so, but we must have weapons. Boduoc, you will tomorrow take the whole of my band and descend to the plain, fall upon the town of Castanium at daybreak; the bands of Victor and Marsus will accompany you and will be also under your orders. My orders are strict, that no one is to be injured unless he resists. Tell the inhabitants that we wish them no harm. Ransack the armourers' shops for arrow and javelin heads, and search all the private houses for weapons; also bring off all the brass, copper, and iron you can find, with every axe head and chopper in the town. We can erect charcoal furnaces here similar to those we used at home, and so provide ourselves with an ample store of missiles. Bring off from the carpenters' shops any seasoned wood you can find suitable for the making of bows. Touch no gold or silver ornaments of the women--the metals are useless to us here--neither take garments nor spoil of any other kind. I would show them that, until driven to it, we are not the foes of the people at large. Above all frighten no woman; let them see that we, though gladiators and outlaws, are as well disciplined and as humane as their own soldiery."

Accordingly at sunset Boduoc marched away at the head of two hundred men, and returned to the mountains late on the following afternoon with a large store of arms and metal, Beric's orders having been scrupulously carried out.

"You should have seen the wonder of the people," Boduoc said to him, "when they saw that we meant them no harm, and that we touched neither person nor goods save in the matter of arms. They gave us their best to eat, and many even accompanied us some distance on our return, overjoyed with the clemency we had shown the town."

There was no lack of charcoal, and in many places the stacks had been left by the charcoal burners untouched when the bands first appeared among the mountains. Those who had been accustomed to the smelting of metals at home were appointed to cast heads for arrows and javelins, others cut down and split up tough wood and fashioned the shafts, others made bows; strong parties were set to work to fell trees and form obstacles in defiles where the rocks rose steeply, while others piled great heaps of stones and heavy rocks along the edges of the precipices. As yet there were no signs of the expected fleet, and when the preparations were complete the bands again scattered, as it was easier so to maintain themselves in provisions; and, a party being left to watch for the arrival of the Roman legions, Beric returned with his band to his former station.

"There will be plenty of time to gather again before they move forward," he said to their lieutenants. "They will have to collect the carts from all the country round, to land their stores and to make their arrangements for victualling. They will know that it is no easy task that they are undertaking, and that they have desperate men to meet. It will be a week after they land at the very earliest before they leave Cosenza."

For a fortnight Beric remained quietly passing the greater portion of his time at the farmhouse with Aemilia.

"It is terrible to me that you are going to fight the Romans, Beric," she said.

"I have no desire to fight the Romans, it is they who want to fight with me," he replied; "and as I have no desire for crucifixion, or any of the other forms of death which they bestow upon their captives, I have no choice but to resist. As you do not think any the worse of me, Aemilia, for having fought your countrymen before, I don't see that you can take it to heart that I am going to do it again, especially as you have very small reason to be grateful to them for the treatment that you and yours have received at their hands. You must remember, dear, that as my wife, you are a Briton now, and must no longer speak of the Romans as your people. Still, were it not for my countrymen, I would gladly bury myself with you in some cottage far up among the hills of Sicily, and there pass my life in quiet and seclusion. But without a leader the others would speedily fall victims to the Romans, and as long as the Romans press us, I must remain with them."

At the end of the fortnight a messenger arrived saying that a great fleet had arrived at the mouth of the Crathis River.

"I will from time to time send a messenger to you, Aemilia," Beric said as he took a tender farewell of his wife, "to tell you how matters go with us; but do not alarm yourself about me, for some time there is little chance of close fighting."

The bands gathered in their full force above Cosenza, and during the week that elapsed before the Romans advanced renewed their labour at various passes through which it was probable that the enemy would move. Some of the men were already skilled archers, and the rest had spent their time for the last fortnight in incessant practice, and could manage their weapons sufficiently well to be able to send an arrow into a crowded mass of men.

It was with a feeling of satisfaction that the Roman column was seen one morning issuing from Cosenza and moving up the road that there crossed the mountains. Once on the crest they proceeded to cut down trees and form a camp. While they were so occupied the gladiators remained on the defensive. Light armed troops had been pushed by the Romans into the woods, but after being permitted to advance some distance the sound of a horn was heard, followed instantly by a flight of arrows, and then by a rush of the gladiators, who drove these light armed troops before them, killing many, till they reached the protection of the spearmen.

Again and again during the ensuing week the Romans endeavoured to penetrate the woods, heavy armed troops accompanying the archers. Before they had penetrated far into the forest they found their way arrested by obstacles--lines of felled trees with the branches pointing towards them, and these were only taken after severe loss, the defenders shooting through the green hedge, which was only broken through when working parties with heavy axes came up covered by the spearmen. One party, pushing on incautiously, was suddenly attacked on all sides, and after pouring in their missiles the gladiators charged them, broke the ranks of the spearmen, and destroyed the whole party, three hundred in number.

After this the advance was delayed until the fortified camp was complete and stored with provisions. Then the Roman army moved forward, and was soon engaged in a succession of combats. Every valley and ravine was defended, invisible foes rolled down masses of rock among them and a hail of arrows, and it was only when very strong bodies of archers, supported by spearmen, climbed the heights on both sides that the resistance ceased. The Romans halted for the night where they stood, but there was little sleep for them, for the woods rang with war cries in many languages. The sentries were shot or stabbed by men who crawled up close to them. At times the shouts became so threatening and near that the whole force was called to its feet to repel attack, but in the morning all was quiet. As before, they were attacked as soon as they moved forward. No serious opposition was offered to the columns of spearmen, but the light armed troops who covered the advance and formed a connection between the columns were exposed to incessant attack.

The third day the Romans, after another disturbed night, again advanced. This time they met with no opposition, and as they moved cautiously forward, wondered uneasily what was the meaning of this silence. Late in the afternoon they learned. They had advanced, each man carrying three days' provisions with him. Beric, being aware that this was their custom, had during the night led his men some distance down the hillside, and making a detour occupied before morning the ground the Romans had passed over. At midday a great convoy of baggage animals, laden with provisions, came along. It extended over a great length, and came in straggling order, the men leading their animals, and making their way with difficulty through the thick trees. Five hundred Roman soldiers were scattered along the line. Suddenly the sound of a horn rose in the woods, and in an instant, at points all along the line of the convoy, strong bodies of men burst down upon them.

In vain the Roman soldiers tried to gather in groups. The animals, frightened by the shouting and din, broke loose from their leaders and rushed wildly hither and thither, adding to the confusion. Greatly outnumbered, and attacked by foes individually their superiors both in strength and skill of arms, and animated by a burning hatred, the Romans could do little, and the combat terminated in a few minutes in their annihilation. The men with the convoy were all killed, a line of gladiators having been posted through the woods, both ahead and behind it, before the attack began, so that no fugitives might escape either way to carry the news.

The animals were then collected, and their burdens taken off and examined. The flour was divided up into parcels that a man could easily carry on his shoulder, and a large number of skins of wine set aside. All that could not be taken was scattered and destroyed, and the animals then slaughtered. As soon as it became dark the band descended the mountain side, marched for many miles along its foot, and then again ascended the hills, ready to oppose the Roman advance; but there was no movement in the morning. Surprised and alarmed at the non-arrival of the train by nightfall, the general sent a strong body of troops back to meet them with torches. These in time came upon the bodies of the men and animals, and at once returned with the news of the disaster to the camp.

"This is a terrible blow, Pollio," the general said to his son-in-law. "We had reckoned on an obstinate resistance, but did not dream that the gladiators would thus oppose us."

"It puts me in mind, Muro, of the work in the fens of Britain; and indeed more than once I have thought I recognized the war cries with which the Iceni attacked us. The strategy is similar to that we then encountered. Can it be possible that Beric is again opposing us? I heard during the short time we were in Rome that the Britons in the palace of Nero had risen and escaped. I was too heartbroken at the fate of my uncle and his family to ask many questions, and was fully occupied in our preparations. My first thought would have been to find Beric out had I not been met on landing with the news of the disgrace and death of Norbanus, and I shunned the palace of Nero as if the pestilence had been there. No doubt Beric would have left with the other Britons, and in that case he may well be at the head of those opposing us."

"The tactics they are adopting certainly look like it, Pollio; and if they continue to fight as they have done so far, we are likely to have no better fortune than Suetonius had in his campaign against them. It is ten days since we left Cosenza, we have made but some ten miles advance among the hills, and we have lost already eight hundred hoplites, and I know not how many light armed troops. At this rate our force will melt away to nothing before we have half cleared this wilderness of rock and forest. Hitherto in their revolts the gladiators have met our troops in pitched battle, but their strength and skill have not availed against Roman discipline. But in such fighting as this discipline goes for little. They are fighting on ground they know, can choose their moment for attack, and hurl all their strength on one point while we are groping blindly."

"But how can they have got through our lines in the night, Muro?" Pollio asked. "Our men were posted down to the edge of the forest on either side of the hills. There were two thousand under arms all night."

"But there was nothing to prevent them, Pollio, from descending far below the forest line and coming up again in our rear. This is what they must have done. Nor have we any means of preventing their doing so, for nothing short of a force strong enough to reach down to the sea on either hand would prevent their passing us. At any rate we must halt here for a time. The whole of our baggage animals are destroyed, and nothing can be done until another train is collected."

The war proceeded but slowly. The Romans indeed made some slight advance, but they were worn out and harassed by incessant alarms. To prevent the recurrence of the disaster to the baggage train the supplies were now carried along the plain at the foot of the hill, and then taken up under very strong escorts directly to the point at which the army had arrived. The soldiers, worn out and dispirited by constant alarms, became reluctant to advance unless in solid order; and in this way five thousand men, taking nine days' provisions with them, made their way through the heart of the hills until they reached the southern slopes, and the sea lay before them. But they occupied only the ground on which they stood, and their passage brought them no nearer to the end they desired. The fact that the army had made a passage right through the mountains was regarded as a triumph in Rome, and believing that the end was near fresh reinforcements were sent to Muro to enable him to finish the campaign rapidly. His reports, however, to the senate left no doubt in the minds of those who read them as to the situation.

"We are fighting," he said, "an enemy who will not allow us to strike him. Three months have passed since I entered the mountains, and yet I cannot say that I am nearer the end than I was when I began. I have lost three thousand men, of whom half are spearmen. The gladiators have suffered but slightly, for they always burst down in overwhelming numbers, slay, and retire. At least twenty times my camps have been attacked; and although I have lost but one convoy, the difficulty and labour of victualling the troops is enormous. If the gladiators would but take to the plain we should annihilate them in the first battle. As it is, it is they who select the ground for action, and not we. The troops are utterly worn out and well nigh mutinous at what they consider a hopeless task. You ask me what had best be done. My own opinion is, that we should retire from the mountains and establish the troops in camps near their foot, so as to restrain the gladiators from making excursions, and to fall upon them when hunger drives them to leave the mountains. Treachery may then do what force has failed in.

"Among such a body there must be traitors, and when the war is apparently ended we may, through shepherds or goatherds, open communication with them. My great fear is, and always has been, that as we gradually press them south they may pour down on to one of the villages on the straits, seize the boats, cross to Sicily, and take refuge in the mountains there, where they could laugh at our efforts to pursue them. I should advise that it should be announced publicly that our army, having traversed the whole mountains of Bruttium without meeting with a foe, the objects of the expedition have been attained, and the enemy may now be considered as a mere mass of fugitives, whom it would be impossible to root out as long as they take refuge among their fastnesses; but that for the present the army will be placed in a cordon of camps round the foot of the mountains, by which means the fugitives will be starved into surrender. If this course is not approved I have but one other to suggest, namely, that the whole of the population of southern Italy should be ordered to take part in the total destruction of the forests of Bruttium. Every tree must be cut down to the level of the soil; every trunk and branch be burnt by fire. The task would be a tremendous one. The loss to the country around by the destruction of the forests, wherein their flocks of sheep and goats and their herds of swine find sustenance and shelter in winter, would be enormous, but thus, and thus alone, I am assured, can these bands of gladiators be rooted out."

Muro's advice was taken, and the exulting gladiators beheld the troops descending from the mountains to the plains below. Their own loss had not exceeded three hundred men, and their shouts of triumph rose high in the woods, and reached the ears of the Romans retiring sullenly down the slopes. In a few days the plan of the Romans became apparent. The camp in the pass above Cosenza was still strongly held, four well fortified camps were established in the plains on either side of the hills, and Muro himself took up his post at Rhegium, where two thousand legionaries were posted. The gladiators again broke up into bands, Beric returning to his former encampment, to the delight of Aemilia.

"You must not suppose that our troubles are over, Aemilia," he said. "We have indeed beaten them on our own ground, but we shall now have to fight against famine. The wild animals have already become scarce. You may be sure that the villagers will be allowed to send no more flocks or herds up the hills to pasture, and before long it will be necessary to make raids for food. You will see that, emboldened by their successes, the men will become rash, and may be cut off and defeated. As for us there is no fear; as long as we can pay for provisions we shall be able to obtain them, for although there may be difficulty in obtaining regular supplies, now that the troops are at Rhegium, all these upland farmers and villagers will continue to deal with us, knowing that if they do not we shall take what we need without payment and perhaps burn their houses over their heads."

It was not long, indeed, before Beric's predictions were verified. As soon as the provisions became scarce the bands on the other side of the mountains recommenced their forays on the villagers, but from the Roman camps parties of soldiers were sent off after nightfall to the upper villages, and the marauders were several times surprised and almost exterminated.

"We must be more and more careful," Beric said to Aemilia when he heard of one of these disasters. "The prisoners the Romans take will under torture tell all they know, and it will not be long before the Romans ascertain the general position of our encampment. The force will dwindle rapidly. In the last two months they have lost well nigh as many men as in the campaign in the mountains. More than that, I have seen several of the leaders, who told me they had determined, seeing that starvation was approaching them here, to endeavour to pass between the Roman camps with their bands, and regain the mountains beyond Cosenza, so as to establish themselves far north; and indeed I cannot blame them. But their retreat adds to our danger. So long as they roamed the eastern hills there was no danger of a Roman force surprising us, but when they have gone some of the captives may be forced to lead the Romans across the hills to our neighbourhood. Boduoc is vigilant and his scouts are scattered far round the camp, and at the worst we may have to carry out my plan of crossing to Sicily. At any rate he has my orders what to do in case of a sudden surprise. If I am absent, knowing every foot of the wood now, he will at once make his way north, leaving it to me to rejoin him as I best can."

But upon one thing Beric had not reckoned. So long as the gladiators were in force among the mountains the country people on the slopes above the straits were glad enough to purchase their safety by silence. But as they heard of one band after another being crushed by the Romans, and learned that parties from the various camps had penetrated far into the hills without meeting with a single opponent, their fear of the gladiators decreased. There were two thousand legionaries at Rhegium. These could crush the band that remained somewhere about the crest of the hills with ease, and they need no longer fear their vengeance. The Roman general would surely pay a great reward for information that would lead to his being able to deal a final blow to the gladiators. The farmer with whom Aemilia lodged had no such thought. He had earned in the last eight months as much as his farm had brought him in the three best years since he inherited it. He found these terrible outlaws gentle and pleasant, ready to lend a hand on the farm if needful, and delighted to play with his children. As to their chief, he was a source of never ending wonder to him. Gladiators were, according to his idea, fierce and savage men, barbarians who were good for nothing but to kill each other, while this tall man bore himself like a Roman of high rank, conversed in pure Latin, and could even read and write. Aemilia, too, had become a great favourite in the house. The farmer's wife wondered at seeing one, with two slaves to wait upon her, active and busy, interested in all that went on, and eager to learn every detail of the housework.

"I could manage a Roman household, Beric," she said. "I did so indeed all the time we were in Rome; but we may have to live in a hut, and I must know how to manage and cook for you there."

In Rhegium life was more cheerful than usual. Many of the upper class of Rome, who shrank from the festivities of the court of Nero and yet dared not withdraw altogether from Rome, had their country estates and villas along the coasts, where they could for a time enjoy freedom and live according to their tastes. Berenice had joined Pollio three weeks before, when she found that he was likely to remain stationed at Rhegium for some time. They lived with Muro in a villa a short distance from the town, and looking over the straits.

"I should feel perfectly happy here, Pollio," Berenice said one evening as she walked to and fro on the terrace with him, looking at the water in which the moonlight was reflected, bringing up into view the boats rowing here and there with pleasure parties with music and lanterns, "if it were not for the thought of Beric. It is curious that he should be mixed up with both our lives. He was my playmate as a boy; he saved me at the massacre of Camalodunum, and restored me to my father. When we left Britain he was fighting against Suetonius, and we expected when we left that the news of his defeat and death would reach Rome before us. At Rome we heard but vague rumours that Suetonius had not yet overcome the final resistance of the Britons, and glad we were when Petronius was sent out to take his place, and we heard that gentler measures were to be used towards the Britons.

"Then, after a time, when we were in Syria, came the news that Suetonius had returned, bringing with him Beric, the British chief, with twenty of his followers, and my father at once wrote to the emperor praying him that clemency might be extended to him for his kind action in saving my life. Then when you came out to Syria Beric's name again came up. You had journeyed with him from Britain to Rome, and he had become your friend. Then a few months afterwards a newcomer from Rome brought us the story of how your cousin Ennia, having turned Christian, had been condemned to the lions; how a British gladiator named Beric had sprung into the arena and craved to fight the lion; how Nero had cruelly ordered him to do so unarmed; and how he had, as it seemed by a miracle, overcome the lion and bound him by strips torn from his mantle. Then again we learned from one who came from Nero's court that Beric stood high in favour with Caesar, that he was always about his person, and that rumours said he kept guard over him at night.

"Then again, when we returned to Rome, my father was at once ordered to take command of an expedition against some revolted gladiators, among whom were, it was said, the British captives who had created a disturbance in Nero's palace, well nigh killed the emperor, and after slaying many of the Praetorians, escaped. After you and my father had left me at the house of my uncle Lucius I made many inquiries, and found that Beric had doubtless escaped with the other Britons, as he had never been seen in the palace that night. I heard too that it had been whispered by some of those who were present at the supper, that the fault had not been his. He had been betrothed to your cousin Aemilia, and Nero, urged thereto by Rufinus, a disappointed suitor, ordered Beric to bring her to the orgy. Upon his refusal Rufinus attacked him, and Beric slew him by dashing his head against a marble pillar. Then Nero called upon the Praetorians, and the Britons ran in to the aid of their chief, and, defeating the Praetorians, escaped. It was the same night that your uncle died and Aemilia was missing. It may be that she fled with Beric, knowing that she would be sacrificed to the fury of Nero. Is it not strange, Pollio, that this Briton should be so mixed up in both our lives?"

"It is indeed, Berenice. There is no one to whom I owe so much. First I owe your life to him, then I owe that of Ennia, my cousin; for although she died afterwards, it was in her father's house, and not a terrible and disgraceful death in the arena. And now we have been fighting against him for months, and though of course we made the best of matters, there is no doubt that we had all the worst of it. We had twelve thousand men against a thousand, and yet Beric kept us at bay and inflicted some terrible blows upon us, for we lost a third of our number. After the first battle there was no longer any doubt that Beric was the leader of our opponents. Even had we not heard them shout his name as they attacked us, we who had fought against him in Britain would have recognized that he was again our opponent; for he used the same tactics among the mountains that he had done in the swamps. We know from prisoners we have taken since that he was unharmed in the struggle with us, and certainly neither he nor any of his Britons have been among the raiding bands whom we have surprised and destroyed. Indeed the Britons never joined in any of the attacks upon the country people before we came hither. I have questioned many of the sufferers by their depredations, and none of them had seen among the plunderers any tall men with light hair. The only time that they have been seen on the plains was a fortnight before we landed, when they entered Castanium and carried off all the arms. The Britons were among that party, and a Briton commanded it; but from the description it was not Beric, but was, I think, his principal follower, a man with a British name which I forget."

"Was it Boduoc?" Berenice asked. "I have often heard him speak of a friend of his with such a name, and indeed he came once or twice to see him when he was with us."

"That was the name--Boduoc," Pollio said. "They behaved with the greatest gentleness, injuring no one and taking nothing, neither jewels, nor ornaments, nor garments, but departing quietly after taking possession of all the weapons in the town.

"Your father reported the fact to Rome, bringing into prominence the fact that this was the first time the Britons had ever descended from the mountains, and that the inhabitants of Castanium were filled with gratitude and admiration for the treatment they received. Last week he wrote to Rome saying that so far as he could learn all the bands that had not been destroyed had gone north, save one composed of Britons and Gauls, about fourscore in number, commanded by the Briton Beric, and suggested that as months might pass before they could be captured, he should be authorized to treat with them, and to offer them full pardon if they would lay down their arms, especially as they had taken no part whatever in the misdeeds of the other gladiators, and had injured no one either in person or property. I know that it was a great disappointment to him, as well as to us, when the letter came yesterday saying that they were to be hunted down and destroyed, and that all not killed in fighting were to be crucified. But we had better go in, Berenice, the dew is beginning to fall."

They entered the villa. The general was alone in the atrium.

"Is anything the matter, father?" Berenice asked, as she saw that he looked disturbed.

"Yes, Berenice, I have received news that as a Roman general ought to delight me, but which, as Caius Muro, your father and the father in law of Pollio, vexes me greatly."

"What is it, father?"

"A man arrived half an hour since saying that he had news of importance to communicate. He was brought in here. He told me he was a cultivator whose farm lay far up on the hillside. For upwards of a year he had, in fear of his life, as he said, been compelled to sell food to the bandits in the mountains. He acknowledged that he had been well paid, and that he had no cause of complaint against them; but he now professed a desire to do service to Rome, for which he evidently expected a handsome reward. I told him I could not bargain with him. He had aided the enemies of Rome, and by his own account his life was forfeited, seeing that for a year he had been trafficking with them, instead of doing his duty and reporting their first visit to the authorities here.

"He said that he was not alone, and that most of the farmers high up on the hills had been compelled to do the same, and had kept silence, knowing that the brigands would have burned their houses and slain their wives and families had they reported aught against them to the authorities, and that, indeed, they were altogether ignorant of the position of the camp of the outlaws beyond the fact that it was somewhere among the mountains. 'What, then, have you to report?' I said angrily, for I hate to have to do with traitors. 'It is this,' he said: 'for some months there has been living a lady, supposed to be the wife of the chief of the outlaws, at a farm next to mine, belonging to one Cornelius. The chief often visits her and stays there; five of his followers live in an out house adjoining the farm, and one of these is always on guard night and day.

"'The chief himself is a very tall young man, and is called Beric by his followers. Four of them are also of his race, tall and very fair like him. There is also a youth who lives in the house. He belongs to the band, but appears to be a native of Rome. He sometimes comes down and makes purchases in Rhegium. The house cannot be approached from below without an alarm being given, owing to the strictness of the watch; but I could lead a body of troops high up above it, so as to come down upon the rear of the house and cut off all escape when another band comes up from below.' I told him that his information was valuable, and that he was to come here to-morrow evening at eight o'clock to lead a party of light armed troops up into the hills."

"And you will send them, father?" Berenice broke in; "surely you will not take advantage of this treachery."

"I have no choice but to do so," the general said gravely. "As a father I would give my right hand to save the man who preserved your life; as a Roman soldier my duty is to capture the outlaw, Beric, by any means possible. Pollio will tell you the same."

Berenice looked at her husband, who stood in consternation and grief at the news. "Do you say this too, Pollio?"

Pollio did not answer, but the general spoke for him. "He can say nothing else, Berenice. To a Roman soldier duty is everything, and were he ordered to arrest his own father and lead him to execution he could not hesitate."

"But I am not a soldier--" Berenice began passionately.

The general held up his hand suddenly. "Hush, Berenice, not a word farther! I am a Roman general. If you say one word that would clash with my duty I should order you to your chamber and place a soldier there on guard over you. Now I will leave you with your husband;" and the general left the room.

"What do you say, Pollio? Will you suffer this man, who saved your wife, who risked his life for your cousin, and is, as it seems, your cousin by marriage, to be foully captured and crucified?"

"I am a soldier, Berenice; do not tempt me to break my duty. You heard what your father said."

Berenice stamped her foot. "Does your duty go so far, Pollio, that like my father you would place a guard at my door if I said aught that would seem to run counter to your duty?"

"Not at all, Berenice," he said with a smile; "say aught you like. I hear as a husband but not as a soldier."

"Well, that is something," Berenice said, mollified. "Well, Pollio, if you will not warn Beric of his danger I will do so. Have I your permission to act as I choose?"

"My full permission, dear. Do as you like; act as you choose; you have beforehand my approval. If you fail and harm comes of it I will stand by you and share your punishment; but tell me nothing of what you would do beforehand. I trust you wholly, but for my sake, if not for your own, be not rash. Remember, if by any means it becomes known that you aided Beric to escape, both our lives are surely forfeited."

"Thank you, Pollio," Berenice said, throwing her arms round his neck, "that is spoken like my husband. You shall know nothing, and I will save Beric."

CHAPTER XXI
OLD FRIENDS

Beric and Aemilia were sitting on the following day in the shade in front of the house, where Porus had erected a verandah of boughs to keep off the sun, when they observed a female peasant and an elderly man ascending the hill. They were still some distance down, and the man spoke to one of the farm men who was on his way down the hill.

"They are coming this way," Aemilia said; "they have passed the point where the paths fork. She seems to find that basket she is carrying heavy, and no wonder, for it is a steep climb under the midday sun."

Stopping once or twice to get breath the two peasants approached.

"She is a good looking girl, Beric," Aemilia said.

"Our host has two or three nieces down in the town," Beric replied; "I expect it is one of them. Yes, she is certainly pretty, and not so browned and sunburnt as most of these peasant girls are."

As they came close the girl stopped and looked at the house, and then, instead of going to the entrance, left her companion and walked across to the verandah. A smile came across her face.

"Shall I tell you your fortune?" she said abruptly to Aemilia.

"It is told," Aemilia said; "to be a farmer's wife. But what do you know of fortunes?"

"I can tell you the past if not the future," the young woman said, setting down her basket. "May I do so?"

"You are a strange girl," Aemilia said, "but tell me what you can."

"I can see an amphitheatre," the girl went on, "a great one, greater than that across at Messina, and it is crowded with people. In the front row there sits a man past middle age and a lady and a girl. In the centre of the arena is a young girl in white."

"Hush, hush!" Aemilia cried, leaping to her feet, "say no more. You know me, though how I cannot guess."

"I see another scene," the girl went on without heeding her; "it is a hut. It must belong to some savage people. It is quite unlike our cottages. There is an old woman there and a man and a young girl. The old woman does not speak to them; she does not seem of the same race; the other two are Romans. The mat at the door is pushed aside and there enters a tall youth.

Not so tall as this man, not so strong; and yet like him, just as a boy might be to a man.

"The girl jumps up and exclaims 'Beric.'"

Beric had risen to his feet also now. "Is it possible," he cried, "that as the boy has grown into the man, so has the girl grown into--" and he stopped.

"Into a young woman, Beric. Yes, don't you remember me now?"

"It is Berenice!" he exclaimed.

"It is indeed, Beric, the child you saved from death. And this is your wife Aemilia, the daughter of Norbanus, who is the uncle of my husband Pollio. And do you not know who that is standing there?"

"Why, surely it is my tutor and friend Nepo;" and running towards him he embraced him with heartiness and then led him to the verandah, where Berenice was talking with Aemilia.

"But why are you thus disguised, and how did you know that Aemilia and I were here?"

"We have come to warn you, Beric. You have been betrayed, and tonight there will be troops ranged along above the house to cut off your retreat, and a company of soldiers will advance from below straight upon the house. My father told me, I think, in order that I might save you, though as a Roman general he could do nought save his duty. Pollio, too, though he said he would willingly give his sanction, knows not that I have come hither. He pretended that his duty as a soldier prevented him from warning you, though I believe that had not I been with him his friendship and gratitude would have been too much for his duty. However, I was with him, and he gave me permission to come; though, mind you, I should have come whether he gave me permission or not. You did not ask permission of anyone when you saved me, and even if Pollio had threatened to divorce me if I disobeyed him I would have come; but as I needed a disguise, and did not like to trust any of the slaves, I took Nepo into my confidence, and he managed everything."

"We are, indeed, grateful to you," Aemilia cried, embracing Berenice warmly. "It was brave of you indeed to come."

"It requires less bravery to come up here with a message, Aemilia, than to run away from Rome with an outlaw who had just bearded Caesar in his palace."

"I did not do that, Berenice. It was not because I was unwilling, but because Beric would not take me with him. I stayed for months in Rome, hidden in the Catacombs with the Christians, until Beric sent for me to join him here; but come inside and take some refreshment, for you must be weary indeed with your long walk up the hill."

"No one else must see me," Berenice said. "There may be inquiries when they come tonight and find that you are gone, and I would not that any should see me."

"No one will see you. The room is situated at the back of the house, and though I shall take the slaves with us in our flight, they shall not catch even a glimpse of your face. I will set them some needlework to do."

They were soon seated in Aemilia's room, and Beric brought in fruit and wine, goat's milk, cheese, and bread.

"There is no hurry for me to return," Berenice said. "The slaves believe that I have gone out to pay some visits, and I do not wish to get back until after sunset. There is so much for Beric to tell us.

"You do not know, Beric, how often Nepo and I have talked about it, and how we have longed to see you, and I believe that what drew me first to Pollio was his praises of you. But before you begin there is one thing I must tell you. My father has received private news from Rome; there is a report there that the legions have proclaimed Galba emperor, and that ere long he will be in Rome. At present it is but a rumour, and of course at court all profess to disbelieve it, and Nero openly scoffs at the pretensions of Galba; but the friend who wrote to my father says that he believes it true. Now my father is a great friend of Galba's. They were much together as young men, and served together both in Gaul and Syria; and he feels sure that if Galba comes to the throne he will be able to obtain a pardon for you and those with you, since you have done no one harm save when attacked. He attempted to procure it from Nero, but altogether without success; with Galba it will be different, especially as a new emperor generally begins his reign by acts of clemency. Now, as I have given you my news, Beric, do you tell us, while we are eating the fruit, everything that has happened to you since I last saw you at that hut."

"So much has happened that it will be impossible to tell you all, Berenice; but I will give you the outline of it. The principal thing of all is, that I have taken a wife."

Berenice pouted. "It is lucky for you, Aemilia, that I was not at Rome when Beric arrived, for I had as a girl always determined that I should some day marry him and become a British chieftainess. He had not seen you then except at Massilia, and I should have had him all to myself at Rome, for you did not get there, Pollio tells me, until months later."

Aemilia laughed. "I should not have entered the lists against you, Berenice. It was not until after he saved Ennia from the lion in the arena that I came to love him."

"Well, I must put up with Pollio," Berenice said. "He is your cousin, and I have nothing to say against him as a husband; he is kind and indulgent, and a brave soldier, and all one could want; but he is not a hero like Beric."

Beric laughed. "You should have said a giant, Berenice, which would have been much nearer the truth. And now I will tell you my story;" and during the next two hours he gave her a sketch of all that had passed since they had last parted in Britain.

"There, Cneius Nepo," Berenice said when he had finished. "You never thought for a moment that your pupil, who used to pore with you over those parchments, till I often wished I could throw them in the fire when I wanted him to play with me, was to go through such adventures--to match himself first against Suetonius, and then against my father, both times with honour; to be Nero's bodyguard; to say nothing of fighting in the arena, and getting up a revolt in the palace of Caesar."

"I expected great things of him," Nepo said; "but not like these. I fancied he would become a great chief among the British, and that he might perhaps induce them to adopt something of our civilization. I had fancied him as a wise ruler; and, seeing how fond he was of the exercise of arms, I had thought long before the insurrection broke out that some day he might lead his countrymen to battle against us, and that, benefiting by his study of Caesar and other military writers, he would give far more trouble to the Romans than even Caractacus had done. But assuredly I never dreamt of him as fighting a lion barehanded in a Roman arena in defence of a Roman girl. As to marriages, I own that the thought crossed my mind that the union of a great British chief with the daughter of a Roman of rank like your father would be an augury of peace, and might lead to better relations between the two countries."

"That dream must be given up," Berenice said seriously, "there are two obstacles. But I have no doubt Aemilia would make quite as good a chieftainess as I should have done. Some day, Aemilia, if you return to Britain with Beric, as I hope you will do, and Pollio becomes a commander of a legion, I will get him to apply for service there. It is cold and foggy; but wood is a good deal more plentiful and cheaper than it is at Rome, and with good fires one can exist anywhere. And now it is time for us to be going. We will take another path in returning down the hills, so that any one who noticed us coming up will not see us as we descend. Nepo's toga and my stola are hidden in a grove just outside the town, and it will be dusk by the time we arrive there. Kiss me, Aemilia; I am glad that I know you, for I have heard much of you from Pollio. I am glad that Beric has chosen so well. Goodbye, Beric; I hope we may meet again before long, and that without danger to any of us. You may salute me if Aemilia does not object--I told Pollio I should permit it;" and she laughingly lifted up her face to him. "He never used to kiss me when I was a child," she said to Aemilia. "I always thought it very unkind, and was greatly discontented at it. Now, Nepo, let us be going."

Beric and his wife stood watching them until they were far down the hill. "She makes light of it," Beric said; "but it is no common risk she has run. Nero can punish women as well as men, and were it to come to his ears that she has enabled me to escape his vengeance, even the influence of her father might not avail to save her."

"I shall remember her always in my prayers," Aemilia said earnestly, "and pray that she too may some day come to know the truth."

Beric did not answer. Aemilia had explained to him all that she knew of her religion, but while admitting the beauty of its teaching, and the loftiness of its morals, he had not yet been able to bring himself to believe the great facts upon which it was based.

"We must be moving," he said, and summoned Philo, who had been much surprised at Beric's being so long in conversation with strangers.

"Send Porus to me," he said, "and bid Cornelius also come here."

The two men came round to the verandah together. "We are betrayed, Porus," he said, "and the Romans will be here this evening."

Porus grasped the handle of his dagger and looked menacingly at the farmer. "Our good friend has nought to do with it, Porus; it is some one from one of the other farms who has taken down the news to Rhegium. Do you order the others to be in readiness to start for the camp. But first strip down the hangings of our room, roll them and the mats and all else in seven bundles, with all my wife's clothing and belongings."

"We need leave little behind. We can take everything," Porus said. "The six of us can carry well nigh as much as the same number of horses, and Philo can take something. I will see about it immediately."

"Now, Cornelius," Beric went on when Porus had left, "you must prepare your story, and see that your men and the rest of the household stick to it. You will be sharply questioned. You have only the truth to say, namely, that some of my band came down here and threatened to burn your house and slay all in it unless you agreed to sell us what things we required; that, seeing no other way of preserving your lives, you agreed to do so. After a time a young woman--do not say lady--came with two attendants, and you were forced to provide her with a room; and as five men were placed here constantly, you still dared give no information to the authorities, because a watch was also set on you, and your family would have been slain long before any troops could arrive here. What you will be most closely questioned about is as to why we all left you today. They will ask you if any one has been here. You saw no one, did you?"

"No, my lord. I heard voices in your room, but it was no business of mine who was with you."

"That is good," Beric said. "That is what you must say. You know someone did come because you heard voices; but you saw nobody either coming or going, and know not how many of them there were, nor what was their age. You only know that I summoned you suddenly, and told you I had been betrayed, and that the Romans would soon be coming in search of me, and therefore I was obliged to take to the mountains. But go first and inquire among the household, and see if any of them noticed persons coming here."

"One of the men says that he saw an old peasant with a girl who asked which was my farm."

"Then that man must go with us to the mountains. He shall return safe and unharmed in a few days. The Romans must not know of this. This is the one point on which you must be silent; on all others speak freely. It is important to me that it should not be known whether it was man or woman, old or young, who warned me.

"I do not threaten you. I know that you are true and honest; but, to ensure silence among your household, tell them that I shall certainly find out if the Roman soldiers learn here that it was an old man and a girl who visited me, and that I will take dire vengeance on whomsoever tells this to the Romans. Discharge your man before we leave with him, so that you may say truly that those the Romans find here are your whole household, and maintain that not one of them saw who it was who came to me today."

"I can promise that, my lord. You and the Lady Aemilia have been kind and good to us, and my wife, the female slave, and the hired men would do anything for you. As for the children, they were not present when Balbus said that he had been questioned by the old man, and can tell nought, however closely they may be questioned, save that Balbus was here and has gone."

"I had not thought of that," Beric said. "Better, then, tell the soldiers the truth: you had two serving men, but we have carried one away with us."

In half an hour all was ready for a start. The two female slaves, although attached to their mistress, were terrified at the thoughts of going away among the mountains, although Aemilia assured them that no harm could happen to them there. Then, with a hearty adieu to the farmer and his wife, Beric and his companions shouldered the loads, and with Balbus, Philo, Aemilia, and the two female slaves made their way up the mountain. As soon as they started, Beric gave orders to Philo to go on with all speed to the camp, and to tell Boduoc of the coming of Aemilia, and bid him order the men at once to prepare a bower at some short distance from their camp. Accordingly when the party arrived great fires were blazing, and the outlaws received Aemilia with shouts of welcome.

"I thank you all," Beric said, "for my wife and myself. She knows that in no place could she be so safe as here, guarded by the brave men who have so faithfully followed her husband."

So heartily had the men laboured that in the hour and a half that had elapsed since Philo had arrived a large hut had been erected a hundred yards from the camp, with a small bower beside it for the use of the female slaves. A great bonfire burnt in front, and the interior was lighted by torches of resinous wood.

"Thanks, my friends," Beric said. "You have indeed built us a leafy palace. I need not exhort the guards to be watchful tonight, for it may be that the traitor who will guide the Romans to the house where we have been stopping may know something of the mountains, and guessing the direction of our camp may attempt to lead them to it. Therefore, Boduoc, let the outposts be thrown out farther than usual, and let some be placed fully three miles from here, in all the ravines by which it is likely the enemy might make their way hither."

Three days later Philo went down to learn what had passed. He was ordered not to approach the house, as some soldiers might have been left there to seize upon any one who came down, but to remain at a distance until he saw the farmer or one of his household at work in the fields. He brought back news that the Romans had arrived on the night they had left, had searched the house and country round, had closely questioned all there, even to the children, and had carried off the farmer and his man. These had returned the next evening. They had been questioned by the general, who had admonished the farmer severely on his failure to report the presence of the outlaws at whatever risk to his family and property; but on their taking an oath that they were unable to give any information whatever, either as to the outlaws' retreat or the persons who had brought up the news of the intended attack by the Romans, they were released.

Balbus was then sent back to the farm with presents for all there, and it was agreed that the camp should be broken up. The general would, in compliance with the orders of Nero, make fresh efforts to hunt down the band; and as he knew now the neighbourhood in which they were, and treachery might again betray the spot, it was better to choose some other locality; there was, too, no longer any occasion for them to keep together. They had the mountains to themselves now, and although the wild animals had been considerably diminished, there were still goats in the upper ranges, and swine and wild boar in the thickest parts of the forests. It was also advisable to know what was passing elsewhere, and to have warning of the approach of any body of troops from the camps round it. Accordingly, while the Britons remained with Beric, who took up his quarters in the forest at the foot of one of the loftiest crags, whence a view could be obtained of the hills from Rhegium to Cosenza, the rest were broken up into parties of five. Signals were arranged by which by smoke during day or fire at night warning could be given of the approach of an enemy, and also whether it was a mere scouting party or a strong column.

For another three months they lived among the hills. Their life was rougher than it had been, for they had now to subsist entirely upon the spoils of the chase, and bread made of ground acorns and beechnuts, mixed with a very small portion of flour. The latter was obtained from lonely cottages, for Beric insisted that no villages should be entered.

"There may be soldiers in every hamlet on the hills, and I would have no risk run of death or capture. Did a few of us fall into their hands it would encourage them to continue their blockade, but as time goes on, and it is found that their presence is entirely fruitless, they may be recalled."

For the first few weeks, indeed, after the failure of the attempt to entrap Beric, parties were sent up into the hills from all the camps, for as the remaining band of gladiators was known to number under a hundred men, it would be no longer necessary for the assailants to move as an army; but after marching hither and thither through the forests without finding any signs of the fugitives the troops returned to their camps, and a fortnight later the greater portion of them were either transported to Sicily or sent north, a few hundred men only remaining to watch for the reappearance of the band. From time to time Philo went down to Rhegium to gather news of what was passing. As the farmer had not been troubled since the visit of the troopers, they renewed their relations with him, except that they abstained from purchasing food of him lest he should be again questioned. Nevertheless he occasionally sent up by Philo a skin of wine as a present to Beric.

"So that I can swear that I have sold them nothing, and that they have taken nothing, there is little chance of my ever being asked if I made them a present," he said.

He was surprised one day by a visit from a Roman, who informed him that he was secretary to the general, and whom, indeed, he had seen when brought before him.

"Do you still hear aught of the brigands, Cornelius?" he asked. The farmer was taken aback by this question.

"No harm is intended you," Nepo said. "The general may have reason for desiring to communicate with the band, whose leader at one time stayed in your house, and which is now the last remnant of the gladiators among the hills. The search for them has been given up as vain, and probably he will receive orders from Rome to withdraw the troops altogether and to offer terms to the gladiators. At present he cannot communicate with them, and he would be glad for you to renew your connection with them, not to assist them by selling them food or receiving them here, but that you should arrange some means of communication with them."

"I might manage that," the farmer said. "It is true that once or twice some of them have come down here. They have taken nothing, and have come, I think, more to learn what is passing without than for any other purpose; but it may be some time before they come again."

"At any rate," Nepo said, "when they do come, do you arrange for a signal, such, for instance, as lighting two fires on the crest above there, with plenty of green wood, that would make a smoke which would be seen for many miles away. This smoke will tell them that there is a message for them from the general. I give you my word as a Roman that no treachery is intended, and I myself, accompanied perhaps by one officer, but no more, will bring it up here and be in waiting to see their chief; so you see I should place myself much more in his hands than he in mine."

It was but a few days before Beric received this message. It filled him with hope, for remembering what Berenice had said about the proclamation of Galba as emperor, it seemed to him that this life as a fugitive might be approaching its end. For himself he was perfectly happy. He and his Britons lived much as they had done at home. It required hard work to keep the larder supplied, but this only gave a greater zest to the chase. They sighed sometimes for the cool skies of Britain, but in other respects they were perfectly contented.

Since the soldiers had been withdrawn they had had no difficulty in obtaining the two things they most required, flour and wine, and, indeed, sometimes brought up sacks of grain and jars of honey, from which they manufactured a sweet beer such as they had drunk at home, and was to them far better than wine. Beric, perhaps, was more anxious for a change than any of his followers. Aemilia seemed perfectly happy, her spirits were as high now as when he had first known her as a girl at Massilia. She was the life and soul of the little band, and the Britons adored her; but Beric remembered that she had been brought up in comfort and luxury, and longed to give her similar surroundings. Although for luxuries he himself cared nothing, he did sometimes feel an ardent desire again to associate with men such as he had met at the house of Norbanus, to enjoy long talks on literary and other subjects, and to discuss history and philosophy.

"It is good," he said one day to Aemilia, "for a man who lives among his fellows to have learned to enjoy study and to find in enlightened conversation his chief pleasure, but if his lot is thrown far from towns it were far better that he had known nothing of these pleasures."

One morning Boduoc, who had gone up early to the summit of the crag, brought down the news that he could make out two columns of smoke rising from the hill over Rhegium.

"I hope to bring you back good news tomorrow, Aemilia," Beric said as he at once prepared to start. "I may find Nepo at the farm when I get there and may possibly be back tonight, but it is full six hours' journey, and as there is no moon I can hardly travel after sundown."

"I shall not expect you till tomorrow, Beric. It were best to arrange that, and then I shall not be looking for you. Even if Nepo is there when you arrive, you will want a long talk with him, and it is likely that Pollio will be with him, so do not think of starting back till the morning."

It was just noon when Beric reached the farm.

"You are just to the time," Cornelius said. "I received an order at daybreak this morning to light the fires and to tell you if you came that the general's secretary would be here at noon. See, there are two figures coming up the hill now."

The moment he saw that they had passed the fork of the paths and were really coming to the house Beric rushed down to meet them, and as he approached saw that they were indeed Pollio and Nepo. He and Pollio embraced each other affectionately.

"I am well pleased indeed," Pollio said, "that we meet here for the first time, and that I did not encounter you in the forests. By the gods, but you have grown into a veritable giant. Why, you must overtop the tallest of your band."

"By an inch or two, Pollio. And you have altered somewhat too."

"The cares of matrimony age a man rapidly," Pollio said laughing, "though doubtless they sit lightly on your huge shoulders. Why, you could let my little cousin sit on your hand and hold her out at arm's length. I always told her that she would need a masterful husband to keep her in order, and truly she is well suited. And now for my news, Beric. Nero is dead. The news arrived last night."

Beric uttered an exclamation of surprise. "How died he?" he asked.

"By his own hand. When the news came that other legions had followed the example of those of Galba, all fell away from Nero, and the Praetorians themselves, whom he had petted and spoilt, having no inclination for a fight with Galba's legionaries, proclaimed the latter emperor. Then Nero showed himself a craven, flying in disguise to the house of Phaon. There he remained in hiding, weeping and terrified, knowing that he must die, but afraid to kill himself. He may well have thought then of how many he had compelled to die, and how calmly and fearlessly they had opened their veins. It was not until he heard the trampling of the horsemen sent to seize him that he nerved himself, and even then could not strike, but placing the point of a dagger against his breast, bade a slave drive it home.

"The senate proclaimed Galba emperor two days before the death of Nero; but as yet all is uncertain. There are other generals whose legions may dispute this point. Syria and Egypt may choose Vespasian; the Transalpine legions, who favoured Vindex, may pronounce for some other. The Praetorians themselves, with the sailors of the fleet, knowing that Galba has the reputation of being close fisted, may choose someone who may flatter and feast them as Nero did. As yet there is no saying what will be done, but at any rate your chief enemy is dead. Muro bids me say that some months may yet elapse before Galba comes to Rome; but that, as he has at present no imperial master, and the senate will be far too busy wrangling and persecuting the adherents of the man whom but a short time since they declared to be a god, to trouble themselves about a handful of gladiators in Bruttium, he will at once collect his troops at Rhegium, and you will be entirely unmolested if you promise that your band will in no way ill treat the people. I know that they have not hitherto done so, and that they will not do so, but the fact that he has a formal engagement with you to that effect will justify him in withdrawing his troops. Indeed, he said that it would be better, perhaps, that a document should be drawn up and signed, in which you pledge yourself to peaceful courses, urging that it was but the tyranny of Nero that forced you to become fugitives, and craving that, as your band has never done any harm to the people, an amnesty may be granted you. This document will aid him when he meets Galba. He will not wait until the latter comes to Rome, but will shortly ask permission from the senate to quit his post for a time, all being quiet here, and will at once take ship to Massilia and see Galba. The new emperor is not, he says, a man bent on having his own way, but always leans on friends for advice, and he feels sure that his representations will suffice to obtain a free pardon for your band, and permission for them to leave the mountains and go wheresoever they will, so that in that case there will be nought to prevent you and your followers returning to Britain."

"This is joyous news indeed, Pollio, and I cannot too warmly thank the general for his kindness to me. As to Berenice--"

"There, there," Pollio said laughing, "let us hear nothing about Berenice. She is a self willed woman, and I am not responsible for her doings, and want to hear nothing more of them than she chooses to tell me."

By this time they had reached the farmhouse, where a meal was speedily prepared, and they sat talking together until evening, when Pollio and his companion returned to Rhegium.

Another three months passed. There was now no lack of food among the outlaws. They still hunted, but it was for amusement, buying sheep and other animals from the villagers, together with all else they required, the natives rejoicing in finding good customers instead of dangerous neighbours among the hills.

At last the signal smokes again ascended, and Beric, taking Aemilia with him, made his way to the farmhouse, where he learned that Nepo had been there with a message that he desired to see Beric in Rhegium. This was sufficient to show that Muro's mission had been to some extent successful, and after resting for an hour or two at the farmhouse they descended the hill. Beric had purchased suitable garments to replace the goatskins which had for a long time previously been worn by the outlaws, their rough work in the woods having speedily reduced their garments to rags, and save that men looked up and marvelled his size, he passed almost unnoticed through the streets of Rhegium to the house of the general. Orders had been given that he was to be admitted, for the sentries passed him without question. As the slave at the door conducted them into the atrium Muro advanced with outstretched hands.

"Welcome! thrice welcome, Beric! Had I not heard from Pollio how you had changed, I should not have recognized in you the British lad I parted with six years ago in Britain. And this is your wife? Pollio, spare your cousin to me for a moment. I am glad to know you, Aemilia. I never met your father, though I have often heard of him as a noble Roman, and I know that his daughter is worthy of being the wife of Beric, not only from what I have heard of you from my son in law, but from your readiness to share the exile and perils of your husband. I see that Berenice has greeted you as if she knew you. A month since I should have said that that was impossible," and a smile passed over his face, "but now I may admit that it may have been. And now for my news. I have seen Galba, and have strongly represented to him the whole facts of the case, and I have, under his hand, a free pardon for yourself and all your followers, who are permitted to go wheresoever they please, without molestation from any. But more than that, I have represented to him how useful it would be that the Britons of the east, where the great rising against Rome took place, should be governed by one of their own chiefs, who, having a knowledge of the might and power of Rome, would, more than any other, be able to influence them in remaining peaceful and adopting somewhat of our civilization. He has, therefore, filled up an appointment creating you provincial governor of that part of Britain lying north of the Thames as far as the northern estuary, and bounded on the east by the region of swamps--the land of the Trinobantes, the Iceni, and a portion of the Brigantes--with full power over that country, and answerable only to the propraetor himself. Moreover, he has written to him on the subject, begging him to give you a free hand, and to support you warmly against the minor Roman officials of the district. I need not say that I answered for you fully, and pledged myself that you would in all things be faithful to Rome, and would use your influence to the utmost to reconcile the people to our rule."

Beric was for a time too overcome to be able to thank Muro for his kindness.

"I have repaid in a small way the debt that I and Pollio owe you," he said. "The senate has not at present ratified the appointment, but that is a mere form, and it will not be presented to them until Galba arrives. They are eagerly looking for his coming to free them from the excesses and tyranny of the Praetorian guard, led by Nymphidius the prefect, who has himself been scheming to succeed Nero, and they will ratify without question all that Galba may request. In the meantime there need be no delay. We can charter a ship to convey you and your British and Gaulish followers to Massilia. Galba is already supreme there, and thence you can travel as a Roman official of high rank. I will, of course, furnish you with means to do so."

"In that respect I am still well provided," Beric said. "Nero, with all his faults, was generous, and was, in addition to my appointments, continually loading me with presents, which I could not refuse. Even after paying for all that was necessary for my band during the past year, I am a wealthy man, and have ample to support Aemilia in luxury to the end of our lives."

"You will, of course, draw no pay until your arrival in Britain; but after that your appointment will be ample. However, I shall insist upon chartering the ship to convey you to Massilia."

The beacon fires were lighted again next morning, and an hour later Beric met Boduoc, whom he had, on leaving, directed to follow with the Britons, and to post himself near the crest of the hills. He returned with him to the band, who were transported with delight at hearing the news. Messengers were at once sent off to the party under Gatho, and on the following day the whole band reassembled, the joy of the Gauls being no less than that of the Britons.

"You will have to take me with you, Beric," Porus said. "I am fit for nothing here save the arena. I have been away from Scythia since I was a boy, and should find myself a stranger there."

"I will gladly take you, Porus, and will find you a wife among my countrywomen. You have shared in my perils, and should share in my good fortunes. You must all remain here among the hills till I send you up word that the ship is in readiness. Boduoc will come down with me, and will send up to the farm garments to replace your sheepskins, for truly Rhegium would be in an uproar did you descend in your present garb. Boduoc will bring you instructions as to your coming down. It were best that you came after nightfall, and in small parties, and went direct on board the ship which he will point out to you. We do not wish to attract attention or to cause a talk in the town, as the news would be carried to Rome, and the senate might question the right of Muro to act upon a document which they have not yet ratified. Therefore we wish it kept quiet until the arrival of Galba at Rome."

A week later the whole party stood on the deck of a ship in the port of Rhegium. Beric had bidden farewell to Muro at his house; Pollio and Berenice accompanied him and Aemilia on board.

"I do not mean this as a farewell for ever, Beric," Pollio said. "I foresee that we are going to have troubled times in Rome. Nero was the last of his race, and no one now has greater right than his fellows to be emperor. Now that they have once begun these military insurrections, for the proclamation of Galba was nothing else, I fear we shall have many more. The throne is open now to any ambitious man who is strong enough to grasp it. Generals will no longer think of defeating the enemies of their country and of ruling provinces. As propraetors they will seek to gain the love and vote of their soldiers; discipline will become relaxed, and the basest instead of the noblest passions of the troops be appealed to. We may have civil wars again, like those of Marius and Scylla, and Anthony and Brutus. I hate the intrigues of Rome, and loathe the arts of the demagogue, and to this our generals will descend. Therefore I shall soon apply for service in Britain again. Muro approves, and when I obtain an office there he will come out and build another villa, and settle and end his days there.

"There is little chance of the troops in Britain dealing in intrigues. They are too far away to make their voice heard, too few to impose their will upon Rome. Therefore he agrees with me that there is more chance of peace and contentment there than anywhere. The Britons have given no trouble since the Iceni surrendered, and I look to the time when we shall raise our towns there and live surrounded by a contented people. You may visit Muro at his house in Camalodunum once again, Beric."

"It will be a happy day for us when you come, Pollio, you and Berenice; and glad indeed shall I be to have her noble father dwelling among us. Whatever troubles there may be in other parts of Britain I cannot say, but I think I can answer that in Eastern Britain there will never again be a rising."

"They are throwing off the ropes," Pollio said; "we must go ashore. May the gods keep and bless you both!"

"And may my God, who has almost become Beric's God, also bless you and Berenice and Muro!" Aemilia said.

Ten minutes later the ship had left port, and was making her way up the Straits of Messina. The weather was fair with a southerly wind, running before which the ship coasted along inside the mountainous isle of Sardinia, passed through the straits between that and Corsica, then shaped its course for Massilia, where it arrived without adventure. There was some surprise in the town at the appearance of Beric and his followers, and they were escorted by the guard at the port to the house of the chief magistrate. On Beric's presenting to him his appointment, signed by Galba, and the safe conduct for himself and his comrades, the magistrate invited him and Aemilia to stay at his house. There were many officials to whom Aemilia was known when she dwelt there with her father, and for ten days they stayed in the city. The Gauls of Beric's party proceeded to their various destinations on the day after they landed, Beric making a present to each to enable them to defray the expenses of their travel to their respective homes, and obtaining a separate safe conduct for each from the chief magistrate. Bidding adieu to their friends at Massilia the Britons started north.

While in the town Beric obtained for his twenty followers a dress which was a mixture of that of the Britons and Romans, having the trousers or leggings of the British and the short Roman tunic. All were armed with sword, shield, and spear. Aemilia travelled in a carriage; the two female slaves had been given their freedom and left behind at Rhegium. Beric was handsomely attired in a dress suitable to his rank, but, like his followers, wore the British leggings. A horse was taken with them for him to ride when they passed through towns, but generally it was led by Philo, and Beric marched with his men. They took long journeys, for the men were all eager to be home, and, inured as they were to fatigue, thought nothing of doing each day double the distance that was regarded as an ordinary day's journey.

At the towns through which they passed the people gazed with surprise at Beric and his bodyguard, and warm sympathy was shown by the Gauls for the Britons returning after their captivity in Rome. On arriving at the northwesterly port of Gaul, Beric learned that London, Verulamium, and Camalodunum had been rebuilt, and that the propraetor had established himself in London as his chief place of residence. Beric therefore hired a ship, which sailed across the straits to the mouth of the Thames, ascended the river, and four days after putting out anchored at London. Beric and his followers were surprised at the change which had been effected in the six years which had passed since they saw it a heap of ruins. A temple of Diana had been erected on the highest point of ground. Near this was the palace of the propraetor, and numerous villas of the Roman officials were scattered on the slopes. A strong wall surrounded the Roman quarter, beyond which clustered the houses of the traders, already forming a place of considerable size.

Upon landing Beric proceeded, accompanied by Boduoc, to the palace of the propraetor, to whom he presented Galba's letter especially recommending him, and his own official appointment. Celsius, who had succeeded Petronius as propraetor, had received Beric sitting; but upon reading the document rose and greeted him cordially.

"I have heard much of you, Beric, since I came here," he said, "and many have been the entreaties of your people to me that I would write to Rome to pray Caesar to restore you to them. I did so write to Nero, but received no reply; but my friends keep me acquainted with what is passing there, and the story of your combat with the lion in the arena, and of your heading a revolt in Nero's palace reached me. As it was about the time of the latter event that I wrote to Caesar, I wondered not that I received no answer to my letter. After that I heard that you had been giving terrible trouble in Bruttium to Caius Muro, and little dreamed that my next news of you would be that Galba had appointed you Governor of the Eastern Province."

"It was upon the recommendation and by the good offices of Muro," Beric said. "I had been brought up at his house at Camalodunum, and had the good fortune to save his daughter's life at the sack of that city. He knew that I had been driven by the conduct of Nero into revolt, and that, even though in arms against Rome, I and my band had injured and robbed no Roman man or woman. He represented to Galba that, holding in high respect the power of Rome, and being well regarded by my people here, I should, more than any stranger, be able to persuade them of the madness of any further rising against the imperial power, and to induce them to apply themselves to the arts of agriculture, and to become, like the Gauls, a settled people contented and prosperous.

"These arguments had weight with the emperor, who, as you see, has been pleased to appoint me governor of the province that my people occupied, together with that adjoining on the south, formerly belonging to the Trinobantes, and on the north occupied by a portion of the Brigantes."

"I think the emperor has done well, and I look for great results from your appointment, Beric. I am convinced that it is the best policy to content a conquered people by placing over them men of their own race and tongue, instead of filling every post by strangers who are ignorant of their ways and customs, and whose presence and dress constantly remind them that they are governed by their conquerors. Where do you think of establishing yourself-- at Camalodunum?"

"No. Camalodunum is a Roman town; the people would not so freely come to me there to arbitrate in their disputes. I shall fix it at Norwich, which lies midway between Camalodunum and the northern boundary of the province, and through which, as I hear, one of your roads has now been made."

After staying three days in London as the guest of Celsius, Beric started for the seat of his government, attended by his own bodyguard and a centurion with a company of Roman soldiers. The news that a British governor had been appointed to the province spread rapidly, and at Verulamium, where he stopped for two days, crowds of the country people assembled and greeted him with shouts of welcome. Beric assured them that he had been sent by the emperor Galba, who desired to see peace and contentment reign in Britain, and had therefore appointed a countryman of their own as governor of their province, and that, though he should make Norwich the place of his government, he should journey about throughout the country, listen to all complaints and grievances, and administer justice against offenders, whatever their rank and station.

Above all he exhorted them to tranquillity and obedience. "Rome wishes you well," he said, "and would fain see you as contented beneath her sway as is Gaul, and as are the other countries she has conquered and occupied. We form part of the Roman Empire now, that is as fixed and irrevocable as the rising and setting of the sun. To struggle against Rome is as great a folly as for an infant to wrestle with a giant. But once forming a part of the empire we shall share in its greatness. Towns will rise over the land and wealth increase, and all will benefit by the civilization that Rome will bring to us."

He addressed similar speeches to the people at each halting place, and was everywhere applauded, for the Trinobantes had felt most heavily the power of Rome, and all thought of resistance had faded out since the terrible slaughter that followed the defeat of Boadicea.

Beric did not turn aside to enter Camalodunum, but kept his course north. The news of his coming had preceded him, and the Iceni flocked to meet him, and gave him an enthusiastic welcome. They were proud of him as a national hero; he alone of their chiefs had maintained resistance against the Romans, and his successes had obliterated the humiliation of their great defeat. Great numbers of those who came to meet him owed their lives to the refuge he had provided for them in the swamps, and they considered that it was to his influence they owed it, that after his capture they were allowed to return to their native villages, and to take up their life there unmolested by the Romans.

The members of his band, too, found relations and friends among the crowd, and it added to their enthusiasm that Beric had brought back with him every one of his companions in captivity. Aemilia was much affected at the evidence of her husband's popularity, and at the shouting crowd of great fair haired men and women who surged round the escort, and who, when Beric took her by the hand and bidding her stand up in the chariot presented her to the Iceni as his wife, shouted for her almost as enthusiastically as they had done for him.

"What a little insignificant thing these tall British matrons and maids must think me, Beric!" she said.

"We all admire our opposites, Aemilia, that is how it was that you came to fall in love with me; these people can have seen but few Roman ladies, and doubtless there is not one among them who does not think as I do, that with your dark hair and eyes, and the rich colour of your cheek, you are the loveliest woman that they ever saw."

"If they knew what you were saying they would lose all respect for you, Beric," she said laughing and colouring. "We have been married nearly a year, sir--a great deal too long for you to pay me compliments."

"You must remember that you are in Britain now, Aemilia, and though in Rome men regard themselves as the lords and masters of their wives it is not so here, where women are looked upon as in every way equal to men. I expect that you will quite change under the influence of British air, and that though I am nominally governor it is you who will rule. You will see that in a short time the people will come to you with their petitions as readily as to me."

As soon as Beric established himself at Norwich he set about the erection of a suitable abode; the funds were provided as was usual from the treasury of the province--a certain sum from the taxes raised being set aside to pay the share of the national tribute to Rome, while the rest was devoted to the payment of officials, the construction of roads, public works, and buildings. Long before the house was finished a child was born to Beric, the event being celebrated with great festivity by the Iceni, contrary to their own customs, for among themselves a birth was regarded rather as an occasion of mourning than of rejoicing.

Beric set vigorously to work to put the affairs of the province in order; he appointed Boduoc to an important office under him, and to act for him during his absences, which were at first frequent, as he constantly travelled about the country holding courts, redressing grievances, punishing and degrading officials who had abused their position or ill treated the people, and appointing in many cases natives in their places. Bitter complaints were made by the dispossessed Roman officials to Celsius, who, however, declined in any way to interfere, saying that Beric had received the fullest powers from Galba, and that, moreover, did he interfere with him it was clear that there would be another revolt of the Iceni.

Galba fell, and was succeeded by Otho, who was very shortly afterwards followed by Vespasian, a just, though severe emperor. Complaints were laid before him by powerful families, whose relations had been dismissed by Beric, and the latter was ordered to furnish a full explanation of his conduct. Beric replied by a long and full report of his government. Vespasian was greatly struck alike by the firmness with which Beric defended himself, and by the intelligence and activity with which, as the report showed, he had conducted the affairs of his province; he therefore issued an order for the disaffected officials to return at once to Rome, confirmed Beric in the powers granted him by Galba, and gave him full authority to dismiss even the highest Roman officials in the district should he see occasion to do so.

Roman towns and stations had sprung up all over the island, roads and bridges opened the way for trade. Now that the tribal wars had ceased, and the whole people had become welded into one, they turned their attention more and more to agriculture. The forest diminished rapidly in extent; the Roman plough took the place of the rough hoe of the Briton, houses of brick and stone that of rough huts; intermarriages became frequent. The Roman legionaries became established as military colonists and took British wives. The foreign traders and artisans, who formed the bulk of the populations of the towns, did the same; and although this in the end had the effect of diminishing the physical proportions of the British, and lowering the lofty stature and size that had struck the Romans on their landing with astonishment, it introduced many characteristics hitherto wanting in the race, and aided in their conversion from tribes of fierce warriors into a settled and semi-civilized people.

Among the many who came to Britain, were some Christians who sought homes in the distant island to escape the persecutions at Rome. There was soon a colony of these settled at Norwich under the protection of Aemilia. They brought with them an eloquent priest, and in a short time Beric, already strongly inclined to the Christian religion, openly accepted that faith, which spread rapidly throughout his government. Porus was not long in finding a British wife, and never regretted the day when he left the ludus of Scopus and joined his fortunes to those of Beric. Philo embraced Christianity, and became a priest of that church.

A year after Beric came to Britain he and Aemilia were delighted by the arrival of Pollio and Berenice with Caius Muro. The former had at the accession of Otho, with whom his family were connected, obtained a civil appointment in Britain, and at Beric's request Celsius appointed him to the control of the collection of taxes in his district, there being constant complaints among the people of the rapacity and unfairness of the Roman official occupying this position. Pollio therefore established himself also at Norwich; Muro, with whom came Cneius Nepo, taking up his residence there with him, and as many other Roman families were there, neither Aemilia nor Berenice ever regretted the loss of the society of Rome. Pollio proved an excellent official, and ably seconded Beric in his efforts to render the people contented.

Had Beric foreseen the time when the Romans would abandon Britain, and leave it to the mercy of the savages of the north and of the pirates of North Germany and Scandinavia, he would have seen that the extinction of the martial qualities of the British would lead to their ruin; but that Rome would decay and fall to pieces and become the prey of barbarians, was a contingency beyond human ken, and he and those who worked with him thought that the greatest blessing they could bestow upon their country was to render it a contented and prosperous province of the Roman Empire. This he succeeded in doing in his own government, and when, full of years and rich in the affection of his countrymen, he died, his son succeeded him in the government, and for many generations the eastern division of the island was governed by descendants of Beric the Briton.

THE END

Milton Keynes UK
Ingram Content Group UK Ltd.
UKHW010313220224
438247UK00004B/514